BRIAN KIRK

WE ARE
MONSTERS

This is a **FLAME TREE PRESS** book

Text copyright © 2020 Brian Kirk

FLAME TREE PRESS
6 Melbray Mews, London, SW6 3NS, UK
flametreepress.com

Distribution and warehouse:
Baker & Taylor Publisher Services (BTPS)
30 Amberwood Parkway, Ashland, OH 44805
btpubservices.com

Thanks to the Flame Tree Press team, including:
Taylor Bentley, Frances Bodiam, Federica Ciaravella, Don D'Auria,
Chris Herbert, Josie Karani, Molly Rosevear, Will Rough, Mike Spender,
Cat Taylor, Maria Tissot, Nick Wells, Gillian Whitaker.

The cover is created by Flame Tree Studio with
thanks to Nik Keevil and Shutterstock.com.
The font families used are Avenir and Bembo.

Flame Tree Press is an imprint of Flame Tree Publishing Ltd
flametreepublishing.com

A copy of the CIP data for this book is available from the British Library
and the Library of Congress.

HB ISBN: 978-1-78758-379-5
PB ISBN: 978-1-78758-377-1
ebook ISBN: 978-1-78758-380-1

Printed in the US at Bookmasters, Ashland, Ohio

Printed and bound in Great Britain by Clays Ltd, Elcograf S.p.A.

BRIAN KIRK

WE ARE MONSTERS

FLAME TREE PRESS
London & New York

For Anne, who helps quiet the
voices in my head.

PART ONE
EXPERIMENTAL MADNESS

CHAPTER ONE

No matter how many times he saw the syringe, the needle always looked too long. Too menacing. Less like an instrument of healing than one of pain. Another crude tool, in a long line of others, created to manipulate the human mind. And attempt to make it sane.

Dr. Drexler dipped the needle into a small vial labeled in his indecipherable scrawl and filled the syringe. He pulled it out and held it up, driving aside fleeting memories of prior failures, and consulted the imaging screen revealing the anatomy of the patient's brain. He prepped the needle, dispersing air bubbles that could easily cause an aneurism, and then placed its beveled tip between the man's eye and the bridge of his nose, just above the tear duct. He paused, held his breath, then pushed the needle through.

The patient, strapped to the examination table with thick leather bands, issued a solitary protest – "Get your Christing hot pocket off my hand" – then fell silent. It was the most coherent phrase he'd uttered all day.

Alex Drexler watched the needle emerge on the monitor screen, traversing the trillions of neurons that comprise our personalities, our speech patterns, our smiles, gliding towards the rice-sized gland in the center of the brain – the nexus of perception, the third eye. The needle bumped against the target's side, and he hissed through pursed lips – this is when his hands were wont to shake – then pierced the pineal gland and depressed the plunger.

Fortune favors the bold, he thought. Followed by, *Christ, I hope this works.*

He withdrew the needle and set it down on the instrument tray. A drop of blood ballooned from the wound, which Alex captured with a cotton ball, applying pressure with his thumb until it clotted. He removed the scanning device from the crown of Mr. Connelly's head and set it aside. Then, he waited, standing and pacing the cramped confines of the claustrophobic operating room, trying to keep his mind from considering the implications should the experiment fail. Again.

The man began to stir. Alex forced himself to walk slowly to his side, conducting the diagnostics check with forced composure. The man's vitals were strong, his breathing even. He waited sixty seconds and checked the man's eyes. Minimal dilation.

Good, good.

He glanced over his shoulder and gave the okay to the stout man standing behind the reinforced window, the R&D Director for Philax Pharmaceuticals. The man's terse nod might have been a sign of approval, or it might have meant "no, this proves nothing." Given his stern expression, it was difficult to decipher the subtle gesture. This was their fifth patient and Philax was losing patience.

Alex turned back to his test subject.

"Mr. Connelly?" he said, then paused and waited. Ten seconds passed and he said it again, this time in his most soothing bedside tone. "Mr. Connelly?"

The man's eyes rolled in their sockets and his lids fluttered. He frowned, muttering something unintelligible, and then his mouth sprang open so wide Alex feared it would pop at the hinge. He rocked from side to side, gurgling through his gaping mouth, and then stretched taut against the table, corded tendons rippling the skin of his extended neck. He convulsed, once, twice, the examination table rattling in the silent room, and then he stopped and lay still.

Seconds passed before he stirred again. Then, dazed, he raised and shook his head, and fixed his eyes on Dr. Drexler. He tried to sit up, but rebounded against the heavy restraints.

"It's okay," Alex said, placing a hand against the man's chest. "Just relax."

The patient surveyed the small examination room, then returned his attention to the doctor. He blinked to bring Alex into focus.

"How are you feeling?" Alex asked.

Mr. Connelly considered the question, smacking his mouth. "Thirsty," he said.

Alex smiled, filled a small paper cup from the sink and tilted it against the man's mouth, waiting as he took a few tentative sips.

"Better?"

"Better."

"Good." Alex put aside the cup and turned back to his patient. The man held his gaze, his eyes clear and focused for the first time in weeks, showing no sign of the paranoid delusions that had led to his recent incarceration.

"You may be feeling a bit disoriented," Alex explained, pulling up a stool and rolling it near the patient's head. "That's okay. Do you know where you are?"

"Some type of hospital room, looks like," the man said. He noticed the observation window and furrowed his brow. "Who's that?" he said, withdrawing his gaze from the Philax rep and squinting his eyes.

"That's a colleague of mine," Alex said, straining to keep the irritation from his voice. He was opposed to the executive's presence in the observation room, but Philax always insisted on having someone oversee the procedure. He rested a reassuring hand upon the man's arm and forced another smile.

"Can you tell me why you're here?"

Mr. Connelly relaxed against the bed, staring towards the ceiling, silent. Then he smiled, his long, tangled teeth fanning out like arthritic fingers. He raised his head and stared at Alex as though seeing him for the first time.

"Yeah, y'all said if I let you run tests on me, I could be let go."

Alex shifted in his seat. He preferred not to focus on how Philax prospected for patients, nor on the state hospital's overeagerness to clear its forensic cells. Early release for a bipolar mother was one thing, freeing a violent schizophrenic in the throes of a psychotic episode was quite another. Once again, he cringed to think what Eli would do if he found out about this. *That's why he won't,* he prayed.

"Well, let's just make sure you're fit for discharge first. Do you feel any pain?"

Mr. Connelly surveyed his body, raising his arms and legs as far as the restraints would allow. "Yeah, these straps are killing my arms. How about you unbuckle them for me?"

"Let's keep them on for now. We need to make sure there are no side effects from the medicine we administered."

Mr. Connelly flexed his arms, straining against the straps; the electronic pulse on the heart rate monitor began to quicken its pace. Then, he stopped and settled down. "Shit. Can't you just loosen 'em some?"

"Okay. Sure," Alex said, wishing he had thought to request a guard. He looked over at the overweight Philax executive behind the reinforced, double-pane window and wondered how much help he would be should Mr. Connelly become unruly. The man's expressionless stare revealed nothing. He could just as easily have been mentally optimizing his investment portfolio as contemplating a rescue plan. Alex reached over and loosened the armbands by a couple of notches, studying the patient's eyes for hidden motives.

"Better?"

Mr. Connelly stretched his arms and rubbed his wrists. "Yeah, that's better." He relaxed against the gurney, the slightest smile tugging at the corner of his mouth, his eyes bright and clear.

Alex had to resist rubbing his own hands together. An hour ago the patient had been extremely agitated, his gaze distant and wandering, his speech jumbled and disjointed. The refined formula appeared to be working. Perhaps it was finally fixed.

Don't get too excited, Alex urged himself. *We've been farther than this before.*

"Good. How about your head? Are you experiencing any pain or tingling? Anything out of the ordinary?" The man had been arrested for slinging his feces at a pack of nuns while screaming about demonic penguins. Alex wasn't sure *ordinary* held the same connotations for Mr. Connelly.

"Not as far as I can tell. Feel a bit sleepy, is all."

"Well, that's to be expected from the local anesthetic. But your diagnostics are all on track, and you're showing exceptional tolerance towards the medication so far. What I'm most pleased to see is—"

Mr. Connelly went rigid and his eyes opened wide. He snaked his head back and forth in an attempt to see beyond Alex's body. Then his lips peeled back in a grimace and he flattened himself against the bed. "Hey! Where did he come from?" Mr. Connelly said, his frantic eyes focused on something over Alex's shoulder.

Alex's chest clinched, his stomach became a roiling stew. Still, he managed to regain eye contact with his patient and keep his head from hanging.

"As I explained. He's a colleague of mine, here to make sure everything goes smoothly."

"No, not the fat fuck. The faggot, that little queer boy behind you." Mr. Connelly started tugging at his arm restraints in an attempt to break free; sweat began to texture his brow. "What, is this some kind of trap? I ain't no queer bait! Let me fucking go!"

"Settle down, Mr. Connelly," Alex said, taking a cursory look over his shoulder. The Philax exec looked stunned.

Shit, shit, shit! Alex spun back around and grabbed another syringe from the medical tray, this one containing a sedative. He stuck it in the patient's arm and depressed the plunger. Within seconds Mr. Connelly was settling down, his body relaxing against the bed, his eyelids sinking low.

How about that? Medicine that actually works.

"You're okay," Alex assured Mr. Connelly. "Everything's okay."

Mr. Connelly's voice was a sleepy slur. "Goddamn queer." He rolled a heavy head on a lubricated hinge. "Almost got me."

"You're okay," Alex repeated. He gave the man a light pat on his chest. It was all posturing at this point. Anything he could do to salvage a sixth trial.

But he didn't see the Philax rep standing behind the window, trembling and growing pale in his hand-tailored suit.

★   ★   ★

It had been seven years since the man had last seen his son. Since he had thrown him out of the house for coming out of the closet. The boy had moved to San Francisco, last he'd heard, where he'd contracted HIV. He hadn't bothered to pay for a funeral. Hadn't even brought his body home. He'd just sent a check to the crematorium to cover the expenses. He didn't know what they had done with his ashes. He didn't care.

But the boy had just appeared in the examination room. He was sure of it. And, stranger still, the test patient had seen him too.

I must be losing my mind, he thought. *No more monkeying around with these crazy fucks. That's enough for me.*

*   *   *

Alex was still tending to the test patient, watching the man fall peacefully asleep while his own mind raged. He knew he had to face the Philax executive in a matter of moments. He was trying to figure out exactly what to say.

The problem was that they'd already heard it all before. He forced a dispassionate look upon his face and turned towards the observation window. It was empty.

Alex didn't know whether to be disappointed or relieved.

CHAPTER TWO

The drive back to Atlanta from the Philax research facility took Alex four hours. It felt far longer. He had driven the entire distance in a mental haze, reworking the pharmacology of his proprietary formula over and over again in his mind. Why wasn't it working? Where had he gone wrong?

More importantly, what was he to do now?

Philax represented his last opportunity to prove the efficacy of his experimental compound – one that had worked without fail in the final series of animal trials. Worked so well, in fact, that he had overinvested in its success, borrowing money to purchase the house, the car, the clothes, the lifestyle that he couldn't currently afford. Not solely off his salary from the state hospital, anyhow.

Which brought his thoughts back to Dr. Eli Alpert, Sugar Hill's Chief Medical Director, his boss and respected mentor. In order for the medicine to achieve commercial success, Eli would have to find out about the test trials. There was no way around that. By that point, however, Alex would be able to justify his actions. The benefits of having a medicine proven to treat, if not altogether cure the condition of acute mental illness would outweigh Dr. Alpert's ethical concerns over patient experimentation. Or his issues with the industry's overreliance on pharmaceutical drugs in general.

Still, he knew better than to disclose the project to Eli before selling it to a pharmaceutical firm. Especially now that it looked like he had exhausted his final option.

It was after 11:00 p.m. when Alex returned home. His forearms were sore from squeezing the steering wheel, and he realized he desperately needed to pee. He mashed the accelerator, launching up the long, winding driveway that led to his suburban estate, thin poplars and pines blurring by as he hugged the corners of the meandering drive. He was rounding the final bend before reaching the circular lot when a white flash streaked in front of the car, dashing underneath the carriage before he had time to react. The supple suspension of his Lexus absorbed the shock, but the car still rocked as it bounced over whatever had run underneath. The creature made a tortured sound like the screeching of tires as he slammed the brakes and skidded to a stop.

There was a moment of total silence, even the cicadas suspending their song, and then he heard the scream.

It came from the front of the house, a piercing shriek that continued to build until it threatened to shatter the glimmering sky. He looked up to find his wife, Rachel, running towards him in her canary-yellow robe, its silk hem billowing out from behind. A slipper flew from her foot as she raced forward, eyes bulging, black hair streaming, mouth open impossibly wide, issuing a wavering scream without end.

She was at the window before Alex had a chance to move, pounding on the glass with the meaty part of her palms. For a moment she resembled one of his patients slipping into a manic episode. The ones that ended up strapped to a safety seat, drooling and sedated. He stared up into her face, barely recognizable in its current state of rage, and watched as her palms turned into white crescents as they pounded against the car window. *There's madness in us all,* he thought as pushed open the door.

Rachel stumbled back and then stopped and clamped a hand over her mouth, silencing the scream. The steady tick of the cooling engine became the only sound. She pointed.

Popeye, their West Highland white terrier, lay flattened against the pavement, a coiled string of intestine streaming out from his split belly like an umbilical cord. The pooling blood was black in the dark night with a reflective sheen created by the taillights. As Alex kneeled over the body, he could see himself in the surface of the expanding puddle. He looked too calm. Using the blood as a mirror, he practiced a more concerned expression before turning and facing his wife.

"Shit, honey, I didn't see him. He ran right out in front of the car. Here, don't look." Alex tried to wrap an arm around her shoulders and shield her from the sight, but she brushed him off. Her shock broke and she began to cry.

"No shit you didn't see him!" She hit him on the chest. "How would you when you're driving like Michael fucking Andretti? How many times have I told you? How many?" She punctuated each question with another punch.

"Rachel, stop it. It was an accident. I didn't see him. Please, just go inside."

While attempting to turn her, her eyes flew open wide and she froze in place. "Oh god," she said, looking over his shoulder. Her lip curled in and her face crumpled; she buried it against his neck, convulsing as she unleashed a flood of fresh tears. Alex began to console her, hugging her tight and stroking her back. Then she pushed him away so suddenly he nearly fell.

"Look," she said, her eyes narrowing into hateful slits, motioning behind him with her head.

Alex turned. Popeye's hind leg was twitching, just like it did whenever Rachel scratched his secret spot.

"Honey, please. Go inside."

Rachel reached out towards the dog as if she could summon him back to life. "No. He's in pain. Help him."

Popeye's midsection was flattened, his jaw unhinged, several teeth speckled the concrete like tiny flecks of quartz. Yet, still, the leg twitched. Twitched. Twitched.

"Honey, there's nothing I can do for him. He's gone."

"He's not gone. He's hurting. Oh, Alex, he's in pain. Please."

It was a quiet night. Thin clouds drifted past a bloated moon shining with a silvery glow. Elsewhere lovers stole kisses under hanging willow limbs, but here a dog lay dying on a piece of pressure-washed pavement while Alex wondered if the day would ever end. "Okay. Let me see."

He walked over to Popeye and placed his foot upon the dog's head. Rachel closed her eyes and spun around; she dropped to a knee. Alex looked down, preparing himself to apply the necessary pressure, trying to avoid the fading spark of recognition in the dog's beady eye. Popeye's leg gave one final spasm. His jaw opened and a gout of blood drooled out. Then he lay still. Alex sighed and moved his foot away.

"Okay, it's all over," he said. He approached Rachel in order to help her to her feet. She heard him coming and stood and began walking towards the house.

"Hey," Alex said. "Honey, I didn't—"

"No. Not right now." She walked through the open door and slammed it shut.

Alex's head sagged. He went to the garage and retrieved a garbage bag, then turned and sulked back towards Popeye's body lying behind his car. Rachel's mischievous terrier that he had effectively adopted when they got married, Popeye having come attached to her lap. And he had often felt like Bluto in its company – the brutish rival incapable of providing the same selfless affection as his wife's adoring pet. But their rivalry, imaginary or otherwise, was now over.

So is my sex life, Alex thought and sighed. Trying to shed the feeling that vague forces were conspiring against him. Much like his patients felt when they went off their meds.

He flapped the garbage sack open and used his foot to sweep Popeye's limp body into the bag, not wanting to get blood on his hands.

CHAPTER THREE

Dr. Eli Alpert meditated to quiet the chattering in his mind that he feared would one day drive him mad. The mantra he used, which he would recite until each word relinquished its meaning, was one he had learned from a Hindu monk.

As everything is destined to die, I shall cherish my time with it today.

The monk, who most certainly would have been committed to a psychiatric ward if he'd lived in the United States, had saved the doctor's sanity. Continued to save it still. Yet in times like this, the pesky voice of insecurity would overwhelm the safeguards that had been erected in his mind, skirting past the sentrymen of his subconscious, crumbling the confidence that he'd worked so hard to cultivate. This voice, which was his own, spoke to him in the clinical tone of a physician, telling him that resistance was futile. That life, as he knew it, was over. That the center could not hold.

You are the harbinger of death, it would insist, *only pretending to make man sane.*

And whenever this voice of self-doubt surfaced, the serenity that meditation supplied would be obliterated like the ramshackle hut that it had become. And the madness that lurks within all men would threaten to take over.

Someone knocked on his office door, rescuing Eli from his manic reverie. He swept the mandala from the wall and returned it to his desk drawer. Then he switched on the floor lamp, blinking his eyes against the light, and applied a smile to his face he did not feel.

"Come in," he said.

The door opened and Angela poked her head through. "It's official. The Apocalypse has come to Sugar Hill."

Eli waved her in, motioning towards a guest chair. "You know I hate that moniker."

"Of course. Why do you think I use it?"

His smile became sincere. "How's he doing?" he asked.

Angela leaned back in the chair and crossed her arms, looking up towards the ceiling, thinking. Her suit sleeve pulled back to reveal the cuff of a tattoo that started at her wrist and covered the rest of her right arm. It was as much of it as Eli had ever seen, but he often wondered how many more were concealed under her conservative work attire and what kind of alter ego they revealed.

There had been rumors once, soon after Angela first started, about some lewd behavior at an informal work party, but details had been hazy and had dissipated quickly so Eli had chalked it up to hospital gossip, of which there was plenty. It was a distant blip on an otherwise sterling record that had made Angela Sugar Hill's most respected social worker.

Over the course of the eight years she had worked there, Eli had only seen her ruffled twice. Once when a patient had managed to lop off a clump of Angela's hair with a pair of confiscated scissors, and that was really more about the safety breach than concern over her newly lopsided hairstyle. She had kept it jagged ever since. And had begun streaking it with colors.

The other time was when she had witnessed a patient being harassed by an aggressive orderly. While only standing five feet in high heels, with the petite frame decreed by her Asian genes, she had backed the large, six-foot-tall orderly against the wall and shamed him to tears with her outrage. And, even then, she had fought against him being fired, citing that he had learned his lesson and deserved a second chance.

It was her reputation for composure and compassion that had convinced Eli to assign her to their newest, and most notorious, criminal forensics patient, Crosby Nelson, aka the Apocalypse Killer. And he knew he'd made the right decision.

He sat in comfortable silence as Angela considered her response.

"You know, he's different," she said, finally, leaning forward and focusing on him with her almond-shaped eyes. "Different than what I was expecting, I mean. He's quiet. He's shy. He's…he's really rather sweet. He seems happy to be here. Of course, we have him on 60 mgs of Clozapine, so he's heavily sedated, but…" Angela crossed her legs and clasped her hands in her lap; her sleeves dropped, covering the tattoo, "…I hate how he's been portrayed in the media. He's not the monster they make him out to be. He's just sick."

"Well, that'll all die down now that the trial's over. They'll move on to something else."

"I know; it's just sad. People watch the news as if it were reality, rather than entertainment designed to get ratings. The media creates monsters to sell its stories without thinking about the tarnished reputations it leaves behind. I just hope they decide to run a redemption piece when Crosby gets well." Angela shook her head. "Apocalypse Killer. Like he's some hell spawn from the Book of Revelation."

"Well, he did bring about the end of his victims' worlds."

"True, but if you look at it from his standpoint, he honestly thought he was saving the world. That's the worst part of his disease. The voices he hears? They lie."

★　　★　　★

Angela scanned the walls of Eli's office, admiring the travel pictures taken from several exotic locations. In one, Eli was sitting lotus-style next to a small Indian monk with long, salt-and-pepper hair coiled up in a bun atop his head. They both shared the largest smiles she had ever seen.

She compared the Eli from the picture to the person sitting in front of her, the blanched complexion, the purple smears under the eyes, the tributaries in his skin that seemed to deepen every day. That smile was still there, though. As wide and bright as ever. He offered it now, and it turned back time.

"Perhaps," Eli said. "I wouldn't start referring to him as a hero just yet, however. I doubt the victims' families would care for it. Nor are they quick to accept paranoid delusions as an alibi. Let's just focus on giving him the best treatment we can provide and help bring him peace."

He removed his glasses and rubbed his crinkled eyelids. "Has Alex met with him yet?"

Angela examined her hands, her lips drawn tight. "He's not due back from vacation until tomorrow. I was hoping he would have been here for the orientation meetings, but—"

"I'll meet with Crosby today. Alex can take over when he returns. Do you recall where he went?"

Angela shook her head, a few strands of purple hair fluttered across her face and she tucked them behind her steel-studded ear. "He didn't say."

"Well, I hope he comes back rested. We're going to need all hands on deck as we get Crosby integrated into our family." He stood and grabbed his hospital jacket from the coat rack. "And let's lose the nickname. I don't want to hear that from anyone on staff. Last thing we need is the patients referring to Crosby as the Apocalypse Killer."

"Absolutely," she said, standing and following Eli to the door. *Perhaps they'll call him hero instead.*

CHAPTER FOUR

When he first saw Crosby softly snoring on his slim mattress, hands tucked between his knees like a toddler, a voice jumped into Eli's mind. One he hadn't heard in years.

"Rule number one: Never wake a sleeping giant.
"Rule number two: If you do, put the son of a bitch back to sleep."

It was the voice of Sergeant Reynold Wagner, the platoon leader from his single stint in Vietnam. Sergeant Wagner was a handsome man in his mid-forties, with a full head of thick brown hair and a deceptive smile that showcased a neat row of ivory teeth. Eli was relieved when he first met him, thought he'd gotten in with a competent and reasonable commander who would lead them safely through the messy tangle of that futile war.

Eli had never been more wrong. The man proved to be a cold-blooded killer, as dangerous as the most deranged patients in Sugar Hill's criminal forensics ward. Yet, under the sanctions of war, Wagner was considered a hero and showered with ribbons and rewarded with rank for his good work. In retrospect, it was Eli's first encounter with insanity.

Eli served a year as a medic under Wagner's command soon before the publication of the Pentagon Papers and Nixon began bringing troops home. Even then, Eli hadn't been cut out for conflict, preferring to resolve disputes through reason and understanding rather than resort to violence.

Sergeant Wagner referred to him as Dr. Pussyfoot, even when Eli was smeared in soldier blood, hacking off ruined limbs, saving men's lives. He had earned the moniker during a raid on a Vietcong encampment that they ambushed, catching the enemy unaware and slaughtering them in their sleep. Eli followed the last infantry group into the enemy camp, a small clearing in the jungle with bamboo lean-tos and makeshift bunkers. Soldiers were busy piling dead bodies to burn, but there were dozens of Vietcong still writhing on the ground, injured, pleading for mercy in their strange alien tongue.

Without thinking, Eli began to offer aid. He was giving morphine to a young soldier, little more than sixteen years old by the look of him, who had taken a cluster of gunshots in his stomach, just below the sternum. The pain had to be unbearable. His feet were skittering in the jungle soil, his head thrashing, crying out like a woman in the throes of childbirth. Just as he injected the needle into the boy's stomach, Sergeant Wagner yanked Eli by the back of his collar, twisting it until it cut off his windpipe.

"Just what the fuck do you think you're doing there, Dr. Pussyfoot?" he said, speaking softly into Eli's ear. A few men looked over and smirked. "Mind explaining why you're wasting good American morphine on the enemy?"

Eli opened his mouth to speak and Wagner twisted his shirt collar another notch, wrapping it around his fist so that all that came out was a choked gurgle. His eyes began to bulge while pressure built within his brain.

"Just whose side are you on? Had we not gotten him first, he would have happily killed any one of us." Wagner shoved Eli forward, bringing him face to face with the dying boy. "And he would not have taken mercy on you."

Sergeant Wagner pulled his sidearm reeking of burnt cordite in the stifling summer air. He pressed Eli against the young Vietcong soldier until their noses touched. The morphine had taken effect and the boy's eyes were free of pain, but bright with fear. They jittered behind his slanted sockets, dry and aware of his pending death.

"I can't have enemy sympathizers in my company." Eli's vision began to blur, his chest burned. His brain thumped along with his heart. Then Wagner loosened his grip and Eli gasped for air. He shoved the pistol into Eli's hand and pressed the barrel against the soldier's head.

"You never wake a sleeping giant," Wagner said, curling his finger around Eli's, pressing it against the trigger. The boy's eyes went wide, frozen in place, locked on to Eli's just a couple of inches away. "But, if you do, you put the son of a bitch back to sleep."

*   *   *

Eli blinked, and the hospital room came back into focus. Crosby stirred on the bed and rolled onto his back. He opened his eyes and raised his head, noticing Eli standing in the doorway, then pushed himself onto an elbow and yawned.

"Sorry to wake you," Eli said. He walked forward and held out his hand. Crosby flinched as if it were a venomous snake. "I'm Dr. Alpert, Medical Director here at Sugar Hill. I wanted to welcome you to our facility and make sure you were settling in okay. How's everything so far?"

Cautiously, Crosby sat up and swung his legs over the side of the bed. He rubbed his eyes with the heels of his hands and shook his head.

"My head feels…" he paused, and shook it again, as though trying to dislodge the word, "…empty."

Eli consulted the patient's records. They had started him on a maximum dose of Clozapine at the prison before transferring him to Sugar Hill. Eli would have preferred to wait and see how Crosby reacted to other forms of treatment before prescribing such a strong antipsychotic, but the penitentiary physicians weren't apt to take any chances with a high-profile patient displaying violent paranoid delusions. No one would get in trouble for sedating him with industry-approved pharmaceuticals, regardless of whether it compromised the efficacy of less invasive forms of therapy.

He closed the folder and stared down at Crosby Nelson, the man whom the media had dubbed the Apocalypse Killer. He looked older than thirty-two. His horseshoe of black hair was cropped short, outlining a cove of pale skin featuring several pockmarks and pale scars. His face was gaunt, yet the skin hung loose as if left in the sun too long. And his dry, cracked hands were wrinkled and tanned yellow from nicotine. In the cramped, ten-by-ten hospital room, he even smelled old. The musty, acrid smell of dead skin.

"That spacey feeling is normal. It's from the medicine you've been prescribed. It should dissipate as you acclimate to the medicine. If not, we'll switch you to something else. Something that your body will tolerate better."

Crosby looked up, his eyes wandering. He smacked his lips a few times, like a cow chewing cud; then he slumped forward and stared down towards the floor. "Maybe I just need to sleep some more," he said.

"Actually, it's just the opposite. Getting up and moving around will make you feel much better than lying down. We'll have you on a physical therapy routine by the end of the week. Once we determine—"

Crosby pushed himself to his feet. He staggered forward on unsteady legs and shook his head, windmilling his arms to get the blood pumping. He raised his arms over his head and began to lean side to side, stretching. Then he turned towards Eli and crouched down into the three-pointed stance of a defensive lineman.

"Red forty-two! Red forty-two!" he said, pawing at the ground with his back foot like a bull.

Eli held out his arms and began backing towards the door. "Not right now, Mr. Nelson. We can hold off on physical activity until our therapy session."

An orderly rushed in and stepped in front of Eli.

"Hold on," Eli said. "Let's not escalate the situation."

"Red forty-two! Red forty-two!" Crosby called out.

The orderly pulled pepper spray from his belt holster and pointed it at Crosby.

"There'll be no need for that," Eli said calmly. He put a hand on the orderly's shoulder and maneuvered around him, pushing him back out of the way. "We're okay."

Eli squatted down in order to get eye level with Crosby. "We'll have plenty of time for exercise," he said. "But now is not the time. Let's sit back down, okay?"

"Ready. Set. Hut one! Hut two!" Crosby raised an arm behind his back as though preparing to charge.

Eli set the patient folder aside and placed his hands on the ground to brace himself.

The orderly stepped forward, preparing to pull Eli to safety.

Then Eli launched forward, swift for a man nearing seventy, and stutter-stepped around Crosby's crouched body.

Crosby fell forward, off-balance, and took a knee. "False start!" he cried. "That's a false start." He looked up at the orderly. "Come on, Ref. Where's the call?"

The orderly was hunched over, pepper spray outstretched, wide eyes on Eli for guidance.

Eli prompted him to signal a false start.

Slowly, the orderly straightened, palmed the pepper spray and rolled his hands over one another, signaling the penalty.

Crosby clapped his hands together and stood. He turned towards Eli and smiled. "That's five yards. Loss of down."

"You got me," Eli said. He walked over and raised his hand for a high five. Crosby slapped it. "You got me on the hard count. Where did you learn that?" He placed a hand on Crosby's back and guided him back to the bed, helping him take a seat.

The orderly pocketed his pepper spray and shook his head as he shuffled out the door.

"Played a couple of years in high school," Crosby said. "Could have played college, but I didn't care for any of the coaches. They were all recruiting me, though."

Eli knew he was lying. Crosby spent his college years delivering pizzas and servicing johns in public restrooms. He hadn't attended a single day of high school.

"Well, we don't play much football here, but we have plenty of other exercises to keep you fit. We could get you to show us some plays, though, if you'd like."

"Yeah, I could," Crosby said, crossing his arms and nodding his head. "I know them all."

"I'm sure you do," Eli said.

The cramped room contained a small bed with a thin foam mattress and a shelf that served as a writing desk, although the patients weren't permitted pens. The smooth cinder-block walls were painted glossy white and barren. There were no mirrors. No windows. In the center of the ceiling, a square vent leaked stale air. It was difficult to sit long without claustrophobia setting in. Some patients found the confines comforting, like a dog in a crate. In others it led to crippling bouts of anxiety. Crosby seemed like the former.

He lay back on his bunk, cushioning his head with his hands, and stared contentedly above. "I know this place ain't what it seems," he said. "But it hasn't been half bad so far."

Eli left space for the words to expand. Farther down the hallway, a patient began to sing the refrain from "Old Rugged Cross." It was the sound of an angel in mourning. He admired it for a moment before responding, "I'm glad to hear that." He held his hand out again, and this time Crosby accepted it. "We're all here for you. To help you with whatever it is you need. We're family here. We all help each other out."

Someone knocked on the door and Eli turned to see Angela walk in. "I hear you boys have been roughhousing," she said, a strained smile on her face, her eyes scanning the room.

"Yeah, it looks like we've got ourselves a star player if we ever put a football team together," Eli said. He squeezed Crosby's hand a final time before letting go. "It was nice to meet you, Mr. Nelson. Angela here is the best social worker we have. She'll take great care of you. And tomorrow your primary therapist, Dr. Drexler, will stop in to introduce himself. You're in good hands." He squeezed Angela on the shoulder as he walked by, and waved from the door before he left.

★   ★   ★

The orderly was waiting for Eli in the hallway – Devon Jackson, a tall twenty-something who looked like he was still outgrowing his baby fat. He kicked off the wall when he saw Eli and came up next to him.

"Hey, Dr. Alpert. Man, you can't be pulling that crazy shit in here. You gonna—"

Eli stopped so suddenly Devon ran into him. He rebounded even though he outweighed the doctor by over seventy pounds. Devon took another step backwards when he saw Eli's eyes, and almost flinched when Eli grabbed his arm and yanked him close.

"Don't ever use that word in here. Do you understand?" Eli's voice was low, nearly a whisper, but it struck Devon with the severity of a shout.

"Say what? Shit?"

"No. *Crazy.* Or any of its synonyms – *psycho, loony, insane.* I don't even want to hear you say *strange, weird* or *different.* Such language is not tolerated in the presence of my patients."

"All right, but look, I got a job to do. How's it going to look if some crazy-ass—?" Devon bit his lower lip and shook his head. "Sorry, if some patient, especially one up in forensics, attacks a doctor on my watch? Man, I'll lose my job for that."

"First, I am not a doctor. I am Chief Medical Director—"

"I know that. Man, that's what I'm saying—" Eli tightened his grip on Devon, who rolled his eyes and sighed like a toddler being scolded by an ineffectual parent.

"As Chief Medical Director, my responsibility is for the well-being of my patients. That takes precedence over your concerns for my safety. Rule number one..." *never wake a sleeping giant*, "...is to establish trust. Without trust, patients resist treatment. Without treatment, they don't get well.

"Rule number two..." *if you do, put the son of a bitch back to sleep*, "...is to treat them with dignity and respect. Getting pepper-sprayed or forcibly restrained does not constitute humane treatment. It is strictly a last resort. You'll remember that while on my watch."

"And what if he were to have jumped you in there? What then?"

"Then, I trust you would have been there to help me subdue him."

Devon pulled his arm away. "That ain't how Dr. Drexler do things. I can't be second-guessing what I'm supposed to do all the time. That's how someone gets hurt."

"Well, then, I'll be sure to reiterate my position to all staff. But that is how we do things here. We treat patients with the respect we would expect for ourselves. Understood?"

"You the man," Devon said. He smirked and gave a two-finger salute before he turned and walked away.

Eli continued down the hall, scowling. *"That ain't how Dr. Drexler do things."* He'd have to have a talk with Alex when he returned. He could sense some tension with Angela when he'd mentioned his name, and now this. Perhaps he'd given his protégé a bit more leeway than he was ready for. He couldn't afford any loose ends with the board review looming.

Just the thought of the upcoming board meeting caused Eli's stomach to clench. He knew his resistance towards more traditional care methods and modern medicine was unpopular. But how ignorant of history must everyone be to immediately embrace new therapeutic methods without erring on the side of caution. During the last century, every decade had ushered in a new form of treatment to be crowned the new cure, from bloodletting to waterboarding to shock therapy to lobotomy to innocuous pills that steal a patient's personality. The only form of therapy that has ever stood the test of time is humanistic – to treat patients like people, not deranged beasts.

If it weren't for Sugar Hill's sterling record for patient recovery, Eli knew he would have been replaced long ago. And, even still, his job was in jeopardy. More than that, his legacy. Which is why it was so important for Alex to carry the torch forward. To ensure that his humanistic philosophies endured and to avoid the pitfalls of the past.

As Eli made the turn back towards his office, he recalled his first job as a young psychiatrist, and another voice whispered in his head. This one his own. *You are the harbinger of death. Only pretending to make man sane.*

CHAPTER FIVE

The building was made up of 6,452 bricks. He had counted every one. And, like snowflakes, no two were the same.

They varied in color from orange to peach, to pink, to crimson, to red. *Blood red*, Jerry thought. They varied in texture, some rough and jagged, others flat and smooth. When he closed his eyes, he could picture each one being picked up, slathered with cement and placed in its own special spot by the bricklayers, stacking them in a staggered line, side by side, one atop the next. The surface of each brick was porous, pricked with hundreds of tiny air holes. On certain days, Jerry could hear them breathe.

The building's breathing was comforting. It was the calm, steady breathing that marked the rhythm of routine life. Never ragged. Never labored. It reminded Jerry of being a little boy and falling asleep with his father on the couch after returning home from Sunday brunch. Rocking to the gentle rise and fall of his father's chest, tucked under the soft throw blanket like some stowaway aboard a seafaring ship. The building walls would expand and contract with the same reassuring regularity as his father's chest, and, at such times, the entire world would come alive, unveiling its hidden beauty, disclosing ancient secrets through whispered words.

His companion landscaper, Manny, plucked a dandelion from the flowerbed and began to stuff it in his bag, but hesitated. He raised it to his face and studied it. "Ain't these supposed to grant you three wishes?" he said.

Jerry had dropped the garden hose and was standing catatonic, paralyzed by the overload of information, the brilliant spectrum of colors, the dance of inanimate objects, the truth and connectivity that unite all things. He was back on his father's chest, but it was Earth's heartbeat that he was hearing, and it was more than his human mind could take.

"Nah, that ain't it," Manny said. "Just one wish, if you blow on it like a birthday candle." He closed his eyes and took a deep breath, holding it in. Then he opened his eyes and blew across the bulb, sending dozens of feathery dandelion seeds floating through the air. "Ha! Looks like I'm getting laid tonight," he said, turning and smiling up at Jerry. Manny shook his head and pushed himself to his feet. *Damn, poor muchacho's lost his marbles again.*

"Hey, Earth to Jerry!" he called as he came walking up, waving his arms before Jerry's vacant stare. "Yo, back to reality, *mi amigo.*"

Jerry remained motionless; the only sign of life was the occasional blinking of his eyes. Manny removed his garden gloves and used them to wipe sweat from the back of his neck. "Shit," he said, scanning the grounds for nurses or guards. The expansive lawn was empty at the moment. That was good.

Manny grabbed Jerry by the shoulder and shook him back and forth. "Hey, wake up, man. Jerry! Jerry! Man, they're going to take you off detail, bro. They're going to put you back inside. Come on, *amigo.*"

A reedy sound escaped Jerry's mouth. It sounded like he was trying to speak. Manny put his ear near Jerry's lips. "What's that? Come on. Talk to me, Jerry."

"I can see," Jerry said in a small, wavering whisper, "the world speak."

"Shit!" Manny said, spooking a sparrow, which leapt from the roofline of the storage shed and flew to the fountain in the center of a seating area near the building entrance. It hopped into the water and began bathing itself as the building doors swung outward and two orderlies strolled through. Their mouths were open, shoulders shaking, but their laughter came seconds late, a slight delay as the sound traveled across the open air.

One looked like Carl, who Manny shared smokes with on occasion. He wouldn't create any waves. The other, though. It looked like Devon, that loudmouth man-child who acted like he was second in charge behind Dr. Alpert. Devon was the gatekeeper of hospital gossip. His eyes and ears were everywhere.

Manny bent over and retrieved the hose, then put his arm across Jerry's shoulders and started walking him towards the door to the supplies building. They only made it a few shuffling steps before Manny heard Carl call from across the yard. He cursed and looked back over his shoulder. Carl was waving a hand in the air and trotting forward, Devon keeping pace with his long, lumbering stride.

Manny waved back as he stared sideways into Jerry's eyes. They were blank, his pupils constricted down to little pinpricks. A string of drool dripped from his slack mouth. He placed the hose back in Jerry's hand and wrapped his fingers around it, then pushed him closer to the flowerbed. The spray fell a few feet short.

"Yo, Manny! What's up, what's up?" Carl said as he approached, slapping Manny's hand and bringing him in for a half hug. Devon stayed back and lifted his head in a curt greeting before shifting his weight and gazing off across the yard. It felt as though a timer had started. Carl pointed to Manny's pocket and said, "You got a couple extra smokes?"

"Yeah, yeah." Manny reached into his pocket and pulled out a crumpled pack of Camels. He shook out three sticks and passed them around.

"Yo, let's go take a seat," Manny said, trying to corral them back towards the central seating area. Carl turned to go, but Devon stood in place.

"Nah, man. I'm straight right here. Some crazy motherfucker be creeping up on us back that way. That's what I'm trying to take a break from." Devon reached out and grabbed Manny's lighter and sparked his smoke. He tossed it to Carl who wasn't looking, so it bounced off his shoulder and hit the ground.

"Man, no patients are going to bust up on us. It ain't break time," Manny said.

"Still." Devon shrugged and took a deep pull off his cigarette, exhaling the smoke through his large, pimply nose.

"Whatever," Manny said. He met eyes with Carl and they both took a drag to hide their smiles. "Come on. Let's at least get in the shade." Again he tried to walk them around the corner of the supplies shed.

This time they turned and began to walk away, and then Carl spun around. "Hey yo, Jerry! Come have a smoke," he said.

Manny cringed as Jerry continued facing the storage shed, saturating a single patch of grass. Carl looked at Manny and raised his eyebrows. Manny shrugged. "Man, he don't want to be bothered, come on."

"Yo, what's up with him?" Devon said, then walked forward and peered over his shoulder. "Man, he's all fucked up." Devon waved his hand in front of Jerry's face. "You're supposed to report this shit," he said.

Manny smiled. He came forward and patted Jerry on the back. "What? Man, you know how Jerry gets. He'll snap out of it any minute. It ain't nothing."

"Yeah, I know how he gets. He gets batshit crazy. He ain't supposed to be out here when he's like that." Devon took another drag, squinting at Jerry through the ribbons of smoke, then exhaled the plume directly into his face.

Jerry blinked his eyes and flared his nostrils. Just like that, his body reanimated and he looked around.

Manny came forward and put his hand on Jerry's back. "Hey, brother, you okay—"

Jerry jerked away from him, frightened. His eyes grew wide and his mouth peeled back, baring his tobacco-stained teeth. "Put that away," he said, leaning back. "You're burning me."

"Hey, it's cool, it's cool," Manny said. He dropped the cigarette and held up his hands. "You're all right."

Carl followed cue, stubbing his cigarette out under his shoe and showing his empty hands. Devon took another drag and stepped forward. "Ain't nobody burning you," he said.

"Get that away from me," Jerry said, cowering back another step.

Devon kept coming forward. "It's just a cigarette," he said, holding it out in front of him.

Jerry raised the hose, plugging his thumb into the spout, and sprayed Devon with a fan of water, extinguishing the cigarette and soaking his clothes.

Devon held out his hand to block the spray, then his lips peeled back in a sneer of rage and he charged. He collared Jerry around the neck and hip-tossed him to the ground, landing on him with all his weight. The hose went flying from Jerry's hand, flopping on the ground like an angry snake.

Jerry squirmed and tried to bridge his back, but he was stuck under Devon's larger frame.

"What the fuck?" Manny said, rushing forward and trying to pull Devon off of him.

"Back off!" Devon gasped, already short of breath. He cranked

Jerry's neck, watching as his face turned from pale to pink to purple. "I'm trying to subdue him."

Jerry began to kick frantically with his legs, and Devon squeezed tighter still, crushing his face against his chest, arching his back. Then Devon screamed in pain and released him. He raised his arm and checked under his armpit, hissing in pain. "Motherfucker bit me." Driblets of red began to emerge through his blue shirt. He stalked forward and Manny restrained him from behind.

"That's enough," Manny said.

Devon turned and shoved Manny backwards.

He had to pinwheel his arms to keep from falling.

"I told you, man. That's why you can't have crazy-ass motherfuckers running free out here. I don't care whose brother he is. You in it as much as he is for covering up."

Manny walked past him and helped Jerry stand up. His eyes were still wild, his breathing ragged and wheezing, but he allowed Manny to help guide him back towards the hospital.

"You okay?" Manny asked as they approached the building entrance.

"The world is hurting," Jerry said. He had started to tremble. "They want to burn the world."

Manny patted him on the back as he ushered him inside. "You're okay," he told him. "You're okay."

CHAPTER SIX

Alex awoke to an empty bed. He pulled aside the sheets and skulked into the bathroom to shower. *What a fucking nightmare,* he thought, wishing that it were.

He had dumped Popeye's body in the outdoor garbage bin before coming into the house, but that wasn't good enough for Rachel. She wanted him buried.

"Where the fuck do you want me to bury him?" Alex had yelled, finally losing his temper. "In the fucking flowerbeds?"

"Bury him under the dogwood."

This had made him laugh. "Right. How fitting."

Rachel hadn't found it funny.

It had taken him an hour of strenuous digging to realize there was no way to penetrate the root system directly under the dogwood. And he was not willing to dig up the expensive zoysia that had just been sodded last spring. In the end, he buried Popeye in an unceremonious grave back behind the outdoor AC units. It saved him from having to make a headstone.

Alex turned the shower handle to hot in an effort to scour away the residue from the previous day. First, his failed test trial. His fifth and, most likely, final test trial. For Philax, at least. Not that he had any additional suitors. The Philax opportunity had virtually fallen into his lap; otherwise he never would have sought it out. But his overconfidence in the medicine's success had buried him in a financial hole so deep he could scarcely see a way out. Not without selling off most of their assets, coming clean to Rachel, exposing his lies to Eli. None of those were viable options at the moment. Comparatively, Popeye had gotten off easy.

He dried off and dressed in his pleated pants and starched shirt, posing in front of the mirror for the fiftieth time before heading downstairs for breakfast. He smelled fresh coffee and wasn't sure whether to be happy or apprehensive. That meant Rachel was still home.

She was at the breakfast table, huddled over a coffee mug, her long, black hair twisted into a loose ponytail and slung over her right shoulder. Pale sunlight streamed through the bay window behind her like a stage light spotlighting a somber scene. Alex paused at the entrance and watched as she raised the mug to her mouth with both hands and took a pensive sip. Her eyes were distant, and for as long as he watched she never blinked.

"Morning," Alex said as he entered the kitchen.

Rachel kept staring straight ahead.

He walked to the breadbox, pulled out a bag of bagels and sliced one in two. He smothered each side with cream cheese and began eating it at the kitchen counter.

"Your phone has been ringing all morning," Rachel said.

He glanced to where he had left it recharging. "Okay," he said.

Rachel lifted her head. She looked more weary than angry. Smudges darkened the undersides of her eyes and the lines framing her mouth appeared deeper than usual. "No," she said. "It's been ringing all morning. You should check it. Like, now."

Alex activated the phone and peered at the display screen. There were five missed calls from Sugar Hill, two from the main line, two from Angela and one from Eli. A flash of heat erupted in his chest. *And the hits just keep on coming.* Rachel watched as he listened to the messages, and took a long sip of her coffee as he set the phone down.

"Goddammit," he said, bracing himself against the counter with both hands.

"What?" Rachel asked, sounding concerned. He saw an opportunity in her tone of voice and let the silence stretch. After several seconds, she asked again, "Honey, what is it?" Over his shoulder he could see her straighten and begin tugging on her hair.

"It's Jerry," he said. He turned and faced her, marshaling his most sympathetic expression. "He's had another episode and has been committed. They're holding him at the hospital."

"Oh no. What happened?" Rachel said. She had set aside the coffee cup and was now fiddling with her sleeve. Alex poured himself a cup of coffee and took it to the table, huddling over the mug with a heavy head, as Rachel had before.

"I don't know. That's all they said. I guess I'll find out when I show up."

"But…" Rachel scooted closer to Alex and placed a hand on his arm, "…is he okay?"

Alex shrugged. "Depends on how severe it is. They're not likely to give him another work detail, that's for sure."

"What? But, that's terrible. How could they do that? They know Jerry. Isn't there anything you can do?"

Alex sighed. He placed his hand on hers and squeezed, then looked into her eyes. "I'll do everything I can."

★   ★   ★

As boys, Alex had always looked up to Jerry, his older brother by four years. They shared a room until Jerry became a teenager, and it had felt like an exclusive clubhouse where Alex was the initiate, becoming indoctrinated in all the secret ways of the world. Jerry had introduced him to comics, which they would read together, huddled under a tented bedsheet with an electric lantern, rooting on Batman, the Hulk and Hawkeye as they brought justice to a miscreant society.

Inspired by their cartoon superheroes, they had set out to form their own real-life dynamic duo. Jerry had created costumes to conceal their alter egos. A black ski mask for him, with zigzagging lightning bolts etched onto each cheek. And, for Alex, an old pair of tighty-whiteys turned upside down, with crude holes cut out for the eyes. Jerry was Bolt Lightning. And, due to the faded brown stain that ran down Alex's forehead, he was called the Streak. Alex was too enthusiastic about their escapades to realize that he was literally the butt of his brother's joke.

Their first mission was to rescue the neighbor's cat, which Jerry had planted in a tree. It was an old, overweight Cheshire that had been declawed. And when placed upon the branch, had fallen contentedly asleep.

Jerry pointed up to the limb of the old elm, maybe fifteen feet above the ground, struggling to keep from laughing at the sight of Alex's eager eyes framing his wash-resilient shit stain. "There's nothing I can do. The electric powers of Bolt Lightning will set the tree aflame. It's up to you. This is a job for…" he paused, biting the side of his tongue, "… the Streak!"

Alex had been overcome with excitement. Unfortunately, his climbing abilities were not up to the task. He was shimmying out onto the limb holding the snoozing cat when he slipped and fell, pinballing off a branch below and breaking his arm on the ground.

Still, the first thing Alex asked for when he returned from the hospital was his mask. Disgusted, his mother had thrown it away. So Jerry made another one. To Alex's delight, the new one had an even darker streak.

As they grew older, Alex's admiration for his big brother slowly turned to envy, as the vast differences between the two became more pronounced. Jerry was their father's son: handsome, charismatic, athletic. Popular at school and successful in sports. Whereas Alex appeared to have emerged from another gene pool altogether, always buried in a book, more interested in science than chasing skirt.

Their father would take them fishing and Jerry would reel them in, one after the other, while Alex organized the tackle box and dissected the worms. After school, the house was always filled with the gregarious laughter of Jerry's friends, while Alex would stay holed up in his room, reading the *Encyclopedia Britannica* for fun.

Still, Jerry would make a point to include Alex in his endeavors, asking him to join in on a pickup baseball game or catch a movie. Even inviting him to high-school senior keg parties when Alex was only in the eighth grade. But by then Alex had either lost interest or was intimidated by Jerry's activities. He was clumsy where Jerry was coordinated, shy where Jerry was sociable, weak where Jerry was strong.

The last time they played catch, their father interrupted after watching from the window, too agitated for words. He spent the next hour working to correct Alex's form. Trying to teach him not to throw like a girl.

When Jerry left for Ole Miss on a full baseball scholarship, their father cried. Later, he got drunk. He started with a small glass of rye whiskey before dinner, then poured another, this one slightly larger. By the time dinner was through, he was on his fifth glass, the amber liquid shimmering just below the brim, a single cube of ice quickly succumbing to the drink's fiery heat. By then, Mr. Drexler had stopped crying, but his eyes were still rimmed with red, and his grief had turned to aggression.

"You got some big shoes to fill," he said. They were sitting at the four-top kitchen table with three place settings. The empty space in front of the fourth had felt like a memorial. There was a crescent-shaped water stain where Jerry's glass used to go. His mother was clearing the table, sniffling. She had been crying all day as well.

"I know," Alex said. He didn't know what else to say. His brother had only been gone a few hours, and the mood in the house had already changed perceptibly. It had darkened. The familiar sights and sounds of each room now seemed foreign, inhospitable. He was beginning to feel like a stranger, as if he had learned he was an orphan and no longer welcome, and would soon be asked to leave.

"What do you know?" his father said, sneering, taking a large sip of whiskey and hissing against the burn. "What can you possibly know when all you do is sit in your room by yourself, doing what? Reading about a bunch of stuff other people have gone and figured out? Try living a little. You don't want to waste your whole life reading about the experiences of better men." His hands clenched into fists and he grimaced like a man preparing to fight. He chewed his tongue. "Boy, you've got big shoes to fill. I want you to know that."

"Don, please," Mrs. Drexler said. She opened her mouth to say more, then exploded into tears and buried her face in a dirty dish towel. Her crying was not quiet. It was the apotheosis of sadness, great heaving wails that sounded like a wounded water beast. It overwhelmed the small kitchen nook, cramming itself into every corner.

"Damn it, look at your mother," Mr. Drexler said. He began to squirm in his seat and his face began to twitch, turning darker shades of red as he worked to rein in his emotions. "Look at her, damn you." Then his lip curled in and he began crying again himself. An ugly, unpracticed cry after decades of disuse.

"What do you want from me?" Alex stammered, raising his arms in supplication. "I miss him too." Then he broke down as well, as much from fear and confusion as from sadness over Jerry's departure.

The three of them sat and cried together, each harder than the other. But the crying did not bring closeness. It felt more like shame. Like they were all exposing sides of themselves they never meant the others to see.

Finally, Alex pushed away and put himself to bed, falling asleep to the sound of his mother crying and his father's slurred, angry speech.

The experience awoke something in him, however. A new sense of determination. Not to follow in his brother's footsteps, exactly, but to push himself to the limit of his own potential. And he found that potential to be immense, rising to the top of his class at school, winning national awards for his projects in science.

Still, it hadn't been enough to win his father's respect. He remained an outcast in his own home, even as he began earning the admiration of his instructors and accolades from the science community for his pronounced intellect.

Then, they received the call. It was from Jerry's college roommate. Jerry was acting strange. He was losing weight, behaving erratically, violently. He was convinced that there was a conspiracy on campus, that it had all been a trap to lure him in and control him. To get information from him. Information that only he had.

The night Jerry had left for college was nothing compared to the night he came back home. To Mr. Drexler, the world had lost coherence. The shy science nerd was excelling and the promising sports star was self-destructing. It was like a personal insult from God. It was also the night Alex decided to begin studying psychology, igniting the chain of events that led him to his present place.

★   ★   ★

Alex patted Rachel on the hand and squeezed it again before letting go. "I should go. I'll keep you posted."

Rachel grabbed his hand and looked at him with her large, expressive eyes. The look was like telepathy, a show of silent support.

"I'm sorry," she said, giving a deep nod that suggested she meant for more than just Jerry. "Call me as soon as you can. Okay?"

"I will," he said, and kissed her cheek. Then stood from the table and set off for Sugar Hill, a half-concealed smile on his face.

CHAPTER SEVEN

Sugar Hill rose before him as he crested the hill, its central spire reaching up to pierce the leaden sky. The narrow lane leading off the main road towards the facility was lined by cedars and large oaks draped with flowing strands of Spanish moss. It was the oldest mental health facility in Georgia, first established back in the early 1800s as a plantation for a wealthy farmer. The man's wife had been from humble beginnings and grown eccentric under the weight of their wealth, supposedly showering gifts like pearl necklaces and frilly lace cravats upon various farm animals that she had grown affection for. When the husband mistakenly butchered her favorite cow, which she'd raised up from a calf, and had it served for supper, she snapped, falling into a bleak, babbling despair that she never could recover from.

As penance, the man granted his plantation to the state. His wife needed treatment, and he wanted her to feel at home.

While the facility had been expanded to accommodate hundreds of patients (thousands during a grim period of overcrowding that was largely omitted from its written history), the architecture remained true to its origins. The main building was red brick with white accents, two-story with a columned entrance and a wide front porch featuring rocking chairs. White picket fences fronted the facility. The taller, wire-mesh ones with razor wire were farther back and harder to see.

The staff parking lot was around the side, with a special, card-access entrance. The facility offered the impression of genteel charm, but it was as guarded and secure as any state penitentiary. And, at times, could be just as dangerous, if not more so.

Alex took a deep breath before sliding his card through the entry slot and punching in the passcode. *Remember, back from vacation,* he thought.

Inside, Sugar Hill shed its architectural ancestry, taking on the sterilized appearance of a traditional hospital with white cinder-block walls and green-flecked linoleum floors. The staff entrance was deceptively quiet.

It led down a short hallway, lined with written warnings and security instructions, to a large steel door with electronic locks. Once through this security entrance, however, the final buffer between the patients' realm and the outside world was removed and the chaotic sounds of insanity echoed from within its inner depths.

Alex strolled past the security desk, offering a curt wave to the two orderlies stationed there.

An elderly African-American patient wearing a loose-fitting hospital gown was walking the hallway. She offered Alex a gap-toothed smile as he passed by, then stopped and spoke to his back. "Swoosh! He goes, he goes. Swoosh, he goes!" she said, sliding her hands together and shuffling her feet.

He kept walking as her rambling voice and discordant two-step faded to a murmur behind him. He turned the corner and opened the door to his office, a small room crowded with bookshelves surrounding a wooden desk covered with paperwork. The only form of wall art was the framed psychiatry degree from Emory. A whiteboard was crammed into a corner, featuring a red triangle bordered by half-erased acronyms.

Alex dropped his briefcase and checked his messages. Eli wanted to see him. ASAP. So did Angela.

He checked his appearance in a handheld mirror that he kept in the top desk drawer, and set off to see his brother instead.

★　　★　　★

He found Jerry in the dining area, hunched over a tray of uneaten eggs, shriveled sausage links and scorched toast. His head was hanging down, hiding his face behind a curtain of unkempt hair. The room was filled with the sounds of clanging trays and incoherent chattering, but Jerry seemed deaf to the chaos around him.

Alex sighed and sat across from him, crossing his legs and resting an arm across the table, drumming his fingers. "Jerry," he said. There was no response, so he said it again, then slapped his hand against the table a couple of times and shook Jerry's breakfast tray. "Hey, Jerry."

Slowly, Jerry raised his head; a string of saliva was rappelling from his bottom lip down to the collar of his paisley gown. His eyes were glazed, but a glimmer of recognition caused him to furrow his eyebrows and lean closer. His mouth attempted a feeble smile before going slack once again. He mumbled something that sounded like, "I'm humble pie."

"Hey, brother," Alex said, shielding the disappointment from his eyes. "How you doing?"

Jerry checked over both shoulders and then leaned as far across the table as possible, planting an elbow into the plate of scrambled eggs. "Where've you been?" he asked in a low, conspiratorial voice. He reached out and grabbed Alex by the wrist. "Are you part of this?"

Alex sighed. "I'm sorry, I've been away." He placed his hand on top of Jerry's and searched his eyes. "Part of what?"

"They've got me locked up. Like a chicken. They took my eggs. Now I'm in a coop."

Alex ran a hand through his thick, wavy hair. The same shade of black as Jerry's, except shorter. "Jerry, you're not locked up. You're just being held for observation. You're sick again, and we need to get you well. I'm going to get you home just as soon as I can. I promise."

"No, that's not it. I saw." Jerry emphasized his statement by pointing to his eyes. "The big one knows," he said, scanning the room again. "He tried to kill me."

Alex studied his hands. *They've got the dosage too low,* he thought. *Damn it, Eli.*

"Well, I'm going to get to the bottom of things. Okay? We'll get you back home as soon as we can. Just try and relax."

Jerry opened a packet of cigarettes lying on the table and lit one, inhaling deeply and blowing rank smoke into the air.

"Shit, Jerry, you can't smoke here." Alex grabbed the cigarette from Jerry's mouth and dropped it into a cup of orange juice. He looked up and saw the large orderly, Devon, rushing over and waved him off. Devon paused, assessing the situation, then raised his hand and walked back to his place along the wall.

Jerry watched Devon walk away, then turned back to Alex with narrowed eyes. "What have they told you? What do you know?"

"What do I know?" Alex said. He swirled the cigarette butt in the juice cup, turning the orange liquid gray. "Let's see. I know that today is Tuesday. I know that Santa Claus isn't real. And I know that running over your wife's dog is not the best way to get laid. As far as the conspiracy involving whatever it is you think you've seen, I know that it's due to a chemical imbalance occurring in your brain that we'll correct with a combination of medicines."

Jerry laughed, stretching his pale skin across a gaunt, skeletal face. "The medicine makes you blind," Jerry said. "Why don't you just cut out our eyes? Take them with you. Look through them and you'll see what I see."

Alex frowned. The primary pursuit of his research was working to understand the nature of psychotic perception. In order to do so, he first had to gain a better understanding into the nature of regular perception, which was an enigma. Where did consciousness come from? From the mind? From a nonlocalized source? No one knew. Cognitive mapping studies had failed to find a source for conscious thought. And the mind was incapable of unraveling its own mysteries.

What really comprised the core of his theoretical work, however, was trying to understand the biological need for altered states of consciousness. Why did the mind have the capacity to create delusions? To hallucinate? To perceive the unreal? And why, so often, did such altered states appear to the perceiver as the actual reality? A world more real than this one?

While at Emory, Alex had been intrigued by a grant-funded study into the effects of certain hallucinogenic compounds. As a top student in the psychiatry department, his inquiries had granted him an invitation to participate in the research, to assess the study from a therapeutic point of view.

The central compound under examination was a potent hallucinogenic called Dimethyltryptamine – a naturally occurring neurotransmitter found in almost all forms of life, including the human mind. It was believed to be produced by the pineal gland, released during REM sleep and times of extreme stress, such as in the moments before death. An endogenous drug responsible for dreams and death's white light. When concentrated amounts were injected into patients, it produced profound states of altered consciousness. Ineffable experiences that seemed to result from a scrambled mind. Except...

Except many of the reports featured similar descriptions. Strangers with dissimilar backgrounds were having shared experiences. Life-altering experiences featuring complex geometric patterns which participants invariably referred to as the "true fabric of reality." Wild journeys to other dimensions where contact was made with alien entities who possessed primal wisdom. Encounters with an energy field described as the God source where participants reported feeling perfect love and understanding.

Underneath all of these shared themes was the unifying belief that whatever the test subjects had experienced had been real. As real as the laboratory in which the experiments were being conducted. A belief that persisted in the minds of the test subjects long after the experiments had concluded.

While Alex did not believe that these visions or hidden realms were real, he accepted that the participants believed them to be. Just as a person suffering from a psychotic episode will consider his or her delusions to be actual reality. It was a trick created by the release of chemicals to stimulate our minds during sleep and protect us from existential stress. Why it seemed to be encoded with archetypal images or capable of accessing our subconscious was still a mystery. But controlling its production by the pineal gland was something Alex had learned to do. It was the core function of the experimental compound that he had created and tried to sell to Philax.

"If you don't want us to see, why don't you just cut out our eyes?"

Alex opened his mouth then closed it. He scanned the room, observing the patients. Some sitting catatonic before full plates of food. Some rocking back and forth, mumbling incoherently. Some gazing towards the ceiling with agonized expressions, as though watching the Rapture descend.

"What *do* you see?" Alex asked his brother.

Jerry nodded his head and leaned back. "The source," he said. "The truth." He tapped his temple and pointed his finger at Alex. "I see what's hidden, and that's why you've got me locked up like a chicken in a coop."

"Jerry, you're not—"

A hand came down on Alex's shoulder. "There you are," Angela said. Her lips were pressed tight, her dark eyes burrowed into his own. Then she looked over at Jerry and smiled. "Hey, Jerry! How are you feeling this morning?"

"I'm fine," he said robotically, then bent over his tray of food and began poking at his eggs.

"That's great. Mind if I borrow your brother for a minute?"

Alex reached out and grabbed Jerry's hand. "Hang in there, big guy. I'll get you home just as soon as I can."

Jerry looked up through his curtain of hair. His eyes jittered and he squeezed them shut and shook his head, as if to clear his mind of what he'd just seen.

CHAPTER EIGHT

Angela sped away from the table, towards the exit, making Alex jog to catch up. She pushed through the hydraulic door without holding it open, so it rebounded against him.

He shook his head and followed her through.

Once outside, Angela slowed. She kept her voice low. "I've been calling you all morning. Where have you been?"

Alex pointed back towards the cafeteria. "Where you just found me. With Jerry. What the hell happened?"

"It would have been better to have had this conversation before you met with him."

"Well, that's too bad. I'm more concerned with his well-being than with sticking to protocol. He's not a regular patient, you know. And he's not being treated properly. His dosage is off."

Angela nodded. "That came from Eli."

"Yeah, I figured."

They turned a corner that opened onto a large recreational room with card tables and televisions bolted to the walls. It was empty during breakfast hours but Alex still led them to a back table by the window, near the far wall.

Alex eyed the wall before he sat down. It was covered by a mural painted by a former patient. The mural, with its Picasso-esque abstractions, was a representation of the Garden of Eden with a man and woman scantily covered by leaves. They were surrounded by all forms of smiling wildlife, predators at peace with prey. Lions stood comfortably beside zebra; wolves nuzzled sheep. A diamond-patterned snake presented a red apple to the woman. Carved into the apple's skin was the pyramid with the all-seeing eye from the dollar bill. The woman was smiling, but a single tear trickled down her cheek. The sky featured the vast cosmos, a tapestry of darkness and stars, distant planets and foreign galaxies. There was no sign of the sun.

They sat and Angela sighed. She scanned the room and then propped her elbow on the table and placed her chin in her hand.

"Look, I'm sorry. It's been a shitty couple of days. It's just—"

"Hard when I'm away," Alex said, smiling.

Angela gave him a mock look of impatience.

"Come on, you can admit it," he said, teasing. "You missed me."

"No," she said. Her legs were crossed and her top foot began to tap the air. "You just always pick the worst time to take off."

"What a coincidence. It couldn't be that things just happen to run smoother when I'm here?"

Angela cupped her hand to muffle her voice. "It's gotten worse," she said.

Alex leaned forward. "Eli?"

She nodded. A crease formed between her eyes and her brows came together. "The new forensic patient, Crosby Nelson, who you were supposed to meet with, by the way, was admitted this week. Eli met with him instead, and there was some sort of an altercation."

"Jesus, what happened?"

"Evidently Crosby got down in some sort of a football stance like he was going to charge him. One of the orderlies stepped in, but Eli ordered him off. He played chicken with him, or something. I don't fully understand."

Alex barked laughter. "Wait. He did what?"

"I'm telling you, I don't know. I came in after. He... I guess he pretended to play football with him."

Alex was all eyes. He shook his head. "That's crazy. So what happened?"

"Thankfully nothing. Somehow he got Crosby to settle down. The orderly's pissed, though. He wants to file a complaint."

"Who is it?"

"The big guy, Devon. Which is another thing. He had a run-in with your brother. Jerry bit him."

"Christ, this week has gone off the rails." *And that doesn't even account for my failed test trial or my wife's dead dog.*

Angela nodded. She leaned back in her seat and crossed her arms.

From the hallway behind her an orderly pushed a supply cart with a squeaky wheel. From farther down came a deep howling, as if from an angry primate. Alex looked over his shoulder and frowned at the painted wall.

"That's why I wanted to see you first thing," Angela said.

"Well, my first priority is Jerry. Have any charges been filed?"

"No. There're some discrepancies surrounding the story. A groundskeeper, a friend of your brother's, is apparently saying that Devon used unnecessary force."

"Yeah, Jerry's not violent. You know that."

"I know. But his condition is just so unpredictable."

"Well, he's on the wrong medication. I need to talk with Eli about that. And Crosby. I'll need to visit with him too. What's his schedule?"

"We have a therapy session later today. Can you make it?"

"Sure." Alex checked his watch. "Anything else?"

"What about Eli?"

"What about him?"

"The review meeting is coming up. I'm worried."

The far hall filled with the sounds of shuffling feet. Two female orderlies came bounding around the corner with bright smiles fixed to their faces. They turned and began greeting the patients as they filed in, shouting in cheerful tones.

"Come on, y'all! Good morning. Good morning. Y'all want to play some games? Let's play us some games, y'all! What do you say?"

Alex stood and rapped his foreknuckle against the top of the table. "That's Eli's problem," he said. *I've got enough of my own,* he thought as he walked away.

CHAPTER NINE

What Randall Rothschild missed more than anything was music. He had lost all his friends, had grown distant from his family, had never had a girlfriend, although he had fallen deeply in love with a girl he hardly knew, a freckled redhead who played a central role in his lyrical prose, always smiling, always batting her emerald eyes.

But the only thing he longed for outside the asylum walls was to attend a concert. To stand front row, eyes closed, sweaty head bobbing, basking in the magic of live music, the symbiotic connection occurring between souls.

Dr. Alpert had bought a guitar for Randall to play. An acoustic guitar, but that's what he preferred to play anyway. It had a blonde body blending into an amber frame and he called it Doreen, named after his secret love. Her voice had been just as sweet.

Sometimes Eli would bring it by and ask Randall to play for him, and he'd conjure up the songs from his old lo-fi albums, written in the dank basement of his parents' house. Songs written during the highs and lows of his manic episodes. Some happy, some sad – all the honest feelings of an unvarnished soul.

Once Eli had cried. It was a silly song about the harrowing courtship between two frogs that had caused him to weep. He had seemed happy, though. He had been smiling, at least. And had thanked him when he left.

This time Eli had decided to return the favor. He walked up and placed an iPod with a docking station on the table in front of Randall. "How about some Nirvana from the *Unplugged* show in '94?" he said. He pressed a button and Kurt Cobain began strumming the guitar, a melancholy ghost risen from the grave.

"Ahh," Randall garbled. He clapped his palsied hands together and smiled around his crooked dentures. His right knee began to jitter, but not in time to the beat. He sang along, his voice mild and melodic.

Eli sat down across from him. He was unfamiliar with Nirvana's music, but knew it was Randall's favorite band. Or had been. He could see why. There was the same plain, unaffected angst in the singer's voice that he heard in Randall's. It was the voice of suffering.

The song ended and Eli hit pause.

"I thought you'd like that," Eli said, which was only half-true. He also knew that the singer's suicide had marked a turning point in the progression of Randall's psychosis. It's when he had begun to see the demons.

Randall hugged himself. His smile made him look ten years younger, even with the top denture hanging ajar. It reminded Eli of the teenager who had first been committed many years ago. "It's…it's…awesome," Randall said, drawing out the last word into a droning *om*.

"What's your favorite song?"

"On this album?" Randall opened his eyes and leaned forward. "It's a cover of 'Oh, Me' by the Meat Puppets. Track eleven."

Eli found the song and pressed play.

It was slow, melodic, moody, dark. Randall fell into a type of trance listening to it. He dropped his head and rocked back and forth, his shaggy hair hanging over his eyes. One particular lyric stood out to Eli as he listened, something about infinity stored deep inside oneself.

It brought back memories of Rajamadja, the enigmatic monk whom he had met in India. His guru. His savior. Rajamadja's death, in many ways, had made the same impact on Eli as the singer's suicide had on Randall. It was as if his guardian angel had left him to grovel alone among the demons. The ones from his past, adding an eerie ground mist to the graveyard of his mind.

★　　★　　★

After returning from Vietnam, Eli decided to pursue a career in psychiatry, initially helping treat returning veterans suffering from post-traumatic stress disorder. A disorder he himself had suffered from, even if he'd been unwilling to admit it at the time.

Every so often he'd see a patient get that look in their eyes. The panic-stricken look of impending doom. It would take him right back to the clearing in Xuan Loc, lying nose to nose with the injured soldier while Sergeant Wagner handed him the hot pistol reeking of burnt cordite. He would begin to tremble, just slightly. And he would become Dr. Pussyfoot all over again.

His first staff position was at a state mental hospital in Tuscaloosa, Alabama. He was twenty-seven, a credited psychiatrist ready to rid the world of mental illness. It was the mid-seventies, and America seemed to be pulling out of its collective state of insanity, normalizing itself. Except in the institutions, where the living conditions were approaching historic lows.

The Chief Medical Director of the Tuscaloosa Sanitarium was Dr. Walter Francis, an acclaimed physician who switched to psychiatry in order to satisfy an intellectual curiosity, more than a genuine desire to cure the mentally ill. The hospital was grossly overcrowded and equally underfunded. The staff was comprised mostly of poorly educated security guards with bad attitudes. They lacked compassion. Worse, they lacked understanding. To them, the patients were subhuman, deranged beasts in need of taming.

To Dr. Francis, they were merely test subjects, human curiosities for his medical experiments. He did not pretend to understand the nature of mental illness, as did so many of his contemporaries of the time. Rather, he sought to discover its cause by way of identifying its cure. His thesis was that the cure would inform the cause. Thus, he explored all the various forms of therapy known at the time, including many of his own imagining.

In many ways, the environment inside the asylum was worse than any battlefield Eli had ever experienced. More gruesome and far more traumatic. This was a one-sided war waged against patients who lacked the weapons to fight back. And neither side ever won.

As in Vietnam, Eli began to sympathize with the patients, fighting to protect them from the treatments that were designed to cure them. In one case he got too close.

Her name was Miranda. She had been committed to the hospital by an adulterous husband complaining of excessive excitability and paranoid delusions. She wasn't suffering from delusions; her husband was cheating. The excitability part was true, though. She was pissed.

She was strolling through the gardens when Eli first met her, smoking. It was early August and she was sweating, her frizzy, blonde hair clinging in dampened strings to her face, blanketing her back. When she walked up to Eli, she twisted her hair into a bun and held it on top of her head. Her neck was slender and smooth, blemished only by the fading bruises seen under the jawline. A bead of sweat trickled down her neck in mesmerizing spurts and joined the pool collecting in her clavicle. Eli was struck with a shocking desire to suck it dry.

"What this place needs is a swimming pool," she said, taking a last, long drag from her cigarette before grinding it into the garden soil with her shoe. "Right over there." She pointed to an expanse of grass framed by flowerbeds.

It has several, Eli almost said, thinking of the submersion pools where they held patients underwater until they lost consciousness. Surprisingly, patients experienced a relatively high rate of recovery after submersion therapy. It helped them overcome their fear of death, by showing them its face.

"I'm not sure that would be such a good idea," Eli said instead.

"And why's that?"

"Well, what if someone drowned?" When he blinked he saw a snapshot of Miranda tied to a submersion gurney, inches below the surface, eyes wide with panic as she thrashed against the straps.

Miranda looked back towards the long brick building and scrunched her nose. "That would be a welcome relief for most of the people here," she said. Then she shifted her weight and fanned herself with her free hand. "It's just so blazing hot. And boring. I've played about all the bingo I can stand."

Eli smiled at her, squinting against the sun wavering high overhead. A bead of sweat dripped down his spine and a mosquito squealed in his ear. He couldn't think of anything to say, so he nodded and began to walk away.

"No, wait," Miranda said. "Please, just talk with me for a minute. Please?"

"It's best if we do that during a therapy session. I'll be happy to talk with your social worker about setting one up."

"I don't need therapy," she said. Her eyes glistened wet for a moment, but she fought away the tears. "I just want to talk normally. Not in some structured setting. Not about my nonexistent phobias or my private feelings.

"People come in here. Some of them…" her lips flapped as she blew out air, "…some of them are pretty messed up. But there are plenty of others who have nothing wrong with them at all, as far as I can tell. But then they're put in this place and treated like they're crazy, spending every day with people who really are crazy, removed from everything that's familiar to them, with nothing at all to do but sit and, and…" She held her arms out to her sides in frustration. Her hair tumbled down from her head and framed her face. Her clear-blue eyes were quicksand.

"And, well," she continued, "it starts to make you feel a bit like you are going crazy. You start thinking, 'Why am I here? What happened? How did this become my life?' And then you think of the life going on outside these walls. Real life. And it's going on without you. And every day that you're stuck in this place is one more day you'll never get back. And you think, 'What's wrong with this world if a normal, sane person can be plucked out of it and placed in this pocket of insanity? What kind of world could allow that?'

"Only a world that is in itself insane. So, that makes us all insane. And if that's the case, then who determines who's sick and who's well? Why do you get to wear the doctor costume and I have to wear the patient one? What's the point of this game and who sets the rules?"

Eli frowned down at his feet. The grass growing between them had ragged edges from a dull mower. Below it, microscopic bugs burrowed and built subterranean cities. Several surely lay dead under his shoes.

He lifted his head and looked at Miranda. The sun reflected off her sweaty face. "Real life happens here too," he said. "Life happens wherever you are. It's all in what you make of it. What you do with the opportunities you're given."

"That's easy to say when you have the luxury of choice. You have the opportunity to leave whenever you like. I don't. You have the opportunity to eat whatever you want. I don't. You…you choose to be here. I don't. I feel like I'm some shadow version of myself, stuck in this nightmare world while the real me is still outside, enjoying her life. And I feel that I'll never make it back to that other version of myself." The tears returned, and this time she couldn't stave them off. "And I'm scared."

Eli felt an urge to rush forward and take her in his arms. "Look… I…I…" he stammered. He was sweating freely now and he wiped the back of his hand across his wet brow. "So a pool would make things better?"

Miranda sniffled and flipped a strand of hair over her shoulder. She looked at Eli from below arched brows. Then she laughed, her slender shoulders beginning to bounce up and down. She leaned her head back and her laughter rose up towards the sun. It was pretty and musical, like a snippet of birdsong.

Eli snorted then began laughing himself.

Miranda composed herself. "Yes, it would make things slightly better, I think."

Eli looked around. An elderly man was lurching their way, mumbling obscenities to himself.

"Well, I'll see what I can do." He reached out a stiff arm and patted Miranda on the shoulder.

She grinned and looked away. She began therapy under Dr. Francis the following day and never was the same.

★　　★　　★

The refrain of the cover song came around again – infinity stored deep inside – and Eli rubbed his arms to dampen the gooseflesh prickling his skin. He turned off the iPod and began packing it away.

Randall continued to nod his head as the beat lingered in his ears. "That's heaven," Randall said.

Eli smiled. "I'm glad you liked it."

"No, I mean, that's like a real connection to heaven. The afterlife exists inside that song."

Eli leaned back, inhaled through his nose and held it. His eyes landed on the mural painted against the far wall, the beasts living harmoniously in the garden of original sin. "You mean, this musician lives on through the recording, making him eternal?"

Randall shook his head. He combed the hair out of his eyes, but it fell right back in place. He looked at Eli through jagged strands. "The song we just heard is a second- or third-generation recording of a live performance by a band of men blessed with special talents granted by God. That song is not eternal because it was recorded. It is eternal because it was written before time began. It precedes the stars. Trace it back to its origin and you find God. It was composed in heaven. To hear it is to experience the divine."

Eli was encouraged by the clarity of Randall's words. Music always elevated him to a higher level. A place of articulate intensity. *Music and laughter,* he thought, *are among the most effective forms of therapy.*

"That's a beautiful way to think of it," Eli said. "Do your songs come from the same place?"

"Not all of them," he said. "Some are just sounds I make with my mouth. Some, though…" Randall began to drum his hands against his leg, "…some come from something beyond me. I just share it. The Creator speaks through all of us in various ways." He smiled and pointed to his head. "Not all of the voices we hear are imaginary."

A flash of heat seared Eli's chest, and he had the sudden urge to grasp Randall by the hand and escort him out of the hospital. To free him like some rare and beautiful bird that had been confined to a cage. *What if this whole time,* he thought for the thousandth time, the tremors beginning to seize his hands, *we've been working to fix people who aren't broken? And if that's so, then what have I done? What am I doing? What am I to do?*

Eli stood and gripped the briefcase handle hard to steady his hand. "We all hear voices," he said, attempting to control his own. "It's all a matter of how we react to them. How they make us feel. What they make us do." He thought of Crosby and his heartbeat slowed. Crosby's imaginary voices had convinced him to kill. That was clearly a sign of a disorder, not some form of divine persuasion.

Eli concentrated on his breathing. *Insanity is suffering; your job is to relieve suffering.* Rajamadja's manic smile and tittering laugh came to mind. *Not all insanity is suffering, though.*

He heard Miranda's melodic voice, *"Who determines who's sick and who's well?"*

His heart began thumping again, this time in his throat. He forced a smile and directed it at Randall, his wrinkled skin creating a landscape of canyon valleys. "We'll do this again," he said and walked away, weaving between pockets of patients on his way to the door. Many of them were mumbling to themselves or to something unseen. He wondered what they heard.

CHAPTER TEN

"There are forces working to bring about the end of the world," Crosby said. Cool air rushed through the large vent overhead. He placed his hands under his legs to warm them. "There's a war going on behind the scenes. I'm a soldier of God."

Alex nodded his head as if Crosby had just told him that he enjoyed playing racquetball. "What forces?" he asked.

"Demonic," Crosby said, chewing his lower lip. "The legions of hell led by Satan himself. It's an ancient battle that's nearing its end."

"And…" Alex held a fist to his mouth as he cleared his throat, "… you've seen these demons?"

"I've seen their shadows."

"Please explain."

The therapy rooms had all been given names. It was one of Eli's initiatives to create a more calming hospital environment. This one was called Tranquility, which, in Alex's experience, was a misnomer. Nowhere else had Alex heard more irrational ideas or observed more erratic behavior. It did have a tabletop rock garden, though, to reinforce its theme.

"The demons take human form. They look just like you and me."

You and I look nothing alike, Alex thought, staring at the scrabbly man before him.

Crosby continued, "But their shadows show their demonic form."

"You'd think they'd only come out at night, then."

Crosby furrowed his brow; his chin dimpled. "Well," he said, thinking, "that's true. I guess it's 'cause most people can't see them, so they feel safe."

"Ah." Alex grabbed the tiny rock-garden rake and began combing the sand. "And why do you think that is?"

"Why what is?"

"Why is it that so few people can see them? Why hasn't God called upon more people to join the war?"

"It's not that simple. It goes deep, deep, deep. Society has been blinded through cultural engineering. God has been removed from our everyday lives and replaced with false idols. People worship money, material things, movie stars. It's all part of a plan to distance us from our true nature. From our divine past."

Crosby's past was far from divine. According to his patient file, he had been raised by a single mother who, by all accounts, was mentally ill herself; a condition she treated with a mixture of meth, men and gallons of cheap vodka. He had been sexually assaulted by more than one of her transient boyfriends and moved to a foster home after he found his mother murdered at the age of fourteen. Strangled, presumably, by a boyfriend, a pimp or a drug pusher. The case had never been solved. The fact that Crosby had been able to eventually secure a job and stay off the streets was indeed a miracle, but Alex doubted that it had anything to do with God.

"And, so, God's soldiers. How do they avoid being blinded by these cultural distractions?"

"Um, well, I know from my standpoint, first of all, I don't own a TV. Well, I do, but I don't have all the channels. Only a few. Just the basic ones."

"So, cable is Satan's most effective weapon?"

Crosby puffed his cheeks and blew out a gust of air. "It's complicated," he said.

"I imagine so." The miniature rock garden was becoming a series of rigid lines pockmarked with pebbles. "Have you seen any demon shadows here?"

"Not yet."

"And why do you think that is?"

"The pills, most likely. They put your head in a fog so that you can't see clearly. But I don't mind. I'm not sure I want to see the demons no more. I'd rather just live my life. You know what they say, ignorance is bliss."

Sounds like something social engineers would say.

Alex had been a staff psychiatrist at Sugar Hill for over eight years. During that time, he had learned that there was no way to reason with schizophrenics during one of their episodes. To argue against their paranoid delusions would only work to implicate you in the plot. To encourage acceptance, as was Eli's primary philosophy, only encouraged the patient to further indulge in their delusion.

In Alex's experience, words could not fix the break in a psychotic's ability to perceive the world rationally. Although words could facilitate the break. Traumatic words, rather. When the closest people in your life – the ones who are supposed to protect you – cause you harm, a fracture in your psyche can occur. This fracture creates uncommon levels of stress, which can lead to the release of chemicals that alter your conscious mind. Suddenly your subconscious begins to manifest into your reality. Your demonic mom becomes a shadow figure following some stranger on the street. To the psychiatrist, this is called projection. To the psychotic, it's considered reality. And the only cure is to stop the frazzled neurons in the brain from misfiring, to stem the flow of chemicals that alter perception.

Current medications only masked the symptoms caused by this imbalance. Alex's drug would cure it, resetting the patient's mind to function properly. Then, and only then, could any form of talk therapy provide a therapeutic purpose for someone with a severe psychotic disorder. Only then would such a patient be in a position to comprehend the connection between prior events and their present condition.

But this is Eli's hospital, Alex reminded himself, *so, until my drug is approved I must continue to offer lip service to this schizophrenic, as if it will make a difference.* He checked his watch and refrained from rolling his eyes. *Besides, I can't afford to be fired.*

Crosby placed his elbows on the desk and leaned over for a better view into the rock garden.

Alex felt conspicuous under his stare. He opened his mouth to address Crosby's latest comment, but couldn't remember what he'd said. He pushed the box of sand and small rocks across the table to Crosby, who accepted it with the wide eyes of a toddler receiving a puppy on Christmas morning.

He grabbed the rake and immediately scrambled the meticulous lines.

Fuck this, Alex thought, *let's get to the point.* "Let's talk about the attacks," he said.

The central air cut off and the only sound in the small room was the scrape of the tiny rake through sand.

Crosby frowned. "What about them?"

"Well, let's talk about them. What was going on that day? Who were they? What were you thinking at the time?"

Crosby began to draw a stick figure in the sand, a circular head with a narrow neck and long, angled arms. He exhaled heavily. "I had gotten the message earlier in the day. I knew to be on the lookout. I had to be ready." He added hands to the ends of the arms, with sharp, pointy fingers. Claws.

"How did you receive the message? What did it say?"

Crosby flipped the rake over, holding it like a pen. He tilted his head to the side, examining his work, and his tongue pushed against his lower lip.

"I was walking up to the gas station to get a pack of smokes and a Mountain Dew. It was nice outside, sunny, not too hot. A few clouds in the sky, just floating up there, not moving at all, although there was a bit of a breeze. Then I knew something was coming because they started to glow. Not from the sun or nothing. It was like a light was shining from inside the clouds, almost too bright to look at."

He drew a pair of legs with clawed feet.

"I put my hand up to shade my eyes..." he pantomimed the movement, squinting up at the acoustic-tile ceiling, "...and the clouds began to change shape. I could see these faces. They looked all nice and smiley. And then their faces changed and they became mean and evil looking. I looked around, but no one else seemed to notice anything. I knew it was meant just for me."

He drew two intersecting circles over the chest and placed a pebble in the middle of each one. Breasts.

"Then there were some words that formed underneath the clouds. They came from the Bible, I think. Some Scripture. Said that in the final days, demons will walk the earth. And the righteous will be called upon to smite them down."

Alex nodded. "And what book in the Bible is that passage from?"

Crosby shrugged. "I don't know for sure. I haven't looked it up. It just sounds like something from the Bible. Maybe it was a direct message from God."

"But that's what it said?" Alex read from the line he had written down, "In the final days, demons will walk the earth. And the righteous will be called upon to smite them down."

Crosby shrugged again. "Something like that. I don't recall word-for-word."

Sure sounds like God. Vague, indirect and easily misinterpreted. "And you took that to mean you were being called upon to kill?"

"Sort of, but I was mostly just...I don't know, amazed. My whole body was buzzing. It was like I had been shot up with some high-grade speed. Everything was super bright and crystal clear. I could see every little detail and hear every sound. It was like I'd been dialed into a higher frequency."

That's not God, Alex wanted to say. *That would be textbook schizophrenia, my friend.* "What happened next?"

Crosby turned his attention back to the busty stick figure in the sand. He added two oblong eyes and slashed vertical slits in their center.

"I went inside the gas station, feeling like I'm floating on air. I walk up to the counter to ask for a pack of smokes and then I see this bright light out the corner of my eye. I look over and it's a hunting knife in a glass case beside the counter. It was all natural looking with a rustic wooden handle with an ivory stripe in it. All the other ones were made of steel, with knuckle guards and metal spikes, like something a serial killer would carry. But this one was different. It was like the kind of knife an Indian chief would've used in a ceremony. Or to scalp somebody."

It was most likely made in China. "Go on," Alex said.

"So, I knew that I was meant to have it. That it was part of the message. But I didn't have enough money."

"How much did it cost?"

"I don't know, I didn't even look."

Alex's amusement was only betrayed by the rapid blinking of his eyes.

"But then the cashier's phone starts ringing, back on the far side of the booth. He turns to answer it and starts yapping in some foreign language. Then it's like he's in an argument. He starts getting angry and raising his voice. He holds up a finger, like he wants me to hold on, and walks through the door to a back office or something and I'm left all alone in the store with that old knife that's glowing bright as the sun."

"Convenient timing," Alex said.

Crosby chuckled. "A little too convenient is what I'm thinking. So I check the case and there's this notch where a padlock is supposed to go but there isn't one attached. The case is just sitting there unlocked, and the knife is shining so bright it's about to blind me. So I open the lid and lift it out, but I don't have anywhere to put it or nothing, so I just kind of tucked it up against my arm and walked out the door. First thing I ever stole in my life."

Crosby's criminal record proved otherwise, but Alex didn't contradict him. Instead, he let silence settle into the room. He shifted in his seat and it squeaked.

"When I walked out, the clouds had come together in a kind of line, like a conveyor belt flowing in a single direction. I looked up ahead and it made a ninety-degree turn at an intersection a couple of blocks down the road. It was like it was telling me where to go."

Crosby leaned back over his drawing. He drew horns on the head and a crooked mouth with two triangular teeth.

"I followed it for a few turns and then it ended in a wide, flat storm cloud over this small group of people. Thunder rumbled, and it cast a dark shadow over the spot where they were standing. I looked over and there was nothing unusual about any of them. They were just standing together, talking. But then the cloud cover cleared and the sun shone through and I could see their shadows."

His hand hesitated over the drawing in the sand. He lowered the rake and drew a large erection rising up from between its legs ending in a diamond tip. He leaned back and admired his work.

"And then?"

Crosby's face turned into a scowl. He raised the rake and then slammed it down into the center of the rock garden, scattering the sand. He looked across the table at Alex; his face became calm.

"And then I did what God wanted me to."

Tranquility my ass, Eli, Alex thought as he brushed sand off the front of his shirt.

CHAPTER ELEVEN

Alex didn't realize how much he had been dreading encountering Eli until he saw him round the corner of the hallway up ahead. A jolt of adrenaline raced through his system and his initial instinct was to turn and walk away.

Antiquated operating system, Alex thought, striding forward. Fight or flight made sense when facing a hungry predator, not a familiar colleague whom one is slightly anxious to see. *Perhaps I'll make a drug one day to cure that as well.*

He quickened his pace and fixed a large smile to his face as he closed the distance, extending his hand.

"Welcome back," Eli said. "I've been looking for you."

"I know, sorry. It's been one of those days. You know, with the Jerry situation and everything." Eli was two inches taller than Alex, but appeared to be shrinking with age. They stood nearly eye to eye without Alex having to elevate onto his toes, which he was prone to do. Angela often joked behind his back that he should just wear platform shoes.

"Right, well, we have several issues to address. Is now a good time?"

Alex examined his watch as if it held his schedule. "Yeah, sure. Your office?"

"Why don't we get some air?" Eli said.

They started out walking side by side silently. Then the quiet became tense. Alex could sense scrutiny in the silence. *Has he found out about the test trials, somehow? What "issues" was he referring to?* Every step felt like a lost opportunity to say something, every stark footfall a gavel strike sentencing his guilt.

He pulled out his iPhone and opened the email app in order to feign a distraction. He dropped a step behind Eli and let him lead the way, tension pulling his chest tight.

★　　★　　★

Eli walked out onto the courtyard, an extended stretch of dark-green grass walled in by hedgerows. Flowerbeds lined the perimeter and the concrete walkways that led up to a large water fountain featuring a young maiden pouring water from a stone vase. Eli always thought of the woman in the fountain as Miranda, finally at peace in her pool.

He walked to a bench on the far side of the fountain and gestured for Alex to sit, then joined him.

"What a mess," Eli said, shaking his head.

★   ★   ★

Alex's heart began to hammer. He nodded gravely. "I know," he said, hedging his bets.

"Under normal conditions this is something I'd prefer to let slide, but given the circumstances, particularly with the review meeting pending, I just don't know that I can."

Alex continued to nod his head, watching the fountain recycle its water while his mind raced through his most rehearsed justifications.

"But this impacts you more than me," Eli continued. "I want to hear what you have to say."

When Alex first decided to solicit a buyer for his experimental medication, he knew he'd have to perform test trials to prove that it worked. The best course of action at that point would have been to pursue a grant to help fund his laboratory work. That would have eliminated the need for secrecy. But he knew it would also have driven a wedge between Eli and him. And Alex was not willing to relinquish his position as a potential successor to Eli at Sugar Hill. It was better, he had decided, to keep his good standing at the hospital and pursue placement with a pharmaceutical company on the side. But he always feared having to face Eli before his plans came to fruition. And he hadn't yet considered how he would handle it. "Well, obviously I think it may be time we reconsider our approach," he said, speaking hesitantly.

Eli crossed his legs and laced his fingers around his knee. "How so?"

"I mean in terms of treatment. I'm not sure the current plan is working."

"Given recent events, I would tend to agree. So, what would you recommend?"

Alex sat up straighter. He turned towards Eli. *Maybe this won't be so bad after all.* "Well, for starters, a different approach to therapeutics. We need medicine that does more than dull the symptoms. We need something that addresses the root of the problem. A medicine that—"

"Doesn't exist," Eli interrupted. He shook his head and sighed. "Medicine won't fix Jerry's condition. You know that. I'm surprised to hear you say so, given his history."

Alex was nearly trembling with adrenaline. When Eli mentioned Jerry, however, it all drained away, leaving an acrid taste in his mouth and a ringing in his ears. "Well," he said, mentally switching gears, "I'm just basing this off a brief meeting with him this morning. His dosage is clearly off. He's still displaying severe paranoid delusions. He...I understand that he assaulted an orderly? He's never been violent before."

"I suspect that he stopped taking his meds," Eli said. "According to Manny he had been acting peculiar for a few days before the incident. We haven't been able to get a straight answer from Jerry. I was hoping you could help get to the bottom of it. I've prescribed 20 mgs of Clozapine to be taken under supervision while we determine what caused the episode."

"That's what I thought. Eli, that dosage is too low."

Eli sat still, staring at the lady watering the fountain. "You know how I feel about antipsychotics. But I won't interfere with your recommended treatment plan. Unfortunately, we can't continue to offer vocational training while he's unstable."

It was Eli who had set up the vocational program at Sugar Hill. It helped provide purpose and offered structure to outpatients still struggling with mental illness, two essential components for recovery and quality living. And it was Eli who'd suggested that Alex enroll Jerry in the program, had, in fact, held the landscaping position open with him in mind, knowing how much he liked to be outside.

Alex had been hesitant at first, unsure that Jerry was capable of handling any level of responsibility, given his condition at the time. But he'd agreed to give it a shot. More out of an obligation to Eli than any optimism that it would help Jerry's well-being. But it had, almost immediately.

Jerry had come alive while performing remedial tasks in the courtyard. He had made friends with the other workers, even some members of the hospital staff. In just a few weeks his malaise had lifted and he had become nearly self-reliant, getting up by himself each day and preparing for his shift.

After a couple of months, Alex had been able to help him find an assisted-living center where he'd moved in on his own. He had become happy, coherent, and even displayed some of the characteristics of his old personality.

In many ways, Eli had helped bring his brother back. It was a gift Alex was not quick to forget.

"I know," Alex said. "I was afraid of that."

"I don't believe that medication is the only answer, though, Alex. I worry about a complete relapse. I would be reluctant to strip him of a constructive outlet. I can help find a temporary position for him with a work-release program for more severe cases. Once we get him stabilized, he's welcome to return to work here."

"I'll think about it," Alex said. *I've got some more pressing problems at the moment,* he thought. "First, I'm going to have him released and brought home. Rachel can watch over him and make sure he's taking his meds."

Eli nodded and said nothing. Alex's wife was not a nurse.

The silence threatened to become uncomfortable again, so Alex broke it. "I met with our new patient, Crosby. We've got our work cut out with that one."

Eli seemed content to sit forever in silence. Alex couldn't bear it. "I hear that you had a run-in with him yourself," he said, and immediately wished he hadn't.

Eli arched his eyebrows. "What did you hear?"

"Nothing, just that there was some sort of a confrontation. That he threatened to tackle you."

Eli appeared fascinated by the fountain. His mouth was clamped shut.

Alex waited, waited – the gurgling water echoing the sound of his rising blood pressure – then continued, "And that you got in the way of an orderly attempting to subdue him. The man's dangerous, Eli. I know your stance on the use of force, but you can't put so much trust in these patients. The man attacked a group of people with a hunting knife, for Christ's sake. And you're…" *old,* he almost said, "…coming up on a critical review meeting. Think how it would look if you facilitated an assault."

★ ★ ★

It was true, Eli knew. Had he been involved in a physical conflict with Crosby, it would give the board an excuse to reassess hospital protocol.

It would support their argument for tighter restrictions, fewer patient liberties, more medical intervention. It would undermine much of the progress he had made to bring a more humane approach to the hospital. And it would likely hasten his exit. Something he was becoming less convinced was such a bad thing anyway.

So long as Alex can carry the torch, he thought, which he had begun to question recently as well. He needed to be sure.

"Perhaps you're right," Eli said and rubbed his eyes. "I don't need to be as involved in patient care. It's past time I turn those responsibilities over to you and concentrate more on hospital operations."

★   ★   ★

Alex pressed his lips together to keep from smiling. When they'd walked outside, he'd thought it was to discuss his dealings with Philax Pharmaceuticals. Now it seemed as though he was cementing his position as the next Chief Medical Director of Sugar Hill. When he inhaled it inflated his chest, and he liked the way it made him feel. "You've set the guidelines, Eli. I'll just be following your lead. I hope that I've proven myself capable of continuing your ideals."

Eli's nod was slight. He placed a hand on his stomach as though from a pang of indigestion. "I'll tell Angela that I'm placing you in charge of patient care. We'll need to be aligned as we prepare for our review meeting. You know the battle we face with the board."

It was a board member who had put Alex in contact with the Philax representative in the first place. He was intimately familiar with the battle over the appropriate use of antipsychotic medicine at the facility and the board's desire to take a more active approach. Not to mention their willingness to accept money from pharmaceutical companies. Had he sold his experimental medicine to Philax, he would not have been the only one positioned to benefit financially.

Alex smiled and gave a conspiratorial nod to Eli. "You know I have your back," he said.

They both turned and faced the fountain, admiring the pretty lady forever filling her pool.

CHAPTER TWELVE

For Jerry, some days the world made sense; its great cosmic mystery could be explained in the life cycle of a chrysanthemum. The seed gets nutrients from its environment, grows and blossoms into a flower, unveiling its vibrant beauty, disseminates its pollen on the wings of the honeybee, then wilts and returns its essence to the earth, enriching the soil for chrysanthemums to come.

Some days, though, the world is a roiling stew of insanity. A cacophony of discordant voices, of contradicting ideas, of irrational impulses, of impossible images. During such days, the flower becomes a creature of dark complexity – a carnivorous species with nefarious fangs and acidic saliva, waiting to devour whatever wanders too close. The flower, then, is both a thing of beauty and an instrument of death. It simply depends on perspective – an unstable, unreliable, inconsistent filter for assessing reality. Reality became even more unpredictable when the filter malfunctioned, when it was removed.

The absence of the filter allowed Jerry to see beyond the veil of reality. A stark look into the raw chaos of the cosmos where life operates on a subatomic scale, a swirling soup of photons coalescing into the image of expectations. An indifferent energy field of infinite possibilities made material through the force of the collective unconscious.

The world is illusion; we only pretend it's real. That was the purpose of the filter, to make the mystery appear mundane. To make it safe to smell the flowers.

The pills provided an artificial filter, a murky lens through which the world assimilated itself into its familiar form. But it was nothing more than a false representation of the way the world should look, according to the makers of the medicine. Not the creator of the world.

Still, Jerry didn't know which was better. The chaotic view behind the veil or the predictable sights supplied by the fabricated filter. These were his thoughts when Alex walked through the door, and Jerry saw both a beloved sibling and a hostile stranger. Then a shadow emerged from behind Alex, and Devon walked into the room.

"What do you say we go home?" Alex said. He was holding a small, scuffed suitcase containing Jerry's few personal belongings. He set it beside the door and smiled. His smile wavered the longer he stood there waiting. "Come on, Jerry, let's get you out of here."

Jerry blinked and stood, holding out his hands as the room swayed underfoot. He struggled to keep his head from sagging and to move his feet forward. That was one thing about the fabricated filter. It produced a heavier world.

"That's it. Take your time," Alex said, placing a hand against Jerry's back and guiding him towards the door.

"Will you escort him out?" Alex asked Devon. "I'm going to load up the car."

"Not a problem," Devon said, circling behind Jerry as Alex stormed out the door.

When the footfalls had faded, Devon grabbed Jerry by the arm, digging his fingers deep, pinching the median nerve against the bone.

"Don't think I forgot about you," Devon growled into Jerry's ear. "Think you can get away with biting me? No, sir. Not a chance. I'm gonna hunt your crazy ass down like a rabid dog."

Jerry turned his head and looked up into Devon's face. The filter revealed a pudgy black man in a crisp blue shirt, but he feared what was behind the veil. He tried to speak, but his tongue was a dead thing, decaying in his mouth.

"Crazy-acting motherfucker," Devon spoke through the side of his mouth, relaxing his grip as they ventured into the hallway. He smiled as a nurse passed by. "You're weak, is all you are. Weak in the mind. You ain't gonna get no pity from me, you biting-ass bitch. I'm gonna pay you back." He gripped his arm again and every few steps would grind the nerve against the bone.

They approached the doorway to the doctors' parking lot and Devon waved at the station nurse.

"Aw, you leaving us, Jerry?" she asked.

His half-lidded eyes hid the pain. When he tried to speak, all that came out was spit.

"Well, don't be a stranger."

Devon opened the doors and pushed Jerry through. "You may be getting out of here, but I'm gonna come pay you a visit. You can believe that."

Alex was waiting in his car by the curb, the engine idling. His wife was holding open the rear passenger door. Devon walked Jerry up to the car and helped him inside.

"There you are, Dr. Drexler. Need anything else?"

"No, that's all, thanks."

"Anytime." Devon gave Jerry a final pat on the arm. "See you around, partner," he said, and closed the car door.

Jerry's arm continued to throb, but after a couple of minutes he couldn't remember why. The motion of the car rocked him in his seat, and every time he blinked, it seemed like he was somewhere different. A highway. A parking lot. A sidewalk. A hallway. A door. Like pictures in a slideshow. That was another problem with the filter – it often lacked fluidity.

He was with a woman now. She held him gently by the arm as he shuffled forward. A curtain of glossy, black hair concealed her face. He swayed as he walked and his arm pushed pleasantly against her breast.

He blinked again and was now staring at a plate of food – a fried chicken leg, mashed potatoes soaked in gravy, a small pile of green beans. He heard voices and tried to lift his head, but it was too heavy. It was like a cinder block attached to a flower stalk.

"Now that he's home it should get better," he heard a voice say.

Home, Jerry mused, looking around, recognizing the familiar interior for the first time. The threadbare floors, the ticky-tacky walls, the hand-me-down furniture with sagging seats and scuffed surfaces, matching only in their uniform lack of design. Was this his home, this transitory outpost for wayward wanderers? This box that had been lived in by dozens of others and would surely be lived in by dozens more.

He hadn't chosen to live here, had he? Of all the places he could live in all the cities and all the towns and villages and as-yet-undiscovered places on this orbiting rock, why here? Whose choice had that been, if not his? In this infinite existence of limitless potential, why was he assigned to this particular reality and what was the point? Better yet, how could he break free?

CHAPTER THIRTEEN

When Alex was a kid he used to imagine what it would be like to have dinner at his big brother's place after they grew up. It was nothing like this. Huddled around a small square table listing a bit to the right. Its faux wood top warped from water spills and spotted with shadows cast by dead moths lying in the light fixture above. The peach-colored carpet was a leopard skin of stains and reeked of mildew, and he could hear *Jeopardy* playing at full volume through the paper-thin walls.

Jerry didn't seem to mind his living conditions, however. He hardly seemed awake, for that matter, with his half-lidded eyes staring blindly at his plate of food. The higher dose Alex had prescribed appeared to be working. Drowsy was better than delusional, as far as he was concerned.

At least Rachel's attitude had improved. She hadn't even made a remark when Alex picked up dinner from Popeye's, only realizing the correlation to the name of her flattened dog after placing the steaming bag of food in Rachel's lap. Sympathy always brought out the best in her.

"He shouldn't require too much of your time," Alex said, talking to Rachel in front of Jerry as though he weren't there. Glancing at his unfocused eyes made it clear that he wasn't really. *"If you don't want us to see, why don't you just cut out our eyes?"* Alex speared a stack of green beans and used it to scoop up a bite of mashed potato. "Just check in every couple of days to see how he's getting along and show him a familiar face."

Rachel began to nod her head, cutting into her chicken breast after excising the skin. She displayed the intense concentration of someone being assigned a secret mission from the director of the CIA. "How long do you think it'll be before he's able to return to work?"

Alex dabbed the corners of his mouth with a crumpled paper napkin. He glanced at his brother, then quickly averted his eyes. "There's no telling. I don't even know that he'll be allowed back. We're just going to have to take it day by day."

Rachel sighed. She looked at Jerry and shook her head. "I don't get it. He was doing so well. What happened?"

"What do you mean, 'what happened'? Schizophrenia happened. It's the nature of the disease. He's always going to have these..." Alex twirled his drumstick in the air like some whimsical conductor, "... episodes. The best we can do is help minimize them with medicine."

Jerry's apartment always gave Alex the creeps. There was something surreal about it, like visiting an alternate reality where his brother had been replaced by a psychotic imposter. *This is not where you were meant to end up,* he thought, recalling their shared bedroom, their childhood bond. His hero had become his patient. His father's favorite son had become a burden. But he knew that Jerry still lived somewhere deep inside that scrambled mind. That was the most troubling part – to think of the brief moments of lucidity when the old Jerry would awaken to this new life and wonder where things had gone wrong.

"Hey." Rachel sat up straight in her seat; she placed her hands flat atop the table. "What about the medicine that *you're* working on? When will that be ready?"

Alex plugged his mouth with a chunk of fried chicken. He wasn't ready to tell her about his failure with Philax. He wasn't yet sure what had even happened or how to fix it. And he was afraid it would lead to further questions regarding their finances that he was equally unprepared to address. He rolled his hand in the air to pantomime progress as he chewed the chicken into paste. Eventually he had to swallow, and Rachel was still staring at him expectantly.

"Well..." she prompted.

"Soon," Alex said. "The tests have been successful so far."

"I ain't no queer bait!"

"We're just waiting on final clearance from the FDA, then we should be ready to move into the development phase."

"That's great!" Rachel clapped her hands together and held them against her chest. She took a deep breath and leaned forward. "I'm sorry, I... Well, with the events from last night I forgot to ask how things went." A strand of hair fell across her face and she tucked it away. "So it works," she said, her eyes sparkling, her full lips stretching into a wide smile.

Alex shrugged. "Yeah. I mean it hasn't been officially approved yet, but..." He looked into her eyes and saw the enamored girl who had once been awestruck by his intelligence. He returned her smile, basking in her sudden adoration.

"But, yeah, it works."

Rachel lowered her voice. "Well then, why don't you use it to treat Jerry? I mean, isn't that what it's for?"

Alex, who had just taken another bite of chicken, nearly choked. He coughed into his napkin and took a small sip of tea, his face turning red. The sound of his swallow was enormous in the quiet room. "It's still a ways from being available for commercial use. It could take some time." *Especially now that I don't have a prospective buyer or any way to even test modifications to the compound.*

Alex turned and looked at Jerry, his once handsome brother who had wasted into this gaunt, withered shell of his former self. *He's still in there, though.*

Rachel seemed to read his mind. "Forget about commercial use. What about family? What about your brother? If it works, couldn't it help get him well? Couldn't it help bring Jerry back?"

"Eli would never allow it."

"Why should Eli have any say in how you treat your brother? And..." Rachel reached a hand towards Jerry and began stroking his arm, "...if he's not being treated at the hospital, why would Eli have to know?"

Jerry began to rock back and forth. He hadn't eaten. Rachel placed a fork in his hand and guided it towards his plate of food. He raked it through the mashed potatoes, then fed it into his mouth and moaned. Whether from satisfaction or disgust, Alex wasn't sure.

Rachel smiled and continued, "I mean, it's your formula. You created it. Forget all the rules and regulations. If it can help Jerry get well and he's under our care, I don't know why we have to wait for some bureaucratic commission to tell you it's okay to use. All that should matter is what's best for Jerry."

Alex looked at Jerry and his faraway eyes; a tan patina of mashed potatoes coated his slack tongue. It had been over ten years since his father had come by to visit. He couldn't handle seeing his son in this state. And it seemed as though he had written Alex off as well; no modicum of success would ever make him worthy of his father's respect.

But what if he was able to bring Jerry back to his former self? What would his father think of him then? And if in treating his brother he was able to work out the kinks of the compound in order to sell the formula to a future buyer, well, wasn't that what the fancy pharmaceutical execs referred to as a win-win?

"We'll have to keep it quiet," Alex said.

There was a sparkle in Rachel's eye; she shimmied in her seat and quietly clapped her hands.

"And this means you'll have to keep a close eye on him."

She pointed two fingers towards her wide-open eyes.

"But, yeah. It's about what's best for him."

"Alex, it's the greatest gift you could ever give him."

It's the greatest gift I could ever give my father, he thought, then raised his cup of tea. His cheeks ballooned as he blew out a gust of air. *And it just might help save us from financial ruin.*

"To Jerry," he said.

Tears welled in Rachel's eyes as they touched paper cups.

CHAPTER FOURTEEN

"You're not going to want to watch this," Alex said as he reached into his medical bag and began pulling out supplies. The sedatives had taken effect and Jerry was resting peacefully on the bed.

"Sure I do. I want to help," Rachel said. She was standing at the end of the bed, holding Jerry's sock-covered feet and massaging their soles.

Alex pulled out the syringe and set it on the bedside tray. He moved aside so that Rachel could see the seven inches of gleaming steel.

"Oh." She took a step back, releasing Jerry's feet as though they carried some contagious disease.

"Exactly. I'll call for you if I need anything."

"Okay." She took a last look at Jerry with those telepathic eyes. It was a sad expression, but Alex knew the intent. She was wishing him well. She eased the door closed on her way out.

Alex turned and inspected the machinery procured from the hospital storage room. The equipment, which was designed to scan and monitor brain activity during surgery, didn't receive much use under Eli's tutelage. Alex wasn't worried about anyone realizing it was gone.

His only concern was for the refinements he had made to the formula. That had been a much more complicated task. The chemical compound he had created was designed to regulate the release of neurochemicals that control the way we perceive reality. Branches of this compound, however, represented some of the strongest hallucinogenic chemicals known to mankind.

In previous tests, patients had experienced moments of total lucidity soon after receiving the medicine, followed by heightened hallucinations. Alex's hypothesis was that the malfunctioning brain of a schizophrenic was flooding the patient with hallucinatory neurochemicals in response to the compound's attempt to suppress their production. The compound simply wasn't strong enough. So he had made it stronger, upping the amino-acid profile against the tryptamine suppressors.

He was reluctant to test this more potent version of the formula on his brother, but at least he would be on hand to help if anything went wrong.

"How are you feeling, Jerry? Still with me?" Alex asked, happy to see that all his vital signs were strong.

Jerry mumbled as if talking in his sleep.

"Good."

The syringe sat empty on the tray, the long, sharp needle pointed in his direction. From this angle, it looked like the stinger on some alien wasp. And in a way it was. Only, he had developed the serum and it had yet to prove venomous. Ineffectual, maybe. But not harmful. Still, it felt strange to be using it on Jerry.

He closed his eyes, remembering, for a moment, the first time he'd been stung.

★   ★   ★

He was mowing the yard to earn his weekly allowance. Five dollars for forty-five minutes of hard work (his father required that he bag the clippings). It was mid-August; the air was hot and humid, but the ground was dry from a three-week-long drought. The mower kicked up plumes of dust as he pushed it in orderly rows. And the dull blade crushed twigs into splinters, stirred up rocks and flung them into the unprotected skin on Alex's shins, face and arms.

That's what he thought they were at first, the stings. Just shards of wood ejected from the blade. But then the wasps got under his shirt and began stinging his back. He stopped the mower then and screamed in pain, but the low drone of the engine kept on purring. It was the angry war chant of the wasps as they swarmed his body and attacked.

It felt like someone was stabbing him with an ice pick. He spun within a circle that he couldn't escape. He didn't realize what was happening, only that something was hurting him and wouldn't stop.

Then he heard Jerry calling his name, saw him running hunched over while swatting at his head and neck. He reached Alex and ripped off his shirt, tearing it straight down the middle like he'd seen Hulk Hogan do on TV. Right then, Jerry seemed just as strong, just as heroic as that muscle-bound pro wrestler whom Alex had idolized. Then he lowered his head and pushed Alex across the yard towards the house. Just bulldozed him away from the horde of wasps.

The pain intensified when they got inside, once the adrenaline drained. It was like his veins were filled with shattered glass. It dropped him to the floor, where he began screaming and flopping about like a fish on dry land.

His father came in, looking more upset than concerned. "What's the matter with him?"

But Jerry was there, by his side. "You're tough, Alex!" he said, trying to bolster his confidence and fill him with strength. "Toughest kid I know! Come on, show me how tough you are!"

And somehow it worked. Jerry's words acted like a salve, dulling the pain and pumping him full of some misbegotten pride. He wanted to be as tough as Jerry said he was. He at least wanted to try.

★   ★   ★

The memory faded as Alex grabbed the syringe, hefting it in his hand. *Not nearly as tough as you,* he thought, then dipped the needle into the vial and filled the chamber to the designated mark. Jerry's words echoed in his mind as he leaned over, placing the needle's tip against the inside of his brother's eye socket and angling it upward. "You may feel a little pressure, but it shouldn't hurt." *I hope,* he thought.

He could sense the faintest tremor threatening his fingers, so he pressed forward and pushed the needle through. *Be tough, brother.*

It only took a few seconds and the needle was out. Alex returned it to the bedside table and plugged the puncture wound with a ball of cotton. Jerry's vital signs remained strong. Now, the only thing to do was wait.

Alex was rising from his chair when Jerry began to convulse violently, his body thrashing against the bed. Alex grabbed Jerry's head and held it steady, clamping his jaw closed. It took all of his strength to hold it in place.

"Okay, I could use a little help in here," he called out, trying to sound calm.

Jerry's back was arched high overhead and his legs were pumping like pistons, causing the pinewood bedframe to screech against the floor.

The door burst open and Rachel rushed through. She stopped as soon as she saw Jerry's condition and spun back around. "Jesus, what'd you do!" It was the panicked voice from the night Popeye died.

"Grab his feet. I need you to help restrain him."

Rachel peeked over her shoulder and winced. She thrust clenched fists down by her side and stomped. "Please! Make it stop!"

Jerry's throat became tight, bloated; he wasn't getting any air. His body went rigid, his hands curled in and his toes pointed down. He began to gurgle – a protracted *nnnnnhhhhgggg* – and his mouth began to foam. Then the convulsions returned, more fearsome than before.

"Goddammit, get over here!" He had to insert a breathing tube. He needed to help Jerry get air. He looked around the cluttered bedroom, the walls closing in, the seconds slipping away.

Maybe it'll look like natural causes. Even his internal voice sounded scared.

"Rachel! Now!"

She turned. Her face crumpled in disgust. She shook her hands as though they'd been stung. "Just fix him! Hurry! Hurry!"

Alex stared at her in disbelief. *He's going to die because of her.* Then the realization hit him. *No, he's going to die because of me.*

He released Jerry's head and used his hands to pivot, swinging his legs up over Jerry's body, straddling his hips and pinning him against the bed. He placed his palm against Jerry's forehead and pushed it back to open his airway, but his tongue was clogging his throat.

Alex looked around, searching for his cache of medical supplies. But this was not a hospital room or even a test lab. It was just the small, dingy bedroom where his brother was about to die.

Jerry's face was turning purple. Spittle continued to foam from his lips. Alex pried open Jerry's mouth and shoved his fingers through his teeth, grabbing the tongue and pulling it forward. A reedy gasp escaped. Then another. Alex dug his thumbnail deep into the tongue tissue to maintain his grip as his brother struggled to breathe. Shallow and hitched at first, catching in his throat, and then deep and unrestricted.

Alex let go of Jerry's tongue and it fell back into its natural place. His breathing became regulated. Then his body began to relax, so Alex slid off and stood beside the bed.

Jerry's eyes fluttered, revealing two crescent moons, and then they sprang open all the way. The eyeballs rolled backwards, and Jerry squeezed his eyes shut. When he opened them again they remained in place. They found Alex and fixated on his face. There was life behind them, a spark of lucid recognition.

Rachel released a ragged wail, and Alex and Jerry both turned their heads. She was bent over, hiding her face behind both hands. Her shoulders hitched as she silently cried until her next exhale, when she released another loud, wavering wail.

Jerry sat up, a concerned look on his face. But Alex stayed him with a hand on his shoulder. He propped a pillow behind his brother's back so that he could sit upright against the headboard. He checked Jerry's vitals, slightly nodding his head. "Just take it easy," he said.

Jerry looked at Alex, swallowed and winced in pain, pointing to his throat. "Water," he croaked.

"Rachel, go get Jerry a glass of water," Alex said.

Rachel nodded and left the room.

Alex exhaled. His collar was damp with sweat, his hands tingling. He wiped them on his khaki pants as he continued to monitor his brother.

Rachel returned with a glass of water sloshing in her unsteady hands and set it beside Jerry. He mouthed the word *thanks*, then grabbed the glass and took a sip. He winced again and set it back down.

Quiet descended, thick and oppressive, save for Rachel's sniffles. They grated on Alex's frayed nerves. "Do you mind waiting outside?"

Rachel looked insulted. "What? No, I want to help."

"Help, huh?" Alex shook his head. "A little late for that, don't you think?"

"Oh, screw that, Alex. You didn't tell me that that was going to happen. You said you'd worked out all the kinks. You could have killed him."

Alex stood and stepped in front of Jerry to block his view. "That's enough," Alex hissed. Spittle flew and a few strands of hair fell across his forehead. Rachel glared at him and he glared back, red heat rushing to his face.

A dog began barking in the distance, the high-pitched yap of a small terrier. It continued for several seconds and then stopped with a sudden yelp like the sound of a screeching tire. Silence returned to the room.

Rachel blinked and looked away, confused, eyes cast down in contemplation.

Alex cocked his head, then turned.

Jerry was looking up at him, a wan smile on face. "Streak," he said, his voice barely a whisper.

Alex returned to Jerry's bedside. He stared down into his brother's eyes. One pupil was fully dilated; the other was constricted down to a tiny pinprick. As he watched, they switched places, the dilated eye constricting while the constricted pupil expanded wide. They went back and forth several times before becoming the same normal size.

"How are you feeling?" Alex asked.

Jerry scanned his body as though assessing himself. He looked over at Rachel, then back up at Alex. He lifted his left hand off the bed and closed it into a fist. His thumb shot up in the air. "Good," he said softly. His lopsided smile expanded. "I feel good." He looked up at Alex, his eyes bright and full of wonder. "What happened?" he said.

"I administered some medicine. It should help you to feel..." He searched his mind for the right word.

"Like me," Jerry answered for him, smiling wider still.

Alex smiled back down at his brother. "Yes," he said. "Like you."

CHAPTER FIFTEEN

The window was no longer a window. It had become a tableau, its surface etched in staggered lines of golden Sanskrit, luminescent letters that produced a radiant glow in the gloom of the group-therapy room. This one was named Serenity.

The message was encoded in an ancient language that Crosby had never learned, yet it was easy to decipher its meaning. The translation came to him in a calm and resolute voice heard in the center of his head, offering a dire warning. He scowled as he scrutinized the people sitting in chairs arranged in a circle, hiding behind their placid masks. *The battle wages on,* he thought.

"What else can we do to help ourselves when we begin to hear voices?" Angela said, smiling as she scanned the faces before her. *She knows,* Crosby thought, but kept silent. He looked at the floor behind her, but she didn't cast a shadow. No one did in the dimness of this gloomy room.

The flabby retard with the wobbly teeth raised his hands. Randall, Crosby thought his name was, but wasn't sure. He hadn't paid attention during introductions. He wasn't interested in a support group comprised of loons.

Angela nodded her head in Randall's direction.

"I've come to just think of it as a kind of radio station that only plays in your head. That way I can just listen without getting all wrapped up in what it's telling me. And it makes it easier to tune out. Kind of like changing channels, you know?"

"Yes, that's an excellent technique," Angela said. Her smile was the second brightest object in the room, only outshone by the window and the radiance of its divine word. "Has anyone else tried to think of the voices as if they're coming through the radio?"

"What if the voices you hear *are* coming from the radio?" The patient's nicotine-stained fingers were frayed with hangnails that he compulsively picked and nibbled with his teeth. "What do you do then?"

"Well..." Angela rubbed her knees as she considered the question, "...first, you would need to be able to distinguish between a real radio announcement and one that you're imagining."

Crosby thought the old man sitting next to Angela was sleeping, until he exploded in a fit of laughter. "That's right, that's right," he jibbered. "You be all thinking the radio's not the radio, then the radio's the radio and you're thinking it's not the radio, and then it's the radio that's the radio. Whoo-eee!" His chin dug back into his chest and he appeared to return to sleep.

Hangnail brought a finger to his lips and peeled away a strip of skin. "Sometimes the radio tells me I got a worm in my stomach, and the only way to get it out is by electrocuting my intestines."

"Hmmm..." Angela pondered, "...that would probably be an example of a time when you're imagining what you're hearing."

"I got a worm in my stomach too," said a burly man whose bushy beard nearly joined his eyebrows. "Its name is José and it makes me drink tequila."

The old man awoke to fresh laughter. "That's right, that's right, that's right, that's right," he said for a full minute, until the others joined in and took up the chant.

Crosby watched as Angela attempted to restore order, pressing down with her hands as though closing an imaginary box. She was so small and fragile looking, with her highlighted hair and china-doll face. He knew, though, that demons often disguised themselves in angelic forms. He wouldn't be tricked again.

His mother came to mind.

She, too, had been beautiful. Tall, with long, thin legs and a tiny waist. A slender, swanlike neck supporting an oval face with a shallow cleft in her chin. She had thin lips, brittle, blonde hair and a severe smile, but her pale-blue eyes could make men shiver, as from ice. And she always had one by her side.

But what Crosby remembered most about his mother was her hands. Bony, clawlike talons that crushed his little fingers and skinny arms as she dragged him along behind her, or yanked him out of a chair or from the bed or off the floor. She had sharp, knotted knuckles, like bone spurs, that would flame white when she made a fist, and burn like cold fire when she crashed them into his spine. And short, sturdy nails that would gouge red lines of raw flesh whenever she raked them across his skin.

Her hands appeared prim and delicate until she got mad, and then they would curl into vicious claws with thick, wriggly veins that snaked up her spindly arms.

"You need to learn to pull your own weight," she'd say as she dragged him through the back alleys leading to their many motel rooms across countless towns. *"I need you to act like a man."*

He supposed that's what she was trying to teach him whenever she brought another man to his room. He wasn't sure what he was supposed to learn from those lessons, but they always ate better for a day or two after, so he thought he must be doing something right. Finally pulling his weight.

And the training had come in handy after he had finally been set free. After he'd left her dead on the floor, the life choked out of her. He always knew how to bring in a few extra bucks to keep from being evicted from his ramshackle motel room, or whenever he'd missed too many meals.

Still, he knew now what his mother was. Knew what lay hidden behind her pretty facade. That's why he'd had to escape.

The room was still a cacophony of laughter and shouting voices, but the sound faded to the background as Crosby leaned forward. He squinted, forcing his eyes to focus, trailing them down Angela's long, athletic arms to where they ended. Her hands. Prim and delicate with short, sturdy nails and sharp, knotted knuckles. A few wriggly veins were beginning to emerge as she clapped them together in an attempt to establish control.

He sat back in his seat and crossed his arms. Finally, the group settled down, gasping and wheezing like an old engine on empty.

"That was good, that was good," Angela said once the room grew quiet. She directed her brilliant smile towards Crosby. "How about you, Crosby?" she said. "We haven't heard from you yet. Do you have anything to add?"

He tilted his head to one side and sucked in air. He held it, then released it in a whoosh. "Do you ever hear voices inside your head?" he asked.

"No, I can't say that I do."

Crosby grunted. "You don't ever hear a voice when you're in the shower, maybe singing a little melody, or when you're driving, shouting at the car in front of you, or when you're at the grocery store, reminding you that you're low on milk?"

"Okay, yes. Sure, we all have an internal monologue expressing our thoughts. There's a difference, though, between the voice our mind uses to articulate our thoughts and auditory hallucinations. Those are the ones that we're discussing now."

"So it's fine for you to hear voices in your head but not us?"

"I'm not saying that there is a right or a wrong, just that there is a difference. Oftentimes, hallucinatory voices create unwanted stress and lead to destructive behavior. We would want to minimize that, wouldn't we?"

"You mean control it. Yeah, I know how certain thoughts can be scary for people in positions of power. It's a form of censorship. Everyone hears voices in their head, but some are considered crazy, others sane. Depends on what the voices are saying, it seems."

"That's an interesting point," Angela said. She checked her watch and then slapped her palms against the top of her thighs. "Unfortunately, we're about out of time. We'll pick back up tomorrow where we left off."

Angela showed her smile, but it had lost its light; the darkness in the room deepened. Crosby looked back at the window, which had become a window again. But he had received its message loud and clear.

I know why you keep your lights so low, he thought as he scanned the floor again for shadows. *You may appear sweet on the outside, but I know what you are underneath.*

Angela stood and started to direct the patients towards the orderlies who had come to escort them to the next item on their itinerary. When she walked past Crosby, she placed a firm hand on his shoulder and squeezed.

CHAPTER SIXTEEN

She cupped her hand over the shot glass, slammed it against the bar – carbonated tequila sprayed out on all sides – and drank it down. The bartender's whistle shrieked. Stacy reached out and shook Angela's head.

"Fucking *opa!*" Angela yelled.

"Opa?" Stacy's laughter turned the word into seven syllables. She held Angela's head steady so she could look into her eyes. "What are you talking about, opa?"

"Isn't that what you say when you take a shot?"

"Yeah, if you're in ouzo drinking Greece." They both paused, the music blaring in the background, then brayed laughter into each other's faces. "I mean… You know what I fucking mean." Stacy pushed Angela's head playfully away.

"Sorry, it's been a while since I've had a tequila slammer," Angela said. "I've forgotten the etiquette."

"Yeah, right. Like, two weeks?" Stacy smirked.

"Oh shut up," Angela said, feigning indignation.

"Then I'll remind you. You're now supposed to stumble up to some cute guy on the dance floor and let him finger fuck you in a booth near the back."

Angela snorted. "Right. I'd forgotten that part. I'll be right back." She spun the barstool around and pretended to hop off.

The bar was beginning to thin out, but a throng of people still pressed against the small corner stage where a cover band blasted Southern rock songs from the seventies. And a ragtag group of gamblers still huddled over tables in the pool hall. Red embers flared like demonic fireflies, while threads of smoke shapeshifted in bands of blue light. Bleary-eyed loners sat at the bar, staring at nothing while downing their drinks in synchronized sips. A string of faded shamrocks encircled the banister overhead, leftover relics from a St. Patrick's party many months, or years, ago.

"I fucking love this place," Angela said, spinning back around to face Stacy.

"This place is a shithole," Stacy said as she lit a cigarette.

"I know. That's why I love it." She reached into Stacy's pack and pulled out a cigarette for herself, leaning over for Stacy to light it. The band started playing "Statesboro Blues" and a drunken cheer erupted from the crowd. Angela shot an arm up in the air and bellowed, "Wooo-hooo!"

Stacy leaned back and clapped her hands, laughing. "You crack me up," she said.

Angela returned the laughter, then blew smoke up towards the ceiling, adding to the gray haze overhead. "Why's that?"

"'Cause you're like this Dr. Do Good by day and Little Miss Devil by night."

"More like Dr. *Feel* Good," Angela said, turning and ordering another round of shots. She placed her cigarette in an ashtray and tousled her hair, resetting the spikes. "I've got to blow off steam after work. Otherwise, I'd go—"

"Crazy?"

Angela rolled her eyes and smiled. "You know what I mean."

"I can imagine. So how are things at the old nuthouse?"

Angela backhanded Stacy on the arm. Then swiveled the stool to face her longtime friend still sporting the same frizzy, highlighted hair from high school. Still applying thick coats of concealer like spackling over blemished skin. The dim recesses of back-alley bars were Stacy's natural habitat. Angela couldn't remember the last time she'd seen her old friend in the unforgiving glare of daylight.

"I don't know. It's good, I guess. In a completely fucked-up kind of way." She grabbed the cigarette from the tray. Twin creases dimpled her cheeks as she sucked in smoke. Her voice became husky as she exhaled. "I swear, the longer you work in a place like that, you start to lose perspective over who's really sane. I'm starting to think that we're all a little bit crazy. It's all just shades of gray."

The shots came. Warm kamikazes filled to the brim. They clinked glasses before choking them down, chasing away the taste with beer that they'd ordered to back the shots.

Stacy propped her elbow atop the bar so that she could feed the cigarette into her mouth simply by rotating her wrist. "My ex-boyfriend used to have me step on his balls with stiletto heels. Trust me. I know what you mean."

"No way! That banker? What was his name – Hank?"

"Henry. Yeah, it turned him on. He wanted to drink my piss too."

Angela almost sprayed beer across the bar. "No way! Did you do it?"

"Fuck no. What, I'm supposed to piss into a chalice and serve it on a silver platter? Gross. That was too much. Even for me."

"I never would have imagined," Angela said, shaking her head in wonder.

"Well, that goes back to what you're saying. We're all fucking nuts." She motioned to the bartender. "Another round, *muchacho*."

Angela's eyes brightened. She gave a mock cheer. "There's something liberating about the idea of losing it. About just letting go and giving in to our natural inhibitions. It's too stressful trying to be perfect all the time. I mean, do you think what's his name, Henry, would want his balls stomped on if he wasn't so repressed in his everyday life? I feel like we only get to be ourselves, I mean our true, authentic selves, a small fraction of the time that we're alive. The rest of the time we're putting on an act for others.

"And it's such a lame act, with all these stiff social graces, this pretentious etiquette. The perfect posture. The smug, insincere smiles. Safe topics of conversation. Fucking manners. I mean, who came up with this stuff? Whoever it was, was a fucking dork."

Stacy did spray beer. She wiped her mouth with the back of her hand and sighed. "It's true. We're all expected to act like the most uptight asshole."

"Seriously. That's why I love places like this. Here, no one gives a fuck. Everyone's just out to have a good time. But, I mean, look at the setup. It's dark, so we can't see each other very well. It's like we're hiding in the shadows or something. The music's loud, so it disrupts our normal speech patterns. There are all sorts of games and distractions."

The bartender slid the shots in front of them.

Angela pulled hers close. "Not to mention everyone's completely wasted," she said, her words beginning to slur. "Everyone's got some vice to help compensate for the fact that they have to pretend to be someone else. It's like our own mini-rebellion."

Stacy narrowed her eyes, squinting through the helix of rising smoke.

"Right. Some people get hammered." She nodded sagely. "Other people just hammer their nuts."

Angela looked sidelong at Stacy. They both held serious expressions for a moment, then burst out laughing. "I can't believe you actually walked on Henry's balls," she said, her shoulders shaking.

"The things we do for love."

Angela's barstool was bumped from behind. She turned to face a tall man wearing a Stetson hat pulled low over deep, wide-set eyes. Long, wavy hair cascaded down his neck, and a thick mustache was perched above his mouth. His smile bloomed in the blue light.

"Hey, cowboy," Angela said, smirking.

"You ladies look to be having a good time," he said in a deep Southern drawl. "Mind if I join in?"

Angela inspected him through narrow slits. "I don't know. You'll have to answer a few questions first."

"Shoot," he said.

"Okay. Well, are you a real cowboy, or are you just playing pretend?"

The man smiled. "Depends on how you define cowboy. I guess I herd things from place to place and spend most my days on the open road. I can sing songs by the fire and am handy with a rope. I can tie a heck of a knot."

Angela looked at Stacy and arched her eyebrows. "You're good at tying things up, are you?"

He took a step closer. Light chased the shadows from his eyes. They were cobalt blue. "If something gets too wild on me. Sure, I just tie it down." He rested his arms across the back of her barstool, forcing Angela to lean away.

She smiled and sucked deeply on her cigarette. "Okay. Well answer me this, have you ever had your balls walked on?"

Stacy bent forward and snickered into her hand.

"What, you mean by a woman?"

"I don't know. You tell me."

His smile became slanted. He reached out and placed a heavy hand on Angela's thigh, giving it a firm squeeze. Angela pressed her legs together, clamping his hand between them. Heat rushed to her face as she held his gaze.

"I can't say that I have," he said. "Personally, I prefer pleasure over pain."

Angela relaxed her legs, allowing him to slide his hand up another inch. She reached a hand around his neck and leaned forward, sliding her smooth face against his rough stubble. "Hi, cowboy. I'm Angela."

He turned his head so that the corners of their lips were touching. "Dale," he said. "What're you drinking?"

"I'm done drinking," she said, chugging the last of her beer and hopping off the barstool. Her legs buckled as she hit the ground, the alcohol rushing to her head, and she latched on to his arm for balance. "I want to dance." She grabbed Dale's hand and led him towards the dance floor. She looked over her shoulder at Stacy and shrugged.

Stacy rolled her eyes and smiled, then turned back towards the bar.

Angela threaded her way through the throng of people, spilling drinks as she careened off shoulders, pulling Dale behind. Sweat trickled down her side as the warmth of the crowd washed over her. She turned to face him and the room kept spinning.

Dale was a head and a half taller than her. When he pressed his hand into Angela's lower back, pulling her close, the soft flesh of her lower belly pushed against his groin. She felt him harden, and began to move against his stiffening member.

He stepped forward, his lead leg slipping between her thighs, and began to grind his hips. The crowd pressed against them from all sides as they started gyrating to the pulsating music.

Angela wrapped both arms around his neck and gazed into the dark shadows obscuring his eyes, biting her lower lip.

The band began a slow, swampy version of Creedence Clearwater's "Run Through the Jungle." Angela turned, reaching overhead and caressing Dale's neck, pushing back against him. He wrapped his arm around her waist, placing his hand on her stomach. She grabbed it with her other hand and moved it lower, moaning as he thrust his hips forward, driving the full length of his erection against her soft backside.

Angela closed her eyes. Her head felt heavy; she let it sway from side to side. Her mind wandered then returned without recording where it had been. The temperature continued to climb and her top clung to her chest. Dale's hands felt slippery against the skin of her thighs.

For a moment, she forgot who was behind her. She had to turn to refresh her memory. Her legs turned rubbery so she leaned against him, forcing him to carry her weight. Her face fell into the crook of his neck and she began to kiss it, running her tongue along its length, tasting his salty tang.

★   ★   ★

"Let's get some air," he said, turning Angela and pushing her back through the crowd. She wobbled, and he wrapped an arm around her to hold her steady, guiding her towards the back of the dance floor.

"Hold on, I just need to check on my friend."

"She's gone," Dale said.

Angela scanned the bar. Stacy's seat had been filled by someone else. She was nowhere to be found.

"Where'd she go?" Angela slurred.

"Come on. Maybe she went outside." Dale walked Angela towards the exit.

The lot was quiet. The air outside was cool. A single streetlamp bathed the cars in a dull, sickly light. Moths careened against its yellow casing, casting erratic shadows across the cracked and pockmarked pavement. Angela laughed for no reason while Dale shuffled her along.

"Are you gonna fuck me?" Angela cupped Dale's crotch. "Are you gonna ride me, cowboy?" She continued to snicker, then slurped back a string of saliva from the corner of her lips.

Dale stopped beside a dark-green Camaro with tinted windows and shiny chrome wheels. He fumbled in his pocket for his keys and then opened the passenger door. He reached in and pulled the seat forward, then grabbed Angela and pushed her into the back, where she landed and bumped her head against the far armrest. Dale followed her in, closed and locked the door.

Angela scooted herself onto her elbows, attempting a seductive stare. Her eyes were half-lidded; her lips looked raw. Her chest heaved as she stifled an emerging burp and tried to play it off by tossing her hair out of her eyes. When she did, her head banged against the side panel.

Dale looked down from above, grinning, massaging his cock through the fabric of his pants. He reached down and grabbed Angela's panties from underneath her skirt and pulled them off, lifting her legs in the air, driving her head into the corner of the car seat. He pushed the hem of her skirt up until she was fully exposed. She closed her eyes and spread her legs in anticipation. It felt like she was sinking; she started to drift. The last thing she heard was the sound of Dale unzipping his pants.

★ ★ ★

Angela awoke to a honking horn and the sound of laughter.

"What's up, egg roll? You need a lift?" A male voice, young.

She opened her eyes and the world spun around her. It stretched and swooned before assuming its proper form. Her head was buzzing, as from an electric charge, and her eyes felt like they'd been pickled in salt. Finally, she was able to focus on the face peering out from the car window. A young man with splotchy skin, wearing a mesh ball cap, its folded bill pulled low.

"Hey, girl. Come on, let's party," the man said. "The night's still young."

She was sitting on the pavement, her legs splayed out before her, leaning against a chain-link fence. "Fuck off," she said, holding a hand up in a feeble attempt to hide her face.

"Fuck *off*? That's not very ladylike. How about we fuck *you*, instead?" Laughter erupted from the car as it drove away, spraying loose gravel in its wake.

Squinting, Angela surveyed her surroundings. She was in the parking lot of a bar. It was nearly empty; just a few cars remained. The neon sign above the door was dark. The bar was closed. Angela vaguely remembered being there earlier. She had been drinking with Stacy. And then… She couldn't remember.

Her purse was beside her. So was her underwear, crumpled in a ball. She reached into her purse and pulled out her phone, then dialed Stacy. Stacy picked up on the third ring.

"Hey, cowgirl. Where are you?"

Angela groaned. "Back at the bar." Her voice sounded deep and gravelly. "I don't know what happened. I'm here, and I'm all alone."

Stacy sighed. "Shit. Are you okay? Do you need a ride?"

"I don't know. I mean—" Angela began to cry. She grabbed a handful of hair and pulled. "Can you come get me? I'm all alone."

"Yes. I'll be right there." There was a pause. Then, "Jesus, Angela. Why do you always do this?"

"I don't know." Angela grabbed her underwear and lurched to her feet. She brushed pebbles of gravel from the backside of her legs.

"No," Stacy sighed. "You never do."

CHAPTER SEVENTEEN

Alex saw Eli walk through the restaurant entrance. He took a small sip of water and stood. "Here he is," he said, looking at Rachel, then at Jerry. "You okay?" he asked his brother.

Jerry winked. "Better than ever." It had been just over a week since Alex had administered the medicine, and Jerry was almost unrecognizable. His eyes were clear and focused. His clothes were clean, his hair trimmed and neatly combed. His face had filled out from the weight he had gained. And his wide smile reflected the charm that had been absent since adolescence. "Like a new man," he said.

"More like your old self," Rachel said, a smile brightening her face. She hadn't been able to shed it since the procedure.

Alex caught Eli's wandering eye and waved.

Eli nodded and started walking their way.

"I don't mean to sound like a broken record, but..." Alex said quietly to the table.

"Don't worry. We won't say a word," Jerry said.

Rachel pantomimed locking her lips and tossing the key.

Eli came up behind Rachel and squeezed her shoulders, then he turned and shook Alex's hand. But his eyes were on Jerry the whole time. He stepped towards him with an outstretched hand. "Hi, Jerry," he said. "It's great to see you."

Jerry hesitated. For a moment his eyes lost focus and he appeared confused. His mouth sagged open.

Alex and Rachel exchanged a concerned look.

Then Jerry smiled and took Eli's hand. He pulled him into a hug. "Sorry, just messing with you. It's great to see you too." He released Eli and held him at arm's length, gazing into his eyes. "Clearly, I think, for the first time."

Eli turned and looked at Alex in wonder. "You weren't kidding.

His recovery is..." he searched his mind for the word, "...well, it's encouraging, to say the least."

"Oh pooh! It's a miracle," Rachel said.

Alex shot her a look.

She averted her eyes and took a long sip of water.

"Here, let's sit down," Alex said. They all took their seats around the circular table, Eli and Rachel sitting between Alex and Jerry. The waiter came, and they ordered drinks. Only Rachel ordered wine.

"So," Eli said, addressing Jerry, "how are you feeling? I mean, you look fantastic."

"That about sums up how I feel." He motioned across the table towards Alex. "Thanks to my bookworm brother over here."

They all laughed. Laughter had come easier for Alex these last few days. "Watch it, jock," he said, and they laughed harder still.

The laughter subsided and the table became quiet. Eli's smile switched off like a light. He turned to Alex and said, "So, how did you do it? From what you've said, and what I'm seeing, this is more than simply a suppression of symptoms. There's been a complete transformation."

Alex leaned forward and crossed his arms. His eyes fixated on an invisible spot in the center of the table. A crease of concentration formed between his brows. "It was the meds, Eli. I know that's not what you want to hear, but..." he trailed off and shrugged, "...it came down to prescribing Jerry the right medication."

"Which was what? Put my prejudice against certain pharmaceuticals aside. If we can achieve these kinds of results, I'll be happy to prescribe the same treatment to all our patients."

Alex saw Rachel's head turn towards him, and he resisted the urge to reciprocate the stare. The buzz of background conversation grew louder as he considered the safest response. He imagined the murmuring noise resembled the frenetic scramble of a psychotic mind.

"I'll let you in on the secret," Jerry said, and all eyes shifted towards him. "Although, I'm not sure if it's available for public consumption."

Alex pinched his lips and tried to silence Jerry with his eyes.

Jerry gave him a discreet wink, then flashed a smile at Eli. "It's Rachel's home cooking. A few days of good ole-fashioned comfort food from the kitchen of my sister-in-law will set any man straight."

Alex's laughter was strained, but it blended in with the others'. "Well then, Rachel," Eli said. "Looks like we'll need to find you a position in our kitchen."

"Sure, we can talk terms later," Rachel said. "But, I'll need for people to sign a release form on pasta night. My *arrabbiata* can set off a fire alarm."

Jerry made a sizzling sound, then gulped down his glass of water while fanning his face.

The waiter returned as their laughter faded, and they placed their food orders. For Alex, it was a welcome respite.

He was considering ways to redirect the conversation, when Eli spoke. "So, Jerry, I certainly hope you plan to rejoin the grounds crew at Sugar Hill. We'd love to have you back."

Jerry leaned back and crossed his legs, clasping his hands around his right knee. "Well, you know I appreciate the offer, Dr. Alpert, but…" He uncrossed his legs and leaned his arms against the table, then sat back and crossed them once more, then leaned forward again. His face turned red and his eyes began to roam. "I mean, if you need me there, I guess I can, but—"

Alex straightened. "You okay, Jerry?"

Jerry stopped fidgeting. He pressed his palms flat against the table, as though suppressing his distress. His body slowly relaxed; his face lost its flush. "Yes. Yes, sorry, I'm fine. It's just…well, I'm not sure how safe it would be for me to go back." He attempted a smile and failed. His eyes showed fear. "I think I might have made an enemy on my way out."

Eli frowned. "With who?"

"I'd rather not say." Jerry took a drink of water and began crunching an ice cube. "Anyway, it's history. I'd rather focus on the future." He turned and looked at Eli.

★　★　★

There was something strange about his eyes. The pupils. One appeared more dilated than the other.

"It sure beats worrying about the past, wouldn't you say?"

Eli leaned forward to get a better look into Jerry's eyes, but was interrupted by table service. A staff of waiters had arrived with their plates.

"Who ordered sirloin?" The waiter was a young Vietnamese man. He was wearing gray kitchen rags that resembled army fatigues. He looked young. Too young to be working at a restaurant like this.

"Over here," Eli said and raised his hand.

The server walked over. When he saw Eli his eyes narrowed, and his lips pulled back in a sneer. He circled behind Eli's seat and bent over his shoulder, brushing against him as he placed the plate on top of the table. He lingered for a moment, then turned his head towards Eli. "Enjoy, sir," he said into Eli's ear, quietly, just barely as perceptible as a resonance of wind. His breath was overwhelming, however. It reeked of death.

Eli stiffened. He grabbed a fork and clenched it in his fist. "Thank you," he said, shying away from the face that was far too close. He locked eyes with the server, just a couple of inches away from his own, and recalled with total clarity the night from the raid on the Vietcong encampment.

"No, sir. It is you whom I should thank." The server's eyes were still locked on Eli's. His lips still pulled back in a knowing sneer. He reached into the pocket of his waistband and pulled something out. The table light caught the edge of a serrated blade.

Eli gasped and threw himself backwards, the chair screeched against the tiled floor as it almost toppled over. He was starting to turn and stand when the server reached out and removed Eli's table knife, calmly setting the steak knife in its place.

"Whoa," Alex said. "Everything okay, Eli?"

Eli was panting. The white-knuckled hand clutching the fork was trembling. He attempted to swallow, but the saliva caught in his throat.

"Sorry, sir," the server said and began laughing, his lips stretching wider to reveal small, gleaming teeth. He grabbed the knife and pantomimed slicing meat. "For your steak, sir." He pointed the blade at Eli and wagged it back and forth in the air, staring with eyes that Eli could never forget. Innocent eyes filled with a mixture of hatred, supplication and fear. "Don't worry. It's already dead." He continued his stilted laughter while pleading through his haunted eyes, the others at the table joining in as though in on the joke. Then he returned the knife to the table and stood back so the other servers could deliver the remaining dinner plates.

Eli's wide eyes remained pinned to the Vietnamese boy, as he scooted his chair back to the table. The young man Sergeant Wagner had forced him to kill.

Jerry leaned towards Eli, pretending to whisper with a raised voice that could be heard by the entire table. "I appreciate the gesture, sir, but it's not necessary."

Eli arched his eyebrows as though creating a question mark.

"You don't need to try quite so hard to make me feel comfortable." Jerry put on the face of a schizophrenic shying from the shadows of imaginary men. He stopped and smiled. "That's all behind me now." He glanced at Alex. "I hope."

"Right. Just a bit jumpy, I guess," Eli said, still clutching the fork in his fist. "I haven't been sleeping very well." He loosened his grip and set the fork down on the table. He used his napkin to pat beads of sweat from his upper lip and chin. "So," he said, his voice wavering ever so slightly, all the blood having drained from his face. "What were we talking about?"

"Nothing," Jerry said. "Just the people from our past." His gaze lingered on Eli. His pupils had returned to their normal size. "And the fact that they can't hurt us anymore."

Alex raised a glass to toast with. "To the future," he said.

Eli's water rippled as he raised his, and he cringed as the glasses clinked together. "To the future," he forced himself to say before grabbing the knife and slicing into his steak, grimacing as the juices ran red.

CHAPTER EIGHTEEN

It struck Eli the moment he turned off the lights. Panic. Thrusting him into a private world of faceless fear, a suffocating state of certainty that insanity was descending. Darkness came crashing down upon him like a coffin door, but his body was the crypt – a claustrophobic box in which he'd be buried forever. He turned the lamp back on, but it didn't help. The enemy had arrived and it wasn't deterred by light. The enemy resided within his mind.

Eli threw aside the sheets, clutching them in his hands as he writhed against the flash of searing fear. *Breathe*, he thought. *Breathe, breathe, just breathe.*

But his breath came in shallow gasps as his mind braced against the pending descent into insanity. *Breathe, just breathe!* He opened his eyes in hopes that the familiar setting of his room would soothe him. Instead, it all appeared foreign. Worthless artifacts collected while creating a life that had led him to this. *I've made too many mistakes,* he thought. *They can never be undone. They are me. I am thee.* His bowels loosened and he raced to the bathroom.

There, the tremors began, causing him to shake as though freezing. When he finished with the toilet he stumbled back to the bedroom and collapsed into his reading chair, pulling a throw blanket up over his naked chest. He closed his eyes and focused on his breathing. But the ghosts lived in the darkness, and they were restless. Tonight, they had come to haunt.

Miranda's face bloomed in his mind, filling the entire field of his inner eye. It was all that he could see. He threw open his eyes, and yet she remained, her image imprinted on the lenses within.

Ghosts are real. Eli groaned and swiped a damp hand across his sweaty face. *They're memories. And they stay with you for eternity.* The thought made him dry heave.

★　　★　　★

The orderlies had her cornered, huddled against the wall of her room like a trapped animal. Eli was waiting behind, forcing himself to remain calm and allow her to be taken. "The stronger the medicine, the harsher its taste," Dr. Francis was fond of saying, and he was standing just outside the doorway.

"Please don't!" she screamed, but Eli blocked out her pleas, focusing his attention on the task at hand.

The orderlies yanked her to her feet, wrenching her arms behind her back and forcing her forward.

"No! Please! Please don't!" she cried, her long, unkempt hair covering her face, eyes streaming tears, strings of saliva stretched wide.

In his mind's eye she looked deranged. But she also just looked scared.

Eli visited with her afterwards. She was depleted, docile. Restful, actually. The therapy seemed to have worked. They were getting somewhere.

"How are you feeling?"

Her eyes fluttered, a smile flitted across her face. She stretched her arms overhead like a contented kitten and purred. "Tingly," she said.

"Emotionally. Tell me what you're feeling."

"Hmmm. Well, I've been thinking about my sister. She's younger. Just by a couple of years. Her name's Susan, but we call her Suzie. She's never had much luck with boys. She's...not all that pretty. But she's sweet. She's my Sweet Little Suzie."

Eli's instinct was to smile, but his training told him to shield his emotions. Silence is the breeding ground for sharing.

"I teased her growing up," she said, and her face grew somber; her eyes began searching the distance for something unseen. "I was ashamed of her looks, that we were related. Like it was a reflection on me. That her ugliness was a blight on our bloodline. Something I needed to distance myself from.

"And then she was always so shy. So insecure. Like she couldn't stand up for herself. And she didn't have any friends, while I was always real popular. It embarrassed me, so I teased her. So people wouldn't associate me with her. It protected me. Or my image, rather.

"But at home, when we were alone together, we would sometimes talk, or play a game, or do each other's hair or makeup, and it seemed to make her so happy I felt like I was doing something good. Like I was doing her a favor. Like I was compensating for the times when I teased her. That maybe it all balanced out.

"But then the next day at school I would ignore her or call her names if we crossed paths in the hall, and it would start all over again. It was a cycle that I finally grew out of when I went to college. Just sibling rivalry, I figured. All a part of growing up.

"We're friends now, but there's still this bit of distance between us. I always thought it was because she's so shy. And insecure. She still doesn't do well with boys. But I've come to realize that I'm the reason she's so insecure and shy. That, by teasing her, I made her that way. If I had accepted her, so would have everyone else at school. But when I rejected her, she never had a chance. She never had anyone to turn to, no one to validate her, to lift her up, to boost her confidence. I was the one person she should have been able to rely on, and I let her down the most.

"She has every reason in the world to hate me, but she doesn't. She loves me. Maybe more than anyone else in the world. And it gets me thinking about how I used to define beauty, and I realize I had it all wrong."

Eli wanted to take her hand and hold it, but he busied himself with his notebook instead. "So you used to fixate more on outer appearances, and now you see the value in one's inner character."

Miranda rubbed the back of her neck; she said it was tender from the convulsions induced by the electric shocks. "Now I see how I've been a shitty sister, and that I'm responsible for my sister's struggles in life, and I just want to get out of here and be with her and see if we can start over. See if I can help undo the damage I've already done."

Eli wanted to sign her release forms and help facilitate the reconciliation with her sister. Instead, he crossed his arms and scowled. "The best thing you can do for your sister is get yourself well."

Miranda pulled her long, tangled hair into a ponytail. There were red blotches on the undersides of her arms that weren't there a week ago. "I don't know how else I can say it. I'm not sick."

Eli didn't think she was. "That's for Dr. Francis to decide."

When her husband visited the following week, Miranda attacked him, raking her nails across his cheeks and pummeling the back of his head with her fists. He had presented her with divorce papers, citing insanity as grounds. He was smiling when they pulled Miranda off of him, even though his lips were bleeding and his teeth were etched in red. Her display was apt to save him a lot of money in alimony. He still made a point to personally admonish Dr. Francis for the poor prognosis.

"She's worse off than when I brought her in," he said. "Surely she's in no condition to be released."

"We'll make the necessary corrections," Dr. Francis assured him. He immediately prescribed the maximum-strength antipsychotic and switched her treatment from electrotherapy to the submersion tanks.

Eli escorted her back to her room after the first session. He held her lightly by the arm as she shuffled her slippered feet across the linoleum floor. Her hair was still damp and it clung to her pallid face. Water pattered down the back of her gown, dripping to the floor. She was shivering as she laced her arm through his and leaned her head against his shoulder.

"It's not so bad," Miranda said.

She had gone calmly into the tub. It wasn't until they strapped her into the seat and the water began to rise that she had begun to struggle. But she had settled down again once she became submerged. Her eyes had remained open the whole time; tiny bubbles had percolated from her right nostril as she stared up at Dr. Francis, her hair fanned out like a halo of seaweed. She had smiled right before her breath ran out. Then she'd begun to strain, holding on for as long as possible, rocking against the straps, mouth pursed tight until she couldn't hold her breath any longer. And then her mouth had burst open in an explosion of bubbles. Her chest had heaved three times before she became still and the orderlies rushed in to release her.

"Dying, I mean," she said.

Eli felt conspicuous with Miranda's head resting against his shoulder. He shrugged it off and wrapped an arm around her waist to keep her steady. He had started to question the purpose of Dr. Francis's treatment programs, but remained silent and let Miranda speak.

"I mean that's all that life is, isn't it? Dying. One day at a time. And if there's such a thing as reincarnation, it's not just one day of death that our soul must endure, but an eternity of it. So, in a way, this has prepared me for the rest of my eternal life, which I plan to spend dying." She inhaled, and water rattled in her lungs. "Fortunately, it's not so bad."

She tried to pull him onto her bed when he lowered her down, and pouted when he resisted. "Please? I don't want to be alone right now," she said. Her blue eyes were bloodshot. Her lips were pale and speckled with white flakes of chapped skin. "Just hold me."

Eli closed the door and sat on the bed beside her. He raised his arm and held it in the air, hesitating.

Then Miranda leaned against his body and he lowered his arm onto her shoulders. She nuzzled up against his chest and pulled his other arm around her and burrowed close. She continued to shiver. When she spoke her teeth clattered.

"I no longer know who I am," she said. "I mean, I don't remember who I was before I came here. I can't remember how I used to feel or what I used to think about. I feel like I've become someone else. I feel like a stranger trapped inside myself."

"Dissociative thinking is common among certain disorders," Eli said. "That's perfectly normal."

A bubble of snot burst from Miranda's nose when she laughed. "Perfectly normal, huh?" she said and wiped her face against his chest. "So, is that how you feel?"

"No, I don't feel that way."

"Well, then it seems like we should switch places. If it's such a sign of normality, maybe you're the one who needs help."

"I just mean that in the case of certain mental states, such thinking is to be expected. It's treatable, though. Our goal is to get you well again."

Her breathing, still rattling with water, became deep and even, her words sluggish. "But what if I was well before I came in here, and it's this place that's making me sick?" She started sliding down his chest.

He stood, placed her head against the pillow and stretched her legs to the foot of the bed.

She smacked her mouth a couple of times and yawned. "I don't want to die again," she whispered before falling asleep.

Eli pulled the blanket up to her neck and ran a hand along her arm. "Don't worry. You won't."

He kissed her cheek before leaving; by then she was asleep. It was an act that could have gotten him barred from practicing psychiatry. But it seemed to be what she wanted. And it satisfied a desire that had been building within him as well.

He decided he could fight his conscience no longer. He filled out a Recommendation of Release form that night. He would help Miranda find a place to get back on her feet, even if it was in the guest room of his small apartment.

But he never got the chance to present the forms to Dr. Francis. She was found hanging in her room the next day. A note had been written, addressed to him.

> *Today I die so that I may live again.*
> *I am afraid, but only a little.*
> *Please be as kind to others as you were to me.*
> *Love them so hard it drives you insane.*

It was a request that he feared was becoming prophecy.

★ ★ ★

"As everything is destined to die, I shall enjoy my time with it today." Rajamadja's childlike voice pierced through the painful memory, banishing it back to the past where it belonged.

Eli grabbed on to that voice like a life raft, and the raging waters of his mind began to calm. His heartbeat slowed, his breathing settled, he stopped shaking. He pulled aside the blanket and sighed.

"All you have is the present moment," his guru's calming voice spoke from beyond. *"Just breathe. Just breathe. Just breathe."*

"But," another voice broke through, *"you are still a product of your past. Your soul carries yesterday's ghosts. And they stay with you forever."*

A bolt of electric fire burned up from Eli's bowels and he went running for the bathroom.

CHAPTER NINETEEN

While Eli had seemed uneasy at dinner, he appeared downright disheveled the next day. Alex had known something was up when he saw the email from Eli calling for an urgent staff meeting that same morning. It had been sent at 1:55 a.m. *This can't be good,* Alex had thought. He had been both right and wrong.

Eli arrived to the meeting looking tired and confused, like he had gotten little, if any, sleep the night before. He swayed at the front of the room on unsteady feet and spoke with a raspy voice, coughing hoarsely into his hand.

The apparent purpose of the meeting was for Eli to reiterate his stance regarding the humane treatment of patients. It was a lecture the senior staff had heard many times before, and there didn't seem to be a purpose for it now.

Whether it was due to repetition or Eli's weakened condition, Alex wasn't sure, but the room turned on Eli, voicing complaints that he was unprepared to address. Several of the nurses spoke out in favor of modern therapeutics and criticized what many considered to be outmoded practices on the hospital's behalf. Devon stood up and questioned Eli's safety protocols, citing the near altercation with Crosby. It was the first time Alex had seen people say to Eli's face what they had been whispering behind his back. And Eli was caught off guard.

As more people began voicing their grievances, the backlash grew so severe Alex felt obligated to intervene. He stood up and hushed the room. And, with just a few placating lines, rescued Eli from the outcry while simultaneously appeasing the senior staff members' valid concerns. He then called the meeting to a timely close.

Yes, the meeting had been both bad and good. Bad for Eli, good for Alex. *Looks like this succession plan may be enacted even earlier than expected,* he thought as he pushed open his office door, floating on a cloud of euphoria.

The message light was flashing on his phone. He checked his voice mail and found two messages waiting for him. One was from Rachel, the other from Mac Childress, his financial advisor. They both sounded equally distressed.

Who to call? Who to call? he thought, still basking in the afterglow from his impromptu performance. He leaned against his desk as he dialed the first number, smiling as the line picked up on the first ring. Mac was always quick to answer.

"Yo, MC. Just got your message. What's up, my man?" Alex always felt compelled to present a cooler, more carefree persona for Mac. Like he was some streetballer with stacks of cash.

"Alex, I've got some bad news." The fictitious image had become harder to hold up as of late. Alex circled his desk and sat down.

"Ah shit, Mac. You got any good news we can start with?"

"Good news," Mac pondered. "Well, you've got your health. A better than average golf game. And a beautiful wife that most men would kill to share a bed with each night."

Mac had met Rachel once, and the way he'd undressed her with his eyes should be against the law. "Keep on piling on the bad news and men won't have to go to such lengths to take my place."

Alex could hear Mac's mind weighing his possibilities during the following pause.

"Hey, why don't you quit fantasizing about my wife, and get to the point," Alex said.

"Sure thing, buddy," Mac said. "Look, remember how we talked about getting more aggressive with your portfolio given this influx of new money you have coming in? Well, as I was quick to caution, the more aggressive we get, the more risk we assume."

If Mac had issued a word of caution, Alex hadn't heard it. In fact, it was Mac who had encouraged Alex to invest in higher-risk ventures, prattling off a list of can't-miss investments while they sipped top-shelf scotch at his country club's bar. Alex had already consumed six beers on the golf course, causing him to double-bogey the back nine. *"The market's depleted, buddy,"* Mac had said. *"Prices can't go any lower. It's a gold mine for people like you with a large stream of capital to invest. You'll make a killing."*

It seemed as if Mac always preferred to meet in person when

discussing spending money, but preferred to speak over the phone when discussing losing it.

"Okay?" Alex prompted.

"Well, I hate to say it, but we took a hit, friend. We got run through the wash with a couple of overseas tech firms. It's nothing we can't rebound from, but I'm going to need for you to settle up on what you owe."

While on the golf course, just about the time he had cracked open his sixth beer, Alex had begun to blab about the money he expected to start pulling in from a pharmaceutical sale. He had exaggerated a bit, suggesting that it was already a done deal and revealing figures that were well beyond what he could expect even should the deal have gone through.

Listening, Mac's expanding smile could have housed a family of four. He had pulled the hidden latch on his golf cart humidor and cut two Cuban cigars, handing one to Alex and lighting it with a butane torch. *"Congratulations, buddy. Let's post up at the bar and talk about putting that money to work."*

Alex had explained that the money wasn't currently available, but Mac had offered to cover him. Had said the firm did it all the time for high-net-worth clients, at a nominal fee. Alex had resisted for the duration of the first scotch. But after the second one, he'd agreed. They'd celebrated with a third, and that was the last thing Alex could remember.

"Sure," Alex said, stalling. "But here's the deal. I'm still waiting on it to come through. There're some..." he began shuffling papers for no reason, "...legal technicalities that we're working out. But it shouldn't take long. I'll have to get back to you."

The silence on the other end resembled the center of a black hole. Finally, Mac spoke. "Don't fuck with me here, Alex. The firm won't hold out for long. Shit, I shouldn't have even covered you in the first place. We're talking about a lot of money. They'll look to put a lien against your assets until their losses are recovered. I can buy a little time, but not much. The sooner we clear this up, the better. Then we can work out a plan to get you out of this hole."

Alex closed his eyes and saw Popeye's blood-matted body lying in the ditch that he had dug. "Right. I know. I'll be in touch," he said, and hung up the phone.

It rang before he could pull his hand away. He brought the receiver back up to his ear.

"Dr. Drexler," he said.

"Hey, honey. Jesus, where have you been? Look, I think you need to get over here." It was Rachel and she sounded even more frantic than she had on her message. "It's Jerry. He's acting…strange."

Alex felt an electrical current shoot up his spine, causing him to straighten in his chair. "Strange how?"

"Like, you know, bad. Like he's having an episode, only worse. He's acting extremely paranoid. Aggressive even. He's…he's scaring me."

"Be specific. What's he doing?"

There was a rustle on the other end of the line. When Rachel spoke again, her voice sounded muffled and muted, like she was cupping her mouth with her hand. "Shit, he just walked into the room."

"So what? Honey, what's the problem?" Alex's voice took on a panicked edge.

Rachel pulled away from the receiver. Her voice sounded remote. Alex heard her say, "Jerry, what are you doing with that?" More rustling. "Please put that away."

Alex shifted the receiver to his other ear and pressed it hard against his head. His eyes turned to slits as he strained to hear. "Rachel, what's he doing?"

She whispered into the receiver, her voice wavering, "Honey, he's scaring me. He's holding a knife, and he's looking at me really strangely. It's like he doesn't recognize me." She apparently turned her head away from the phone. Her voice was distant. "Jerry, what's wrong, honey? I'm talking to your brother. Please tell me if anything's wrong so we can help you." Alex heard a mumbled, indecipherable voice in the background. Then Rachel responded, "Who are you talking about? I don't know who that is. Jerry, nobody is going to hurt you."

Alex gripped the phone in both hands and squeezed. "Rachel," he said. She didn't respond. He spoke louder, "Rachel, honey, head for the bedroom. I'm going to call the facility and have them send help."

Rachel's voice was high-pitched and trembling, like she was struggling to choke back tears. "Okay. I…I… Okay, yeah. I think I can…"

Alex heard shuffling and heavy breathing, rustling as the phone brushed against her clothes. Then he heard the sound of a door closing and ragged breaths.

"Rachel? What's happening?"

"Honey, I'm so sorry. I just don't know what to do?"

"What the hell is going on?"

There was silence on the other line. Then she whispered, "He's right outside the door." Now her voice sounded louder and away from the phone. "Jerry, everything's okay. Just give me a minute and I'll be right out. Okay?" It sounded like she was walking across the room. "I'm sorry, this just caught me off guard. He's been doing so well, and then this comes out of nowhere. He's got this look. It's like a dog defending its litter. The distant eyes. The tilt of the head. I'm sure it's nothing, but it's starting to scare me. Now with the knife."

"It's okay. Are you safe?"

"Yes, I think so. I mean, yes, I'm sure it's fine, it's just—"

"No, you're doing the right thing. Where did he get a knife?" There was a rule against sharp objects at the assisted-living-facility apartments, even childproof scissors were prohibited.

"I have no idea. He just walked in with it." Alex heard a distant knocking sound. "Wait," Rachel said. "There's someone here. Thank god, that was fast."

Alex frowned. He hadn't called the facility.

"Jerry, wait. Let me answer it," he heard Rachel say. He heard the door open and Rachel walk through. "Jesus," she said. "Jerry's tucked himself in the corner. He's shaking. What is going on?"

Alex had stopped listening. His mind was spinning, obsessing over the implications that this apparent regression would have on his plans to begin clinical tests on his refined formula. Clearly the new formula worked. It must be a matter of maintenance and treatment frequency. That should be an easy fix.

Alex's attention returned to the phone. He heard another knock, closer now, and a deep voice muffled by the door.

"Here, let me call you back," Rachel said.

"No, keep me on the line."

"Okay." Alex heard a door open. Rachel sounded surprised. "Oh hi. Wow, that was fast. Alex must have alerted you. Thank you for coming." There was a pause; then Alex heard a deep, mumbling voice and Rachel respond, "Right, come on in. Oh, look at this little cutie? Is he yours? I had one just like him."

Alex cringed as a burst of barking came blasting through the phone. "Hey, down boy," Rachel said. Her voice was drowned out by a series of sharp, high-pitched barks. She sounded panicked. "No! Down! Hey, please help get him off me!"

A jostling sound came from the other end, and then the phone went dead. Alex sat there listening to the drone of an open line.

He pulled the receiver back and furrowed his brow. He dialed Jerry's line and listened to it ring. Next he tried Rachel's cell phone. No answer.

Slowly, he stood up and walked stiffly towards his office door. He threw open the door and began to run, his leather-soled shoes slipping on the linoleum as he gathered speed. Alex slid blindly around the corner, breaking into a full sprint, and then was sent crashing against the wall as he collided into someone on the other side.

"Damn, Dr. Drexler. You okay?" Devon said, reaching out a hand to help Alex to his feet. "Where you rushing off to?"

"Family emergency," Alex said as he stood, pushing past Devon and scrambling down the hall. He glanced over his shoulder before rounding the next corner and saw Devon looking at him through crooked eyes like he was crazy.

If you think I'm crazy, you should see my brother, Alex thought as he windmilled around the next turn. *Oh wait. You already have.*

PART TWO
INNER DEMONS
CHAPTER TWENTY

The parking lot was filled with police, their silent rooftop lights flashing red and blue, like beacons of sorrow. The residents, all either disabled or mentally ill, stood dressed in their robes and unkempt clothes behind a barrier of yellow tape. They made for an unruly group of spectators. Much of the staff was on hand, attempting to settle them down.

Alex maneuvered through the crowd and approached the officer standing sentry beside Jerry's apartment door.

"Sorry, no one's allowed in," the man said.

"What's happened?"

"You'll need to step back, sir." The officer placed his hand upon the Taser clipped to his belt.

"This is my brother's apartment. My wife's in there." Alex looked over the officer's shoulder at the closed door, its flimsy pine surface withholding some grim secret.

"Sir, we have your wife. She's with the paramedics, but she's doing fine."

Alex was too wound up to feel relief. "What about my brother?"

The officer's shifty eyes answered for him. "Sir, please clear this area and we'll fill you in on everything we know."

Alex turned and located the ambulance. His eyesight felt enhanced, his senses intensified. The scene was now moving in slow motion, while he was operating at regular speed. The crowd of onlookers became a snapshot of staring faces. He saw a man with Down syndrome slowly sip red liquid through a straw. They met eyes and the man offered a friendly smile, raising his right hand as though taking an oath.

The ambulance came rushing towards him in a silent tunnel and he staggered on wobbly legs, feeling the strange distortions of a world rearranging itself into a different place. One harboring a dark secret behind a flimsy pinewood door.

Rachel was breathing into an oxygen mask. She was pale. Damp hair clung to her face and wound around the plastic tubing leading to the oxygen bag. She was breathing deeply at the urging of a female medic who was rubbing her back. A policeman stood by the back of the van, looking on with obvious impatience. When Alex approached, her eyes went wide and she began hyperventilating. The cop cursed and turned his back.

"I'm her husband," Alex said as he entered the van.

Rachel tore the mask off her face and wrapped her arms around his neck, nearly cutting off his air.

He grimaced, then noticed the medic watching him and changed his expression to concern. He repositioned his hands from Rachel's rib cage, where he had been preparing to push her away, and placed them on her back, pulling her tight.

"It's okay. It's okay." He summoned his most soothing voice. "Take deep breaths."

The policeman walked up to the back of the van and leaned in. "Sir, I understand that emotions are running high right now. But it's important that we collect a statement from the witness as soon as possible."

Alex felt Rachel nodding against his shoulder. She inhaled, sniffling against a blockade of snot, swallowing a wad of saliva. She pushed back. Color was returning to her pallid face, splotches on her cheeks and scarlet rivulets streaming up from her neck.

"It's okay. I can talk."

She took a deep breath, tucking frizzed hair behind each ear with trembling fingers, looking at Alex with red-rimmed eyes. He saw the tears well up, her lower lip curl in, her chest begin to hitch.

"Christ, will you give her something, please?" he said to the paramedic. She became much calmer after the shot.

Alex saddled up next to her on the bed and leaned over. "What happened?" he asked.

The policeman hopped into the van and placed a pen against his notepad.

Rachel stared up at the gray-cloth ceiling and sighed. "The door rang," she said. "I answered it. It was that guy from the hospital."

"What guy?" Alex said.

Her eyes floated as they peered inward, trolling for a memory in her medicated mind. "I don't know. The one who helped Jerry to the car. The large African-American man."

"Devon?"

Rachel nodded her head slowly. The drugs were making her drowsy. "He had a dog with him." Her tongue became obese. It struggled to lift itself up from the bottom of her mouth. "It was Popeye," she slurred. "He attacked me."

Alex's lips formed a white line. His ears turned red.

The policeman inhaled, hesitated and then spoke. "Who's Popeye?"

"Our dog," Alex said.

"So, this guy..." the cop consulted his notes, "...Devon, he came to the door with your dog?"

"No," Alex said. "That's impossible."

"Sir, let's let your wife answer."

"Go ahead, but you'll have to disregard what she says."

"Why's that?"

"Because our dog's dead. I buried him last week."

"Okay," the cop said slowly, tapping the pen against his teeth. "So this dog resembled your recently deceased pet."

Rachel shook her head. It rocked back and forth on loose bearings. "No, it was Popeye. I know it was. He even had—"

"Look, just keep going," Alex cut her off, his voice strained.

"No, wait, hold on," the officer said. "Let's back this up."

"Listen." Alex glared at the cop. "I don't give a shit about the dog. I'd like to know what the fuck happened to my brother."

"Sir, I understand. That's what I'm trying to determine as well."

"Just shut up, then, and let her tell the story."

The cop's jaw muscles clenched, his eyes narrowed. He turned towards Rachel and nodded. "Go ahead, miss."

Rachel exhaled through rubbery lips. She lifted her hand an inch off the gurney and let it drop back down. "Popeye chased me back into the eating area. He was barking, biting at me. I ran around the table to get away, but he followed me. When I came around the other side, I looked up and saw Jerry and the orderly fighting. They were fighting over the knife. The man, he was so much bigger. He took the knife." Rachel's voice was trailing off, becoming softer and harder to hear. "He was smiling. Jerry turned to run, but he grabbed him from behind. He pulled him back, and—"

The cop scooted forward. "Wait, wait. What knife? Who had the knife?"

"Good Christ!" Alex shot off the gurney and stormed out the back of the van. He marched straight for the apartment door. The door opened before he could reach it and two paramedics came out, wheeling a stretcher with a thick, white sheet draped over the outline of a body. A murmur erupted from the spectators and they pressed forward. Two policemen stepped up to perform crowd control. Alex skirted past the distracted officers, following the paramedics to the van. This one black, sans siren. It was in no rush to reach its destination. The morgue.

"I'm Dr. Drexler." He reached into his pocket and pulled out his identification card. "I'm family."

"Sir, I'm sorry," one of the men said. He dealt with death every day and still his sympathy looked sincere. He moved out of the way as Alex walked forward.

"I need to see," Alex said. He reached out towards the head of the gurney and pulled aside the sheet.

Jerry looked just like he did when they had shared a bedroom, asleep on his back, with the sheets pulled up to his chest. The soft glow of moonlight shining through the bedside window, turning his pale face blue. But this wasn't sleep. He was much too still. And his face was far too pale, his lips more purple than blue. There were just a few specks of blood freckling his cheeks, but the ragged gash running across his neck was still seeping. It was like a canyon ridge with a stagnant riverbed at the bottom.

The paramedic grabbed the sheet from Alex and pulled it back over Jerry's head. It fell against his face and outlined his features. A few drops of blood spotted the sheet and spread.

It didn't make sense. He had just seen Devon. Had literally run into him on his way out of Sugar Hill. Rachel must be mistaken.

Well, of course she was. She was hysterical. Delirious, convinced Popeye had returned from doggy heaven to exact his canine revenge.

The sound of the ambulance doors shutting startled Alex. He took a step back, blinking, as the engine started and the ambulance drove his brother away.

That left...*the dog. What about the dog?*

He turned and jogged back to the van where Rachel was being questioned. She offered a bleary smile when she saw him, a sedated grin.

"Honey, what happened to the dog?" Alex said, hopping back inside.

"You mean the imaginary dog?" the cop replied.

Alex ignored him. "Where did it go?"

Rachel raised her head from the pillow. She fought to focus her eyes. Her lips moved, but Alex could hardly hear her. He moved closer and asked again.

This time Rachel raised her hands in front of her face, mesmerized as though they held some mystical import. "Poof," she said, spreading her hands outward like a magician making something disappear.

"What?" Alex said.

"When Jerry died," she whispered, laying her head back down and closing her eyes. "Popeye just...disappeared."

CHAPTER TWENTY-ONE

The police came after Devon with their guns drawn, nearly causing a riot in the hallway of Sugar Hill. Patients scattered, squawking, flailing their arms like quail being flushed from a field. Orderlies chased after them and tried to instill order as the police formed a circle around Devon and forced him to face the wall.

Eli had been sitting alone outside, reflecting on his ruined staff meeting while staring at the stone maiden filling the fountain. Miranda's pool.

He had not, therefore, received the cop's cursory warning call. When he heard the commotion, he came running up the hallway, weaving through the startled patients, nearly too stunned to talk.

"What is this?" he said when he reached the nearest officer. The man's head was shaved in a flattop that showed his pink scalp. Loose skin was bunched together in a series of rolls at the base of his neck. He looked bored as he watched two other policemen drive Devon into the wall, while a third wrenched his arms behind his back in order to apply handcuffs.

"Stand back, sir," the officer said, placing a heavy hand against Eli's chest, shoving him backwards. The weariness he had felt just moments before was replaced with a wash of adrenaline. He swatted the officer's hand aside and stepped forward, getting right into his face.

"I'm not going to step aside. I'm in charge of this hospital. Tell me what's going on."

The officer inched forward, his rotund belly pressing against Eli's like a cannonball. "We have a warrant to bring this man in for questioning. I advise you, sir, not to interfere."

"On what charge?"

"Murder."

Eli's eyes flashed wide. The surge of adrenaline left him like a reverse tide. He turned and stared at the side of Devon's face that was not smashed against the wall. "Jesus," he said. "Of whom?"

"A former employee and outpatient of yours." The officer looked at Eli with disdain, as though he were partly to blame. "Jerry Drexler."

"I didn't do shit!" Devon yelled when he saw Eli talking with the officer. "Hey, Dr. Alpert! I been here all day. Man, tell them I didn't do this shit."

Devon's outburst provoked a series of wild hoots from the riled-up patients. Suddenly, it seemed as though the whole hallway was jostling.

The scene took on a surreal quality, almost like déjà vu. The colors turned dull, the sound became muted. Everything slowed way down. Eli shook his head and tried to focus as his vision took on a grimy film. "When?" he said, the word resounding hollowly in his ears.

"When what?"

"Jerry. The... When did it happen?"

Devon's dulled screams were fading farther away. The officer reached out and gripped Eli by the elbow. His expression softened. He now looked concerned.

"Hey. You okay, there?" the officer said.

Eli's knees buckled and he staggered forward.

At the same time, Devon pushed back from the wall and began struggling against the men arresting him.

This reignited the patients into a wild frenzy. The orderlies were hopeless against the horde as they rushed forward, colliding into Eli and the officer from behind.

The officer released Eli and he went sprawling to the ground, his face crashing against the floor. The linoleum tiles smelled of scoured rubber. They felt gritty against his face. He barely felt the feet trampling on top of him, rocking his limp body back and forth as the light dimmed from white to gray to nothing.

CHAPTER TWENTY-TWO

Angela was finishing up in the bathroom when she heard the commotion. Her bowels were rebelling from the night before. She washed her hands and stared at herself in the mirror. Her eyes were puffy. Her skin was red and chapped, her hair frayed. The lack of sleep was finally catching up with her. *Why do you do this to yourself?* she asked herself for the thousandth time.

She stood, staring into her eyes, seeking out the strength she knew was there. Somewhere inside. The part of her that performed so well at work. The part of her so capable of helping others, yet still bent on destroying itself. *Where does the one person end and the other begin?*

The commotion continued. In fact, it was escalating. She turned off the faucet and waited for it to pass. She wasn't sure her head could take it.

It didn't pass. It continued to swell, taking on an even more riotous tone. Something was wrong.

She opened the door and started off towards the patients' wing. Now that she could hear the screaming more clearly, she quickened her step. She stuck her head into Eli's office. It was empty. Farther down, she checked in on Alex's. He wasn't there. She raced to the end of the hallway and scanned her keycard to access the patients' area. She went through.

A few patients were wandering the hallway, clutching their heads and crying. But the main commotion was coming from around the corner, down by the nurses' station.

When she rounded the corner, she stopped, stunned. She had never seen Sugar Hill so out of control. The orderlies, far outnumbered, were being overwhelmed by a swarm of patients rushing towards what appeared to be a team of police. She started forward, slowly, wondering what she could do to contain the patients. Trying to determine how best to help diffuse the situation.

Then she glimpsed something on the ground. A path parted between a sea of legs and she saw Eli lying head down, his face turned towards her. His eyes were open, but empty. They looked straight through her. His head was being stomped like a soccer ball as people scrambled over and around him and the police fought to push them back. His body was caught in the middle of the scrum.

Angela shot forward, seeing Eli's face through tunnel vision. Everything else faded into the distance. She had reached the edge of the scrum when someone grabbed her from behind, wrapping arms around her waist and lifting her up into the air. She kicked her feet and squirmed as she was carried back down the hallway, then thrown into a patient's room. She landed and spun around.

Crosby was shutting the door. He turned around, leaned back against it and looked down at her. He was breathing heavily. Blood leaked from his nose. She must have hit it with her head as she squirmed to break loose. He wiped a hand across his lip, smearing the blood against his cheek, staining his whiskers red. When he saw the blood on his hand he smiled.

"I see you," he said. He bounced off the door and stalked towards her. His smile held no humor, his eyes lacked humanity. Crosby was not there. Something else had taken over. "You don't think I do, but I do." He pointed at her, accentuating each word with a thrust of his finger. "I. See. You."

Angela got a knee underneath her and started to rise. She saw Crosby prepare to spring, and froze, holding up her hand and softening her eyes. "Everyone seems a bit excited right now. Let's not let our emotions drive our actions, okay? Please, Crosby, take a seat. Let's talk." She knew the smile she showed looked more sincere than it felt. It was one of her many skills.

It faltered, though, when he stepped forward and kicked her in the face. She fell backward. Her face felt cold where he had kicked her. She smelled metal and tasted it deep in the back of her throat. She groaned and looked up. He was hovering over her, straddling her with his legs.

"Think I don't know what's going on?" he said, peering down from above. His head eclipsed the overhead light, casting his face in shadow. "Think I don't know what this place is?"

The cold fire of the kick was now a hot throb, a heartbeat inside her head. "Crosby, there's nothing going on. Please don't hurt me."

"Of course that's what you'd say. But you don't understand. I see." He pointed to his eyes with a rigid finger, his lips contorting into a snarl. Spit flew when he screamed, "I see!" He grabbed a fistful of hair and slammed her head against the ground, then brought his foot down in the center of her stomach. "Lock me up in Satan's lair? Think I don't know where I am? Think I don't know why I'm here? But I'm not blind like the others. I see how things really are. I've got the divine light to guide me."

He released her hair and she arched her back, gasping for air. Her throat bulged as it fought for oxygen. Just as she inhaled her first lung-shuddering breath, Crosby hop-stepped and kicked her in the ribs. She rolled into the kick and clutched her side. It didn't hurt nearly as much as her head, but she wanted to appear beaten, broken. Her hair fell across her face, providing a screen through which to peer. Crosby was still hovering over her, his face a red ball of rage.

He leaned closer. His lips peeled back, revealing clenched rows of bloodstained teeth, and he hissed until his face began to shake. Spittle flew and gnarled veins writhed up the front of his neck. His face looked like it was about to pop from the pressure.

Then he opened his mouth and screamed. An insectile scream beyond the scope of human range that threatened to burst Angela's ears. It continued, rising in volume, lasting long after he should have run out of air. She was surprised by how loud her whimpering sounded when he finally stopped.

Crosby dropped down on top of her, straddling her with his knees. He put his hands around her throat, curled his fingers and squeezed. He made a sound like *hnnnnnnnggghhh* as he put all his force behind the choke, biting down on his white-encrusted tongue.

Angela's eyes bulged open. They felt like they were about to burst. Flecks of black appeared on the edge of her sight and expanded inwards. She began to pray for the first time since she was a little girl. To a god she felt had forsaken her, begging his forgiveness for a life of sin.

The door sprang open. An orderly rushed in. He launched forward and tackled Crosby from behind, ripping his hands from Angela's throat. They rolled when they hit the ground and Crosby wound up on top.

He postured up and began raining punches down from above, striking the orderly on the side of the head and neck.

Angela stumbled to her feet. It felt like a knife was stuck in her side. She shuffled forward, hunched over, and wrapped an arm around Crosby's neck, allowing the orderly to scoot out from underneath him. Together, they tackled Crosby to the ground and fought to contain him. It took multiple elbows to Crosby's temple to get him subdued.

"Go get help," the orderly said, panting. She hesitated, chest heaving. So many thoughts raced through her mind that they canceled each other out.

Crosby stirred, he opened his eyes. They locked on to Angela and he bared his teeth and began struggling again.

"Get the fuck out of here!" the orderly said.

Angela stood and hobbled out the door.

CHAPTER TWENTY-THREE

"Say that again?" Alex said, crinkling his face as though that would improve his hearing. He had just returned home from the police station. Rachel was upstairs, asleep on their bed. He couldn't believe it was only 4:30 p.m. The rules of natural law did not seem to apply to time today. He switched the phone to his other ear. "Hold on, I can hardly hear you. Did you say Eli was attacked?"

"No, *I* was," Angela said, her voice a raspy whisper. "By Crosby. Eli's in the hospital, though."

There were still five unheard messages awaiting Alex on his iPhone. He couldn't imagine what other blissful news they would bring.

"Look, I've got a bit of a situation here myself. I'll call you back as soon as I can."

He canceled the call and closed his eyes. His phone began ringing again and he sent it directly to voice mail. Message number six.

He felt complicit in dramas beyond his comprehension, like he was on the tip of some winding gyroscope that was starting to wobble. He didn't know how to hold it together or why the responsibility should fall to him. He hadn't done anything wrong. All he'd tried to do was help. And just when things were starting to get better, some psycho had come along and brought it all to an end. Had killed Jerry. Had murdered his brother.

Why? Alex thought. He rubbed his eyes with the heels of his hands and twin images bloomed behind the lids. His brother's pale-blue face lying against the gurney. His ragged throat split wide. Jerry had never hurt another person in his life. Who would want him dead?

He realized that his father didn't know. And that he would soon find out. Find out that Jerry had died while under his care.

But he was murdered. It wouldn't matter. In his father's eyes, he would somehow be to blame.

Alex opened his eyes and checked the rest of his messages. One was from Angela, another was from the morgue. The hospital where Eli was staying had called. So had a member of Sugar Hill's executive board – Steve Price, the grandson of one of the founding board members. Steve fancied himself an enterprising entrepreneur, although all he had managed to do up to this point in his life was squander half his trust fund on misguided ventures.

He was also the only other person affiliated with Sugar Hill who knew about his test trials. In fact, he had introduced Alex to an executive with Philax Pharmaceuticals, seeing the potential payout should the medicine ever make it to market. Alex hadn't spoken with him since his most recent experiment, but he was certain Philax had. Steve's message was brusque.

Great, Alex thought. *Might as well get it over with.*

"Hi, Alex," Steve answered right away, sounding serious.

"Steve."

"Christ, buddy, what a day."

Alex snorted air through the speaker. "No shit," he said.

"So, have you seen him yet?"

"Seen who?"

"Eli. Who else?"

"No, not yet." Alex walked to the wet bar and began fingering bottles. "Actually, I've been pretty tied up today with a family emergency. I haven't heard exactly what happened."

Steve's laughter was hesitant at first; then it took on the warm delight of a professional gossip about to pop a virgin ear. "Full-scale riot. Patients and police fighting one another. Eli either fainted or was knocked out. He's being treated at the hospital for a concussion. One of the social-worker chicks was attacked, almost killed. It's a full-blown fucking mess, my friend."

Alex couldn't understand why Steve was smiling. He could hear it in his voice through the phone.

"What were the police doing there?"

"Arresting one of the orderlies for murder. That's the icing on the cake."

Murder? Then it hit him. "Devon," he said.

"Who?"

"The orderly who was arrested. Was his name Devon?"

"Fuck if I know. Some big-ass black guy is what I heard. Put up some kind of fight."

Alex shook his head. He was certain that he'd run into Devon on his way over to Jerry's. While Jerry was still alive. It didn't make sense.

"You know what this means, don't you?" Steve said.

Alex didn't, but he kept quiet.

"Alex?"

"I'm here."

"Buddy, Eli's out. He's completely lost control over the hospital. We're going to be recommending you as his replacement. It'll be announced at the board meeting. There will be a bit of a transition period, but the job's basically yours. Congratulations."

There wasn't much about the situation that felt celebratory. Perhaps it *was* time for Eli to move aside, but still. Not under these circumstances. "That's great," Alex said, forcing himself to sound enthusiastic.

"Damn right it is. I told you we would make this happen. Now we can finally bring the hospital into the twenty-first century. Speaking of which, how are we coming along with our clinical trials? When will the meds be ready for market?"

Perhaps he *hadn't* spoken with the folks at Philax. "Still working through some kinks," Alex said.

"Shit, Alex," Steve said. "Damn it, that's not so good, buddy."

Alex crunched the phone against his shoulder. Eli had been hospitalized, Angela assaulted, Devon arrested for murder, and this was the bad news? Alex felt the increasing weight of some responsibility he couldn't quite see.

Steve broke the silence with a sigh. "Look, here's the deal. It would greatly help your position here if you could hurry things along. Sugar Hill is going to take a major PR hit for this fiasco. We need to respond with a strong statement. Changing medical directors is one thing. Having a medical director who has pioneered one of the greatest therapeutic breakthroughs in the field of psychiatric medicine is quite another. Get the difference?"

"Sure," Alex said. *And if my brother hadn't just been murdered you'd have the breakthrough you need.* Still, the refined formula had worked. At least for a while. "Philax is out, though. I've fixed the formula. It's ready. I just need funding."

"Philax is out?"

Alex recalled the image of Mr. Connelly's panic-stricken face. "Ah yes. They're done."

"That was my last contact, Alex." Silence returned.

Another call beeped in and Alex checked Caller ID. It was Angela again. Silence persisted until the phone indicated that she had left a message.

"Well, you're just going to have to get creative," Steve said.

"What does that mean?"

"That's for you to figure out. Here's the deal. I need you to prove to me that the formula works. You do that and I can get you funding. I can't get someone to front the research. Not again."

"But how am I supposed to prove that it works, without someone to fund the research?"

"You'll have to figure it out. Listen to me. I pushed for you to get this position based on the understanding that you would be introducing this medicine. If that's not the case, we may have to reconsider our decision. Is that clear?"

The other line beeped again. Alex didn't even check it. "I'm with you," he said to Steve and ended the call. Then he grabbed an unopened bottle of rye whiskey from the back of the wet bar and filled a glass to the brim.

"Here's to me," he said to the empty room and took a fiery sip.

CHAPTER TWENTY-FOUR

It was hard to tell who looked more hungover, Alex or his dad. Both of their eyes were bloodshot and swollen, which was fitting for the occasion, although neither had been crying.

Don Drexler hesitated when he entered the viewing room and saw Alex standing in the corner. He scowled and shuffled in. Alex's mother followed meekly behind.

It had been nearly four years since Alex had been in the same room with his father. He looked shorter than he remembered. His hair had thinned and turned entirely gray. Still, the room took on a charge when he entered, like the formation of a storm cloud.

He walked up to Jerry's casket, took a brief look inside – Jerry's burial shirt concealed his sutured neck – then shook his head and turned his back. He walked to the sofa against the far wall and sat. His shoulders slouched and his heavy hands hung loose between his thighs.

Mrs. Drexler approached the casket and placed a kerchief against her nose and began making a series of hitching, high-pitched squeaks.

Alex felt unwanted in their presence. Like an intruder.

"Where's Rachel?" his father said.

"Home."

His father smirked as though this were some expected insult. "She was there, wasn't she?"

"She was."

He made a sound that resembled a laugh. "And where were you?"

"I got there as fast as I could."

"But you were too late."

Alex's mother continued to stare into her dead son's face and squeak. "I don't get it," his father said. He turned and looked Alex in the eyes.

Alex felt a stab of heat sear the center of his chest. It traveled up his neck and burned his face. "Isn't this what you do? Aren't you supposed to fix these people?"

"What people?"

"You know, crazy people."

Alex didn't respond.

"And you couldn't even fix your own brother? I don't get it. I really don't."

"Jerry was murdered, Dad. How was I supposed to fix that?"

Mr. Drexler dismissed the comment with a wave. He scratched his head, causing random hairs to stick up. He exhaled and frowned, and his face folded in on itself. "I don't know, Alex. You're the doctor, not me. But if I were a doctor, I would have worked harder to help my own family. I know that." He looked over towards the casket. From his angle all he could have seen was Jerry's nose. "Jerry could have been anything he wanted. He was special, that kid. Just sick, is all. And with a doctor for a brother who never could get him well. I wonder about that. I really do."

His father stood. He walked over to his wife and grabbed her by the arm.

She turned and buried her face against his neck.

He looked back at Alex. "You made all the arrangements?"

"I did."

His father knocked on the casket door. "And this rickety piece of shit is the best you could do? I thought you could afford better. Guess your brother's only worth so much."

Alex started forward and then stopped. He jammed his hands into his pockets and squeezed them shut with a force that threatened to crush his fingers. He *had* saved Jerry. He *had* made Jerry well. There was no way for him to explain this to his father, however. For his father, the successful son would always remain the failure. Only now, he had failed in the most unforgivable way. And there would never be another chance for redemption. Future successes would only accentuate the fact that he had failed where it mattered most. He had failed to heal the favorite son.

His father and mother left the room without looking back.

Alex waited a minute and then approached the casket. He peered down onto Jerry's face.

He looked like a mannequin. His face appeared plastic, his lips like pale wax. Only his neck showed any signs of imperfection. The skin was pulled unnaturally taut as it fed into Jerry's shirt collar. Beneath which, Alex knew, was a ragged line of sutured skin that would never mend.

The studies using Dimethyltryptamine had unexpectedly led to a series of questions regarding death. Regarding the possibility of an eternal soul. A significant percentage of the test patients were convinced that they had ventured beyond the veil of our material world while under the influence of the hallucinogen, to view what lies beyond. They spoke of a timeless place of ineffable wonder, filled with an overwhelming sense of unconditional love.

In all such cases, these experiences produced profound changes in the subject's outlook on the nature of reality. Atheists found God. People with depression found joy. The terminally ill found peace. Death, to these voyagers, lost its frightful allure.

Alex had always considered these experiences to be nothing more than hallucinations, mental phenomena dredged up from the pits of the subconscious. Now, for his brother's sake, he hoped that there was some glint of truth in these otherworldly reports.

But science told him otherwise. Death was darkness. Death was decomposition. If we live on, it's in the stomachs of earthworms or the weeds that arise from our rotten corpse.

For the first time since Jerry's murder, tears threatened to spring from Alex's eyes. He couldn't remember the last time he had cried, and was surprised by the searing pain that came with his attempt to quell the surge of emotion.

"I'm sorry," Alex said. His words were thick and sodden. "I'm so, so sorry." His vision blurred and he wiped his eyes with the sleeve of his silk suit. His brother's plastic face came back into focus. "I hope they were right." The tears welled back up, blurring his brother's features, turning Jerry's face into a soft, crystalline ball of brightness. "I hope you're finally at peace."

Alex leaned down and rested his hands on the edge of the casket, one stacked atop the other. His lips curled in, his chest grew tight. A piqueish squeal escaped him. His face contorted as he fought to hold it in, but the tidal surge of emotion overwhelmed the levee built to keep it at bay. He thrust his head against his hands and wept.

CHAPTER TWENTY-FIVE

Psychic handcuffs. That's what they were. The drugs. The demon's elixir that had been shot into his veins, dulling his visions, turning him into the undead.

Crosby was staring into his lap. Had been for hours. His muddled thoughts sludged through tar pits, only to be sucked down into the goopy mess. His mouth felt mammoth, like a gaping cave.

Yet a spark of his true self still remained. He could sense it fluttering around in the dark hollows of his mind, evading talon-like shadow hands that tried to grab it and tear it to shreds.

"The bitch," he slurred. Not even a slur, more like a moan. "Demon bitch." His useless tongue clogged his throat. Thick drool drenched his toes.

Inside his mind, his fluttering essence spoke in snippets.

Get.

Message.

Pain rain.

Cold bitch.

Almost.

Shadow fuck knuckles.

Again.

He was in a small room. Alone. A guard was posted outside his door. A small window set high in the wall cast a slanted crosshatched square of light that crawled slowly across the floor. The door was made of thick metal and had a thin waist-high rectangle to pass things through. The air was stale and made a soft hum. It stirred a few lank strands of hair against his bald head.

Crosby was slumped forward. He tried to sit up straight, but invisible hands were pushing against his head and neck. Hands. Everywhere, hands.

Murky voices now drifted from the hallway. Muted sounds that seemed to travel from beyond the horizon across the curvature of the world. A metallic clap came, like an anvil strike, and the heavy door swung open. Two men entered lacking shadows. Their shuffling feet sounded like the slither of snakes.

"This is the one all the fuss has been over?"

"That's right."

"The what? Doomsday Slayer?"

"Apocalypse Killer."

"Oh, that's right. Because he thought he was saving the world from annihilation."

"His report just mentions demons."

"Hmm. So what does that have to do with the end of the world?"

"I'm not sure. The Rapture maybe?"

"Ha! Got to give it to the media, they know how to sell a story."

"Yep."

"What's he on anyhow?"

"One thousand milligrams of Thorazine."

"Jesus. I'm surprised the son of a bitch's still breathing."

"Well, we're waiting on Dr. Alpert to return for instructions. It could be he's moved to the state pen."

"Won't happen. He's already been found not guilty by way of insanity. All additional crimes would fall under the same plea. Besides, Eli would never release him. He'd try and mother him back to health. And just look where that got him."

"How *is* Eli?"

"He's fine. Bumped his head, is all. He'll be released today. Anyway, it's no longer his problem. This is Dr. Drexler's hospital now."

"Oh..."

"Aw hell. Look, that hasn't been officially announced yet. Keep it to yourself for a couple of days, why don't you."

"Right. Sure."

"And keep this one under wraps. We can't afford any more negative attention during the transition."

"So, you want me to...?"

"Oh never mind. Alex will handle it. Let's keep going."

"Right. Okay, this way."

The door clanged shut, echoing for eons. The slanted square of light continued to slide across the floor. And the fluttering spark of Crosby's self spiraled in flight as it fought to evade the imposing grasp of shadow hands.

CHAPTER TWENTY-SIX

Eli unfolded the crumpled slip of paper once again. It had been handled so much by now it was as soft as cotton. He stared at the handwritten words that had begun to fade into the crinkled folds:

Xanax 1 mg
Take as needed.

He'd had another panic attack at the hospital. He had thought for sure it was a heart attack. The pain had been unbearable. He had not been able to catch his breath. He had soiled his bedsheets in his manic state of disillusioned fear.

"This is to be expected." His doctor had comforted Eli after a nurse sponged away the streaks of shit that had smeared all the way down the back of his legs. *"It's common to experience acute anxiety after a traumatic event like you've been through. I'll give you something to help you through it."*

"No, I'm fine. Really," Eli had said, but it lacked conviction. Even still, the physician had been wrong. It wasn't the traumatic episode that worried Eli. He was afraid of the fear itself. The sheer potency of its destructive power. Its ability to instantly crumble the scaffolding that supported the principles and beliefs that he had spent a lifetime constructing.

He had always felt anchored to his core identity, had felt secure in the set of values that guided his life trajectory. Now he felt like a newborn calf walking across a frozen pond. And the potential relief that this prescription slip promised seemed more like stable ground than any of the mental constructs that were wilting, one by one, under the harsh scrutiny of true mental stress. Was this what it was like to go mad?

And, if so, if this was what madness felt like and he were to run to the comforting embrace of a pharmaceutical drug the first chance he got, then what did that say about his professional philosophy? It would be like an evangelical preacher taking a deal from the Devil at the first taste of temptation.

Eli crumpled the paper in his dampened hand. His sharp knuckles pushed against his thin, wrinkled skin. He was so tired the act of squeezing his hand into a fist felt strenuous and made him lightheaded. His brain hurt.

Have I been right or wrong? he thought, then shook his head. That was the wrong question. *Have I caused suffering, or have I relieved it?*

He opened his fist and dropped the crumpled ball of paper into the wastebasket. A twinge of fear caused his heart to flutter. He inhaled deeply and held it. The sense of fear remained.

He exited his bathroom and walked down the dark, narrow hallway of his home, opened the door on the far right and entered. The musky scent of incense permeated the room. Eli placed a fresh stick in the bamboo holder and lit the tip with a match, extinguishing it with a shake. A thin ribbon of smoke slithered through the still air.

Eli placed his meditation cushion in the center of the room and sat. He folded his legs into the lotus position and closed his eyes.

Miranda was waiting in the darkness. Her eyes were wide; a stream of tiny bubbles percolated from her nose. Eli breathed and breathed and breathed, and watched as Miranda's frightened eyes became oblong and slanted. Her pale skin turned tan. The incense took on the harsh smell of burnt cordite. A frightened face now peered back at him through the frantic eyes from which a boy once watched his impending death.

Eli breathed.

He breathed.

He breathed.

And the vision began to fade.

Only to be replaced by another.

The pungent fragrance of incense intensified. Thick ribbons of smoke. Choking smoke. The smell...the smell of roasted flesh. The pyre beside the holy river. A tangle of corpses feeding the flames rising high into the sky turned crimson from the setting sun. Black, roiling smoke from her smoldering remains.

The cancer had spread like wildfire. By the time she received the diagnosis, it was already far too late. The weight loss, the stomach pains, the nausea – these were all symptoms that she had attributed to anxiety over wedding planning. But, no, it had been pancreatic cancer, eating away at her insides while she suffered in silence. Not wanting to complain or cast a negative light on something so wonderful.

Sweet Lacy. His wife who never was.

They canceled the wedding when they received the prognosis. There was simply no point. They took a honeymoon instead. To Varanasi, India, near the banks of the Ganges River. That is where Lacy went to die.

★   ★   ★

Eli was already Chief Medical Director of Sugar Hill when they met. He had given a speech about the history of humanistic psychiatry to a group of psychiatric grads. Lacy approached him after the presentation. She was nearly half his age, but seemed far older. She lacked the wide-eyed exuberance of a recent college grad. And she had an uncanny ability to see straight to the heart of any given thing and understand it completely.

"I respect what you're doing and appreciate you taking the time to talk about it," she said. And she had said it with true sincerity, wanting nothing in return. Only to express her honest admiration. "It's shameful that your psychiatric philosophy is not more widely practiced simply because there's not as much money to be made in it."

Eli had not addressed the financial discrepancy between humanistic psychiatry and other forms of medical intervention. It was an astute insight.

He paused and looked more closely at the tall young lady in front of him. Staring at him through dark, earnest eyes that were at his same level. She was thin, almost too thin – a voracious metabolism that would further disguise her cancer symptoms in the years to come – with long, straight brown hair parted in the middle. She wore a plain khaki blouse with flowing cotton pants and a pair of Birkenstock sandals. A throwback to the sixties. A contemporary flower child.

Eli normally looked to avoid post-presentation banter, but he felt drawn to the young lady before him. She reminded him of someone from a long time ago. "Yes, well, while that may be true, the outcomes from humanistic treatment are reliably superior to other forms of psychiatry. If that's what the patients demand, the industry will have to respond."

She nodded and offered a sheepish smile. "I like your optimism. It's idealistic, but…that's what the world needs. I'd like to see it spread."

"I'd hate to think there's something idealistic about using humane methods to help people with mental disorders." He said it, but he knew exactly what she meant. While it seemed perfectly obvious to him, the industry continued to push antipsychotics as the primary form of treatment, even when the evidence clearly showed superior success rates with more natural forms of therapy.

"Did you know that in Ancient China doctors were paid for preventing illness, and were not compensated when patients became sick?"

"What happened when their patients died?"

Lacy scrunched her nose and peered towards the ceiling in mock concentration. "I think they became obstetricians."

Eli laughed. "Ah, that would be wise. The most certain way to ensure a constant flow of customers."

Eli felt as though the conversation had run its course, but the girl remained in place, gazing at him with frank admiration, delighted eyes expressing genuine interest. A few seconds went by as they simply stared at each other. *Where have I seen this woman before?*

He reached out his hand. "Eli Alpert," he said.

Her handshake felt like a hug. "Lacy Lovechild."

Eli's smile faltered. He felt like she was putting him on.

Lacy blushed under his sudden scrutiny. "Hippie parents," she said and shrugged her shoulders. "Changed it from Palakowski." She smiled in spite of the heat rushing to her face and held his gaze.

"Oh wow. Can't say that I blame them," Eli said. Her perfect white teeth were framed by rose blossoms blooming on her cheeks. He realized he was still holding her hand, and he released it. Reluctantly. He immediately wanted to grab hold of it again. The urge was out of character and he now became aware of the swarm of people vying for his attention.

"Well, it was nice meeting you. I'm glad you enjoyed the discussion," he said.

She remained rooted in place, as though she hadn't heard him, still assessing him with that frank stare. She took a step towards him, leaned forward and spoke into his ear. "It was nice meeting you as well. I hope to see you again."

He felt pressure against his side coat pocket.

It wasn't until three days later, when he took his coat in to be laundered, that he found the slip of paper with her name and number on it. After dealing with so many doctors, her handwriting, with large, looping letters written in purple ink, felt whimsical and free.

You're projecting, he told himself.

Still, he kept the paper with her number on it. Like a talisman, it began to acquire a sort of potency, a palpable charge. In it, his trained skepticism saw fate. Through it, his pragmatism fell victim to visions of fantasy, of grandiose scenarios plucked straight out of a child's fairy tale.

A rush of emotion soon overwhelmed him, growing stronger every day. The fantasy became an obsession, distracting him from his job. He would replay their meeting over and again in his mind, reassessing every minute gesture, replaying every word, even laughing again at their simple exchange and strained bits of witticism. He would close his eyes and hold his hands together, trying to replicate the way her handshake had felt like a hug.

He had spent so much of his life alone, married to his work, he was surprised to realize how much he was missing female companionship. He was shocked by how good it felt to be desired.

But weeks went by and he began to realize how elaborate and frivolous his fantasy had become. He came to believe that he had interpreted the gesture incorrectly. It wasn't intended as flirtation; it was merely a professional gesture, a recent graduate looking for a job. His fantasy came crashing down in a cascade of cold sweats, leaving an empty hollow in his insides. His ballooning heart began to deflate and shrivel.

He threw her number away while leaving work. When he got home, he cursed himself and went back to get it. By the time he returned to Sugar Hill the cleaning service had emptied his trash can and left. He felt a curious combination of relief and remorse. He was finally, irrevocably free of the fantasy that he hated to see die.

When she called two weeks later, Eli was comically speechless. She wasn't. She was disappointed that he hadn't called. She even had the gall to tell him off, albeit in a teasing way. Lacy was undeterred by the difference in age, unimpressed by his prestigious position. She had felt an immediate attraction to the man and his principles and was not ashamed to pursue him. She made this clear by asking him out for their first date.

"Are you going to make me do all the work?" she said.

Eli hadn't said more than seven words since she called, and three of those had been "sorry." He said it again, "Sorry?" His face was on fire, his body felt freezing cold.

Lacy exhaled in mock exasperation. "I would have expected the leader of such a large and respected institution to be a bit more assertive. But that's okay. I'd like to meet you for dinner. How does this Friday sound? I'll even pick up the tab if that's what it'll take."

"No, that's not necessary. I mean, yes, that sounds good. I mean about the dinner, not the check." He stopped and took a deep breath before his runaway words made him sound any worse. "Look, I'm sorry..." he cringed, having said it once again, "...but you've caught me a bit by surprise. I'd be delighted to take you to dinner. How does DaVinci's at 7:00 p.m. sound?"

"Sounds wonderful. I'll see you there."

"Oh sorry, but—"

She hung up just as he was about to offer her a ride.

He looked down and saw that during the two-minute call he had sweated through his shirt.

Despite his initial awkwardness, the date went well. They both grabbed for the check at the same time and ended up holding hands. His was cold and slightly damp, but Lacy didn't seem to mind. He felt a charge just from touching her. Felt authenticated by her blatant look of adoration. She initiated the good-night kiss and it made him feel like a little boy.

Their relationship progressed faster than he would have ever expected. Faster than he'd even pictured in his fantasies.

Lacy was like a form of therapy. For so long Eli had felt conflicted by his innate instincts to treat people with compassion, even those considered to be his enemies, and the resistance he'd met from the masses who shared a different view on how to interact with others. He'd felt outnumbered and wondered why he was the minority. Without realizing it, he had started to become emotionally distant from his patients, denying them the personal bond, the sharing of souls that led to true healing. He had slowly started to conform.

Lacy reawakened his spirit of humane therapy. She gave him validation. She inspired him creatively, driving him to pursue new forms of therapy that delivered outstanding results. She also made him silly. She swept away his stress.

Her pet name for Eli was Alpert-fish. Whenever he was upset, she would suck in her cheeks, pucker her lips, place her hands beside her head like gills and kiss him. "Oh, come here, my sweet little Alpert-fish. Kiss, kiss. Tell me all your troubles."

It was Lacy who first introduced Eli to meditation to help quiet his mind and manage his stress. Later, introducing him to even more enjoyable tantric techniques that they'd employed in the bedroom.

Eli had never identified with any traditional religion, but began reading the books on Buddhism that Lacy brought home and found a connection with its spiritual teachings. He became engrossed in the material and found that it began to positively influence his work. He saw his life pursuit as one to alleviate suffering among the mentally ill. And the four noble truths espoused by Buddhism had applications in treating mental suffering. With Lacy's support, he overcame serious resistance from the board and was able to introduce mindfulness exercises as a form of psychiatric therapy.

Throughout this subtle transformation, this fulfillment of Eli's intrinsic potential, Lacy was always there. Always there with her silly puckered lips, soft caresses to the back of his neck after a long day's work, sweet murmurings during their lovemaking and final moments before sleep. *"My sweet little Alpert-fish. Kiss, kiss."*

Lacy often talked about taking a pilgrimage to India to soak in the spiritual culture pervasive throughout their society. She got her wish when the cancer came.

CHAPTER TWENTY-SEVEN

She was wearing a bridal veil when she told him. "Well, it looks like we can stop paying the doctor." The veil concealed the tears in her eyes but not the sheepish smile on her face. "I'm sick."

The news shattered Eli's dispassionate-doctor facade. He couldn't accept it. She was so young. The wedding was just three months away. They had a whole life planned together. This was not part of the fantasy. He was reeling. He was in shock.

Not death. Not again.

Lacy grabbed his hands and held them. She sought out his eyes and steadied them. "Just kiss me," she said. "I'm still alive. Right here, right now. In fact, in this moment I feel as alive as I've ever felt. And all I want – all I need – is a big, wet kiss from my sweet little Alpert-fish."

Eli's vision narrowed and all he saw was her face, peering at him through the white lace of the veil. She looked every bit the part of a bride. She was beautiful, vivacious. It was impossible to believe that she was dying. He lifted the veil and brought it back over her head. It caught in her hair and pulled it, causing her to gasp in pain. "Sorry," he said. It's what he always said. They looked at each other and laughed. She stepped forward and Eli cupped her face in his hands and kissed her. The moment didn't last long enough.

Lacy seemed to come more alive as she died. Eli found it almost too much to bear. For the first time, death became something other than a clinical outcome for him. It awakened existential feelings that he had never experienced before. The world began to seem absurd, pointless. Faced with the absolute whim of the universe, Eli felt impotent. Powerless and insignificant. How had he ever felt like he was in control or that his life mattered in any meaningful way? He was nothing more than an organic bag of oozing fluids with an ego. Nothing more than a monkey with a conscious mind.

And Lacy's exuberance in the face of death began to seem irrational.

Insane, even. Or was it his inability to accept the most certain of all eventualities that was delusional and insane? Despite himself, he began to resent her. Despite himself, he wished that she were already dead. That would be easier than watching her die.

Or that they had never had met. That would be easiest of all.

Either she is insane, or I am. Or nobody is. Or we all are. Either way, who am I to say? And who am I to keep people caged against their will in asylum cells? Who am I to presume to get them well when I no longer know what being well means?

Eli was in no position to go to India, but he did. By then Lacy looked anorexic. All skin and bones. Yet still she smiled. Still her eyes sparkled and shone. Still she could make him break out in gooseflesh with puckered lips and a "kiss, kiss." Even if in the back of his mind all he could think about was kissing a corpse.

They called it their honeymoon, but Eli couldn't think of a less romantic place to go. Or a less peaceful place to die. The chaos was overwhelming. He shuffled along the crowded streets in a daze as hordes of people scurried past – the smell of incense commingling with that of roasted flesh and the polluted stench of the Ganges River, where Lacy wanted to bathe. In the water beside the pyre where dead bodies burned.

She was wearing a flowing yellow sari with topaz flowers. It was mesh around the middle and left one shoulder bare.

Eli descended the stairs to the edge of the river, staying one step behind her. The river was a splashing mass of humanity, its tepid water gray like after a load of dirty laundry.

Even in the unbearable heat, Eli had no urge to enter the water as he had promised. The sounds of splashing and mad chatter of foreign tongues ceased to be something experienced externally. It was burrowing inside of him, grabbing handfuls of gray matter and smearing it against the inside of his skull.

In an instant he had a striking epiphany. This was all a mistake. Some cosmic prank. He was not in love with Lacy. He had fallen victim to a rush of silly prepubescent hormones at a time when he felt lonely. He had succumbed to the siren song of desire shown by an attractive woman half his age. This was nothing more than a midlife crisis gone out of control. And it had led him to the bank of this filthy river with a strange girl who was about to die.

The world had never felt so small and yet so large. Gravity became an absurd theory that was about to give way, sending him flying off into the whirling cosmos, out to the farthest reaches of infinity. He was disoriented and felt faint. His vision lost fluidity, turning into a snippet of snapshots instead. He had to sit down.

Lacy stopped on the landing that entered into the river. She began to disrobe, unwinding the sari from her body like an exotic offering to the bathers below. Finally, she stood naked, facing the brackish water, her back a birdcage of bones, her gaunt head held high. She descended into the water. She never once looked back.

The sun was a large orange blur. It ate up the atmosphere. Heat waves created a cascading shimmer across its bloated surface as it lumbered towards the horizon.

Lacy lowered herself underwater. Seconds went by, minutes.

Eli began to suspect suicide. He began to question whether or not she had ever actually existed, or if he had followed his fantasy all the way to this anticlimactic conclusion.

Then he saw her, a small turtle shell creating a gentle wake in the flowing water. She had just poked her eyes and nose up over the surface, like a hippopotamus in the African wild. She stayed that way for a long while, occasionally blinking. Just breathing in the noxious stench of the river through her nose and watching the scene around her.

These were two worlds. One real, one unreal. One peaceful, the other chaotic. Eli's mind was incapable of processing the scene as one he could relate with in any way. Therefore, it felt increasingly illusionary. And his inability to adjust aggravated his unease. His life existed on the other side of the planet. There, he held responsibility. People depended on him in important ways. He wondered whether that world still existed or if he had crossed over into this new reality and would have to find his way anew. He could not fathom how Lacy was capable of integrating herself so completely into this frightening environment. Especially when she was so close to crossing over into the most foreign land of all. All he wanted was to take her back to a more familiar place where he could appreciate her final moments. Where he could offer support while she died. Eli began to rock back and forth, holding himself out of fear of falling apart.

Lacy rose higher, the water reaching to just below her emaciated breasts. She cupped her hands in the water and splashed it on her face and poured it over her head. She leaned back and shook her head so that her hair separated into tangled strands. Water flew from her hair and body, glinting like ice in the torrid air.

She began to wash herself, pouring handfuls down her neck and over her extended arms. Every movement was slow and deliberate, sensual. Her nipples became sharp, her body prickled with puckered skin. It was like spying through a hole in the bathroom window as a woman bathed. And then Eli watched in horror as men began to take notice, circling around her and wading closer.

A man approached. His dreadlocked hair was gray and perched atop his head like a cone, his wiry beard wet and plastered to his chest. He was nearly as gaunt as Lacy, with a smile just as wide and twice as bright. They began talking with exaggerated gestures.

Eli could hear their laughter tinkling through the squall of splashing water and chittering tongues. His own crying was silent.

The man appeared to be coaxing her, instructing her to turn around. She did. The man approached her from behind. At first, she covered her breasts in her first act of self-conscious modesty. But the man said something that relaxed her and she raised her arms overhead and began to lean back towards him, falling against the current. The man grabbed her by the forearms and walked backwards so that her body began to float. She looked like a piece of white flotsam in the brown filth. Lacy's face was contorted in concentration, but she soon relaxed and let the water flow around her. Her smile returned.

Others came towards her, men and women both. Naked and clothed. They reached out and began washing her, their hands indiscriminately passing over her breasts and the patch of dark hair between her legs. They lifted her – Eli heard her squeal and laugh – and spun her slowly in a circle as they splashed her with water. They began to chant a spirited song of celebration. They were smiling, their eyes bright. Lacy let her head hang back and her hair drift along the water. Then they brought her back down and eased her to her feet. One by one they touched her head and bowed with their hands clasped before them in blessing and slowly walked away.

Lacy began to wade towards the shore. She faltered and went under, then reemerged, sputtering. She slipped and fell again. Eli tensed as though about to rise, he struggled to see her through the tears in his eyes. She came back up, her head bowed, weakened and in need of help. Eli remained seated. The man with the dreadlocks splashed over and offered support, helping guide her to the shore.

She staggered up the steps, leaving her sari lying on the landing. When she made it to Eli she collapsed into his arms, shivering despite the oppressive heat. Eli pulled her close and held her. Her teeth were chattering, and when she looked up into his face her eyes were glazed and empty. Her body was a shell.

He felt conspicuous holding her naked body, like he was doing something inappropriate and would soon be scolded. She began to shudder, even while her body radiated heat. Her skin felt feverish. Eli rubbed her arms with his hands and pulled her closer, resting his cheek against the top of her head to contain the heat. She reeked of the river, and the polluted water began to soak through his clothes. He fought to keep from cringing.

The shuddering intensified, turning into spasms. She was convulsing. Her teeth were clacking and then her tongue flopped forward and became jammed between her jaws. Blood rushed over her chin and streamed down her neck in bright-red rivulets.

The riverside turned quiet. All Eli could hear was the sound of Lacy straining against the convulsions – a prolonged moan as though from electrocution. Her body went rigid, her eyes opened wide, her mouth turned down in a grimace and her neck extended in a stretch of rigid tendons. It reminded him of shock therapy. It reminded him of…

A tight, reedy exhalation passed through her contorted mouth, pushing out every last bit of air until there was a final gasp followed by a dry click at the back of her throat. Her eyes fixed in place, gazing up over Eli's head at the crimson sky. Her head fell back and her body went limp. Eli eased her to the stone step beside him and stood, looking down on her skeletal frame.

She had never made it out of the water. Whatever comprised Lacy's spirit, her soul, was now flowing along the tide of the Ganges River. Eli had not been able to say goodbye.

The chant began again, the ceremonial song. Shadows emerged around Eli's feet, rippling across Lacy's decimated corpse. Eli looked up and saw villagers approaching, their eyes bright and merry, their combined voices rich and strong. They wore tattered wraps and threadbare saris. Some wore nothing at all. But they danced like they possessed all of the world's riches. They smiled as though eternal joy sprung purely from their song.

They were coming for her – for Lacy – crowding forward, creating a dense wall of writhing humanity. Their chanting grew louder, it echoed in Eli's ears. The dense heat was suffocating. This was not the death he had imagined. The eloquent farewell. The kiss goodbye. The ceremonial closing of the eyes.

Lacy looked like a Holocaust victim shucked from the shower stalls to bake in the oversized sun. And these strangers, these haggardly paupers with their misappropriated song, were not meant to be cast in this last chapter, this final agonizing act.

As they closed in, so too did the world. It was like *he* was being confined to a coffin. He began to ward away the villagers by swinging his arm, his eyes wide and wild, river water and sweat flinging from his clenched fist.

A man stepped calmly from the crowd. It was the man who had first approached Lacy in the river, the one with the beehive of dreadlocked hair and long, flowing beard. He was clearly mad – he smiled like a lunatic in the face of Eli's swinging fist. The man took another step forward; Eli's fist now swung less than an inch from his face, nearly brushing the tip of his nose. He took another step as Eli's arm bounded off his opposite shoulder and returned in a violent backswing.

Eli halted his arm just before it crashed into the man's head. The man didn't even flinch. He placed his hand on Eli's chest, directly over his heart.

It felt like the air cooled thirty degrees. The oppressive wall of people seemed to move several steps back, lifting the sense of claustrophobia from Eli's chest. The tenor of the chant changed; he could hear its beauty; he could perceive its intent. The man before Eli now looked like an angel, like love incarnate.

Eli peered down and saw Lacy as he'd first met her. Comfortable with herself, even in death. And he understood – this was how she had meant it to be.

The man spoke English with an Indian accent. "Do not let your heart rage against her." Eli could feel his heart swell pleasantly under the man's gentle hand. "You have known her many times. Her love will never leave you. Please, my son, be at peace."

Silent tears began to flow down Eli's face. He trapped the man's hand against his chest and closed his eyes and cried. The crowd came forward, touching him, embracing him. Their love was something real, and in it he could feel Lacy's love as well. That, too, had been real. And even though she had died, he knew it would last forever. More, he knew that it had always been.

They lifted Lacy up onto their shoulders and carried her lifeless body to the fire. The sky had turned cobalt blue with a bloody slash along the horizon. A few bright lights were flickering above, ancient fire from the corpses of long-dead stars. *Stardust and death, it's all we are,* Eli thought as he gazed overhead, the night sky now filled with unbridled beauty and inexplicable wonder. *Hello, star. We send our death fire back towards you.*

Sparks whirled upward when Lacy's body landed on the logs. There was a loud crackling, like the fabric of reality was being ripped apart. Her wet body popped and hissed as the flames enveloped her, white steam began to rise. And then she caught fire. The chanting stopped and the people fell silent. They stood huddled together and watched Lacy burn.

Eli turned his head and saw the man standing beside him, the fire flickering in his eyes. The man turned and looked up at Eli and smiled, his teeth unnaturally bright.

"Beautiful spirit," he said.

"Yes," Eli said.

"You have known her a long time."

Eli thought it was a question. "No," he said. "Not long enough."

The man laughed again, a cheerful, infectious laugh.

Eli was shocked to hear himself chuckle.

"No, you have known her many lifetimes. You save her every time."

Eli turned towards the pyre. Lacy's body was engulfed in yellow flame. "There was nothing I could do."

"You did everything you were meant to do. Same as before. Now, *you* must accept salvation. Now, *you* must be saved."

Whatever spell had been cast was beginning to wear off. The man's words began to sound delusional again. Eli nodded in the detached way he would with a patient suffering extreme psychosis. He pinched his nose to stifle the sudden smell of roasted pork.

"Come and find me here tomorrow," the man said.

Eli's flight had been one-way. He hadn't thought about what to do after Lacy died. "Here? How will I find you?"

"Ask for Rajamadja," the man said. And then he fell silent and turned back towards the pyre with its tangle of burning bodies.

Together, they watched as the fire slowly turned to ash.

★ ★ ★

Acrid smoke burned Eli's nostrils. He opened his eyes. The incense had burned down to the stick. He exhaled deeply and assessed himself. His foot was asleep from the sitting position. He untangled his legs and stood. Before him was a picture of Rajamadja, the emaciated monk who had at one time saved Eli's sanity.

"Where are you now, friend?" Eli said, wondering indeed where his spirit was, knowing his body was nothing more than gray ash beneath the blazing fire of the funeral pyre. "Why can I no longer feel you?"

In the days following Lacy's death Rajamadja had opened Eli's eyes to a world he had never known before. To miracles he'd never imagined possible. Psychiatry offered little explanation for the psychic powers the man appeared to possess.

And, slowly, he had revealed to Eli a purpose, a continuation down a path that he was already on. And he had provided Eli with ways to defend himself against the resistance that worked to distract him from his noble pursuit. Ways in which to fight against his destructive shadow self. But that had been such a long time ago.

Eli snuffed the incense stick against the base of the bamboo stand. His hands were damp and trembling; his heart fluttered irregularly in his chest.

Such a long time ago, he thought as he put away his cushion and left the room, turning the lights off on his way out. Leaving, he hoped, the ghosts behind.

CHAPTER TWENTY-EIGHT

The sun was slow to rise; it lifted sluggishly into the sky as though still pondering the absurdity of last night's dreams. It was a pastel yellow, round and cartoonish, casting a mellow warmth that dried the morning dew and gently awoke the chirping insects from their slumber. Rays of white, hazy light streamed through the Spanish moss flowing from the ancient oaks lining both sides of Sugar Hill's winding entrance road. The smell of honeysuckle perfumed the air, accented by a richer scent of wet clay.

Normally, these were the days that convinced Eli that all was right with the world. It was nature's way of telling us to take it easy. To chill. To cast aside our petty problems and understand that everything was going to be okay. But, today, it felt like a facade, a trap. A siren song luring him towards a place of danger, inviting him to let down his guard when he needed to be fully alert.

Projections, Eli, he thought wearily. *You're just projecting again.*

But as he crested the hill and saw the great spire of the main building thrusting skyward, it failed to instill in him the usual sense of profound purpose. Rather, it caused his concussed head to throb.

He pulled into his assigned space and parked. His fingers were trembling. He reached into his pant pocket and pulled out a dime and two quarters. He checked the other pocket – empty.

His heart began to race and his stomach turned sour. Time accelerated and the car walls closed in. He saw the frantic look in his eyes reflected in the rearview mirror and cringed.

Then he remembered the change drawer. He flipped it open and there it was – the Xanax pill, its oval shape and orange appearance providing the calm assurance the morning sun no longer could. He crammed it between his teeth and chewed, relishing its acrid taste, its promised potency. He exited the car, feeling confident in the fortitude of his medicated mind.

He had been away for a full week, his longest leave of absence since his sabbatical to India over two decades ago. He knew the timing was poor with the board meeting approaching, but it couldn't be helped. He hadn't planned for a riot-inducing police siege on the hospital. *Unfortunately,* he thought, *I wasn't able to prevent it either.*

Eli felt oddly detached from the hospital as he made his way through the side entrance. It felt like he'd been away longer than a week. Like changes had been made in his absence – the floor plan altered, the walls given a fresh coat of paint. It reminded him of returning to school after summer vacation, not knowing what the new semester would bring.

The nurses, normally quick to offer a jubilant hello when they first saw him, were hesitant as he approached. Strangely shy.

"Well, hello ladies. How are we this morning?"

The group of three nurses grew silent, as though caught gossiping. "Just fine, Dr. Alpert. Welcome back, sir." Their curt formality was out of character.

He walked closer. He saw guarded expressions, but felt a buoyant sense of camaraderie regardless. The Xanax was beginning to take effect. He stopped and stared at them, a bland smile forming on his face. "What? That's all I get? After spending a whole week in the hospital."

"I thought you was let out on Wednesday," the nurse said. It did little to make Eli feel loved.

"Well, I was, but..." He scanned their impassive faces. *What is going on?* he thought. He almost felt like hanging his head and pouting in an attempt to garner sympathy. He resisted the urge. "Anyway, it's good to be back."

They murmured in agreement and found other things to do.

From down the hall he heard a door close. It sounded like the one to Alex's office.

Jerry, he thought. *Oh god.* He had exchanged messages with Alex, but had yet to actually speak to him since his brother's death. His murder, according to the police. He could understand if Alex wanted a bit of privacy.

He peeked in as he walked past. Alex was at his desk with the phone in his hand. Eli felt a deep sense of compassion for the pain he must feel. The shared pain that he himself felt over Jerry's death. He vaguely realized that the Xanax was responsible for this increasing sense of openness and euphoria. But what did that matter, so long as the emotion was justified? He continued down the hall, passing his own office, ambling along.

Breakfast was just ending and patients were shuffling back to their rooms or to morning sessions. "Morning," he said to each of them as he walked past.

"Morning," a few muttered back.

"Ain't morning to me, commie," said one.

"Fuck your mother," said another.

Each response made him smile.

He passed Randall's room and paused. He peered in and saw him sitting on the edge of his bed, staring at the empty space before him. *Such wasted potential*, Eli thought. Then he had an idea.

He went back to his office and retrieved his key to the supply room. He opened the door and looked around, not noticing the conspicuous absence of the neural imaging equipment. He was too focused on finding a particular item, which he located in the far-back corner, leaning against the wall – the acoustic guitar. He grabbed it and hurried back to Randall's room.

He knocked on the door and entered. Randall slowly turned his head. His eyes were half-lidded and glassy, his lips sunken in. "I've got a request," Eli said, pulling the guitar out from behind his back.

"Huh?" Randall said. He smacked his toothless mouth a couple of times and mumbled, "Huh-uh. I already took 'em. I already took 'em today." Then he saw the guitar, and his eyes opened in delight.

Eli handed it to him. "You still do requests, don't you?"

Randall strummed the guitar, playing a series of full-bodied chords. Then his fingers picked the strings like a banjo, faster than Eli would have thought possible. Just as suddenly, he pressed his hand against the strings to dampen the sound. "I'll play any damned thing you want to hear!"

He broke into a brief medley, blending the songs together: "Sweet Home Alabama," followed by "Midnight Rider" and finishing it off with "The Seeker" by The Who. He riffed hardest on the last song. Eli thought for sure he would snap the strings.

The strumming faded away, and once again Eli was struck by the drastic change that music produced in this patient. Just moments ago the man had been nearly catatonic. Now he sounded like he was ready for the recording studio. Eli applauded.

Randall cradled the guitar and bowed his head at Eli's reaction. "So, what do ya want to hear?"

Eli crossed his legs and thumped his lips with a finger as he thought about it. "I was always a big Beach Boys fan."

"Ah," Randall said, returning his hands to their playing positions. He began to strum the opening to "Sloop John B," one of Eli's favorites. Then he began to sing in a clear voice inflected with boyish emotion – this was what Eli had come to refer to as Randall's authentic self. The one before the disorder. It was better than listening to Brian Wilson himself.

Eli watched enraptured, losing himself in the music, the Xanax stripping away his usual inhibitions. He joined Randall in the final chorus, their voices rising to full volume as they sang about feeling so broke up they just wanted to go home.

Eli felt hot tears burning the corners of his eyes. He hadn't ever considered the last lines from a patient's point of view. But hearing Randall bellow out each lyric with such heartfelt passion, Eli knew that he too perceived the significance beyond that which the Beach Boys had originally intended. It felt like a moment of understanding. A moment shared.

Eli composed himself. He looked at the concrete wall to keep from crying. "You know, Brian Wilson, the lead singer and songwriter for the Beach Boys, suffered from mental illness. Spent years in a mental health hospital like this one, actually."

"Yeah?" Randall was gently strumming the guitar with his eyes closed, quietly humming to himself.

"He did. You know, it's always interested me, that fine line between genius and mental illness. It doesn't seem as though true originality can come from a completely stable mind."

Randall shook his head in pleasure and continued to strum.

"Why do you think that is, Randall?"

Randall quieted the strings. His bloated face, with its sunken lips and protruding cheeks, made him look like a frog. He scratched a patchwork of boyish whiskers that would never form into a beard. "Well," he said in his raspy voice, "I guess it's because they have access to the thoughts of God. The only people who can get away with that without being called crazy are preachers. And I'm not sure that they actually do what they say they do. Talk to God, I mean. They're the really crazy ones, you ask me."

Eli leaned over his knee. "What do you mean?"

Randall began to play again. The strings squeaked as he switched chords. "It's the ideas, the songs, the music – they don't come from the brain. It's more like the brain is a radio antenna. It picks up on the songs and ideas from a higher source.

"I guess most people are just tuned in to a channel that lets them see the world a certain way. The normal way. And all the people gifted with genius, they're able to tune in to a channel set to a different frequency where God plays DJ. In their mind they hear angels sing, but it don't always sound like you see in the movies, with golden harpsichords and what have you. It sounds like Jimi Hendrix and Nirvana too. It looks like street graffiti and comes in the form of pornography. People just don't ever relate that with God, but that's what it is.

"But I guess it's enough to fry the mind, sometimes. Or maybe it's just so different from what people are used to that they call it crazy because they don't know what else to call it. It's genius, but it's crazy too."

"You're right," Eli said. Their conversations always seemed to veer towards this general point. "Half the patients were put in here because they claim to talk to God. But preachers do the same thing and they're put in positions of power and praised. That's an oversimplification, of course, but it's an interesting insight."

Eli pressed his palms against his legs and prepared to stand. Randall stopped playing the guitar and extended the neck towards Eli for him to grab. Eli took it away and Randall's eyes glossed over, that sparkle began to fade. He slouched forward and began gumming his lips.

Eli paused. "Hey, why don't you hold on to this?" he said, knowing that it was breaking policy. "Just try and keep it quiet, okay?"

"For real?" Randall's gaping smile revealed red, puckered gums.

"Sure, why not? Listen to the angels for a little while. Let me know what they say."

He handed the guitar back and Randall's eyes began to shine.

CHAPTER TWENTY-NINE

Alex heard Eli talking with some nurses in the hallway.

The phone had not been his friend lately, bringing nothing, it seemed, but bad news. He was relieved nonetheless by the timing of this current call. He saw Eli peek in through the window just as he pressed the receiver to his ear, and blew out a pent-up breath as Eli moved on.

"I understand congratulations are in order, Dr. Drexler. Chief Medical Director. That's got a nice ring to it, wouldn't you say?"

It was Bob Bearman, the chairman of the board. He had been surveying the hospital during Eli's absence, assessing its condition. The Bearman family had made their money farming peaches before getting into politics. The man had no formal experience in psychiatry, but that hadn't kept him from obtaining the hospital's highest rank. As he said, "Let the shrinks handle the madhouse. Leave the business to the businessmen." And it was through this mentality that many of Sugar Hill's decisions had historically been made.

Fortunately, Eli's regime had made Sugar Hill one of the most successful state-run hospitals in the nation. But "times they were a-changin'," and Mr. Bearman hadn't been especially discreet about the board's pending decision to out Eli and replace him with Alex. The word had spread like wildfire throughout Sugar Hill while Eli was away.

"Well, thank you, sir. I don't know that it's been officially announced, however."

Mr. Bearman sounded like he lived with a peach pit perpetually lodged in his gullet and was constantly attempting to clear it from his throat. "Oh, don't give me that unofficially, officially horse jizz. You're our guy. All that's left is pure formality."

"You mean telling Eli."

"Eli's been out nursing a damn headache because he couldn't keep the crazies under control. I got more pressing problems on my plate than worrying about him."

Mr. Bearman's heavy, congested breathing filled the line. His chest phlegm quaked. "Look, I won't lie. This is going to cause a stir. Especially in light of recent events. We need to get out ahead of this thing. We need to decide how this thing's going to be scripted out, and you're going to play a big part in that."

"Certainly. I'm happy to do whatever's needed."

"That's good. That's what I like to hear." Mr. Bearman rattled the peach pit around in his throat. "I have it on good authority that you've created some kind of miracle drug to cure mental maladies."

Alex shot up in his chair as a painful electrical current coursed through his body. *Goddamn Steve!*

"Well..."

"Look, I know it's hush-hush..."

Yeah well, it's too bad your lips are looser than a geriatric nymphomaniac.

"...but that's going to be what gets us through this temporary period of turbulence. We need you to put it to work."

The painful electrical current came back for a second pass. "I'd be happy to, sir, but the medicine hasn't been formally approved for consumption. I'll need to conduct successful clinical trials before we take it to market."

"Sure, that's fine. That's what I mean."

Alex slumped forward, relieved.

"I've got that all taken care of."

Alex lifted his head. "Well, that's great."

"You're damn right it is. Now all you got to do is prove that it works. It does work, don't it?"

The stronger formula and heavier dose had effectively cured Jerry before he'd been...what? Killed by a man who wasn't there, accompanied by a dog that was dead. Problems for another day.

"Yeah, it works all right. It's unbelievable, actually. Groundbreaking. It regulates levels of a particular neurochemical compound located—"

"All right, all right. Look, I don't need all the damn scientific details. I just need to know that we can rely on you to make this work. Do I have your assurance?"

Alex knew that his professional future with Sugar Hill hinged on his answer to this question. And that this was likely his last real opportunity to get his medicine approved for therapeutic use, which would alleviate all his financial troubles. "You have my guarantee. So, where will we be conducting the test trials?"

"Where? What do you mean, where? Seems like you have a perfectly suitable test lab right there."

"What, here?"

"Yes, there! You do work at a mental hospital, don't you? You do have patients to treat, don't you? Well, treat them. That's what I'm talking about. You start to show positive outcomes for your patients – groundbreaking results, as you said yourself – well then we got ourselves quite a nice story to tell. Eli will be old news. That poor girl getting herself nearly killed won't matter so much. Especially when her assailant makes such an astonishing recovery. That's the story we're going to write, you hear me? And you're going to be the damn author."

"You want me to test the medicine on Crosby?"

"He's your patient, ain't he?"

"Yes, but…"

"So, what's the problem?"

Alex's mind searched for an excuse and came up empty. Crosby was as good a candidate as any. But he was a news story. If something happened to go wrong, there was a chance it could go public. But publicity seemed to be what Bearman wanted, assuming that it would all go well. Which it would. The formula had been fixed. It was a matter of maintenance, which he would be on hand to administer.

"Nothing. It's just that he recently committed an assault. Charges may be filed against him. Wouldn't it be better to work with someone a bit more stable? You know, hedge our bets a little?"

"Look, either your medicine works or it doesn't. You say it does. Then it shouldn't matter who we choose. That Crosby fella makes the most sense from a political standpoint. Plus, he's put up in solitary confinement, so you have an isolated space to perform the tests without getting any interference from other patients. It's the most controlled environment you're going to find."

Bearman cleared his throat. "Listen, Alex, I don't think you fully appreciate what we're doing for you here. Frankly, I'm surprised to hear any reservations from your end. Just do your job and everything will be fine. Or maybe we should be looking for someone else."

"No! No, no. I don't mean to sound ungrateful. I am *very* grateful. This is all great, really. I just… Things have been crazy lately."

"I heard about your brother. Killed by an orderly, from what I hear. That's another knock against Eli, you ask me. Hiring a killer to protect hospital staff. Not such a good move."

Devon couldn't have done it, you big, fat malignant fucking tumor! "Yeah, well, I'm honored to have your trust and to be given this opportunity. I won't let you down."

"I'm sure you won't. I have your guarantee, after all. I'll expect to see progress at next week's board meeting."

Mr. Bearman ended the call. Alex looked at the receiver as though he'd never seen one before. He was being handed everything he'd ever wanted. He should be tap dancing on his desk. But there was something about the offer that didn't sit right with him.

It was the way Eli was being treated. It felt like an insult after all the good he'd accomplished for the hospital and its patients.

His career has run its course, Alex thought. *Hell, even I was undermining his trust. Conducting the test trials behind his back. A confrontation like this was simply a matter of time. This was the only real conclusion, no matter what.*

In fact, Alex thought, *this is even better. Let Mr. Bearman and the board shoulder the blame. I was just following orders. And, it's not like Eli hadn't screwed up, either. It's not like he shouldn't have seen this coming. I'm just being sensitive, is all. Just being a good friend.*

There was no way his father could call him a failure anymore. Not once he became the Chief Medical Director at one of the nation's oldest and most respected state hospitals. Not once news got out about his miracle cure.

If only he'd had a chance to show how it had saved Jerry.

CHAPTER THIRTY

It wasn't fear that Angela felt. Sure, she was nervous. But in an excitable way. It was more like the feeling you get before jumping from a high dive or speaking in public or unzipping the pants of some stranger you've decided to fuck.

Crosby had taken his best shot at her and come up short. She had to show him that she wasn't defeated. That she wasn't afraid. Danger came with the territory. It was likely what attracted her most to the job. And, despite his attack, Angela was still committed to helping Crosby recover. He hadn't attacked her because he was evil. He'd done it because he was sick. And it was her job to help him get well.

They were trying to remove him from her care, but she wouldn't let them. They owed her as much.

She reached into the medicine cabinet, bypassing the Tylenol and grabbing the bottle of high-strength Percocet instead. Her face still hurt from where Crosby had kicked her. Her pussy was sore from a recent one-night stand. Battered or not, she'd still found time to party. Angela shook her head, thinking about the snippets of fuzzy memory from the last few nights that still caused residual shame.

She popped open the top to the pill bottle and scooped one out, then another. *Fuck it,* she thought and took out two more. She put them in her mouth and swallowed. She closed the door and left the medical-supply room, turning and making her way to meet Alex, where he stood waiting for her outside Crosby's isolated cell.

CHAPTER THIRTY-ONE

The forensics wing of the hospital was separated by a series of electronically locked doors that were under constant video surveillance. The main reception area was monitored by armed guards. This was the part of the hospital devoted to Sugar Hill's most violent mentally ill patients, home to the criminally insane.

Angela passed her keycard through the final scanner and showed her ID badge to the guard manning the reception desk. He handed her a sign-in form, which she filled out.

"You the one he got to, huh?" the guard said. His blonde hair was spiked in the back, as though he'd just awoken from a nap. He was chewing gum. It crackled in the small confines of the reception space. Despite its minty freshness, his breath smelled stale.

Angela signed her name. "Which way?" she said.

The guard sighed and raised his eyebrows. The gum switched sides. "Come on, now. A little thing like you, they'll eat you alive. Let me be your escort." His eyes scanned down the length of her body, settling on her legs. "You may need someone to watch your back."

"That's okay." She licked her thumb before grabbing a sheet of paper. "Besides, you look busy."

"Nah, I can—"

Angela began ripping sheets of paper from the registration form and letting them flutter to the floor.

"Aw hell. He's back down there in solitary. Room 13C. Now, stop that already."

"Thanks." She dropped the clipboard that held the rest of the sign-in forms and started walking towards solitary row.

The forensics wing was like an underground barracks. Lacking windows, it was filled with harsh artificial light. Beastly screams echoed down from distant chambers. When the bellows faded the fluorescent bulbs buzzed like electric insect traps. Angela's shoes created a hollow clomping in the cavernous acoustics of the concrete tunnels. She couldn't shake the feeling of being followed.

For at least thirty years, people had reported seeing ghosts in this section of the hospital. Two in particular. One was claimed to be the spirit of a serial killer who had been convicted of raping then killing over thirty young men and keeping their mummified corpses arranged throughout his house like mannequins. He was known to have taunted the male guards while he was alive, revealing himself in obscene ways, fondling guards whenever he could get his hands free.

He was found beaten to death in his locked cell. His penis and testicles had been smashed to an unrecognizable pulp. So had his face. No one had ever been charged with the attack.

He was said to taunt the male guards still, locking them in empty cells, violating them from beyond the grave. It had been a decade since anyone had claimed to have heard the story firsthand, but once every few years a young male guard would wind up getting locked in an empty cell, traumatized and panicked, and would inexplicably quit.

The other ghost was supposed to be the spirit of a young mother of six children, ages ranging from infant to eight years. Police were called in when neighbors began to worry that they had gone missing. They were gone, but not missing. The mother had killed each one and eaten them. She was caught wearing their bones, which had been bleached clean.

People claimed to see her walking the hallways holding her stomach as though hungry, and to hear the macabre clacking of her skeletal jewelry.

Casting aside the historical lore, Crosby was one of Sugar Hill's more notorious patients from a media point of view. The salacious nature of his crimes – and sinister moniker assigned to him by a local journalist – had captured national attention, although the story had achieved greater coverage down here in the Southlands. It had provoked a public debate on the treatment of mental illness and whether or not the insane should answer for their crimes.

And, for a brief period, it had drawn people from neighboring Bible-belt counties, who came to protest Crosby's sentence, or lack thereof. Angela had found it sad. These people, who claimed to have such deep religious faith, seemed to have forgotten the teachings of their Scripture, reverting back to a more archaic gospel. Tooth for a tooth. Eye for an eye. Soul for a soul.

Angela knew that she may be a sinner, but at least she wasn't a hypocrite. Hell, Christ himself had hung out with plenty of drunks and promiscuous women in his day. And who had ever performed a better party trick than turning water into wine? Jesus was okay, as far as Angela was concerned, although she didn't think too many of his followers would like to hear her reasons why.

She turned down the hallway leading from general housing to the row of solitary cells. She had to pass through another locked doorway to get there. When the door closed behind her it felt as though she had entered an abandoned bomb shelter. The overhead lighting was dim, as though the hospital was unwilling to expend undue energy on this wing. The hallway was narrow and long. The cell doors were all lined up against one wall, separated by several feet of stone preventing noise traveling from one patient to the next.

The thick metallic doors had sliding panels to look through, but they were all closed, sealing the patients inside. She wondered how each patient was passing the time in their small, solitary cells, and shivered. It got cold all of a sudden, and she found herself listening for the sound of clacking bones.

Alex was waiting at the far end of the hallway, standing before the last cell. He turned towards the sound of her clomping shoes and held up his hand.

Angela hadn't seen him since Jerry's death and her assault. She didn't know whether to hug him or shake his hand. Who was supposed to console whom? She walked forward with outstretched arms just as he looked down and began fishing in his pocket for a key. He noticed her gesture and looked up just as she dropped her arms and retreated, crossing her arms awkwardly across her chest. Her face began to burn.

Alex arched an eyebrow. He managed to smirk. "Come here often?" he said, parroting a cheesy pickup line.

"On occasion. They've got decent happy-hour specials most Friday nights."

Alex looked around as though inspecting the scene. "Seems pretty dead tonight."

"It caters to an exclusive clientele."

"An eclectic bunch, from what I hear."

"Yeah, it can get pretty rowdy."

"Just my kind of place."

If you only knew, Angela thought, and her smile fell away.

Alex stepped forward, observing the bruises on Angela's face. He used a finger to lift her chin and inspected the purple thumbprints on her neck. "Not too bad," he said. "I expected worse."

"It wasn't nearly as bad as people are making it out to be."

Alex scrutinized her through unbelieving eyes. "Right," he said.

"I'm serious. There was no reason to have him removed from my care. I'm more than capable—"

Alex raised his hand to stop her. "No need to beat a dead horse. You've made your case. That's why we're here."

Her heartbeat had quickened when she felt the need to defend herself. She wanted to appear calm when she met Crosby, however. Then she remembered Jerry's death. She reached her hand out and caressed his arm. "How about you? You doing okay?"

Alex's sardonic laugh sounded like a sneeze. "Peachy," he said.

She offered a sympathetic expression. "Hey, wait," she said, growing more excited. "I heard some good news about you through the grapevine."

Alex held a finger to his lips.

Angela looked around. The hallway was empty. The soundproof rooms were occupied by the state's least trustworthy witnesses. Still, she lowered her voice.

"Well?" she said.

"We'll talk later." He pulled a set of keys from his coat pocket, palming them. Then his face became serious. "You don't have to do this," he said.

"I want to do this. I'm not giving up on him."

Alex sighed. "No one would see it that way."

Angela crossed her arms. "Do I need to beat the horse some more?"

Alex nodded. He lowered his head, thinking. Angela noticed that his hair had sprouted several new strands of gray. "Okay, okay," he said, nodding again. He took a step closer and lowered his voice to a whisper. "I need you to know that the board has taken a special interest in this particular patient."

"Okay?" she said, her eyebrows coming together.

"They are wanting to use him as a…" he mentally rejected several politically insensitive phrases before saying, "…demonstration for the positive new direction that we're heading in."

Angela offered a knowing smile and nudged his arm with her elbow.

Alex's responding smile hardly lasted a second. "They have authorized…no, they have *instructed* us to administer a new therapeutic medicine that is in the exploratory stage of development. This is highly confidential. No one else can know about it. Especially Eli. Is that understood?"

"Sure. My only goal is to get him the best care possible. If this new treatment plan will help him get well, I'm all for it. I have no problem keeping it quiet."

"I mean it. No one can know."

"That's fine. For how long?"

"I don't know. That depends."

"On what?"

"Look, I don't know. I think it's more complicated than the board realizes. For now, let's just focus on what we need to do to prepare Crosby for the new treatment plan." He flipped through the keys until he found the right one. "And getting you out of here without another black eye."

"Ha. Ha," Angela said dryly, but it made her smile. She'd rather make light of what happened than turn it into some serious catastrophe. Violence occurred every day in the sane streets of every city. What did they expect from a mental asylum? All she knew was that she preferred this job with its potential for danger to working behind a desk.

"Okay. Let's see how our good friend's doing." Alex inserted the key and unlocked the door. The bolt slamming back sounded like the crash of a hammer, it echoed down the hall. And then there was just the static buzzing of the overhead lights as the door before them eased open.

They entered.

CHAPTER THIRTY-TWO

Crosby was in a fetal position on his bunk, facing the concrete wall. His hands were clasped under his chin, his knees tucked to his chest. He looked like an exhausted toddler napping during day care. But Angela knew better than to trust his innocent appearance. Just like Crosby believed, appearances could be deceiving.

"They've kept him loaded up on sedatives since the incident," Alex whispered. "I had them halve the dosage two days ago. He should be a bit more responsive by now."

She nodded.

"Mr. Nelson," Alex said in a jovial voice that crashed against the walls of this claustrophobic room. "How are we today?"

Angela thought that "we" was an unfortunate way to address a schizophrenic, but kept it to herself.

Crosby stirred on the cot. He began to straighten his legs and stretch his arms overhead. He opened his mouth in a yawn that seemed to last a year, then blinked his eyes against the dimness of the room in order to focus on his visitors.

He sat up and swung his legs around. He scanned their faces, then their feet. Angela looked down and saw that she was standing in a beam of light flowing through a small square window positioned near the ceiling. It cast a shadow beside her. She quickly stepped away from the shaft of light, and the shadow disappeared.

"Whaddya want?" Crosby's voice was heavy and hoarse. The words seemed to form deep in the back of his throat with little assistance from his lips and tongue.

"We're here to check up on you," Alex said. "See how you're doing. You remember Ms. Drake, I'm sure."

Crosby's eyes were half-lidded; he had to angle his head upward to see her. There was no spark of recognition. He methodically nodded his head. "So?"

"So how are you feeling?" Alex said. He clasped his hands before him and rolled forward onto the balls of his feet.

"Like you don't know," Crosby said in his sluggish tone.

"Only you know how you feel."

Crosby's chuckle was more like a dry cough. "I feel like shit," he said. "Nobody's feeding me. I haven't showered in a dozen years. Haven't eaten a thing. Where is this?"

"You tell me?" Alex said.

"I don't wanna tell you a goddamn thing. You're prolly the one behind all this."

Angela spoke up, using the silky voice that so effectively cast a spell on most men. "Crosby? What's the last thing you remember before being moved to this room?"

Crosby put the first two fingers of his left hand to his forehead as though channeling the memory. His cuticles were raw and crusted with blood. "I...uh... There was a battle. An uprising against the demons. We almost won." He leaned back against the bed and crossed his ankles. The soles of his feet were chapped and chalky white. "Yep, we almost got 'em, but they overtook me. Then they locked me up in here. I don't know where it is though. Doubt I'll ever get out."

"That depends on you," Alex said. "This lady, here? You attacked her. So we've had to confine you for your own safety and ours."

Crosby forced his lids to open wider. He looked more closely at Angela's face. "Oh yeah," he said. "You're the one with the hands."

Angela held her hands up. "Yep, I've got two of them."

"Those are devil hands. They're just like my mama's."

Alex interjected. "Mr. Nelson, you are presently residing in an isolated cell in the forensics section of Sugar Hill Mental Hospital."

"This ain't no hospital. This is goddamn death row."

Alex continued. "Our goal is to return you to general residence where you can enjoy some more interaction with others. But, in order to do so, we need to be sure that you no longer exhibit behavior that could result in another violent outburst. Do you understand?"

"Nah, that ain't it. Your goal is to turn me into a mindless sheep and fatten me up for the slaughter. You can tell your lies, but I don't have to listen."

"Regardless of your attitudes towards us or our intentions, I promise you that we only have your best interests at heart," Angela said in her sweet, sincere voice. "Our job is to get you feeling good again."

"That's right," Alex said. "To start, we'll be taking you off your present medication, which is causing the drowsiness you're currently experiencing, and prescribing a new medicine that will make you feel..." *Like yourself? Who the hell is this man?* "...much better."

"Blah, blah, blah. Whatever. Just make sure they tell that damn chatterhead out by the window to shut the hell up already. Can't hardly sleep with all that bullshit."

Angela and Alex exchanged a glance. "Certainly," Alex said. "We'll tell him to keep it down."

"We'll check back in on you soon," Angela said. She winked at him. "It's good to see you again. You feel better, now."

* * *

Alex closed the door and locked it, flinching at the sound. It was hard to think of the man inside as human, someone who needed to be kept in a cage. This was the ugly secret that mankind kept from society. And this was the person he was supposed to cure.

"Well?" Alex prompted.

"It's impossible to say, with how sedated he is. He's still exhibiting paranoid delusions. He seemed to remember me, but I don't know what he was referring to about my hands. He's a lot calmer, that's for sure."

"I'll have him taken off his medication. It should take a few days to completely clear his system. Then we'll begin the new treatment. Remember—"

"I know. Trust me. I won't say a word."

"Good." Alex pocketed the keys and began to walk past her. She halted him with a hand on his arm.

"So, this new medicine. I mean, what kind of results can we expect?"

Alex frowned while he considered the question. "It'll return him to his former self. The million-dollar question is, what kind of man will emerge?"

CHAPTER THIRTY-THREE

They say time speeds up as we grow older. For Alex, that statement had never felt more true. It felt like he was operating on fast forward – the events of each day whizzing by in a blur. It seemed like just yesterday that he was prepping his test kit for the final Philax trial, and digging a grave for Rachel's dog.

And now, with the news of his sudden ascent to Chief Medical Director, and the new responsibilities resulting from the pending promotion, he hadn't had a moment to reflect back on his brother's death. In fact, it felt like it hadn't even happened. Like time was spinning so fast it had blown right past the event and left it behind in a plume of dust.

What the hell had happened to Jerry? He hadn't heard anything from the police. Rachel was absolutely convinced that it was the orderly Devon who had murdered him. And the fact that Devon and Jerry had had an altercation seemed to provide credence to her claim. But still. Alex had seen Devon on his way out of the hospital. Had run into him while the attack was taking place. It didn't make any sense.

And it left him undecided about what he should do. Should he come forward with this information? Should he contradict his wife's testimony? In essence, call her a liar, or simply confused?

Somebody had killed Jerry, that much was clear. And Rachel had witnessed the event. It must have been someone who looked like Devon, but...

And what about her claim that Popeye was there? Not a dog that resembled Popeye, but the actual dog itself. She had since backed away from her belief that the dog at the apartment had been her former pet. She understood how impossible that would be. But it showed how confused she had been at the time. Alex knew how the mind played tricks during moments of extreme stress. Many personality disorders were a direct result of some traumatic event. It was the mind's defense mechanism. It created delusions to protect itself from the horrors of reality.

He also hadn't had a chance to reconcile his thoughts on his interactions with his parents. His father, in particular. They hadn't exchanged more than five words to each other at the funeral, which Alex had splurged on to avoid further criticism. Money he could hardly afford to spend. But his promotion to Chief Medical Director would fix all that. And the development of his drug, which had been all but green-lighted, would bring about the kind of wealth that would make his recent woes a distant memory.

Not that any of that would matter much to his father. Alex wasn't sure what would. It was like the man had never given him a chance. Like he had a limited amount of love and had spent it all on Jerry, exhausting his supply. If only he could make his father see how much he had loved Jerry as well. That, alone, could provide a bond on which to build. If only he could have seen Jerry while he was on the medicine. Perhaps if Alex could have given his father his favorite son back, then he could have finally found acceptance. Now, he didn't see what he could possibly do to achieve the acceptance he so desired. It was best to just move on.

He was passing by the recreation room on his way back to his office when he heard music playing. It sounded like a guitar. He stopped and cocked his head, listening. Yes, he could distinctly hear the strumming of guitar strings. He hadn't heard anything about anyone hiring a performer. He followed his ears to the source of the sound.

There were half a dozen patients forming a semicircle around someone sitting. They were hooting and clapping their hands, twirling and dancing erratically. And they were smiling, smiling and singing the wrong words to a song that none of them knew.

Alex stormed forward to see who was playing the guitar. It was a bipolar patient, Randall. He had been in and out of the facility since late adolescence. Like Crosby, demons were his downfall. When in a severely depressed state, he saw them in otherwise ordinary people. When he was manic, though, he claimed to see angels. So Alex figured it all balanced out. It was curious how evil archetypes were such consistent memes for the mentally ill. Why did schizophrenics so rarely believe in a conspiracy to make the world a better place?

Alex had never heard the song before. He figured it was an original. The tune was a discordant combination of chords that seemed out of sequence. But there was some offbeat energy to the melody that he had never quite heard before, and it was sending the patients into an ecstatic frenzy. *This is why patients aren't allowed to own instruments,* Alex thought.

"Hey, hey, what's going on here?" Alex said, circumventing the semicircle of patients and stepping in between Randall and them. They kept dancing as though they hadn't heard him. Randall kept playing, singing in a melodic voice, with his head tilted back and his eyes squeezed shut. Alex reached out and grabbed the neck of the guitar, silencing the strings.

"Hey!" Alex yelled to get their attention.

They stopped, startled. One of the women, a patient named Carla who had attempted suicide nearly ten times, began to shake and started crying. "Don't do that," she said, sobbing. "Ohhhhh no no no no no! Don't doooo that!" She clenched her fists and stomped up and down.

An orderly came from across the room and consoled her. The other patients stood petrified in place.

Alex turned back to Randall. He was staring, as though horrified, at the hand holding the neck of the guitar. Alex began pulling the guitar, but Randall wrapped both arms around its body and clamped down.

"No!" he yelled. "It's not yours! It's mine!"

"Where did you get this?" Alex said, grabbing the neck of the guitar with both hands and pulling harder.

"I gave it to him," Alex heard a voice from behind him say. He turned to look. It was Eli. He let go of the guitar.

Eli walked forward. "What's the problem?"

"I wasn't aware that we had authorized personal possession of musical instruments," Alex said, fighting to control his voice.

"Well, I've decided to make an exception in Randall's case. He's a talented musician, and it would be detrimental to deprive him of this outlet. The other patients appear to enjoy his playing as well."

All eyes turned to Alex. He felt put on the spot. He hadn't made the rules, why should he feel guilty for enforcing them? He attempted a disarming smile. His lips began to squirm. "I'm not questioning his ability, Dr. Alpert. It's simply a matter of hospital policy." He emphasized the point through his eyes, but Eli ignored it.

"Alex," Eli said, smiling and shaking his head. There was a curious sheen to his eyes. He came a few steps closer. "You know that we never put policy before our patients' well-being. That guitar is a greater form of therapy in Randall's case than anything else we have to offer. He's an artist; that's his purpose, his ethos. There is no pharmaceutical substitute for that, I'm afraid."

Randall began to strum the guitar again, playing a slow ballad as a backdrop to the doctors' back-and-forth.

Alex felt a strong urge to grab the guitar and smash it against the floor. He snapped his head in Randall's direction. "Stop playing that fucking thing right fucking now," he hissed through clenched teeth.

Randall stopped immediately. His eyes flashed wide and his knees began to quake. "Sorry, d–d–d–doctor," he stuttered. Tears welled up in his eyes. "Here." He held the guitar out for Alex to take.

"Why? Why? Why?" Carla began crying again. "That's good music. Good music!"

Alex felt like the attention falling on him carried a physical weight, something that needed to be resisted. He noticed Randall nudging his hand with the head of the guitar, and ignored it, taking a deep breath. It failed to calm him.

"I'm not trying to deprive a patient of their purpose in life, Eli." The words were bypassing an emotional filter that was temporarily out of order, causing his voice to rise. "But policies are in place for a reason, and I think we're setting a dangerous precedent by making an exception."

"I–I–I didn't m–m–mean to do nothing w–wrong," Randall said. His whole body was now shaking. He had begun to sweat. "I'm not l–l–looking to c–cause any problems. I just won't p–p–play anymore." He dropped the guitar to the ground where it produced a hollow gong. He hid his face in his hands and leaned forward.

"No, it's okay, Randall. I said you could have it. This is a misunderstanding. You've done nothing wrong," Eli said. He stepped forward and was bending down to pick up the guitar when Alex stepped in front of him.

"Perhaps we should talk about this in private," Alex said in a low voice.

"No, this situation needs to be diffused now," Eli said. "The guitar was meant as a form of therapy, not to incite trauma. These situations should be handled more delicately, Alex."

Alex stood his ground. "Okay, sure. Why doesn't everyone get a musical instrument, then? Let's start a goddamn band, why don't we!"

The sarcasm was lost on the patients. They began to stomp their feet and cheer as if starting a do-si-do. One of them, a middle-aged man wearing a coffee-stained undershirt and a pair of baby-blue slippers, reached down and grabbed the guitar off the ground.

"Well, since my baby left me!" he wailed, strumming the guitar discordantly and gyrating his hips. "I've found a new living hell! Down at the door of Insanity Street, in Sugar Hill Hotel!"

The patients began to dance and shout, flinging their arms and kicking their feet. Alex was knocked off balance when a patient backed into him after an overly exuberant pelvic thrust.

Alex placed two fingers in his mouth and issued a piercing whistle. He caught the attention of a group of orderlies and waved them over.

The patients had formed a mini mosh pit. They were colliding into each other in an ecstatic frenzy to the world's worst parody of "Heartbreak Hotel."

Alex grabbed Eli by the arm and pulled him free from the mayhem as the orderlies moved in to establish order. "What do you think you're doing?" Alex said, digging his fingers into Eli's arm.

Eli didn't react to his arm being squeezed. He seemed detached as he watched the patients being detained. He barely blinked as a few were forced to the ground and began to howl in frustration and pain. He turned and looked at Alex with a face devoid of emotion. "I'm trying to help." His eyes were distant and glazed. "That's all. I'm just trying to help."

"This is why we have policies! To avoid situations like this! You know better, Eli. This is why..." *You're getting fired, you idealistic fuck!* "...we can't make exceptions to the rules."

Alex could feel his hand cramping as it gripped Eli's arm. He was shaking it to emphasize each point. Eli hardly seemed to notice. His attention was elsewhere. Alex released his arm and followed Eli's eyes until they reached Randall, still hiding his face, still hunched over in his chair.

"He was so happy before," Eli said. "They all were." He looked at the other patients, now lying face down on the floor.

He faced Alex again. "No." His eyes regained focus, narrowing. His expression hardened. "No, this has nothing to do with the rules. It has to do with the proper treatment of patients. This is not a prison, it's a hospital. These are people, not inmates. There is no reason why they should not be allowed to pursue things that bring them joy.

"This was not brought on by the guitar; it was brought on by a need to establish power and control. These are not your children, Alex. They are adults with the same inalienable rights to pursue happiness as anyone else."

Alex rose up onto his toes and leaned forward. "Sure, except that when these particular adults don't get their way or become overly excited, Eli, people end up in the hospital. Or worse. Your desire to treat them with compassion has passed over into reckless naivety." He looked over Eli's shoulder and saw Angela striding forward. He motioned towards her with his chin. "Not without consequences, either."

Eli turned and watched Angela approach. He winced at the purple knuckle prints that blemished her beautiful face. Her throat mottled with angry streaks of red.

"What happened?" Angela said as she drew closer.

Alex looked to Eli, staring expectantly. The sounds of struggle had died down to a combination of tittering laughter and Carla's sniffling sobs. The patient who had impersonated Elvis Presley had a nosebleed and was catching the blood with his tongue while an orderly restrained his arms.

"What happened?" Eli repeated Angela's question, almost as though asking himself.

Eli watched as Randall was pulled up from the chair. Frightened, Randall resisted, a fifty-year-old face with the eyes of a child. Two orderlies wrestled him to the ground. The impact knocked his dentures loose; they hung crookedly from his mouth, like some costume prop. He was crying and struggling to breathe with a knee digging into his back.

"Randall was playing his guitar," Eli said, still watching the struggle unfold. His voice was monotone. "That's all. Just playing a guitar. I gave it to him. It soothes him. It's the one thing he understands."

The orderly grabbed Randall by his elbows and hauled him to his feet. He looked up and saw Eli staring at him. He opened his mouth to speak and his dentures fell out and clattered to the ground, the right-front tooth popping loose when it landed.

"No!" Randall yelled through his rubbery lips. "My neeet!"

The orderly allowed him to pick them up from the floor. He cradled them in his hands, crying as he was ushered back to his room.

"I didn't think instruments were allowed," Angela said.

"They're not. This is why," Alex said.

"That's not true," Eli said.

"Excuse me?" Alex squinted his eyes and cocked his head.

"The patients were behaving peacefully before you intervened in an aggressive manner. That's what ignited the situation."

"There wouldn't have been a situation had you not ignored hospital policy!"

"Policy," Eli said with a hint of disdain. "We are not here to enforce policies established by people who don't know the first thing about mental care. We are here to create the most conducive environment for the restoration of mental well-being. Policy is nothing more than an excuse to establish power and control. Power and control breed abuse. They trample compassion. They wilt the spirit. They imprison the soul. What policy lacks is nuance. It's painting Mona Lisa's smile with a spray gun."

"What the fuck does that have to do with a goddamn guitar, Eli?" Alex said, looking to Angela for support.

She shook her head and shrugged.

Eli sighed. "If you came upon a man peacefully playing a guitar for a group of people who all appeared to be enjoying it, would you step in and break it up?"

"What? That's not a fair comparison."

"Why not?"

Alex chuffed. "Because outside these walls it's allowed; inside it's not."

"They're just walls, Alex. Inside, outside, it's all the same. These are not a different breed of people. They just have different problems."

Alex lowered his head and waved his hand. "I'm sorry, Eli, but you've taken this too far. I don't have time to explain to you the problems with ignoring the rules of a psychiatric ward. I would have thought you would have had some sense knocked into you the other week, but apparently not. Perhaps the board will be able to make you see your mistakes more clearly."

There was a pause within which an electrical current formed.

Angela studied her feet.

"You're out of line," Eli said.

"We'll see who's out of line," Alex said.

The expression of shock and confusion on Eli's face was hard to behold, but Alex held firm. Eli had created this mess; it was why he was being replaced. And Alex had more on his mind than worrying about another grown man's feelings. Even if it was the man he had always looked up to as a mentor.

"What's that supposed to mean?"

"Don't make me spell it out for you, Eli. Open your eyes, already. You think you can keep causing hospital riots without some repercussions?"

Alex didn't wait for a response. He turned and stormed away.

★ ★ ★

Angela remained in place, tapping her foot. She wished she hadn't intruded. She flicked her hair back and offered Eli a sympathetic expression. It quickly turned to concern.

His face had paled. He looked lost and confused. In a matter of minutes he had aged thirty years and no longer projected the authoritative image of his profession. He now more closely resembled a patient.

"I don't get it," Eli said, turning his sunken eyes towards Angela, frowning at the sight of her damaged face. "All I want to do is help people. But everyone just winds up getting hurt."

Angela stared back in silence. While she was hurt, she wasn't in pain. The Percocets had taken that away, and left her with nothing to say.

CHAPTER THIRTY-FOUR

It took four days for the antipsychotics to clear Crosby's system. Alex didn't prescribe any other medications to moderate the withdrawals. He wanted Crosby free from all pharmaceuticals as quickly as possible in order to begin testing the new formula.

He had instructed the orderlies overseeing the solitary wing to minimize their contact with Crosby while the drugs were leaving his system. They didn't need much incentive to comply. Crosby had become hostile by the end of the second day when the sedative effects of his antipsychotics had stopped working. He had to be confined to a restraining chair by the dawn of day three.

It had taken six strong men to pin Crosby to the chair and clamp down the restraining straps. Fueled by extreme paranoid delusions, Crosby's strength was superhuman. He was convinced that he was being imprisoned by a cabal of demonic entities disguised in human form and that his survival depended on escaping. Due to his state of heightened aggression, the orderlies had issued a request to sedate Crosby before restraining him, which Alex had denied. Now one of the orderlies had required stitches to sew an ear back to his head and another was at risk of losing an eye.

The guard on duty glowered at Alex as he signed the entry form. "Damn creep can stay in that chair the rest of his life, for all I care. I ain't getting him out."

"Don't worry. You won't have to." Alex shifted the medicine kit back to his right hand. It looked heavier than it was, its contents consisting of sanitizing liquid, gauze, several vials of his experimental formula and a stainless-steel needle seven inches long. "Crosby won't be harming anyone again. I can assure you of that."

"Too late for Kelvin and Jessie, I guess."

The thin smile Alex offered lacked any semblance of sincerity. "I'll have Crosby apologize in person as soon as he gets well." He turned and started down the hall towards the row of solitary cells.

The scanning equipment was already waiting for him outside Crosby's cell. Given the board's endorsement, he no longer needed to operate under complete secrecy. And Eli had all but walled himself up in his office since their confrontation a few days before. It seemed he'd gotten the not-so-subtle hint after all.

The hallway housing solitary row was silent. It was eerie to be among such disturbed people and not hear a sound. *It's like a dungeon down here,* Alex thought, rubbing his arms to ward off the cold. It felt twenty degrees cooler surrounded by these dark concrete walls.

He checked the equipment, testing the straps and turning on the scanner. It beeped with a steady, rhythmic consistency like a metronome, in contrast to the stampeding beat of his racing heart.

There was a strong sense of expectation associated with the moment. Like his life had all been in preparation for this. Like every decision he had ever made had served to pave the path leading to this place and time. And any slight deviation, any alternate decision, no matter how small, would have shifted his trajectory in a different direction. But it had not. It had led him here. And in this moment, Alex felt a disorienting sense of predestination, a superstitious premonition which he quickly cast aside.

Fortune favors the bold, he thought, smiling, then inserted the key into the lock and opened Crosby's door.

The chair was facing the doorway. In it, Crosby sat upright, strapped to the chair with thick restraining bands wrapped around his legs, torso, arms, chin, mouth and forehead. His head and body were completely immobilized, but his face contorted into a baleful rage when Alex entered the room. He began to buck against the seat with what little force he could muster.

"Relax," Alex said.

A single step brought him to the cot against the far wall, where he placed his medical kit. Calmly, he walked back to the hallway and returned with the scanning equipment, rolling it next to Crosby's chair. He turned and shut the door. It clanged when it closed. After the echo faded, the room fell quiet, save for the muted snuffling of Crosby's futile struggles against his restraints.

"I know what you think," Alex said, watching Crosby dispassionately. "I know what you see, rather. Instead of seeing me as I really am, a doctor who is here to help you, you see a demon who is here to harm you." Alex eased open the medical kit and withdrew his supplies, laying each of them on a piece of cloth that he placed atop the cot. "I know there is nothing I can say to convince you otherwise. That is the nature of your illness." He moved over to the monitoring equipment and began to connect the scanning sensors to Crosby's head.

Crosby watched his movements through eyes that were wide and glistening.

"All I can do is administer medicine designed to alleviate your symptoms so that you can see the truth for yourself."

He walked back to the cot and began to prep the needle, filling it with his refined formula. The one that had set Jerry free.

One cc. Two ccs. Three ccs. This was as large a dose as Philax would allow.

He began to withdraw the needle from the vial, then stopped, thinking. There was no executive looking over his shoulder now. He paused then pushed the needle back in until it clicked against the bottom of the glass vial and pulled the plunger once again.

Four ccs. Five ccs. The liquid kept climbing up the lines.

He watched as the last bit of solution was sucked up into the syringe, and then flicked it with a finger and pressed the plunger slightly to dispel any air bubbles. With the chamber filled, the plunger was so long he almost had to operate it with two hands.

He approached Crosby, angling the beveled end of the needle towards the inside of his right eye.

Beads of sweat burst to the surface of Crosby's skin. His face began to tremble, his jittery eyes opened wide. The electronic beep tracking his pulse produced a frenetic beat.

Alex stared into Crosby's manic eyes, observing the mixture of hatred and fear. "Take one last look at your demons," he said, placing the needle tip against Crosby's tear duct. "And tell them goodbye." He pushed the needle through.

CHAPTER THIRTY-FIVE

Crosby had no idea where he was. He hardly knew who he was, for that matter. There was a slight itching sensation in the corner of his eye and when he went to rub it he realized that he couldn't lift his arm. He tried to look down but was unable to lower his head. He cast his eyes downward and saw that he was restrained. *Strange*.

Then he noticed a man standing before him, scrutinizing him with extreme interest. The man looked vaguely familiar, but he couldn't identify from where. He was clearly a doctor of some kind, but this looked nothing like a hospital room. It looked more like a prison cell. He opened his mouth to speak, but it was obstructed in some way. *What the fuck is going on?*

The man before him smiled. He began to nod his head. He appeared immensely satisfied with something. Was this some kind of sadistic killer? Had he been abducted and brought to some sort of torture chamber?

An image shot into his mind, as clear as any photograph. The image was that of the man standing before him, but he was bent over and looking at his face reflected back in a puddle of blood expanding out from the belly of a mutilated dog. It was as though he was peering out through the man's own eyes, observing a memory.

Then the image changed and he was looking out through the same set of eyes onto another face with features similar to those of this mysterious doctor *(murderer?)*, although not quite the same. The other face was bluish gray, as though drained of blood, with a raw gash running across its gaping neck. A dead man's face. Someone freshly slaughtered. He blinked and the image disappeared.

"Welcome back," the man said. "You're doing great so far. Everything looks perfect. How do you feel?"

Crosby mumbled. He was confused. The man seemed sincerely concerned with his well-being, but was clearly some deranged killer based on the images he'd just seen. What was going on?

"Sorry." The man chuckled. "Don't suppose you can say much with that strap around your mouth. Here…" The man reached down and removed it. "How's that?"

Crosby didn't know what to say. He racked his brain for its most recent memory and came up blank. What had he been doing before this? How had he gotten here?

Another sequence of still frames shot across his mind's eye. Long needles stabbing into eyeballs, a large black man wielding a bloodstained knife, a bleary-eyed father figure crying over a glass of whiskey. He knew he should feel fear, but he didn't. Instead, he felt a deep sense of confusion, inadequacy and shame. He felt guilt, but for what he could not say.

"Where am I?"

The doctor/killer leaned forward and checked his eyes, lifting each lid to get a better look. He squinted and frowned. "Are you feeling any pain?"

Aside from the slight itch in the corner of his eye, he wasn't. He tried to shake his head, but couldn't.

"That's good. You've got a bit of dilation occurring in your eyes, but that's normal. Just take it easy and you should start to feel better soon."

He closed his eyes and breathed deeply. The air smelled of urine and mildew. It smelled like…

Mother, he wanted to say. But that didn't make sense. Why would he associate such a smell with his mom?

Hands began to choke him, thin, bony hands hard as stone, cutting off his air. He gurgled as the hands shifted to the back of his neck and thrust his face forward, pressing it into thick shag carpeting reeking of neglect as something thick and rigid entered him from behind, tearing his rectum wide.

He shuddered and opened his mouth to cry out, but the sensation disappeared. He gasped for breath. "What the fuck?" he said.

He was still in the room. He was fine.

"Settle down. You may be experiencing some initial discomfort from the onset of the medication, but it will dissipate shortly."

"Where am I?" he said again.

"You're in the forensics ward of Sugar Hill Hospital."

The name meant nothing to him so he scrunched his face in confusion.

"It's a mental health facility," the man continued. "You're being treated for schizophrenia. Can you recall your name for me?"

Schizophrenic? No. That meant he was crazy, and that couldn't be. *My name?* "My name is…"

"Crosby, you worthless piece of shit! You filthy little come dumpster! You crazy freak! When are you going to start pulling your own weight?"

He scanned the room for the source of the voice. It sounded like it was coming from directly behind him. It was the voice of…

The memories began to seep back into his brain, slowly at first, then with explosive force. The streets, the dirty motel rooms, the men, her hands clawing at his sensitive skin. The men. The men.

"You've got to pull your own weight, you worthless little shit! I don't care how much they come in you! We need to eat!"

Crosby felt a great pressure building in his chest, a burning in the center of his face, a buzzing in the middle of his brain. It felt like his insides had been set on fire, that they were boiling towards some volcanic release, and he began to cry – great wallowing wails – as realization set in and he remembered who he was, why he was here, what he had done, where he had come from.

"My name's Crosby," he blubbered between hyperbolic breaths, snot streaming over the ridge of his upper lip. "And I remember. Oh god. I remember who I am."

The man began to pack up his medical kit, giving Crosby space to cry. He returned and squatted down in front of him so that he was at eye level. He placed a hand on Crosby's knee and squeezed.

"Welcome back, Crosby," the man said. His face became gaunt and flickered pale blue for a second – a jagged line was slashed across his throat – then it faded and he was smiling like he had just won a prize at the county fair. "Now your real therapy can begin."

CHAPTER THIRTY-SIX

Alex had sweated through his second shirt, but not from the humid summer heat. He had been in his air-conditioned office most of the morning, preparing for the arrival of Bob Bearman and the rest of the board members for their biannual review meeting. In less than an hour he would be forced to face Eli, whom he had hardly spoken with since their confrontation over Randall's guitar. He knew that Eli had already been informed of his pending dismissal, and that Alex was to assume the role of Chief Medical Director in his place. Apparently, it hadn't gone over well. Alex hadn't expected that it would. And now that it had already happened, he saw all the things he wished he could have done differently.

Eli deserved better. Especially from him.

There was nothing to do now, however, but press forward. He had wanted to talk with Eli one-on-one before the board meeting, before the change was officially announced, but he had been too busy overseeing Crosby's recovery, which by all accounts was phenomenal.

He knew that his career may well have hinged on how Crosby reacted to his formula, and he couldn't have asked for a better outcome. All the delusional symptoms of schizophrenia had dissipated. What remained was a man with a history of major trauma who was now coherent and able to confront the psychological damage inflicted upon him during childhood. The schizophrenia had been a defense mechanism to dissociate himself from the child being traumatized – a way for him to deflect the pain by externalizing it and assigning responsibility to others. It was no wonder he saw shadow demons in regular people. It was a way for him to excuse the actions of his mother.

Now, however, he saw through the illusions created by his psychosis and accepted his situation for what it was. Without his mental defense mechanism, he could begin the healing process. It was sure to be a major breakthrough in the field of psychiatry. It was everything Bearman had hoped for. And it had all been conducted behind Eli's back. But the board meeting would be more like a direct slap across his face.

Alex reached over his shoulder and tried to peel the soaked shirt away from his sweaty back, but it was plastered down. He sighed, wishing he had brought a spare.

Bearman had met with Crosby personally a couple of days before and had deemed him fit for release from solitary confinement, not that it was his call to make. He had then instructed Alex to have him brought into the board meeting. Alex had discouraged the idea. Crosby's condition, while drastically improved, was precarious. It was not the nearly overnight transformation that had taken place with Jerry. Crosby had more extreme emotional scars that he was just beginning to work through. It was not the time to begin parading him in front of others as an example of psychiatric success. Bearman had reluctantly agreed, but Alex was skeptical.

Someone knocked on his door.

Alex lifted his arm and scowled at the large sweat stain under his armpit, then clamped his arms down next to his sides. "Come in," he said.

The door opened and Angela stuck her head through. "You got a sec?"

Alex began to raise his arm to wave her in, then caught himself and nodded his head.

"Okay, so I'm completely freaking out," Angela said, although her beaming smile suggested otherwise. She sat down on the opposite side of Alex's desk. "What do you think he's going to do?"

For a second, Alex thought she was referring to Crosby and his heart began to stutter. "Who? Eli?"

"Right...like you're not thinking the same thing. Have you talked to him yet?"

Alex looked at his lap and shook his head. "Haven't had time. Been too tied up with Crosby."

"God, this is going to be so weird." Angela's sparkling eyes suggested that she meant exciting.

Alex bent forward. Her phony tone had touched a nerve. "Give me a break. Don't act like you couldn't see this coming. He refuses to embrace the precepts of contemporary psychiatry, he refutes modern medicine, he was hospitalized for a riot that happened while on his watch. As were you, by the way. And one of the orderlies has been arrested for murder. For fucking *murder*. Of my fucking *brother*." He somehow refrained from screaming. But his face was on fire, and his heart was fighting to burst free from his chest. "Let's not act like it's beyond comprehension that the board felt it necessary to make a move. If Eli's upset, that's fine, but it shouldn't be with me. The man did it to himself."

Angela raised her hands in surrender, but she still couldn't wipe the smirk from her face. "Hey, I totally agree. I'm just saying, it's going to be weird. I don't understand why it has to be made into some spectacle during the meeting. He should just be allowed to leave with his dignity. Especially after all he's done for this place."

"Jesus, Angela. You think I have anything to do with this? I don't. I don't agree with how it's being handled, any more than you do, but what do you want me to do about it? Turn down the promotion? Say that they're being unfair? That a man who seems to be slipping in the twilight of his career should be given another chance while I wait patiently in the wings?" He clasped his hands together and squeezed to quell the tremor that was threatening to take hold. "Besides, what does this have to do with you? All you have to do is sit on the sidelines and enjoy the show."

Finally, Angela forced herself to appear sufficiently cowed. "Look, I'm sorry. I didn't mean to set you off like this. I'm just full of nerves. You're right. You haven't done anything wrong."

Alex felt like he was close to breaking his fingers, so he relaxed his hands. He glanced at Angela and noticed that her face still bore light-brown bruise marks from Crosby's fists.

"It's fine. I'm just ready to get it over with." He gave her a sheepish grin. "And I must admit I've got a case of the nerves too."

"Yeah, right."

Alex lifted his arms. They were drenched underneath.

Angela cupped her hands over her mouth to stifle a laugh. It muffled her voice. "That looks like me after hot yoga."

"I have no idea what that is, but if it results in this, it can't be fun."

His phone rang and he answered it, speaking briefly and nodding his head. He hung up the receiver, pulled his suit jacket from the coat hanger and put it on. "Showtime," he said.

"They're here?" Her smile returned.

"They're here."

She stood and straightened her black suit pants and checked her shoes.

Alex came around the desk and placed his hand against her lower back, pushing harder than intended as he ushered her towards the door.

"Let's get this over with," he said as they exited the office. The door slammed closed behind.

CHAPTER THIRTY-SEVEN

Alex could hear Bearman's booming laughter echoing down the hallway. It didn't matter how many times Eli had told him that strange voices and loud noises disturbed the patients, he always preferred to make his presence known. And he became visibly angry when, inevitably, he encountered a patient who had become agitated by his boisterous behavior. He viewed it as a sign of ineptitude on the part of the hospital staff.

Up ahead was the door to Eli's office. Angela and Alex exchanged a glance. They both quickened their steps as they scurried past. Angela looked in while Alex kept his head down.

"He's not in there," Angela informed him. "Maybe he's not coming."

"Not a chance. He's got too much pride. He'll be there."

And he was. But he was not sitting in his customary place of prominence in the middle of the long, U-shaped conference table. Instead, he had picked the more discreet spot where Alex normally sat off to the side. He was the only one in the room. The door clanged when it closed behind them and Eli looked their way.

"Eli!" Angela shouted exuberantly, as if being reunited with a long-lost friend. She hop-skipped on quick, nervous feet over to where he sat and embraced him from behind.

"Nice to see you too, Angela," he said, patting her arm. The heft of his hand felt soft, insubstantial, like a baby bird, and his clothes hung loose from his gaunt body. His attempt at a smile seemed to strain him and leave him short of breath.

"Mind if I join you?" Angela said.

"Sure, be my guest." He tried to pull the seat out for her, but it hardly moved an inch.

She helped him scoot it away from the table and sat down.

Alex was still deciding where to sit when he heard Bearman's booming voice approaching the door behind him. It burst open and he walked through, accompanied by Steve Price and the only female on the board, Linda Sykes. She was a tall, slender lady in her early sixties with an absurd wig of wavy, blonde hair that sat perched above a tight, shiny face that had been lifted twice and tucked. Her stretched lips looked as though they were constantly smiling, but Alex had never met her in a pleasant mood. It was as if she thought the only way to project importance was by pointing out others' flaws.

Bearman nearly bumped into Alex as he barreled through the door. He gargled the eternal deposit of phlegm in his throat and stuck out his hand. "There he is," he said, gripping Alex's hand and pumping it as if cracking a whip, "the man himself."

Alex began to reply, but Bearman pushed past him and started towards the table. Eli and Angela both stood.

"Eli," Bearman said, "I'm not sure they should have let you out of the hospital. Good lord, son. You look like shit."

Eli gripped his chair's headrest with white-knuckled hands. "You've always had a gift for pleasantries, Bob."

"Look, with the condition this hospital's in, I don't blame you. But we're going to get that straightened out, now, aren't we?"

Linda snickered, and Steve was quick to pipe in, "That's what we're here for." He patted Alex on the back as he walked past.

The conference room was the largest, most formal space in all of Sugar Hill. It could accommodate up to seventy-five people, but it had never held more than fifteen at a time. The table was positioned in the center of the room. The rest of the room was wasted space, resulting in poor acoustics and a sense of self-consciousness for each speaker. Except for Bearman, who seemed to love the way his voice filled the air.

Bearman walked to the apex of the table and took a seat, the squeaky chair bemoaning his weight. He slapped his large palms down on the tabletop as though proclaiming his territory. Steve and Linda sat on either side of him.

"This everybody?" he said, drumming his fingers while assessing the empty chairs. He stopped when he saw Alex still standing by the door. "Hell, son. You joining us or what?"

"Yes, of course. Where should I..." Alex hadn't meant to say the last part out loud. He knew it made him appear weak and indecisive. But his nerves were thrumming and the excessive sweating was making him dehydrated. In an attempt to overcompensate for his show of weakness, he walked straight to where Linda was sitting, to the right of Mr. Bearman, and asked her to scoot down.

"What? No," she said.

"Why the hell should she move? Just sit the hell down, already," Bearman said. He grumbled far back in his throat and his face turned a deep shade of red. "Christ almighty! Is this whole place filled with a bunch of loony tunes? If so, we may be in deeper shit than I thought."

Alex and Angela were the only two who offered a commiserative laugh. Eli looked like he was attempting to count the fibers in the carpet.

As Alex eased down into his chair, it occurred to him that Eli was the one who usually opened these meetings, often with a charismatic greeting that provided the perfect blend of professionalism and grace, establishing his position of authority and disarming Bearman and the rest of the board. In the space of a second, Alex realized how much preparation Eli must have put into making these meetings flow so effortlessly, and how little he himself had prepared.

Silence descended as everyone settled into their seats. It persisted for far too long.

They're waiting for me to say something, Alex decided, looking around, desperate for someone to break the silence. And then his own mouth sprang open against his will and began making noise.

"Okay then. Well, thank you all for coming. We've had—"

"Just what the hell are you doing?" Bearman interrupted. "This is my meeting, and we ain't your invited guests. You really are making me wonder if we've done the right thing, you know that?"

"Okay, go on then," Alex said, trying to act defiant, but the room devoured his voice.

Bearman scowled. He attempted to clear his throat. "Look, I'm just going to cut to the chase here."

Both Steve and Linda pursed their lips and began nodding their heads in earnest as if this were the most prudent decision ever made.

"And it ain't like this is going to come as a surprise for anyone here. The hospital's started to attract some negative attention that we frankly can't afford. If allowed to continue for too long, funding will be cut. This, I can assure you. If funding gets cut, it undermines our ability to properly care for our patients. The whole thing begins to unravel, and it ain't going to happen on my watch."

Both Alex and Eli were aware that Bearman's bonus was based on the hospital's operating margin but they kept it to themselves.

Bearman rubbed the bridge of his nose as though what he was about to say pained him. Instead, it just looked like he was stifling a sneeze. "Eli, I know we haven't always seen eye to eye, but you should be commended for the way you've run this hospital for as long as you have. And for many of those years you did a fine job. But these are different times. Medicine has made advancements, and, frankly, you've been slow to keep up. We—"

Eli straightened in his seat. A slight glimmer sparked in his dull eyes as he turned them towards Bearman. "Psychiatry has been making *'advancements'* for as long as I've been practicing medicine. We began with bloodletting and swiftly moved to lobotomy. There has yet to be a form of medical intervention that has demonstrated consistent effects across a broad range of patients, or that has provided sustainable improvements over a significant period of time. The more holistic protocols practiced at this hospital, however, have consistently delivered some of the country's highest recovery rates with the lowest percentages of relapse.

"I understand that you are determined to make a move, but I won't allow for the facts to be misrepresented."

Linda swiveled in her seat. It was impossible to read her expression through the placidity of her surgically flattened face. "Ha!" she cried out as a mockery to Eli's statement. It sounded like the mating call of some predatory bird. "The modern array of psychotropic therapies is a far cry from the barbaric days of lobotomies, Dr. Alpert. To even offer such a comparison is itself an admission of ignorance."

Steve Price chuffed and chimed in, "Seriously, how can you even compare the two? It's like saying aspirin is the same as using leeches to thin the blood."

Eli shook his head, a look of sad resignation on his face. "We use certain antipsychotic medications in our treatment of patients. It depends on the patient and is just one component of a holistic plan."

"You don't utilize them nearly enough. Not nearly as much as is advised. Not only by the standards of modern psychiatry, but by the members of this board, concerned constituents of the state and senior members of this hospital staff," Bearman said and then paused for effect, "Dr. Drexler included."

Alex blanched and averted his eyes, but Eli didn't flinch. "Based on what evidence?" Eli said. "These medications appear harmless because they come packaged in a pristine little pill that fits within our idea of what medicine should look like. But when you spend time with them, like I have, and observe their effects, like I have, you find that they often produce results that are indistinguishable from other, more archaic forms of therapy.

"You will find that they can turn people catatonic, void of emotion or personality. They can cause seizures and uncontrollable tremors. I have patients who claim that the side effects from their prescription medications are far worse than the mental illness that they're designed to fix."

"And these patients, with their extreme impairments, are to be trusted? Taken at their word?" Linda said.

"Yes," Eli said. "My god, these are people – daughters, artists, intelligent mothers and fathers – not a subspecies of human to be treated with suspicion and disrespect. They come here for help. To get better. To return to a life with meaning and purpose. They—"

"Okay, okay," Bearman said. "Clearly we all want what's best for these people." He smiled as he scanned the room, delighting in the supportive expressions of assent. Then his face turned stern. "Let me tell you what's not best for your patients, Doctor. Subjecting them to the dangers of a homicidal killer. Allowing hysteria to spin out of control and turn into a full-scale riot. Taunting violent and unstable schizophrenic patients with godforsaken football drills. That's not good for anyone. Not for you. Not for her..." he pointed towards Angela, whose face still bore the aftermath from her recent attack, "...and not for the reputation of this institution."

"In Dr. Alpert's defense," Angela said, "none of these incidents can be directly attributed to him. And while I'm not opposed to the use of antipsychotic medications, I would like to point out that they have contributed to thousands of deaths, which, by comparison to these outbursts, is the more serious offense."

"Says the lady with the battered face," said Linda.

Bearman stood up and raised his arms like a minister threatening his congregation with the wrath of God. "Look, enough of this talk about the merits of medicine." He lowered his arms and pressed his palms against the table, leaning forward, addressing some imaginary audience absent from the oversized room. "It does us no good to sit here and argue about the past. What matters is the future, and how we plan to push forward."

Again the room became a collection of bobbing heads.

Bearman raised himself upright, puffing up his chest and folding his arms across his protuberant belly. "Regardless of what you say, Eli, the best way to treat people with illnesses, mental or otherwise, is with medicine. I'm sorry that's not as plain and obvious to you as it should be."

Bearman paused to gargle phlegm, pressing a football-size fist against his mouth. He swallowed heavily and then continued. "Hell, if you have such a problem with modern medicine, why not try to make it better? You ever think of that?"

Eli opened his mouth to reply, but Bearman charged on.

"Well, your protégé has. It's not enough to keep patients comfortable, Eli. Our job is to cure them. And it looks like Dr. Drexler is the only one in this hospital who understands that. His discovery will not only revolutionize psychiatric therapy, it puts this hospital on the cutting edge of innovation. That's the position we want to be in moving forward, Eli. Not holding on to the past."

Eli looked at Bearman through glassy, uncomprehending eyes. "What discovery?"

"You mean you don't know?" Linda said, attempting to convey surprise without aid of expression. "You really have fallen out of touch."

Eli looked at Alex for the first time. "What's he talking about?"

Alex lowered his head and addressed the top of the table. "Well, I've been working with a compound. It moderates the release of select tryptamines through neurotransmitters and relieves schizophrenics of their symptoms. Completely relieves them." He raised his head and found Eli's eyes. "Cures them. We've vetted it through clinical trials. It works."

Eli kept his eyes locked on Alex. "You've discovered a cure for schizophrenia," he said, deadpan. "Who are these test patients? Where are the results? Wait..." Eli's eyes went wide. He cocked his head to the side. "Not Jerry?"

"No!" Alex jumped in his seat. "No, of course not. It's all been conducted in controlled environments under careful regulations." He grabbed the front of his shirt and pumped it to circulate air.

"We've seen the results, and they're nothing short of astonishing," Bearman said. "But I don't blame you for being skeptical. Even I was at first. I guess there's no substitute for seeing something firsthand."

Alex sucked in air. The cavernous room closed in until he felt crammed into his own body. *No*, he thought. *Don't!*

"Alex, bring your patient in here. Do us the honor of a demonstration."

"I don't think now's the time—"

Bearman pinned him with a look. "Excuse me? Did we not already go over this?"

"We did, and I said that Crosb...that the patient was still adjusting to the medication and may not be ready for a public evaluation."

"Who said anything about the fucking public?" Bearman motioned to the empty space surrounding the conference table. "I'm talking about an evaluation on the part of this hospital's most senior staff. Is there anyone here who's not qualified or permitted to assess a patient's condition?"

Eli stood. "I'm not sure what exactly is going on here, but I am one hundred percent opposed to subjecting a patient to any form of psychiatric evaluation in this setting. Absolutely not."

"I didn't ask you!" Bearman slammed his hand against the table with the force of a gavel strike. He paused and cleared his throat. "Besides, it's no longer your call."

Eli continued undeterred. "As long as I'm present at this hospital—"

"Dr. Drexler is now responsible for the—" Bearman began speaking over Eli, the two voices colliding in the vacant space of the oversized room. They continued to talk at the same time, their voices rising until Bearman clenched his fists and shouted "Dr. Drexler!" so loud it caused Linda to cup her ears.

Eli stopped and became silent.

Bearman quit yelling. He cleared his throat vociferously as he smoothed down his shirt, his face a dangerous shade of red. "Dr. Drexler," he said sternly, looking sidelong at Alex through glaring eyes.

"We have given you the explicit authority to dictate patient protocol. Perhaps this responsibility is too great for you. Your lack of spine implies that we should be looking for someone else."

Alex stood. At forty-five, he was a man full-grown, but felt like an acolyte preparing to offer counsel to elders. The science behind patient treatment had always been easy; this was a side to the business he had never seen. "Dr. Alpert," he said in a formal voice that sounded phony to his ears, "this isn't your call. You've made your point of view clear, and it has been rejected. It's time for you to step aside now and clear the way for us to move in a new direction."

Bearman beamed. "Well, I'll be. It looks like the boy has a pair after all. Now bring in your man and let's show Dr. Alpert what this new direction is all about."

Eli stood firm. "Alex, you said yourself that this isn't an appropriate setting. You need to establish firm guidelines and hold true to your convictions."

"That's it. I've had enough. Dr. Drexler, is this your call or not? Last chance."

Through the corner of his eye, Alex could see Eli looking at him. He knew better than to try and meet his gaze. Instead, he quickly scanned the rest of the room, taking in their nodding, affirmative faces and expectant stares. All except for Angela.

Her chin was tucked against her chest with her hair obscuring her face. Behind that curtain of hair, Alex was sure she was wearing a smile. The same mischievous smile she had shown in his office, in giddy anticipation of this very moment.

And he knew then that the only way to command the respect that he deserved was by showing the results from his formula. That the evidence would firmly substantiate his position as Eli's rightful heir, and earn him the authority to operate the hospital as he saw fit.

"No, the decision has been made. I'll bring the patient in."

CHAPTER THIRTY-EIGHT

When the door closed behind Crosby it clanged loudly, like it was made of heavy metal instead of flimsy wood. Alex halted for just a moment and cocked his head before ushering Crosby farther into the room. He brought Crosby to the front of the conference table, across from where Bearman sat, and motioned for him to stand still.

"So," he said, "many of you have met this man already. His name is Crosby Nelson. He was admitted into our forensics ward by way of the state after an incident where he attacked a group of citizens with a hunting knife. He was found not guilty due to his mental disorder." He turned to Crosby, looking for him to corroborate his story.

Crosby nodded for him to continue. There was something irregular about his eyes. The pupils appeared to be different sizes, one dilated, the other contracted.

Better make this quick, Alex thought.

"Crosby suffers from paranoid schizophrenia, which causes him to experience visual and auditory hallucinations stemming from delusional fantasies. When he first arrived at the hospital, he believed that he was complicit in a war between good and evil, between angels and demons."

Code blue in cell block one! Code blue in cell block one!

Alex stopped, startled. He'd just heard a loud voice calling out through an intercom speaker that sounded like it was right outside the room. "What was that?" he said.

Nobody answered.

"What was what?" Bearman asked.

Alex scanned the room, confused by the bored, oblivious expressions on the faces staring back at him. "That person on the intercom. Just now. Where did that come from?"

Bearman surveyed the room; everybody shrugged.

Alex shook his head and shuffled his feet. "Sorry," he said. "Where was I?"

Bearman sighed. "We're familiar with his condition, Doctor. Move on to the use of your medicine."

"Right." Alex opened his mouth to continue but paused, remaining stuck in that position. A rush of babbling voices and bustling bodies was now audible through the walls. It sounded like dozens of people were shuffling down the hallway just outside the conference-room door. He noticed that nobody else was reacting to the noise and fought to ignore it.

"The medicine. Yes. We...we placed Crosby on various levels of antipsychotic medications which controlled his symptoms, mostly through sedation, but were unable to...to..."

The sound of activity intensified – feet shuffling, chains clanging, doors closing, snippets of conversation. "Motherfucker better not try that shit on me!"

How could nobody else hear it?

"...to offset his delusional thinking and stop his hallucinations."

Alex began to sweat again. It was dripping down his sides and beading on his face. He wanted to wipe his forehead but was afraid to expose the underside of his arm.

"Hold on one second," he said, and then walked back towards the door and opened it. The hallway beyond was empty, but the sound of bustling activity grew even louder. It sounded like whatever he was hearing was right there in front of him. He turned back around. His face was turning white.

"My medicine...the medicine I'm working to develop, that is, works by—"

"That's enough, Doctor. I'm getting the sense you're not so good under pressure. You look like you're about to be sick. Why don't we just hear from the patient at this point." Bearman waved Alex out of the way. "Step forward, son."

Crosby stepped forward. His shadow stayed behind. It was the dark reflection of a much taller, more slender man. Its head was narrow and angular, its hands long, with thin, pointy fingers. It stalked forward with an exaggerated swinging of the arms as it followed behind Crosby, who shuffled with a more subtle gait.

Bearman pointed a fat finger at Crosby. "I first saw this man a few weeks ago. I can attest to the poor condition he was in at the time. While under Dr. Alpert's care, I might add. He was in solitary confinement, completely catatonic. Didn't even know I was in the room. He was disheveled, drooling on himself. He hardly represented the picture of health and self-reliance that Eli professes to produce under his protocol.

"I can tell you that the person who stands before you now is a completely changed man. The transformation is nothing short of miraculous. Tell us, son. How do you feel?"

Crosby's hands were shaking. He scratched his bald head, and cleared this throat. "I...uh...well, I feel...I feel quite a lot. More than I ever have before," he said. He offered a pinched smile and his chin dimpled as if he might cry.

Alex was not listening to the exchange. His attention was focused on Crosby's shadow, which was moving independently of his body, pacing back and forth behind Crosby's back, swinging its loping, elongated arms.

"Okay. Well, is that a good thing or a bad thing? 'Cause I got to tell you. You look a hell of a lot better than when I saw you drooling on yourself back in that solitary cell."

Crosby opened his mouth, but was preempted by Eli. "I'm sorry, I can't allow this to continue." He stood and walked around the table towards Crosby, placing his hands on his shoulders in a protective embrace. "This is not only unprofessional, and almost certainly detrimental to Crosby's improving condition, but it may be criminal as well. What is this medicine? Who approved it? And who authorized its use?"

"That's none of your concern, Dr. Pussyfoot! Whose side are you on anyway?"

Eli flinched. His mouth sprang open as he glared at Bearman, his head craning forward for a closer look.

Alex watched as the shadow figure approached Eli from behind. It bent forward as though whispering in his ear.

Eli's head swung around, and he looked confused. His roaming eyes fixed on Alex. "What did you say?"

Alex raised his hands. "Nothing." He could hardly hear his own voice over the commotion coming from outside.

Steve and Linda were both scrutinizing Bearman with shocked

expressions, surprised by the extent of his outburst. Even Bearman had a confused look on his face.

An uncomfortable silence pervaded the room.

Crosby broke it, his voice low and hesitant. "This is a fine charade. But, it ain't me you should be concerned with. I can look inside every one of you. There's darkness there. You don't see it, but you will soon."

He took a step forward, separating himself from Eli's faltering grasp.

The room grew dim, but not from a change in the brightness of the overhead lights. They had disappeared. The ceiling was lost in a vast darkness that appeared to have depth, as if the roof had been raised or removed.

"Dr. Drexler says that my sickness was a trick my brain played on itself to protect it from prior traumas." Crosby paused; he looked up into the descending gloom. "I'll admit it's all very clever. But it's not like that. I see that now. My so-called illness protected me, but not from prior traumas. It allowed me to see things that others can't see. It guarded me from dark forces. It protected me from people like you."

Bearman was inspecting the darkening room uneasily. His boisterous laugh reeked of false bravado. "Clearly the patient is still in the process of getting better, but I think we can all agree that the rate of progress is—"

A high-pitched, chittering laugh interrupted him. It came from the encroaching shadows surrounding the room. The walls were no longer visible.

"Who's turning down the goddamn lights?" Bearman's voice had the resonant echo of someone shouting in an empty cathedral.

The lights continued to dim. Yet the shape of the shadow figure became more distinct, as if it gained power from the dark. It was standing in place now, behind Crosby, its legs bent, its arms angled outward, its chest heaving as if it was panting.

"I see now that I am special. For my whole life I have been resistant to the evil of this world, despite its constant onslaught against me. From my own mother, even. But I suppose fighting back will not be tolerated. It landed me here, where my defenses have been stripped away, making me susceptible to evil forces."

Alex could now hear the heavy breathing of the shadow figure. It was a shallow rasp. Hungry.

"What's going on?" Linda nearly screeched as she struggled to stay calm. "Is there a power outage?"

The rasping grew louder.

"Okay. This is fucking weird," Angela said, offering a tittering laugh.

You knew it would be, Alex thought.

The darkness deepened.

Steve jumped from his seat and strode to the nearest light switch. He flipped it up and down, but nothing happened. He took a few steps and tried the door. The knob rattled in his hand. Locked.

"Evil is all around us. Before, I could keep it at bay. But you've taken my defenses from me. And forced me to let it in."

The shadow figure leapt back into Crosby's body as the last glimmer of light faded from the room, casting them in complete darkness.

Linda shrieked like the young woman she wished she still was. It choked off in a wet gurgle.

"And now you'll see where it lives inside each of you."

PART THREE
PURIFICATION
FLAMES

CHAPTER THIRTY-NINE

A dull ball of light pierced the darkness, shining down from above, falling away as Alex passed underneath. Only to be replaced by another that blinked on up ahead as Alex approached, casting a faint oasis of light that he entered. Otherwise, the hallway was completely dark.

Within this first halo of light, Alex merely noticed his shuffling feet moving him forward. He had no idea when he had begun walking or where he was going. An instant ago he had been in the conference room, listening to Crosby address the board. He had noticed Crosby's curious shadow, the lights had gone out, and then…

What the hell happened?

He passed through another cone of light and noticed two additional sets of legs striding on either side of his own. He now felt firm pressure on his arms and the cold constriction of handcuffs around his wrists. He looked to his left to see who was holding him, but he had moved beyond the light and could not see an inch in front of his eyes.

Then he entered another dim halo and the man's face came into view. It was square and compact with a flat nose and firm jaw covered with coarse stubble. The man was wearing a cotton cap with a curved brim pulled low over his wide brow. The cap cast shadows that gave him the appearance of a charcoal sketch. He had no neck.

Alex set his feet and pulled to a stop.

The squat man grunted and barely broke stride as he yanked him forward.

"Wait, hold on," Alex said. He tried to set his feet again and failed.

The men pulled so hard Alex almost fell.

"Stop!" he pleaded.

"Quit your fussing or we'll bring out the spark stick." This came from the man on the right. Alex waited for another flash of light — *How long is this hallway?* — to illuminate the man's face. It took four steps before the wan light washed over them again.

The other man was tall with such clean, smooth skin it looked wet. His jaw muscles bunched as he chewed a wad of gum the size of a robin's egg. He gave a quick finger tap to the cattle prod strapped to his waistband and winked.

"But..." Alex muttered, bewildered.

He was not much of a drinker — unlike his father — but he had overindulged a couple of times early in college. One night he had awoken from a blackout in the backseat of a friend's car, with no idea where he was or how he'd gotten there. The other passengers were looking at him and laughing as though he had been performing a stand-up routine. The experience was so alarming it had stopped him from drinking. This was the exact same feeling.

"Where are you taking me?"

The squat man on the left grunted again. Or perhaps it was a laugh. A light flashed, then darkness. They had been walking at a brisk pace for several minutes, but Alex had not seen anything other than the concrete floor under his feet.

"To your new home," said the man on the left. "It's not far."

In the next circle of light Alex registered their outfits. Police uniforms.

"What am I doing here?"

"You'll have plenty of time to ask yourself that," the tall man said. He turned and inspected Alex, showing more of his boyish face.

He looked familiar. Alex was certain that he'd seen him before.

"Greed, I'd say," the tall man said, and thrust his tongue through the skin of his gum and blew. He sucked the pink bubble back into his mouth. "What say you, Charlie?"

Charlie looked sidelong through a simian eye and grunted. "Vanity," he mumbled.

"Could be," the tall man said, chomping his gum. "Could be."

The hallway up ahead appeared brighter, the beams of light broader. Alex could now see more of the area around them. The walls were lined with prison cells. The shadowed outlines of men hung just beyond the steel bars. Occasionally, the ember of a cigarette would spark red and fade, or a set of fingers would appear and curl around a bar. He heard coughing, he heard shuffling. Otherwise, it was quiet.

"Ultimately, though, only you know why you did it." The man on the right blew another meager bubble, which deflated with a sigh.

"Did what?" Alex tensed. He tried to halt to a stop.

The tall man tsk-tsked and tugged on the cattle prod.

Alex stumbled on.

"Every one of 'em's innocent, eh, Charlie?"

Charlie's throat rumbled like distant thunder.

"Ah, here we are. Just up ahead," the tall man said. "Home, sweet home."

A man was standing beside a distant cell door, a ring of keys dangling from his hand. He was not outfitted like an officer. Instead, he wore an expensive-looking charcoal suit with a striped tie and shiny, black shoes. He was a big man, broad in the shoulders, wide in the belly, and his voice boomed as he issued a greeting while they approached. "Come on, boys! We've got a special spot reserved for our revered doctor, here. It's not quite as cozy as the old asylum accommodations, but it'll do fine for a fraudster such as yourself."

The man's face came into focus as they approached. Alex recognized him right away. "Mr. Bearman?" he said, tentative at first, then with more conviction. "Mr. Bearman, what the hell is going on here? What's happened?"

The big man looked confused. "What's with this guy? Y'all didn't crack his head, did you?"

The two guards waited for the big man to smile before responding. "Not yet, sir," the tall one said, chuckling. The squat one grunted.

"So, just who do you think I am?" The big man stepped forward until their noses were almost touching. Even this close, it was clear who the man was. There was no way he could be mistaken.

"I don't...I don't understand. We were just..." Alex closed his eyes and shook his head violently from side to side. The two guards tightened their grip. He was lightheaded when he opened his eyes, but Bearman was still standing right in front of his face. "I don't understand what's happening," Alex said.

"Looks like you've spent too much time in the loony bin," the big man said, then cleared his throat, rattling a wad of phlegm. "Well, it's too late to plead insanity, I'm afraid. Verdict's in, son. In the great State of Georgia, doctors aren't allowed to experiment on their patients in an effort to make a few bucks." He smiled and assumed a condescending tone. "It's a slight breach of ethics."

The big man turned and inserted a key into the lock on the cell door and swung it open. "But you'll have plenty of time to learn that now, won't you?"

The tall guard chuckled, shoved Alex through the opening and closed the door. "Let me see those hands."

Alex held them up to show that they were empty.

"No, genius. Through the slot there." He held up a key to the handcuffs.

Alex reached his hands through the slot and winced as the guard wrenched his wrists to gain access to the lock before pulling them off.

"There you go. Now go be a good neighbor and greet your cellmates. See what you all have in common."

The big man snorted then leaned back and laughed, holding his formidable gut.

The squat guard's shoulders shook, and his body quaked like seven points on the Richter scale, but he didn't make a sound.

Alex turned around. The cell was small. A single cot was on the left side of the room. Bunk beds were on the right. A metal toilet and sink were affixed to the far wall with a dented mirror covered in grime.

A large black man was lying on the single cot, facing the wall, and Alex could just see the shape of someone sleeping under a thin sheet on the top bunk. He shuffled towards the mirror above the sink, wanting – *needing* – to establish contact with himself. To stare into his own eyes and search them for sanity.

The face looking back at him was his own, but not the one now staring into the mirror. It was him, back in the boardroom where he'd just been, standing in the middle of the room with a catatonic look on his face. Eyes glazed and unblinking, mouth slightly ajar.

He gripped the sides of the sink basin, certain he was about to throw up. Then he heard a familiar voice address him from behind. "Well, I'll be damned. Doctor motherfucking Drexler. Just the man I been wanting to talk to."

Alex turned from the mirror, though the reflected image didn't move, and his heart began to hammer in his chest as soon as he saw the man now sitting up on the cot. It was the orderly from Sugar Hill. Devon. The one who had been charged with his brother's murder.

"Here I been sitting in this cell for weeks, serving time for a crime you know I didn't do." His white teeth gleamed as his mouth sheared back in a sinister smile. He pushed off the cot and stood. "You've got some explaining to do."

CHAPTER FORTY

Angela opened her mouth to scream and felt something placed inside it, nearly causing her to gag. A wafer, it seemed, tasteless and stale. It sat on Angela's tongue like a piece of Styrofoam. A chalice was tipped against her lips, and spoiled wine washed the wafer down her throat.

"From this, the Body of Christ." The wavering voice before her sounded caring and wise.

She opened her eyes, blinked, and nearly collapsed. "What the fuck is going on?" she said, taking a step back.

The row of women around her all sucked in air at once.

The noise startled her and she swiveled her head to both sides.

The women, approximately five on each side, were identical in appearance. Their young, beautiful faces featured pale, flawless skin with full, naturally pink lips. Their blonde, gossamer hair gleamed in the kaleidoscopic sunlight streaming through the stained-glass windows lining the walls overhead. Their shocked eyes were of the purest blue surrounded by the same pristine white as their flowing cloaks. The room was silent as though they had inhaled every sound.

"An ugly word spoken by an ugly girl," one of the girls said and averted her gaze.

Angela looked down and realized that she was the only one wearing black. She stood out like a stain.

"That's not necessary," the priest said. His old, wizened face peered out from beneath his hooded robe. He was weighed down by so many sacramental ornaments it looked like he could hardly stand. They tinkled as he shuffled forward, centimeters at a time, relying heavily on his shaking staff. "Let's leave Sister Drake alone."

"Pardon me, Father, but why must you always protect her? Does it not discourage her growth?" one of the sisters said.

Angela was shocked silent. Her mouthed gaped open, but she was unable to make a sound. What, was she dreaming? Had she passed out?

"We are all children of God. It is his will how and when we grow."

"Then it is our growth that suffers," another said. "As you are forced to spend more time with her than with anyone else."

"I provide attention to those who need it most."

One of the women clucked her tongue and stomped her foot. She turned towards Angela and said, "Why must you shame us, Sister? Why must you continue to shame yourself?"

The two rows of identical women turned as one to stare at her as well. They stood in the same position, they held the same expression. They even blinked their perfect blue eyes in unison.

"I don't...I don't...I don't know..." Angela stammered.

"Well, of course she doesn't. She never does," a sister said. "Ugly words from an ugly girl."

"Please, no more of that," the priest said. He waddled up next to Angela, placing a delicate hand on her arm. He was almost a full foot shorter than she was, his back frail and hunched over. He trembled like a baby bird. "Leave us for now."

The sisters all huffed and turned in the same direction, marching together towards the center aisle and the back exit of the cathedral.

"Come, child. What's troubling you?" the priest said when the women had left the room. His eyes were hidden behind bushy, gray brows that resembled storm clouds. His voice was a dying wind.

Angela began shaking harder than the priest's palsied hand. She scanned the cathedral, noting the ten-foot-tall, stained-glass windows featuring satanic figures glowering down. Below each one was the Greek word *Apokalypsis*. Where it had been bright and sunny just moments before, the light had grown dim.

"I don't know...where did... How did I get here?" she managed to say.

The priest's polite laughter was a wheezing cough. It appeared to pain him, although he maintained his determined smile. "No one understands the mystery of our calling, Sister, until our purpose manifests."

"That's not what I mean." Angela attempted to pull her arm free from the priest's gentle grasp, but he clamped down. His fingers dug painfully into her bicep, pinching a nerve against the bone.

He eased his grip as soon as her eyes registered pain. His face seemed to recede into the shadowed hollow of his hood. "It's not our place to question the Lord's motives," he said. She could no longer see his lips move, and his voice had become deeper, as though someone else's.

Angela spun in both directions, searching for some familiar sign, some familiar face. The priest's hand remained clamped to her arm. His grip as unyielding as granite.

She stopped squirming and turned to face him. All she could see were the faint whites of his eyes from the dark depths of his hood. "You need to help me," she said. "I'm very confused right now. I...I was just somewhere else. And now I'm here. And I don't know how I got here. And I don't know where *here* is. Something is wrong with me."

"Oh, dear." The old man caressed her arm. His wizened face reemerged from within the hood. "You're having another one of your spells, aren't you?"

"I...I don't know what you're talking about."

"Here, come with me." He turned her and began to guide her back towards the pulpit, past the table containing sacraments for communion. She gazed down into one of the gold offering plates and saw herself reflected back in its surface. Her face was blank, sightless eyes gazing out from her seat at the table next to Eli, who had the same lifeless expression.

Angela resisted and pulled her arm free. She began to back away. "Look, I just need to—"

The priest's hands shot out from his sleeves and grabbed her once again, this time by both arms; his fingers felt capable of crushing bone. "I sense a deep unease within you, Sister. That is the mark of corruption. Come, it's time for you to atone for your sins."

The priest forced Angela past the pulpit, guiding her towards a dark wooden door hidden behind it. She dug her feet into the ground but it did no good. The priest's deceptive strength kept propelling her forward.

"Dr. Alpert!" she screamed. "Dr. Drexler! Help!"

The priest's wheezing became a cackle. His gnarled hand left her arm for a brief moment to turn the knob and open the door, then she was thrust through, falling forward into the blackness beyond.

CHAPTER FORTY-ONE

The man lying on the table was going to die. There was nothing that could be done to save him. The bullet had shot straight through his eye, blasting shards of orbital bone into the softness of his brain, bits of which still oozed through the softball-size exit hole in the back of his head.

"Please..." The man's lips were smeared with blood. It splattered from his mouth every time he spoke. "Let me die," he said, just before he did.

"He's gone," a man said. "The children may have him now."

The dead man's head jerked backwards as small hands pulled it by the hair from behind. A hand released his hair and slipped inside the exit hole, entering the pulpy wetness and emerging with a fistful of gray flesh. Clumps of brain-infused blood drained out from the frayed wound, pooling on the tabletop around the man's head. Another set of hands scrabbled from behind the table to scoop it up.

"Hey!" Eli said. He reached out and grabbed the blood-soaked wrist before it could enter the head wound again. "Stop that," he said, circling around the table.

The children were compressed together, as if they shared a single body. Thin arms rose up from the writhing mass like a malformed spider reaching for something trapped in its web. Their sightless, black eyes roamed in random patterns. Wet tongues lolled from gaping mouths set to gorge on handfuls of gelatinous flesh. They cried for their carrion food with keening caws that made a mockery of human speech.

"Let go of him, Doctor. Let them eat."

Eli turned. Dr. Francis was wearing military fatigues.

Behind him a woman sat clutching her hair in clawed hands, crying. "Please don't let him have died in vain," she said.

Eli let go of the boy's wrist and the hand sank back into the skull with a slurp. The children mewled from the recess below.

"One more should do it for today. Eh, Eli?" Dr. Francis said.

Eli spun around. He was in what looked like a small operating room. The ceiling and walls were off-white. The table and instrument tray were metal. The crying lady was sitting on a rubber-cushioned bench. Dr. Francis stood by the door. The children were all crouched in a recessed pit behind the operating table, the head of which, Eli could now see, was angled down in their direction. To offer them easier access.

There was a large window in the left-hand wall, which looked into an adjacent room. Dr. Francis circled around the feeding children to stand beside the window. "Who should it be?"

Eli looked through the window. It was tinted like a two-way mirror. The room on the other side was long and narrow. It looked like a converted racquetball court. Against the far wall stood a row of people lined up next to each other, shoulder to shoulder. They were blindfolded, and their arms were restrained behind their backs. A man wearing military fatigues stood off to the side, holding an assault rifle. The man glanced towards the window and then looked away. Eli recognized his face. It was Sergeant Wagner, the platoon leader from his tour in Vietnam.

It felt like a cold hand had seized Eli's heart and squeezed. Shocks of electric pain traversed from his core down to his extremities, causing them to tingle.

This must be some hallucination caused by my concussion, Eli thought. *I must have fainted back in the boardroom.*

But the scene before him seemed so completely real he even felt a disconcerting sense of vertigo from questioning its authenticity.

Or perhaps it's finally happened. I've lost my mind.

"Dr. Alpert?" Dr. Francis said, slightly concerned. "Which one should we offer next?"

Eli began to concentrate on his breathing. He tried to calm his racing heart. When he spoke, it took every bit of his will to stay composed. "I think we're done for the day." He wasn't sure what they were doing, but he wanted whatever it was to end, and could not give in to what must be a trauma-induced dream or psychotic delusion.

"No!" shouted the woman from her seat. Several of the children mimicked her scream. Or, perhaps, they echoed her desire to continue. "What's the point of stopping now?" she wailed.

"That's enough," Dr. Francis said. "That's our decision to make." He pressed a button on the console next to the window.

Seconds later a young soldier appeared at the door.

"Take Ms. Winniker to the waiting room, please," he said, and the soldier whisked her away.

Her wailing was silenced the instant the door closed, leaving only the slurping sounds of the children spooning brain matter into their mouths.

Dr. Francis peered through the tinted window, crossing his arms over his chest, scratching the mound of gray whiskers on his chin. "We should at least give them one more. The effects have been negligible so far."

Eli peered through the window. There were seven people lined up against the far wall. Despite the distance and the black blindfolds obscuring the top part of their faces, Eli thought he recognized several of them. Two of the girls, in particular. "What do you hope to achieve?" he said, squinting to aid his inspection.

"Excuse me?" Dr. Francis said.

Through the window, Sergeant Wagner pulled his jacket lapel close to this mouth. His amplified voice streamed through the intercom to the right of the window. "What the hell's taking so damn long? Stop pussyfooting around in there. Are we doing another or not?"

Dr. Francis and Eli locked eyes. Dr. Francis cocked his head in hope of prompting a response.

During the silence, the children began keening for more food.

Dr. Francis shut his eyes in apparent disappointment. He pressed the intercom button and said, "Yes, the one on the far right."

"Roger," Sergeant Wagner said. He stalked forward, setting his legs in a shooting stance. He raised the assault rifle and began to take aim.

It's not real, Eli thought, even though he could feel the beating of his heart. Both in his chest and in each temple. He curled his hands into fists and could feel the scrape of his fingernails dragging across each palm. He leaned forward and strained to see the person selected to be shot. He could swear it looked just like…

Sergeant Wagner tilted his head, eyeing the sight at the end of the barrel. He adjusted his feet and secured the stock against his shoulder, his elbow cocked as he prepared to shoot a woman that looked just like Miranda, his patient from long ago.

CHAPTER FORTY-TWO

Crosby first abolished time. It had always caused him distress. Without time, he wouldn't have to worry about being late anymore. Not that he had anywhere to go. Actually, that wasn't true. He had everywhere to go; he just wasn't sure where to start.

Next he got rid of the patients. He didn't kill them, just sent them away, cast them out of his reality. Into which one, he didn't know. But the hospital was much nicer without all that chaotic noise.

Learning how to manipulate his environment would have taken much longer if he hadn't dispelled time. *A millennium,* he thought, but couldn't be sure. Because time no longer existed, it was impossible to tell. In his reality it had all happened in an instant, which still felt rather strange. No, *strange* was not the right word. It was a weak word. Strange did not begin to describe how Crosby felt.

Powerful, was more like it. Omniscient. Omnipotent. Yet, ultimately words are inadequate. They are incapable of describing the act of becoming God.

But, if he were God, what, then, was the beast that had once inhabited his shadow, but had become part of him now. He could hear its harsh breath just beneath his own. Could sense its shadow shape inside his very skin. Its reptilian consciousness casting a dark pall over his liberated mind. Overlaying his thoughts with discordant images. Painting his vision in decrepit colors. Distracting him with instinctual impulses to create chaos, to destroy.

No matter how much control Crosby felt like he was establishing over his abilities, he knew that the beast held power as well. It was as if they had equal stakes in the power they somehow shared.

Was he becoming like them? Like the demon-possessed people he had pledged to destroy? Those evil entities masquerading as healers of the mind?

No. They did not possess the same power as he. He was certain of this. They had been taken completely by surprise when he was called into their meeting. If they were like him, they would have been able to see, as he was able to see. To see inside his soul, as he had been able to see inside theirs and perceive their sins.

He took a last look at these lesser demons in human disguise. Dr. Alpert. Dr. Drexler. The social worker, Angela. The fat director with all of his sycophant followers.

Perhaps they could be reformed through purification. That would be for them to decide. It was no longer his concern. He closed the door on their catatonic faces, staring back at him through sightless eyes. Leaving them to fend for themselves within the worlds created by their subconscious. To find their way back if able to destroy the demons within.

The quiet was disconcerting. Each footfall was the only one in this existence, its hollow resonance reverberating across the vast emptiness of this infantile creation.

It may get lonely, Crosby thought. Such as God must have thought before he made the mistake of creating man. Fleshy creatures with the seeds of demons lodged deep within their corruptible souls. God had been betrayed; Crosby would not allow himself to be.

But still. It would get lonely.

Then he had an idea. *Careful,* he thought, clapping his hands atop his head as if to clamp the idea down. *Ideas are how new universes are born.* An image of living on a double-bacon-cheeseburger planet popped into his mind, and he flinched, expecting it to come true.

Nothing happened. He giggled to himself.

Underneath, the beast quietly growled.

But I could. I could if I wanted. Create all the worlds of my imagining and more.

He shook his head. *No, this will do for now,* he thought, marshaling his runaway imagination and heading towards the recreation room.

When he arrived, he clapped his hands.

It was alive. The mural, it was alive as he somehow knew it would be. A verdant garden from the beginning of time. A cool nocturnal breeze blew across the bushes and rustled the leaves of the great apple tree. The man and woman sat against the trunk of the tree, gazing at the endless stretch of stars above. They stood when they saw him approach, unabashed in their nakedness. The woman raised her arms overhead and yawned, standing up on the tips of her toes. The man crossed his arms and shifted his weight onto his other foot. They both were beautiful. Innocence incarnate.

The beast's ragged breath grew louder as Crosby walked closer, nearing the boundary between the rec room and the verdant garden beyond. He stopped at the edge and stood. The breeze ruffled his shirt and caused the few wispy hairs on his head to flutter. The crisp night air smelled of apples.

The woman reached for him. As did the man. It was the first time he had ever felt wanted by anyone in his life.

Did I create this? he thought. *Are we to begin again?*

He stepped forward, his feet sinking into the soft grass, and reached out for his original creation to receive him. For the circle to become full.

The man and woman stared in wonder at his clothes, pulling at the shirt buttons and feeling the fabric of his pants.

Crosby issued a husky laugh. He found that he couldn't bring himself to disrobe. He pushed their playful hands away and they stopped probing him.

The moon overhead hung low, its blue light nearly as bright as the sun. It cast a double shadow behind Crosby – one much taller and more animated than the other, with clawed hands ending in sharp talons – as he walked towards the tree. He saw the shadow of this other arm reach up beside his own as he grabbed a ripe red apple from one of the lower tree limbs.

From overhead he heard a soft hiss. He looked up and saw the flickering of the serpent's forked tongue, its slitted eyes staring at him with ancient indifference.

And then it all became clear to him. This was his chance to eliminate evil once and for all. To undo the original sin that placed all of humanity on this treacherous path. His divine purpose was grander than he would have ever imagined.

The snake bared its fangs and hissed.

Deep within him the demon growled.

The man and woman shied from him, their faces contorted by fear.

"No," he said, dropping the apple and holding his empty hands out to disarm them.

He didn't see the snake slither closer. He didn't sense it strike. The next thing he knew its fangs were buried deep in the side of his neck while its body wrapped around his throat.

The man and woman screamed, turned and ran.

His shout caught in his throat as the snake constricted. He staggered to his knees, clawing at its body with his hands, and gasped as the bright-blue light from the moon turned to black. A depthless pit of darkness that set his inner shadow free.

CHAPTER FORTY-THREE

Alex had never appreciated how tall Devon was until now, as he watched him rise up from the cot, his head reaching toward the ceiling, shoulders stretching wide, as though expanding into every crevice of this small prison cell, crowding Alex into the back corner, leaving him nowhere to run.

"Christmas done come in July," Devon said as he stalked forward, his top lip curled back in a snarl, his eyes like two narrow slits on a burning furnace. "They brought me my damn alibi."

Alex was still reeling from the sudden shift in reality – from the airy conference room to the cramped confines of this cell. He was certain it must have been caused by a hallucination or, perhaps, he had somehow fainted and was experiencing a lucid dream. But that wouldn't account for the level of sensory detail. The crinkle of Devon's plastic mattress as he stood, the buzzing of the overhead light, the nauseating stench of bad breath and body odor wafting his way. These were not the things of dreams. This was something different.

"Hold on." Alex formed a T with his hands, like a referee calling a time-out. "I need time to think."

"The fuck you do!"

Alex shied away from the shout, but resisted the urge to plug his nose. *What the fuck are they feeding him?* he thought. *Putrefied fish?*

Devon grabbed Alex by the collar of his jumpsuit and pulled him forward. "I already spent too much damn time up in this place, understand? All because of your bitch-ass wife and your crazy motherfucking brother. And you know I ain't done shit. But did you say anything? Hell no. I guess you been too busy, huh? Well you've already taken up too much of my damn time. Time's up, motherfucker. Now you're going to help get me the fuck out of here."

Alex began to shake. He had never felt such fear in his life. Such confusion. Such uncertainty. "I-I…" he stammered. *I don't know where we are!* he wanted to say. *I don't know how I got here!* he wanted to scream. *But I'll do whatever I can to get you, me and anyone else out of here as soon as I figure out what the fuck is going on!* He opened his mouth, but all that came out was a wet jumble of words washed away in a flood of tears.

A second of silence ticked by as Alex stopped blubbering and took a hyperventilating inhalation.

Then Devon spun Alex around and slammed him to the floor, landing on top. He straddled Alex's body, grabbing him by the hair and pinning his head against the concrete with his left hand. He began to hammer Alex's face with his right, punctuating each punch with an animalistic grunt.

The first few punches produced flashes of light in Alex's eyes. The next few brought pain. His face soon became slick with a wetness that created a splat sound for each subsequent punch, like a line cook flattening hamburger patties before slapping them on the grill. The last few blows brought relief, blessed escape. Blackness.

★   ★   ★

"What a waste," he heard, the voice distant, faint. It sounded like whispered words through a neighboring wall. "All that potential, and look what he does with it."

"We're all disappointed." This voice louder, familiar. Female.

Alex shifted and his head shrieked in pain. He nearly passed out again.

"Looks like he's moving," the man said.

"Yes. He's coming around." This from the female. "Honey, can you hear me?"

He strained to open his eyes. They were swollen. A thin sliver of light stabbed through his lids with the sharp edge of an ice pick. He squeezed them shut. His head began to throb. It felt like all of his blood had migrated to his brain. He moaned, rolled over and forced open his swollen eyes again. Two blurred figures stood on the other side of the cell door. Dreamlike wraiths in this insane reality.

"Good god!" the female said.

"Eh, serves him right. He deserves worse."

"He could have been killed."

"I wish he was the one who was dead."

Alex managed to rise up on an elbow. Blood dripped from his chin and plinked in the widening pool of blood below.

It plinked again. Again. Again.

He tried to breathe in through his nose, but it was clogged, busted closed. He blinked and fought to focus his eyes. Finally, he was able to identify the people outside his cell and he tried to get to his feet. But he fell, banging his face on the concrete floor. "Help," he gasped in pain.

"Oh no. You got yourself into this mess. There's nothing we can do," Alex's father said. "You've disgraced us once and for all."

"Stop it. How is that productive?" Rachel said.

"Productive?" Mr. Drexler's chortle devolved into a cough. "If only his supposed medicine had been productive. Then I might still have my firstborn son. Instead of this self-serving fraudster."

Alex wormed his way up to his knees. The room whirled while cymbals crashed against both sides of his brain. Then, his vision steadied and he could see more clearly. "What's happened?" he said.

"I'll tell you what's happened!" Mr. Drexler began, but Rachel placed a calming hand on his shoulder to silence him.

She waited to make sure he wasn't planning another outburst before addressing Alex. "We're going to get you looked at as soon as we can. I bet you have a concussion, but your memory should return soon. I knew it was wrong to put you in the same cell as him."

Alex slowly scanned his cell. Someone was still sleeping in the top bunk, but Devon had disappeared.

"They took him away," Rachel said. "He's being released. Which is ridiculous, after what he did to you. But they seem to sympathize with his position. Wrongful imprisonment."

"But you said..."

"I know what I said. I know what I saw. Or what I thought I saw. I realize that I was wrong. Stress-induced hallucination is what they tell me. But you probably know all about that. It was the formula you experimented on your brother with. It...It drove him crazy, I guess. Jerry...well, he... Alex, your brother killed himself."

Mr. Drexler burst into a prolonged cry of anguish. It was a strange, ugly sound. It reverberated within the small concrete cell, seeming to build upon itself. Watching his father cry had not gotten easier over time.

Alex staggered to his feet. His head pounded heavily, nearly driving him back down to the floor, and then the pounding diminished. "There's no way. That wasn't a self-inflicted wound. Plus, he had been doing so much better. He was like his old self again."

Rachel averted her eyes, shrugged. "I don't know," she said.

"But what about..." Talking caused his brain to throb. He waved an arm around him to reference the room. "Why this?"

"You don't remember?"

Alex shook his head once and winced.

"The formula, Alex. You were testing it illegally. On your own patients. On your own..." she tapered off, motioning towards Mr. Drexler, who had his face buried in his hands.

A trial? A conviction? Impossible. I would remember.

"But I had authorization. I need to speak to someone. Get me Mr. Bearman."

Rachel offered him a sympathetic smile, as though humoring him. "Just wait until your memory comes back."

A booming voice came bellowing from down the hallway. "Okay, folks! Visit's over!"

Bearman's doppelgänger walked up and stepped between Rachel and Mr. Drexler. He peered in at Alex. "Damn, son. You sure got whooped, there, didn't you? Well, not likely to be the last time. Want a word of advice?"

Alex's lower jaw dropped; his mind was void of any possible reply.

"Learn to fight," the man said. He grabbed Rachel and Mr. Drexler by the arms and ushered them away. "Come on, folks. Say goodbye. As you can see, he's in good hands."

And then they were gone. Alex turned around. Despite all the sound and commotion, the man in the top bunk still hadn't stirred.

CHAPTER FORTY-FOUR

The priest scampered into the room, quick as a lizard, and closed the door behind him. A sickly yellow light began to emanate from unseen sources, as though from the very air itself. It spread with a grim luminescence, revealing two rows of white-clad women lining either side of a four-poster bed. Christ hung from a wooden cross on the wall behind the bed, his skin torn and bleeding. His sorrowful eyes bearing the pain of all men.

The priest grabbed Angela up from the floor by her arm. He spoke. His voice had changed again. It sounded even older, ancient. But it also sounded familiar. The inflection of a younger man weakened over eons. "You have fallen back into your old, wicked ways, Sister. You must repent."

The women joined hands and began to sing in a foreign language. Some archaic hymn. Their angelic voices rose to the rafters and rained down with a caustic harmony, their innocent intonations grating on Angela's ears like steel wool. And through the whirling eye of their rapturous song, she could feel the wickedness inside her, the need to be scrubbed clean.

The wan light flickered as if from a candle flame. For a moment, the shadowed interior of the priest's hood receded and she again glimpsed his face. His skin was lucent. The shimmering exterior was a shriveled mask of withered skin and sunken cheeks spotted with lesions. Underneath that surface image was another face. Younger, yet still old. And underneath that, another. This one younger still. And again, layer upon layer of regression. Of regeneration. Of rebirth.

She recognized the middle-aged man within the myriad masks, and his eyes burned with recognition as well. Then the shadow returned to conceal the priest's features, cloaking the many faces with a dark slate without depth, like a puddle of oil.

His voice came from beyond the black hole, echoing all the way back from the beginning of time. "Repent, Sister. You must be made clean."

He thrust her upon the bed. Her head whiplashed when she landed on the firm, unforgiving mattress. She could taste the metallic tang of blood. It smeared on her hand when she wiped her lips.

And the singing grew louder – more earnest – as though fueled by the blood. It caught in the canopy above the bed, refracting upon itself, offering its own refrain.

The hem of her black cloak had bunched up when she bounced on the bed, riding up her legs, showing the sinuous shape of her thighs. The low light showed the smoothness of her skin. She attempted to push the skirt back down in a desperate act of modesty, but it would not budge, as if held in place by unseen hands.

"Unclean! Impure!" the priest shouted. He raised his arms and shook his gnarled fists towards the sky.

"Wicked! Wicked!" the women chanted, incorporating it into their song.

The priest approached the bed. He pulled back his hood. His face was solid again. Just that of the old, wizened man.

The women stopped singing and circled behind him. They reached out to remove his robe. It peeled away from his frail and cadaverous frame. Sharp bones pressed against age-spotted skin. A fine pelt of wispy, white hair sprouted from his shoulders.

The robe fell away completely and the member between his legs rose up like a staff. It was engorged and disproportionately large, pointing at her like an angry accusation.

I'm dead, she thought as she gaped at the distorted figure before her. *I've been sent to hell.*

The women encircled the bed.

Angela searched their faces for a friend. Her eyes flashed wide.

She was looking at herself. The women in white surrounding the bed were all her. Or, rather, a version of her. Pure, clean, unsullied. They wore their white with grace and impunity. They looked at her through her own kind and compassionate eyes.

The priest began to mount the bed.

"Wait," Angela said, surprised that she was still able to voice a word. That she still held some dominion in this twisted unreality. "Please, just stop."

The other Angelas reached out, grabbing her legs and arms, pulling them apart so that she formed the letter X, lifting her, momentarily, up from the bed with the extent of their force. Her hair was grasped and pulled back. She could feel the cloak being pulled farther up her thighs, exposing her groin. She felt a dank heat building down below. A sick, perverse desire.

"No," she cried, but in her mind she heard, *Yes, yes. Do it, do it. I deserve it. I know I do.*

The women began to sing again in that angelic alto that mocked the ugliness of the coming act. The priest crawled towards her, wheezing from exertion, his ornamental chains tinkling like wind chimes. Christ loomed down from above, his agony, forever frozen in time, mirroring her own.

"It's the pain that purifies us," the priest said when he reached her, pushing himself between her legs. "We must die to be reborn."

No, Angela thought, looking up at the leering priest in revulsion. *Not again,* she thought, remembering, feeling once more like a confused and helpless child.

Say it! she thought. *Say it!*

She opened her mouth to scream.

CHAPTER FORTY-FIVE

"Wait!" Eli yelled. He shoved Dr. Francis aside and activated the intercom. "Stop! Don't shoot."

Sergeant Wagner spun in an angry circle, spitting a string of obscenities that went unheard in the soundproofed room. Then he remembered the intercom and switched on his lapel speaker. "What the fuck is the holdup?"

Dr. Francis looked troubled. "Give us a minute," he said, and switched off the intercom. Sergeant Wagner stormed silently across the room, gesticulating like some angry mime.

"What's with you?"

Eli had no idea how to answer. He was far too confused. But to admit as much would be to acknowledge the fact that he had suffered a psychotic break of some kind. But, then again, so would playing along. Both options seemed insane.

"I already told you. We're done for the day. That's enough."

The children's ravenous keening turned into a tortured cry. They were clearly suffering. There was a heart-wrenching quality to their cries.

"Then it's all been done in vain," Dr. Francis said. "What meaning do we give their deaths if it doesn't give life to someone else?"

"I don't understand. Why do they have to die?"

Dr. Francis smirked. "Forming a conscience now? Sorry, Eli. It's too late for that. Morality is fragile in this field. Those who can't be cured die to help those who can. It's the way it's always been."

The desperate cawing of the cannibalistic kids was distracting Eli.

Why try and reason with insanity, he thought.

Because insanity has its own rationality, his mind replied.

The children had emptied the man's head. He could hear their fingers scraping against the inside of his skull.

"Eli, we need another donor for the treatment to take effect. Do they look remedied to you?" Dr. Francis pointed towards the pit of writhing children, their blood-slick arms digging into the dead man's hollow head, their eyes wide, vacant, brackish gore smeared across frantic faces.

Another donor.

Why do they always have to die?

Eli looked back through the window. "Who are they?"

Dr. Francis scoffed. "I really don't know what's gotten into you. Who are they? Christ, Eli. This is your project. When has it ever mattered before? They're donors. They're as good as dead. What is it that you say? 'The greatest use of one's life is to help another live.' They die so that others may come alive. That's their purpose. That's their meaning. Remember, they all volunteered for this. No one forced them to make this sacrifice. They do it for you. For your work. Don't turn your back on them now. Don't make their lives meaningless."

Eli kept waiting to wake up, although he knew this wasn't a dream. His senses were too sharp. His thoughts and actions too organized. His confusion and dismay too intricate and complete.

In dreams, emotions are archetypal – fear, lust, joy, sorrow – there is little nuance. But now, Eli's emotions were a tangled ball of twine, with each frayed thread representing a different line of perception and understanding.

He felt revulsion towards the children gorging on the dead man's brain, but also a keen sense of curiosity and compassion. He wanted to study them, learn their ailment and alleviate their pain.

He wondered who the woman was who had been escorted away. A mother, he assumed. Or perhaps the wife of the donor. Now that she was gone, he desperately wanted to question her to determine her role.

Above all else, however, he felt baffled by the presence of familiar people. His old boss, Dr. Francis. His old squad leader, Sergeant Wagner. And if his eyesight was correct, his old patient, Miranda, now standing among the seven members of the firing squad.

Yet, no matter how real it all felt, it still bore all the arbitrary absurdity of a dream. The exaggerated scenario, the loosely symbolic themes.

This must be either delirium or death. But this is no dream.

There was something empowering about that realization. Something liberating. It diminished his sense of responsibility for making the right decision. It reduced the perception of grave importance. While Eli could not determine what this was or how he'd gotten here, it most certainly had to be a fabrication of the mind – some simulated scenario. And, if that was the case, then he, in essence, could do no wrong. There couldn't be any true ramifications from his actions.

If he was dead, then he needn't fear death. If he was delusional, then he needn't fear for his sanity. It may not feel like a dream, but he may as well treat it as if it were one while he waited to be resuscitated. Or for understanding to arrive.

Unless this is a test, he thought, just as he was about to turn and march out the door. *A test of what?* That made little to no sense, but it was enough to give him pause. Enough to bring his frantic mind's attempt at logic full circle. *A test of my convictions – to see if I can make the right decision, even under the most extreme scenarios. A test I have failed my whole life.*

Eli straightened and strode towards Dr. Francis. He looked him in the eye and, in a stern voice full of conviction, said, "No, there's already been enough death in my name." He pressed the intercom button. His lips brushed the speaker grate as he spoke. "That's it. We're done for the day. No more."

Sergeant Walker glared back through the two-way mirror with a look of anger and dismay.

Dr. Francis reached for the intercom button and Eli grabbed his wrist. He could feel the man's pulse thump as he tightened his grip. "This is absurd!" Dr. Francis said.

Eli almost laughed. "I couldn't agree more."

"What do you think you're doing?"

Eli squeezed the man's wrist until he could feel the rigid edge of bone. "We're going to find a way to help those kids, one that doesn't require anyone to die."

Dr. Francis tried to yank his arm away, but Eli held firm. The man stopped struggling. He attempted a strained facsimile of a smile. It wavered between petulance and pain. "Your morality is misguided. You think you're helping these people by sparing their lives? No, all you're doing is ensuring that everyone suffers in order to make yourself feel better. It's all about the greater good, you self-righteous coward.

"Sacrifice takes strength. It takes courage. You can't play god and cry over the casualties. You must be willing to sacrifice your only son. It's part of the job."

The dead man was pulled from the table into the mewling pit. The kids began to wrestle over the lifeless carcass, fighting over remaining scraps, their cries rising into animalistic screams. It was like listening to an altercation between howler monkeys at the zoo.

Eli released Dr. Francis's wrist and approached the pit. The kids were clawing at one another and gnashing their teeth. The screaming increased in intensity. Urine sprayed in the excitement and wet feces splashed to the floor. The hole in the man's head was being gripped by a ring of little hands, with more scrabbling for purchase, each one pulling in opposite directions. The man's head fractured and split, chunks of skull and scalp were torn free and discarded. His face began to rip, the bone underneath cracking with a popping sound, stretching the skin tight and out of shape – like a rubber mask being removed – which then began to tear. The man's head peeled open like a flower, exposing the inside of his neck. His esophagus stuck up like a stalk.

The children threw the desiccated body to the floor. Eli stood paralyzed on the edge of the pit. The kids below him were like a pack of wild predators. A hand shot out and grabbed the cuff of his pants. Then another, its grip surprisingly strong. The kids below surged towards the side where Eli was standing, reaching up towards him with clawed hands, grabbing his legs and pulling him off his feet, their insane screams assaulting his ears.

He slid towards the pit in spurts, as the hands crawled higher, pulling him closer, his legs extending out over the ledge. He tried to find purchase on the slick tile floor, but couldn't. His hands kept slipping as the kids jerked him towards them. Their strength was extraordinary. Fueled by an insatiable hunger to be healed.

Eli arched his back and looked behind him. Dr. Francis was watching with gaping eyes and a cavernous mouth. Eli reached towards him, stretching as far as his body would allow, but Dr. Francis remained rooted in place. He closed his mouth to swallow, but it sprang open again.

One of the kids wrapped his arms around Eli's legs, trapping them, and pulled. He slid farther out over the ledge. Then others piled on in a human tidal wave and he went over, falling down to the gore-splattered floor.

Kids began clawing at his head as though trying to dig a hole. Others tried to bite through his skull, sinking their sharp teeth into the thin flesh of his scalp.

Eli could feel the cutting of their teeth, the tearing of their hands. He could smell the copper odor of the dead man's blood mixing with the acrid smell of urine and fresh feces. It was ripe, like raw sewage.

This is no dream. This is no dream. The thought became a chant, a mantra. Eli repeated it over and over in his mind – he was screaming now – as he curled himself into a ball, covering his head with both hands.

Pop. Pop. Pop-pop,pop,poppop.

It sounded like fireworks, like M-80s popping in rapid succession.

Then, closer, a fleshier sound, like meat being slapped.

Kids began to fall away. He felt their attack weaken as bodies crumpled to the ground with agonizing cries. Eli uncovered his head and and peered through his arms.

A young soldier was standing beside the pit, the stock of his assault rifle pinned to his shoulder, an unblinking eye peering down the barrel. He squeezed off two more rounds and blood splashed Eli's upturned face as it sprayed from two kids beside him – two pigtailed twins no older than four.

Once their screaming had stopped, the room fell silent. Above the rank odor of gore, Eli could smell burnt cordite. Smoke drifted from the soldier's gun.

Eli rose to his feet, his legs shaking. Blood dripped from his brow down into his eyes, and he blinked it away. He looked down at the massacre. At the tangle of bullet-riddled bodies and blood-soaked limbs. At the adolescent faces turned innocent by death.

The greater good, he thought. *My god, this is no dream.*

CHAPTER FORTY-SIX

Alex didn't think that he would ever sleep again. There was no way to quiet his mind. It was a maelstrom of raging thoughts, questions and suppositions, all encased in an endless loop of circular logic. It would be like trying to take a quick catnap during the running of the bulls.

Meanwhile, the man in the bunk above him appeared to have no trouble sleeping. He hadn't shifted position once since Alex arrived. Hadn't even woken up during his assault. *Probably happens all the time,* Alex thought and shivered. He may have to follow the officer's advice and learn how to fight.

Fighting was something he had zero experience in. Jerry had always been there to shield him from bullies and violent altercations. And Alex had kept Jerry fairly busy.

For such an intelligent child, Alex had lacked common sense and possessed little social grace. He never stopped to think that his technical way of speaking or wry sarcasm could possibly be misinterpreted as arrogant by other people. In his mind, their aggressive behavior was always motivated by misguided jealousies over his superior intellect. He never considered the fact that the fault lay with him and his inability to relate to others or find common ground. He was constantly acting condescending, but he considered that attitude to be an expression of wit, not a display of superiority.

The first time Jerry had ever taken Alex to a high-school keg party was also the first time Alex had ever gotten drunk.

*　　*　　*

It was in an abandoned cul-de-sac surrounded by woods. He stood sheepishly off to the side at first, swilling cheap light beer from a clear-plastic cup, while watching the older students interact. As the alcohol started to take effect, his perception of the scene started to shift. He began to view the revelers as a macrocosm of the quantum world – a field of subatomic particles displaying their cosmic design.

There were clusters of people – whom he now saw as electrons – orbiting around a binding force – a nucleus. There were rogue molecules darting from place to place but never attaching themselves to any single orbit, much like free radicals. And he imagined that if this scene were to be viewed from a great enough distance, it would look very much like our own microbiology seen through a microscope. Which made him contemplate the nature of our biological makeup, and whether or not the world is simply an expression of the micro-universe on ever-expanding scales.

This was, to his inebriated mind, quite a brilliant idea. One that he felt should be shared with others immediately. In a witty, comedic way, of course.

He stumbled from his place perched against a pine tree, feeling an elated sense of giddy weightlessness, like every molecule in his body was reverberating in alignment with his recent revelation. As though the whole universe were awakening to the simplicity of its construction – that all forms of matter were nothing more than expressions of the same quantum activity in varying scales.

Alex smiled, but it wasn't so much a smile as an energy wave activated by a thought. On his pale, pubescent face, sprouting the first black strands of facial hair, the unfamiliar smile bore all the sincerity of a catfish being held up by fishing pliers.

He walked up to a small group of people and said in a loud, brazen voice, "Hiya, Atom! I'm Alex, nice to meet you," then started laughing – snorting, really – uncontrollably. He dropped his plastic cup, splashing beer on a sophomore girl's bare feet. Her name was Betsy, and she was being hit on by a junior jock named Dan.

Dan stood with his chest puffed out, arms cocked by his sides like some gunslinger preparing to draw. "Who the fuck's Adam?" he said.

Alex, still giggling, straightened and swayed. "We are," he said. "We're all atoms, can't you see?" Spittle sprayed from his laughter and struck Dan in the face.

"You little shit!" Dan said, wiping his face as he stalked forward. He placed both hands on Alex's chest and pushed.

Alex flew from his feet and somersaulted backwards when he hit the ground. For a moment he sat there, stunned. Then someone walked over from another group, to catch the action, and Alex pointed and began laughing again. "See. Oh my god! The atom loses an electron and gains a proton. It's true! You're an atom!"

"Who the fuck is Adam?" said the guy who just walked over.

Alex stood up and returned to the group. He studied the girl, Betsy, and then looked back at Dan. "So I guess you're the negative electron," he said to Betsy, forming a circle with his forefinger and thumb. He turned to Dan, his lips squirming in an attempt to quell his smile. "And you're the positive electron," he said, sticking out the forefinger on his other hand. His smile broke wide and he began to snicker as he thrust the finger through the whole in a pantomime of fornication.

Even though he had just been pushed, Alex did not worry about whether or not he was provoking further violence. He assumed that once everyone figured out the joke, and the amazing insight that it related, they would soon be celebrating his comedic genius and brilliant mind. In his alcohol-fueled fantasy he was moments away from becoming king of the party.

Jerry arrived just as Dan cocked his arm to throw a punch. Jerry caught it from behind and curled his other arm around Dan's neck, squeezing so fast Dan never had a chance to take a breath. He eased his grip just before Dan blacked out, and spoke calmly into his ear, "That's my little brother. Leave him alone."

Dan turned, his hands balled into tight fists, but stopped when he saw who was behind him. Jerry stood there, smiling, knowing that the confrontation was over. Dan's face was still mottled red from the rush of blood to his brain and grew darker from embarrassment. He muttered a quick apology as he grabbed Betsy and escorted her away. Betsy gave a lingering look over her shoulder at Jerry, smiling with her eyes as she left. To this day, Alex had never received a look like that from a woman. Not even his wife.

Alex didn't realize how close he had come to getting pummeled. He was too busy considering the quantum equivalent of the altercation that had just occurred. He was still waiting for someone to pick up on his clever reference and applaud.

Jerry walked over, shaking his head. "Hey, bro. Making a few friends?"

Alex burped. The beer was beginning to make him feel sick. "I think…" he said, stifling another belch. *I think we are all one large network of atoms operating on a macro scale,* is what he wanted to say, but his gorge rose again. "I think…" His cheeks puffed out and he turned pale.

"I think you need to walk this way, little buddy, before you blow chunks on my shoes." Jerry led Alex a few feet into the woods and held him upright as he spewed stale beer. He clapped Alex on the back when he was finished. "Happens to the best of us," he said, smiling.

Alex leaned against a tree, steadying himself, and returned the smile. "Tasted just as bad coming up," he said.

Jerry laughed. "Fucking A it does. Want another?"

Alex surveyed the foamy pool of puke and then scanned the hordes of people partying. *The molecules' ecstatic dance.* "Hell yeah," he said as he assumed an unsteady march towards the keg.

"That's my bro." Jerry walked proudly behind him, his protector from the world.

* * *

Snippets of memory chased shoddy theories in Alex's tumultuous mind – none of them bringing him any closer towards understanding where he was or how he had gotten here.

Could I really have suffered some sort of amnesia?

That didn't make much sense. He couldn't imagine what would have brought it on so suddenly. Plus the situation just seemed too… unreal. Staged, somehow. It had all the qualities of a dream, with the sensory characteristics of reality.

Maybe my bunkmate can shed a little light on the situation.

Alex swung out from the bottom bunk. The dull ache in his head was beginning to lessen, but his face felt like it had taken on ten pounds of bloody tissue. He pressed gingerly against his cheek. It was tight and swollen, visible now in the bottom quarter of his eye.

I must make for a welcoming sight, he thought.

The sleeping cellmate was completely covered under a white, threadbare sheet. The overhead light revealed the shadowed outline of his body, like a larva in a cocoon.

Or a corpse under a coroner's blanket. *He hasn't moved.*

Alex stood in the center of the cell, looking for some little movement

– the rise and fall of his chest – some infinitesimal sign of life. There was nothing. The bunk may as well have been occupied by a mannequin.

Maybe it was. Nothing much would have surprised him at this point.

Alex began to make some noise. He scuffed the floor with his feet, tapping it with the soles of his shoes, kicking it with his toes. He cleared his throat several times and coughed with such force it hurt his face.

Still nothing. Not the slightest shift.

Shit, maybe he is dead, Alex thought.

He stepped forward, walking quietly now. Not wanting to wake the man up. The cell was preternaturally quiet, the dull hum from the dim bulb became a roar of electricity.

He took another step. He was almost within arm's reach, his head level with the inch-thin strip of foam serving as the mattress for the top bunk. The man was lying on his side, facing the wall. Alex stopped and held his breath. He cocked his head and listened. All he could hear was the buzzing of the light bulb above.

He shuffled closer, sliding his feet, which made a soft, gritty sound, like sandpaper on smooth wood. He was within arm's reach now. He could reach out and pull the sheet away if he wanted to, like some rank magician revealing the bunny beneath.

That'd be a fine way to get your ass kicked, he thought. *But, then again, I do need to brush up on my fighting.* He may have smiled if his face weren't so sore.

He cleared his throat again, quieter this time. He was now right beside the bunk. Then he said, "Hey." It was just above a whisper, so low he barely heard it himself. Quickly, without thinking, he reached out and poked the bedframe, rocking the bed against the wall, and said it louder this time, "Hey."

The man moved with the motion of the bed, but stopped swaying as soon as it settled down. The sheet remained in place, covering the man from head to toe like a shroud. And that's what it felt like now. A burial shroud.

Alex began backing away slowly. The human-shaped lump on the bunk remained still. They had allowed a man to die in here. He was almost sure of it. What did that mean for him?

He bumped into the steel bars, a crossbar jabbing into his lower back. *What's one more bruise?*

Now that he suspected the man to be dead or, at best, badly hurt, Alex was reluctant to turn away. He wasn't yet sure how the rules worked in this unfamiliar world, but he didn't trust them. He felt like the moment he turned his back, he would hear the bedframe creak and the sound of bloodless feet hitting the floor.

He looked sidelong out the cell door, out into the hallway. It was dark, quiet. He couldn't see beyond the sickly yellow circle of light cast by the bulb overhead. He couldn't even make out the opposite wall.

He turned his head for a better look, but was still unable to see beyond the round perimeter of light. The silence was absolute. Its completeness was impossible. The hallway should have been filled with the racket of other prisoners and the activity of guards. Yet, nothing.

Alex called out, "Hey! I need to talk to somebody!"

The words evaporated into the air. They didn't even echo.

"Hey!" he tried again, the word swallowed by silence. He cringed when he heard the panic creeping into his voice. "I think this guy's hurt in here! I think he might be dead! Someone needs to come look!" No matter how loud he tried to yell, his voice produced the same muted sound, like shouting into a pillow, the words consumed by the dark as soon as they escaped his mouth.

It was like being in a vacuum. He felt like he was in a bubble of existence, like the world ended at the edge of the feeble light. Like he had been placed in a solitary cell in some isolated pocket of the universe. Locked up for eternity with a dead man. The punishment did not fit the crime.

"Help!" he screamed with every ounce of effort his battered body could manage. The only lasting effect was a dull ringing in his ears. Hot tears sprang to his eyes from both frustration and pain. He fought them back. It was the first fight that he won.

"Okay," he accidentally said out loud. "What does it matter," he continued. "It's not like anyone can hear me."

He took a deep breath and stepped forward, his focus so devoted to the shape on the bed it was like tunnel vision.

Alex had little experience dealing with cadavers, if that's what this was. His medical training dealt mostly with the mind. But he had been around more trauma than most ER doctors. He figured he could handle a corpse.

As he approached the bunk, the only thing leading Alex to believe the man was still alive was the lack of smell. While the cell was far from minty fresh, it was not tinged with the cloying stench of decomposition. In addition, the body still held a natural form. It did not appear stiffened with rigor mortis.

Alex rocked the bunk again, causing the body to sway. It soon settled back in place without further movement. "Okay, okay, okay," he said, exhaling. Steeling himself, he reached out his hand and grabbed the man – he assumed – by his arm.

It was neither warm nor cold. Rather, it was room temperature, the muscles hardened, but not rigid with rigor mortis. He rocked the body back and forth. It moved without resistance. Then he pulled the body towards him and it landed on its back. The sheet slipped down to reveal a crown of cropped, brown hair.

He looked back over his shoulder, into the black abyss outside his cell-block door. The overhead light sounded like the idle electricity of an executioner's chair, waiting for the condemned to sit down.

Alex suddenly wished Devon were there. Anyone, even his assailant, his brother's alleged killer, would help ease the tension he felt at this moment. He pinched the sheet just below the man's chin and pulled it down.

The man was definitely dead. His neck was slashed open, the wide wound crusted with dried blood, surrounded by raw, tattered skin. He could see where the esophagus was severed and the stark white of the spinal column. The rest was a pulpy mess.

The man's head rolled towards him. The neck could no longer support it. And the eyes blinked rapidly, as though trying to focus. A raspy gust of air escaped the neck wound, wafting the first ripe scent of body rot Alex's way.

Alex staggered back, feeling a painful shock. The distance provided a new perspective. He was better able to view the man's face. The blinking, animated face that was starting to rise up from the bed, leaving flakes of dried blood behind. He recognized it.

And now knew there were worse things than insanity.

CHAPTER FORTY-SEVEN

It was a scream that had been building within her for decades, growing charged with more and more energy every time she had swallowed it down.

"I said NO! Stop it!" Her face quaked with the force of her rage. Spittle flew from her mouth and blood vessels burst in her eyes. "Don't you fucking touch me!"

The priest paused. The montage of replicated women stopped their song and gasped. Everyone stood frozen in place. From Angela's vantage point, it looked like some pagan ritual gone wrong.

The priest snarled, "You don't get to deny me." But he looked hesitant, unsure.

Angela felt the hands restraining her arms and legs weaken. The eyes looking down at her all became filmed with tears. She flailed her arms and kicked her legs and broke free from their grasp. She fell to the bed and scooted back against the headboard. Jesus gazed down from his cross.

"No. You have no control over me. You cannot take from me. You cannot have me. I won't allow you to." She was no longer shouting, but there was a vital strength in her voice. A vein of power that sounded more sacrosanct than the choir's song.

The priest's erection began to wilt. His outer face shuttered, a spasm of disparate features emerging from the images behind. He was at once both youthful and old, infantile and ancient. A boyish face with elderly eyes and old, dangling ears. A cascading brow with withered skin and lush, sensuous lips. His face continued to morph, cycling through a spectrum of disjointed features and a range of ages.

Then *his* piercing blue eyes appeared and locked in place. Next his nose, porous with dark pits like strawberry seeds. The cheeks became sooty with stubble, the chin dimpled. His hair turned dark and converged in a widow's peak. When his face stopped shifting, his head drooped, as though from exhaustion. Or shame. The women draped him with his robe.

He put it on. He pulled up the hood. And his face receded back into the descending gloom. His voice – his kind and gentle voice – came from the dark. She could just see his lips move. "I do it because I care about you. Because I love you."

The women around the bed no longer shared Angela's face. They each wore their own. And each time she looked they wore a different one, as if representing all the women of the world. They watched in raptured silence.

Angela rose farther up the headboard. She scooted her legs underneath her so that she could move forward. So that she was no longer retreating. "I've spent my whole life receiving your type of love. That's not what it is. It's the opposite. And it's over. I won't accept it anymore."

She moved towards him, her uncle whom she hadn't seen in over twenty years. "No, you hide behind your religion, but it's all a charade. It's the most despicable disguise." She shuffled forward on her knees, hands curling into tight fists beside her. "You're the one who needs to repent. You're the one who should seek forgiveness."

She reached out and pulled the hood back from his head, revealing his face as it had looked when she last saw him. After he had finished molesting her. "You're the one who should seek God."

For a moment, he looked somber, as though shamed by her speech. But then she saw it. The slightest uptick at the corner of his mouth. The barely suppressed smile. The smug look of reproach. It was all she could take.

Her fist flew up from her side and smashed him in the face.

The room flashed – for just an instant it disappeared and she was back in the conference room, where Eli and Alex sat paralyzed, unfocused eyes staring into an empty room – then it reappeared.

Blood spewed from her uncle's nose. He was holding it and mewling in pain.

The women began to murmur. Their hands formed fists and they crowded the bed. A hand shot out and hit him on the head. Another caught him on the back of his neck. "No!" the women said together as they struck him. "It's not what we needed. No!"

He covered his head with his arms to block the punches, his expression turning from pain to fear. "Stop!" he cried.

"No!" the women said, pressing forward, pummeling him with rigid fists.

"Please!" he yelled, curling into a ball. "Stop!"

"No!" They dug their fists into his spine, his ribs, each strike landing with a solid thunk.

"That's enough," Angela said.

She'd said it quietly but the women all stopped at once. They were breathing heavily, their faces flushed. They looked ready to pounce again. Like they were barely restrained.

"It won't do any good. It's done. It just brings us to his level. It makes us ugly like him."

He was still curled in a fetal position, shaking and stammering for them to "stop, please stop."

Angela placed a hand on his back, gently. She lifted him up. His nose was dented in the middle. Blue knots were swelling on the sides of his head. His eyes were shifty, like a cornered raccoon, but they settled as they focused on Angela's. She held his gaze.

She saw him for what he really was, the face beneath the mask. The traumatized child with an illness of his own. She saw in him her patients whom she treated with such compassion.

"We're all victims," she said.

The room sizzled, it flashed, and she caught another brief glimpse of the conference room, like a snapshot into a parallel world.

She thumbed blood from his lip and wiped it on her blouse. She parted his hair to inspect his scrapes. "What you did was due to a sickness. But you never realized that it could be contagious. That it infected me."

His brow knitted together in deep thought or confusion. "I never meant to hurt you," he said.

Angela nodded. Her chin dimpled and her eyes began to burn. "I believe you," she said. "That doesn't excuse what you did, but I believe you never meant to harm me."

His face shook in an attempt to suppress a surge of emotion – it burned red as though he had been holding his breath. Then the emotion broke through and he let out an ugly wail. A man never looked more like a boy. "I'm sorry," he said. "I hate who I am."

"I know," Angela said. "I hate myself too."

And there was truth there. All the self-destructive acts throughout her life had been an attempt to punish herself for self-imagined wrongs she had never committed. Everyone else was worthy of compassion, capable of redemption, but not her. Perhaps her uncle's atrocious acts had planted the seed of self-loathing, but its tendrils had grown deep. It was a cancerous weed that spreads with reckless abandon until someone is able to spot it and wrench it out from the ground.

But another one will grow back in its place. Like weeds, they always will. Their roots go back to the beginning of time.

Angela could not bring herself to embrace the man before her, but she took him by the shoulders and squeezed. She fought for eye contact and found it. "I forgive you," she said.

A smile broke through his battered face. Blood bordered his rust-colored teeth. His face began to age again, rapidly. Wrinkles carving through his skin like the formation of a canyon through a time-lapse camera. He brought the hood back over his head, bringing down the veil of shadow. But, even through the depthless dark, she could still see the faint glow of his smile.

He crawled off the bed, grabbing his walking staff on the way. His array of ornamental chains tinkled as he hobbled back towards the door.

The women followed behind. All except for one. She had poorly cut, crinkly red hair, and a freckled and pockmarked face.

Poor girl could use some concealer, Angela thought, then admonished herself. *No, her face is her face. Who am I to judge?*

The redheaded woman eased up to the edge of the bed. Her eyes were green. Angela was sure she had seen them before. In equally darkened rooms such as this.

"You're ready to see her now," the woman said. She held out her hand for Angela to take. "Come."

Angela had been so consumed by the confrontation that she had momentarily lost sight of where she was. *Dead,* she thought again. *This must be some final test. Some life review to gauge what I've learned.* She reached out and took the redheaded woman's hand. *Perhaps this is where I meet God.*

"Her?" Angela said.

The redhead nodded; her emerald eyes glowed.

"I knew it!" Angela said. *Only a woman could give birth to a world.*

She came down from the bed, feeling the rough-spun fiber of the wool rug under her feet. The room was cool. The candle flames produced golden coronas in the corners of her eyes. They crackled softly on their waxen wicks. Every detail, Angela observed, was intricate and acute. She never thought the afterlife would feel so real.

The woman led her past the column of candelabras. On the far side was a second door that she hadn't seen. It appeared to be made from flimsy pine, covered with a thin, white coat of paint that was beginning to peel.

"She's in here," the woman said. Her wan smile widened to reveal crooked teeth, which she covered with her hand.

"Don't do that," Angela said. "Don't be afraid to smile."

The woman dropped her hand and laughed, but she began to blush. It would take time.

Angela faced the door. "Who's in there?"

"Go see."

Angela looked at her ruffled cloak. She attempted to smooth the wrinkles with her hands, but stopped. It was useless. *What does it matter?* she thought. *Surely God won't be vain.*

She swallowed and saliva stuck in her throat. *I hope.*

She opened the door. And began to cry.

CHAPTER FORTY-EIGHT

"Look what you've done," Dr. Francis said, his face a pale slate of shock. "They're all dead. All of them. You're right, Eli. Too many have died in your name. And here they die still."

Eli swiped blood from his eyes. He almost slipped in the slick pool forming at his feet. The odor was overwhelming. It was one he had smelled before, a pungent mixture of blood, excrement and gun smoke. No other sense was as capable of awakening a memory in such vivid detail. And all of his most poignant memories seemed to be connected to death.

"It's not what I wanted," Eli said. He wanted out of the pit, but felt compelled to stay awhile longer. As some form of penance. "I didn't mean for this to happen."

"It doesn't matter what you want or what you mean to have happen. It's what you allow. How many good deeds does it take to counter the bad? Where does your scale tip? You admonish the sacrifice of one life to save the lives of many, yet sacrifice many to save the life of one. Where is the good in that?"

Eli hung his head. The open eyes of the dead stared up at him in blind judgment. *That's not who I am,* he thought. But was that true? How many had died on his watch? Could he have intervened to save them? Why hadn't he then?

Eli had always considered his work to be righteous. Not in a religious sense, but in terms of doing the right thing. He'd helped to drive psychiatry in a more compassionate and humane direction. He'd treated his patients the same way he would want to be treated.

But had he held true to his noble convictions in the most dire of situations? Or had he cowered and succumbed in the moments that mattered most? Sure, it's easy to act righteous – to do the right thing – when nothing's on the line. But how does one act when life itself is on the line? Isn't that the true test? And, if so, had he passed?

No. He had not.

So, did that make his life a failure? His philosophy a sham?

He didn't know.

Dr. Francis walked back to the intercom. He dismissed Sergeant Wagner and had him disperse the remaining donors from the firing line.

He came back to the edge of the pit and looked down. He shook his head. "I don't know what's gotten into you today. Take some time. Regroup. And we'll start again when you're ready."

He left the room. The young soldier followed him out.

Mere seconds passed before the door swung open again.

Two nurses entered, dark skin against stark-white uniforms from a prior era that made them look a bit like nuns. Their black hair, streaked gray along the sides, was slicked back against their heads, covered by an old-timey nurse's cap. Their faces were shiny, wrinkle-free and smooth, belying their age, with eyes that appeared sharp and wise. One had freckles, the other did not; otherwise, they could have been twins.

"Mmmm-mmmm-mmmm, what a mess," the one with the freckles said. According to a tag on her lapel her name was April. The one without the freckles was May.

"Sure is," May said. "Can't seem to keep his nose clean for long, can he?"

"Nope, not Eli. God help him. Always trying to save the world, but who's going to save the world from him?"

They squatted down and reached out all four arms. "Come on, sugar," April said. "Let's get you clear of this mess."

Eli's arms were smeared with blood; it dripped from his elbows. He could taste it leaking into his mouth from his lips. He didn't want to stain the nurses' pristine white outfits, but had no way to make himself clean. He wiped what he could on his pants.

They both offered quarter-moon smiles. Their teeth gleamed. "Come on, now. Blood don't bother us. Once it's shed it loses all its power. It just washes away."

Eli reached up and they grabbed his arms. He meant to brace his foot against the lip of the pit for leverage, but they leaned back and yanked him free, nearly dislocating his arms from each socket. The nurses were surprisingly strong.

May looked down into the pit and clucked her tongue. "I bet you meant well, though."

"He always do."

More than with Dr. Francis, more than Sergeant Wagner, Eli felt a desperate need to confess his confusion to these two women. He needed for them to help him understand what was going on. He grabbed each by their outer shoulders, staining their sleeves maroon. "Please. I need you to help me," he said. "I don't know how I got here. I don't know where I am."

They exchanged a blank look. It revealed nothing.

"We *are* here to help you, honey," April said.

Eli sighed with relief. "Thank you. Thank you. Please, what is happening?"

"Right now you're talking with us. Pretty soon, we're going to take you back to your office. Help get you cleaned up."

"Right, but..." Eli was becoming impatient. He needed answers. He needed to understand the situation. He needed to know if he had finally gone insane. "I don't know how I got here or what I'm doing. This all seems crazy to me."

Neither April nor May seemed concerned by this statement. It seemed like the most natural thing in the world for him to say. "That's how everybody feels, honey. That's life."

He hung his head. He let go of their shoulders and his hands slumped towards the floor.

The nurses came around on either side of Eli and grasped him by the elbows, as though preparing to escort him down a wedding aisle. They started moving him towards the door.

"Wants all the answers, don't he?"

"Sure, don't we all?"

"But then we don't see what's right in front of us."

"Might as well be blind as a bat to what's right under our very noses."

"You got people want to help you, Eli. You just got to let them."

"Don't worry about what's gone on before or what comes next, just do the best you can every step along the way and you'll make it out okay."

Eli felt exhausted. Taking another step *was* all he could focus on at the moment. If it weren't for their support, he would likely collapse to the floor.

"Some people are happy to make sacrifices – sacrifice their life, even – to help someone along their way. Something like this. Seems like a tragedy now. Senseless and unnecessary. But good will come from it. You just got to allow it to come through."

"The Lord works in mysterious ways."

"If only people knew."

They were walking down a hallway so bright it hurt Eli's eyes. It was clear of people, and quiet. He couldn't even hear the squeak of their footfalls as they shuffled along the glossy linoleum floor. The world was their voices, nothing but their vague and confusing banter.

Aside from the glaring light, the scenery was the same as at Sugar Hill. He saw the door to where his office should be, ahead on the left. They stopped just shy of it and the nurses released his arms.

"Let's get you cleaned up," April said.

May nodded. "Wash this mess away and start fresh."

His name was on the placard by the door, just like at his actual office. The door appeared the same as well, the top half obscured by pebbled glass. He turned and looked at the two nurses. Even in their bloodstained clothes, they looked as beautiful as their springtime names.

"No, I can handle it," Eli said. What he couldn't handle was any more of their clichéd riddles, which did nothing to alleviate his hopeless confusion. If anything, it only added to his sense of unease.

April and May exchanged a look revealing nothing.

"Okay," April said.

"If you say so," May said.

They turned and began walking back the way they had come.

"He's a stubborn one," he heard one of them say, her voice fading.

"Has a hard time accepting help."

"Doesn't see it when it's right in front of him."

"Well, he will."

"Or he won't."

"One or the other."

"That's the only two there are."

"Just hope too many more people don't have to die before he do."

Eli turned the knob – his hand felt like it was coated in honey – and pushed open the door. The office was exactly how he had left it. An oasis of normalcy. He stumbled in and shut the door. *Perhaps I'm back,* he thought. *Back from some fugue state.*

Which would make his bloodstained clothes even more disconcerting.

No. Nothing can be worse than what I've just been through. Even if I've murdered one hundred men in some blind psychotic state.

He shuffled to his desk and collapsed in the chair, unconcerned about smearing blood. His body was tingling with exhaustion, his head swimming. He closed his eyes and took a couple of deep breaths, holding each as long as his lungs would allow. The room smelled like old lemons. Like teakwood. After the vile reek of the feeding pit, it was the most wonderful scent he'd ever inhaled.

Eli opened a cabinet and removed the mandala, pinning it to the wall. He switched on the CD player, turning it to his favorite song – an Indian instrumental featuring the hypnotic strums of the sitar. He spun the chair towards the mandala with its weblike weave of psychedelic designs. He let his eyes lose focus, his lids fall. Everything became a blur. He drew each breath from the stomach, letting it rise up his spine and flow out each nostril, inhaling again in a circular loop, stomach expanding.

Outside was silence, inside the sitar, each string being plucked with expert precision, creating a mesmerizing flow.

Eli began to pray – to what deity, he did not know. Perhaps it was to the wandering soul of Rajamadja, wherever that may be. It was a wordless prayer. It was the channeling of thought through emotion.

If you made me, you must know how I feel. Please make it stop. If there is an infinity, I cannot fathom enduring it. Why must we suffer so much? All of this expressed through a sharp burning in the chest – through indescribable fear. The fear of being stuck inside himself forever.

The player plucked the strings faster. The mandala's weave-like web pulsated and began to spin. Eli's breath became shallow as his panic grew more pronounced.

Fear is deadly. Perhaps my killer has finally come.

The sitar reached a crescendo, a fervent and constant strum. It was a chaotic sound. It was the murmurings of the most manic mind. It threatened to go on like that forever, long after the cooling of the final sun.

Then it stopped. It *paused.* And when it resumed, it was the sound of a regular acoustic guitar being strummed. Perhaps like the one Elvis

Presley used to play. Or every little boy in their earliest imagination.

It was a folk tune, slow and full of backwoods soul, its sound influenced by sweltering summers and the serenading bugs of the bayou. There was a distinct purpose to the player's tune. A heartbeat. A transmission of meaning that transcended verbal translation.

A voice began to sing. An adolescent voice speaking of heartbreak and loss and truths that most men prefer to ignore. Eli recognized the voice. He hadn't heard it in decades, but he knew whom it belonged to now.

His shallow breathing began to deepen. His heart slowed its frantic pace. He realized that every muscle was fully clenched and he felt himself begin to relax.

The guitar stopped, the singer became silent. And then Randall's high-pitched, wavery voice spoke to Eli through the speaker. And panic set back in.

CHAPTER FORTY-NINE

Alex had spent many nights wishing he could hear his brother's voice again, but now he would gladly use every wish a genie could grant to make his voice go away.

It was like listening to a drowning snake – the words slithered through severed pipes. They gurgled and bubbled in stagnant blood. Every utterance was a violent choking heard more through the gaping neck than the moving mouth. And every utterance was an admonishment.

Jerry swung his legs out over the bunk; his head teetered precariously on his severed neck. His eyes were clear and focused. And angry. They were leveled on Alex, and they never wavered.

There was a hitch in Jerry's speech, as though he were struggling to suck in air that wasn't there. "You made..." *gurgle, gasp,* "...me..." *gurgle, gasp,* "...imagine him." *Gurgle, gasp.* "Him!" *Gurgle, gasp.* "And..." *gurgle, gasp,* "...he came."

Alex was paralyzed in place. Jerry could come off the bunk and kill him and Alex would never move. The stark terror of the moment was beyond fight or flight. He would prefer to be struck dead.

"Who did?" Alex mumbled. "Who did what?"

"You...conjured my...killer." Jerry dropped to the floor. His head bobbled and nearly toppled backwards, but his spinal column held it in place. "And...now you've...conjured yours."

"I didn't mean to do anything."

"You...meant to...get rich. You...meant to...get respect.... You didn't...think of...the consequences.... It was...at my...expense."

"No. I thought I had fixed it. I thought that it worked. I wanted you to get better. I wanted to help create a cure."

"You...didn't know.... You did it...any...way."

"It wasn't just me." Alex couldn't believe he was having this conversation. If only he could wake up. Or die. "Rachel talked me into it."

Jerry paused. His neck wound clamped down. The wet flutter of cut and torn tissue must have been a sardonic chuckle. Alex could see the dark humor reach Jerry's eyes.

"Why?" The word came through Jerry's slit neck like a sigh.

The question was too broad. Too all-encompassing. Why what? Why anything? "Why did I test my medicine on you?" Alex asked.

Jerry blinked his eyes rather than risk nodding his head.

And through that plaintive gesture, that innocent desire to know what had caused his death, the ramifications of what Alex had done came crashing down upon him. The finality of his brother's last breath. If he had indeed caused this, then this nightmarish torment was tame compared to what he deserved.

"I did it because…" Alex didn't know what he intended to say next. His mind was blank. He was astonished by his ability to form words. "…because I knew you would let me. Because I knew you wouldn't let me down.

"I wish I could say that I did it to help people. To help *you*. But that would be a lie. I did it because I thought it would make me important. I thought it would make me money and bring happiness, and make Rachel want to fuck me more.

"I thought…" despite himself and the absurdity of the situation, Alex felt a momentary flash of resentment towards his brother, even in this undead, zombie-like state, "…that it would redeem me in Dad's eyes. I thought that if I cured you – if I brought you back – he would finally respect me.

"And I did bring you back. At least I thought I did. He just never got to see it."

Alex cast his gaze towards the ground and held it there. An act of submission. A plea for sympathy. He did not know whether this undead version of his brother was capable of emotion, but he felt like going for the heartstrings was the best chance he had. It was either that or try to take Jerry's head off his severed neck. And Alex was far more comfortable using manipulation than physical force.

The silence became unbearable. He began to sag under the weight of his dead brother's stare. Alex glanced up sheepishly. Like a lost and confused little brother. Jerry looked less sympathetic than he had hoped.

They stood staring at each other for half a minute. It was like the old

stare-downs they used to have in the back seat of their father's Buick
to see which one would be the last to blink. Jerry looked like he could
hold out for several centuries. Alex didn't feel like waiting that long.

"So what is this, Jerry? I'm not dreaming, I know that. Am I dead?
Is this purgatory? Am I being judged?"

"No." And yet Jerry's unflinching stare felt like the harsh scrutiny
of appraisal. As if he were deciding his brother's worth. Deciding what
should be done with him.

"What then? What is this? What are...*you*?"

"You...still have...time."

Alex looked around. The fear was waning. He felt his body
thrumming in the afterglow of adrenaline. "Well, I can't say this is
how I want to spend it."

"That's for...you...to decide."

Alex squinted at Jerry through one eye, as if trying to see through
his charade. "I don't see how I have much say in the matter."

"You...created this. You...created me. The medicine...opens
up...the mind." Jerry stepped forward. He reached out his right
arm and placed it on Alex's shoulder. It was warm and felt oddly
comforting.

"You...still have...time to...make it...right."

There was a flash, like the turning of a channel, and Alex was back
in the Sugar Hill conference room. He was still standing in the middle
of the room. He opened his mouth to gasp, to speak, to...

And he was back in the cell, staring into his brother's pale, blood-
speckled face.

"I am what...happens when...you lie. You can...create any...
world you...choose. Choose...another one."

Then he smiled, one red grin stacked above the other, his lips
yawning nearly as wide as his neck. Blood was crusted in between
his crooked, unkempt teeth. A reeking stench blew out that foretold
of death to come. The smile faded, yet his mouth opened wider,
and wider still. As if it were coming unhinged. As if it meant to
engulf him.

"Choose one..." it came out *uuuuzzz uunnghh*, a low, guttural
growl heard through the gaping esophagus hole; his maroon mouth
yawned wider, "...that doesn't end...like this."

Jerry shot forward, his open mouth a dark cave with stalactite teeth. Alex shut his eyes and was struck by...

...the silence.

He could feel the spacious, cool air. His nerves were still sizzling in anticipation of his brother's bite, but it never came. Hesitantly, he opened his eyes and nearly collapsed to the floor.

The vacant stares of Bearman and his board, Eli and Angela, looked up at him. He was back in the conference room.

CHAPTER FIFTY

The little girl sat on a padded footstool with her legs curled underneath her, gazing out of a wood-paneled window onto the courtyard beyond.

Her hair was cropped short – like she'd worn it when she was eight – with a shelf of bangs cut straight across her forehead. Her knees were knobby and scraped. Her face was still and solemn. She stared out the window without seeing. Her eyes were cast inward, reflecting a sadness towards the horrid images that played within her mind.

The little girl didn't hear Angela's sobbing. She had not reacted to the opening of the door. Nor did she seem to notice as Angela approached her, taking small, tentative steps, each one leading her farther back in time, to an age that she had all but forgotten. To an age she had blocked out.

Angela stopped behind the little girl – she couldn't think of the girl as herself, although that's who it clearly was. She couldn't fathom that she had once been this person. That she had survived and lived still. How had it happened? She had grown up without even realizing it. The two ages seemed to be separated by a vast chasm, yet were tethered by a tattered rope bridge that swayed precariously over the great divide.

She looked over the little girl's shoulder at the landscape beyond. It was an overgrown garden with a dry and decrepit fountain. In the middle of the fountain stood a forlorn woman holding a moss-covered pitcher containing nothing left to pour. The overcast sky was the same slate gray as the tarnished stone.

Angela held out her hand, letting it hover over the little girl's shoulder. Her fingers trembled. Her chest still heaved. She used a technique that she taught her patients to help quiet their roiling emotions, to stop themselves from crying.

Pausing, she focused her mind. Then drew a deep breath in through her nose, mentally counting her many blessings: *I have a great job, I am smart, I have my health.*

She felt a pleasant glow spreading out from her chest as she prepared to exhale through pursed lips, expelling negative energy: *I shed my anger, I shed my hate, I shed my fear.*

She felt lighter. Her wavering wails had already reduced themselves to sniffles. Her hand held steady. It was the first time she had ever attempted the coping mechanism on herself. She had always preferred wine.

The little girl stiffened ever so slightly when Angela rested her hand upon her shoulder – just the most subtle tensing of the neck and tilting of her head. Otherwise, she remained oblivious to Angela's presence. She exhaled a shuddering breath, as though revolted by some imaginary sight, and her shoulders slumped.

And now Angela found that her own mind's eye was awakening to a series of images. They were faint, like film projected by a fading bulb, the objects blurred and unfocused. She rested her other hand on the little girl's shoulder and the mental imagery grew brighter, sharper, clearer.

It was like watching a movie, but she knew that wasn't what it was. She was watching a memory. Her own. One that she had buried in the cemetery of her mind many years ago. She somehow knew it was only now resurfacing due to the conduit provided through her younger self, where it was still fresh. Where it was wreaking havoc on her confused and fragile psyche.

Her mother was looking back at her through the partly open front door. She had to leave for work. She had taken on a second job to cover expenses after Angela's father passed away.

Passed away. That's what they called it. But it was a poor description for what had happened to her father, who had died from a sudden heart attack so severe it had ruptured his aorta, producing a tearing sensation in his chest, killing him while he clutched at his heart, as though trying to rip it out, his feet scrabbling on the floor, his neck distended, eyes bulging, screaming in agonizing pain as shit exploded from his rear.

Passed away. No, he had died hard.

Maybe her mother had known something was amiss. It was hard to tell. She wore a worried expression anytime she was forced to leave Angela alone. But she wore a distrustful expression close to terror anytime she left Angela in the care of her uncle.

Her uncle, the priest. The sanctimonious saint. The transmitter of God's word and terrestrial savior of souls. It would be natural for such a man to want to watch out for his brother's widow and provide care for his niece after his brother died. But he wasn't like his brother had been.

He did not share the same openness to other ethnicities that her father had. He treated Angela's mother, with her Asian ancestry and heavy accent, like a feeble child with a learning disability. And he had not been around much while her father was alive, only showing up with any regularity after the funeral mass was over, which he had presided over himself. Turning it into a sermon that focused less on her father's life, and more on the precarious nature of the parishioners' souls that *"needed to be saved!"*

He had even implied some uncertainty over her father's salvation, due to a relaxed attitude towards religion. Due, perhaps, to being influenced by the dubious theology of her mother's native land.

But this was a man of the cloth, not to be questioned. And he was from her late husband's bloodline, which her mother thought she could trust. So, even if the honest voice of instinct may have insisted that there was something off about her brother-in-law, she decided to ignore it. It was just too big — too dangerous — a hunch to indulge.

The look in her eyes, however, fresh in this motion-picture memory, told the full story. She was worried about leaving Angela alone with this man — reverend, relative or otherwise.

Her mother skulked out the door and closed it. There was no sound in the memory, just sight. So the door shut in silence.

Father Drake turned and smiled — a bright smile with sparkling eyes that said, *Boy, aren't we about to have some fun!* His name was Glenn, but he insisted that everyone call him by the formal title of his ordained profession. Even family.

The memory began to lose its linear narrative. Inner thoughts and emotive overlays began to intrude on the scene, like some omniscient narrator reading a scrambled script.

The scene soured. It darkened, the colors blanching out and burning inward at the edges. The priest's smile became the sinister sneer of a carnival barker inviting kids to see the horrors within the funhouse. His centipede-like mustache scampered above his lips, millions of whiskered legs marching.

He walked towards her, placing a hand first against her neck, and then sliding it down, tracing it along the arched curve of her lower back, palming her underdeveloped behind, pinching it in jest and giggling as if playing a game. Grabbing it painfully before letting go.

But fear was not the emotion sensed within the memory. Nor dread. Certainly not fun.

It was guilt. It was shame. A confused search to determine what she had done to provoke what was to follow. Some flirtatious gesture? Some suggestion of lust? Or, perhaps, some unspoken agreement between the priest and her mother, permitting it to happen? Because there was no other explanation. No way a holy man, no way her uncle would violate her in such a way. No way her mother would allow it. Unless it was her fault. Unless she deserved it.

Young Angela's mind was under duress. It was *squirming*, trying to cope with what had happened and trying to understand why. Trying to pinpoint some moment that would explain it all away. But, in order to do so, she must live through it again. Let it all play out in this exaggerated reenactment which had been warped by the revolting reality of the act.

She knew the word for it: *INCEST*. And she knew it was a dirty word. And that it made her a dirty girl.

Stained. Tainted. Covered in filth that would never wash away.

Angela felt her younger self cringe under her hands, trying to escape from the memory of her uncle undressing her. Of his hands caressing the prepubescent buds growing from her breasts.

And, at the same time, trying to dissect it to figure out what, if anything, she could have done differently. She had permitted it. But had she encouraged it? She shivered. She screamed in silent frustration.

No, Angela thought, and she heard her voice enter into the mind of the memory. It sounded calm and comforting. It was the voice of compassion Eli had taught her to use when consoling patients. *You didn't encourage it. You didn't bring it on yourself.*

She began to run her fingers through the little girl's hair, letting the silky strands flutter back in place. She combed the girl's hair back from the sides, pulling it into the small nub of a ponytail, while she stroked the soft skin exposed on her neck.

It was not your fault. He was disturbed. He was sick. There is nothing you could have done differently. If you had fought, it would have only made it worse.

The darkness of the memory began to diminish. The point of view zoomed in on her uncle. It showed his feverish eyes, his manic, desperate gaze – windows into a mind at war with itself. A mind disgusted by its own depravity. A weakness of constitution unable to overcome its perverted urges. A self-loathing deeper and more despairing than anything Angela had ever experienced. Even in her most compromised moments. Even when she felt she could fall no farther.

He needed help, but there was no one to help him. Even if help meant separation from society. Even if help meant death. He would have preferred those things to being who he was.

His face was contorted in an animalistic expression of hunger, of predatory lust. But it also showed anger and revulsion and shame, all directed towards himself. It was an act of self-flagellation, as much as sexual gratification. He knew Scripture well enough to believe that he was damning his soul. And still he couldn't stop.

You were his victim, and there's nothing that can be done to minimize how awful that was. But he was a victim too. Of faulty genetics, of a damaged brain. He was broken and needed to be either fixed or destroyed.

But you, little Angela, you did nothing wrong. You were a strong, brave girl. You survived. And look at us now! We've gone on to help fix the broken people. We have so much to be thankful for. You'll get over this. You'll move past it.

And what, replace it with booze, blackouts and one-night stands? The connection was so blatantly obvious it was professionally embarrassing that she had never made it before. Well, she had, but in a more general, abstract sort of way. She had never considered that she was still punishing herself over something that was not her fault. That she still harbored all the guilt and the shame.

I will not remain a victim any longer. It's time to move on.

The memory began to fade, losing its immediate potency. It fast-tracked to her mother returning home, exhausted from a sixteen-hour workday. But still making the time to check in on Angela. To make her something to eat. To lay her down to sleep. Only then shutting her own eyes for the few hours she had until it was time to wake up and do it all over again. All for her little girl. All for Angela.

The little girl stirred on the footstool. Outside, a golden shaft of sunlight had penetrated through the clouds and was spotlighting the statue of the lady standing in the empty fountain. It made her glow.

Angela could see the little girl's face reflected in the windowpane. Her eyebrows were still knitted together in deep concentration, but there was a one-sided smile on her lips. Almost a smug, little grin. The girl was smart. She was tough. Angela had a feeling she would make it just fine.

She leaned down and wrapped her arms around the little girl, resting her head against the small crook of her shoulder.

I love you.

And she heard the voice of a young little girl say, "I love you too."

Tears blurred her eyes. She wiped them away as she stood, peering out through the window again at the lady in the fountain. Wait, she had seen this before. Of course she had. It was the courtyard back at Sugar Hill.

CHAPTER FIFTY-ONE

"We're all dead here. We're caught in the in-between."

Randall's voice came through the speaker in a burst of static, as though from a station that was just out of range. But this wasn't a radio. It was a CD player. There was no signal to pick up.

Eli shut his eyes. *What have I done to deserve this hell?*

"We're dead, but we cannot die. We're stuck out here, without eyes to see."

The static made it hard to understand what Randall was saying, but when he played the guitar it came through crystal clear. He was picking the strings, a slow, discordant rhythm that produced a formless beauty, almost an anti-song. His static-laden words, then, became a kind of poetry.

"We've already been here forever, and we're ready to come home."

Eli was intent on waiting out this new, strange scenario. It too would pass. Just like the others.

"Eli, we're scared. This place is scary. We're alone with just our thoughts. Together, but alone. Our thoughts have gone on forever. Will you help us?"

Eli leaned towards the CD player, which as far as he knew didn't have a microphone, and said, "Randall, is that you?"

The speaker exploded with static. Laughter? A scream? He couldn't tell. Then, this crackly but audible, "whooo-hoooo."

"Yes, Dr. Alpert. It's me, but there are others. We've been here for such a long time."

"Where? Where have you been?" *Okay, now I'm talking to my stereo,* Eli thought.

"The in-between. Stuck in nothingness."

"Randall, I don't understand. Can you please explain?"

"He sent us away, but didn't give us anywhere to go."

"Who did?"

"The killer at the end of the world."

"Who?"

"The killer of Raptures."

"Randall, I don't understand."

But then he did. It clicked.

"Do you mean Crosby? You mean the Apocalypse Killer?"

The speaker rattled with static.

"Randall, I don't understand what is happening. How am I speaking with you?"

"We are a part of nothing, but know everything. It's all here. All the information there ever was or will be. I can't explain. But you can control it. You are in control."

"Control what, Randall?"

"Your mind. Your reality. You are in one of the infinite tributaries branching off the river of existence. You need to come back. Come back and bring us back."

"I don't know how."

"Let go."

"Let go?" Eli looked at his hands, which held nothing. "Let go of what?"

"You must let go."

It was a saying he had heard throughout all of the Buddhist teachings: Let go. But he had never understood what it meant. His life was one of service to others. That wasn't something he could just give up. He needed to apply himself, not surrender. What good would he be then?

Besides, he had already lost too much through ambivalence. People had died because he had not shown enough strength. Letting go had not saved any of them. And it would not save Randall now. He needed to fight back against whatever force was afflicting him, whether it was his own mind or something else. That was the only way he would overcome it. Not by letting go. Not by giving in.

"I'm going to figure this out," he said, feeling ridiculous for having a conversation with a CD player.

The first thing I need to do is stop indulging in my fantasy, he thought.

He reached out and turned off the stereo, casting the room into silence where he sat, lost and alone.

CHAPTER FIFTY-TWO

The sense of vertigo was so strong Alex had to hold his arms out for balance. He was back in the conference room, standing before the U-shaped table in the same spot he had been in before...

Before what? What the hell happened?

His heart was racing. Just moments ago his dead brother was lunging forward to bite him, and now he was back here. His return was just as abrupt as his departure. Just as disorienting. *Return from where?*

And to his dismay, everyone was staring at him. Looking at him with stunned, horrified expressions.

I must have had some kind of a stroke, he thought. *Oh god. What a nightmare!*

Then he realized that the faces staring up at him weren't moving. They were catatonic; their only movement was the occasional blinking of their wide-open eyes.

Alex surveyed the room. Crosby was gone; otherwise, everyone else was accounted for. He approached the table, watching to see if anyone's eyes tracked his movement, but they did not. They each continued to stare at some image in the distance that he could not see.

That must have been what I looked like, he thought. *They must all be having the same lucid dream.*

He stared down into Bearman's rigid face, looked right into his bulging eyes. He held his fingers up and snapped them in front of Bearman's nose. There was no reaction.

He walked to the right, scanning the frozen faces. He stopped and slapped his hand down onto the wood table as hard as he could. The smack resounded like a gun blast, but no one moved. No one even blinked in surprise.

The room was silent, completely still. There wasn't even the soft hiss of centralized air coming from the vents overhead. He drummed his fingers on the tabletop just to hear a sound. It had the same hollow resonance as Jerry's coffin lid. His skin prickled and he suddenly felt cold.

There was a gasp to his right – a sudden intake of air. He turned his head. Angela was *looking* at him, but no longer with that petrified stare. She was looking at him. She was *there*.

Angela opened her mouth to speak, but nothing came out. She closed her mouth, swallowed and looked around. The deep lines forming between her brows looked like they would remain there forever. Then she bent forward, placed her head in her hands and began to shudder as she silently cried.

Alex didn't know what to say. He wasn't sure whether or not to admit what had just happened to him. But, whatever it was, it appeared to be happening to the others as well. Something was, at least.

His mind scrambled to figure out the best way to handle the present situation. It came up blank. Then it offered this: *What would Eli do?*

He realized it was true. Eli would know precisely what to do, even in this puzzling situation. And he would somehow make it look easy and obvious. Eli was in no condition to help now, however. His face looked like it had been fossilized. Except for every so often when his eyelids would blink – lightning quick – and then return to that disconcerting vacant stare.

Angela's crying was still silent. He wished she would sob. He wished she would contribute some sound to the vacuum of the room.

Then she raised her head back up and looked at him again. It was the most confused and vulnerable he'd ever seen her. She looked like a lost little girl.

"What's going on?" she said.

Alex shook his head. He turned his back on her and paced the room. He couldn't stand the frightened look on her face. He was afraid it was on his face too.

"Alex?"

He turned. His hands were clasped behind his back. If he couldn't come up with anything encouraging to say, at least he could appear calm. He raised his eyebrows in an invitation for her to continue.

"How long have I been out of it?" Angela asked. Her speech was barely audible. It was all breath.

Alex shrugged. "I'm not sure."

They both looked at the row of vacant stares.

"It's happening to them too," Angela said.

"JESUS CHRIST!" Bearman slammed back against his chair. It came up on two legs, like some boardroom wheelie, and nearly toppled over. His hands crashed against the table when he came back down.

Alex jumped, and Angela yelped with a sound like a hiccup.

"Holy hell," Bearman said, fully animated now, his head swiveling, chest heaving, greasy sweat streaming down his quivering face. "Did I just have a goddamn heart attack?"

Impatient with the lack of response he was getting from Alex and Angela, he turned in his seat towards Linda. He shook her by the shoulder. Then he pinched her cheeks in his fat hands and shook her by the face. Her eyes never left that distant place that appeared to be a world away. And maybe was.

His fingers were digging into her cheeks, creating white dots where they looked like they were about to punch through. "Linda," he was saying over and over again. "Linda, Linda, Linda!" If he squeezed any harder he was sure to dislocate her jaw.

"Stop it!" Angela cried. "Let go of her!"

Alex rushed forward and pried Bearman's hand from Linda's face.

Bearman swung his arms and brushed him off. "What's wrong with her?" he said.

No one answered.

He looked around, observing Steve and Eli, both still in their catatonic states. "Christ alive." It came out as a whisper, in a reverent tone.

Until he had a better handle on the situation, Alex figured it was best to keep silent. He knew Bearman couldn't stay quiet for long.

"Anyone care to tell me what the hell is going on here? Is this some kind of sick psychiatry experiment?"

"I don't know," Angela said, and looked up at Alex for an answer. So did Bearman. They were now both staring at him expectantly. He could stay silent no longer.

What would Eli do?

He would tell the truth.

Alex unclasped his hands and brought them around in front of him. It gave him something to look at. He couldn't meet their manic, pleading eyes. "Look, I'm just as confused as you. I don't know what is going on. I…" Then he did look up, just briefly, to make sure they were still attentive. To make sure they were still there. "It's like I slipped into a dream. I was somewhere else. And it felt like I was there for a long time. I can't explain it." Looking at his hands, with their neat, manicured nails, felt surreal. The sensory experience, the feeling of this being the one true reality, was indistinguishable from how he had felt while locked in the prison cell. He was now unsure which reality had been a dream and which one was real. "Is that what happened to you too?"

"It wasn't a dream," Angela said in a faraway voice. Her eyes had glazed over again. She was distracted by something in her mind. "But it couldn't have been real either."

"I'll tell you what it was," Bearman said. "It was mass hypnosis. That crazy fella, what's his name, somehow hypnotized us all."

"Crosby?" Alex said. He looked around again. "He's the only one who isn't here."

Angela was shaking her head. "Crosby doesn't know how to hypnotize anyone."

"How the hell do you know?" Bearman said. He stood up, wiping the sweat off his brow with his shirtsleeve. He took off his suit jacket, tossed it on the table and shivered. "How'd it get so damn cold in here?" He didn't look cold. Around his collar there was a ring of sweat that went all the way down to his chest.

"I would have known if he knew how to hypnotize. It would have been a major security concern."

Alex was nibbling on his thumbnail. "What was it he said? Right before we...went away?"

"Some crazy bullshit about his defenses against evil being stripped away," Bearman said. "Clearly, he's not cured. That was a major misjudgment on your end, Dr. Drexler. It don't get much more fucked up than this."

Alex dismissed the insult. He barely heard it. He was thinking back to the moment right before he had been transported away. "Right. He said that he could no longer hold it at bay. That he was forced to let it in. And he couldn't control what it wanted him to do."

"The medicine opens the mind." That's what his dead brother, Jerry, had said. Just before going in for a nasty chomp. Alex shook his head to dispel the image.

"That was all part of his act, I bet," Bearman said. "A bunch of mumbo jumbo that helped cast his little spell. Then, when he put us to sleep, he told us what to think. What to dream up. We need to find that crazy fucker. I bet he's escaped." Bearman started stomping towards the door.

Alex was still thinking. It wasn't a bad theory. Like Angela, he knew it would be extremely unlikely for the staff to have overlooked a patient's ability to perform hypnosis, but it wasn't impossible. Something about it didn't seem quite right, though. On the other hand, nothing about any of this seemed quite right.

"But…" Angela still had that vacant, faraway look, "…he couldn't have seeded those…dreams, or whatever they were. It was too personal. There were…things that he couldn't have known."

Bearman swung open the door.

Alex peered over his shoulder. He could see all the way down the hallway to the far wall. It was empty.

Bearman cupped his hands around his mouth and called, "Hey! Emergency! We need some help in here!" His voice echoed down the empty hallway and faded away. He waited a couple of seconds then shouted again, "Hey! Help in here!" The shout faded, and they didn't hear another sound. Bearman let the door slam shut. "Unbelievable," he said. "What kind of lax operation is Eli running here?"

He stormed back across the room to where Angela was sitting. "Too personal, you say? Hell, I don't know. That's probably the subconscious at work. That's elementary psychiatry, isn't it? Freudian, or whatever? It's alarming that I'm the one having to explain this to you guys."

"We need to find Crosby," Alex said.

Bearman gave him a disbelieving stare. "Wow, thanks for the topflight leadership, Captain Obvious. You've probably got a crazed killer on the loose. Not exactly the PR story we were going for, now, is it?"

"Angela, stay here and tend to the others. I'm going to find out what's going on." Alex turned and marched towards the door.

"Must be some code word to wake the others," Alex heard Bearman saying as he opened the door. "What would that crazy fuck think up?"

He walked out to find him.

CHAPTER FIFTY-THREE

The hallway was empty. Alex couldn't hear a sound. That was wrong. The corridors of Sugar Hill were never silent. They were always buzzing with people bustling about, the babble of conversations, the occasional shout or incoherent rant. Even at night, with the skeleton staff, and the patients all asleep, there was more noise than this.

The whole hospital must be stuck in the same state of hypnosis, Alex thought.

Alex started forward, more slowly than he'd intended. He couldn't help it. He was shaken by his experience and spooked by the silent emptiness of the hallway. And, now, as he trod forward, he was confronted with a new sensation, one more disturbing than anything before.

It felt as though nothing beyond his peripheral field of vision existed. Like the hallway behind him had ceased to exist as soon as he had taken a step forward.

He turned, mentally reprimanding himself for giving in to such a ridiculous fantasy. Still, he exhaled in relief to find the hallway still there, along with the door leading back to the boardroom.

But now he felt certain that the hallway behind him had disappeared. That the material world had been reduced to what lay in his immediate field of vision. He was sure that right now there was nothing behind him or beyond the boardroom door. Not now, anyway. If he were to open the door it would all return, but that would be because he *saw* it into existence. Manifest reality had become limited to what he could see, and he was the only one in it.

You're losing it, he thought, turning back around and continuing down the hallway, feeling like the only thing holding the world together was the power of his sight. *Fuck losing it. Whatever there was to lose, it's already gone.*

He came to the intersecting hallway at this corridor's dead end. He looked both left and right. Each direction was empty.

The main nursing station was to the left so he went that way, expecting at any moment to hear voices, footsteps, anything. But all he heard was the squeaky shuffle of his rubber-soled shoes sliding across the linoleum floor.

No one was attending the nursing station. He stood still and cocked his head, but didn't hear a sound.

"Hello?" he said in a voice just above a whisper. It sounded shockingly loud. He still felt like the world beyond his field of vision was nothing but empty space, the absent void that preceded all of creation.

"He-llo-o," he said musically, turning it into a three-syllable song. He felt like the subject of some alien experiment. Or that he was being pranked. His mind reverting back to some juvenile state in the face of this strange and unknowable situation. Silliness had always been his form of bravado.

He rapped his knuckles on the laminate countertop and the hollow knocking seemed to be the only sound left in the universe. He now felt sure that the absence of people somehow extended beyond the hospital walls.

He stood up on his toes and leaned over the countertop to see the workstation beyond it. It looked like it had just been vacated. The computers were still on, cycling through pictures of cute kittens. He saw cans of soda scattered about and a half-finished cup of coffee. Alex walked around the counter and picked it up. It was still warm. Almost hot, in fact. It hadn't been abandoned for long.

Something was seriously wrong. No, that was an understatement. Something catastrophic was happening. And it was unfolding at this very moment.

Whenever you think things can't get any worse, Alex thought, *the world around you vanishes.*

Alex heard something. It sounded like the rattling of a patient's bed, coming from one of the rooms farther down the hallway. Then he heard it again – the metallic clank of bedside braces being shaken. It sounded like it was just three doors down.

He flew forward, was at the door without feeling like he had taken a step. He turned the knob and entered.

The patient in the bed was pale and gaunt, yet beautiful, but Alex couldn't recall having ever seen her before. She was struggling with a nurse who was standing bedside, trying to restrain her arms. The patient turned her head when she saw Alex walk in and cried out, "No! I need to get out of here! I can't do this again!"

Alex could only see the back of the nurse struggling to restrain her. He couldn't tell who it was.

He approached the bed. The patient bowed her back and bucked her legs, the bed jerking across the floor, but she couldn't break free of the nurse's grasp. She stopped struggling for a moment to recoup her strength.

The nurse turned towards Alex. The sight of her stole his breath. She was covered in scar tissue, the stretched and ravaged sinew of burned skin. Her pale face lacked pigment, giving it a ghostly appearance; she didn't have lips. Her nose was nothing but two breathing holes, and she had nubs for ears.

He now saw that she was bald under her nurse's cap. And her skin, every inch of it, was a tortured map of gleaming texture, as though she had been turned inside out. He looked into her eyes and saw that they had the same vacant, distant stare as the people back in the boardroom. Then he realized they were fake.

Her voice was a charred rasp. "Help me with her."

"No!" the patient screamed. "I can't go through this again!"

Alex couldn't move. He felt like he had been paralyzed, his body numb from the neck down. The face staring at him with those sightless marble eyes was a nightmare. A mouthless amoeba in human form. He felt less threatened by the patient than the disfigured thing before him.

"Step back. Let her go," he said.

Was her skin oozing? Oh god. It looked like it was.

The nurse was facing him, but her eyes peered up and to the left – one more aslant than the other. "She's just in shock. It will pass soon," she rasped.

"I'll handle it," Alex said, and stepped in between the burned nurse and her patient. His arms touched her skin and it felt rubbery.

She stepped back and out of the way.

The patient stopped resisting as soon as Alex took hold of her arms. They were cold, unnaturally cold – *corpse cold* – despite the room being warm. He frowned, and looked over his shoulder at the nurse. His frown grew more severe. *How can she see?*

"What's going on here?" Alex asked.

The patient's eyes were roaming wildly. "Don't listen to her, she's not a real nurse. I need to get out of here."

Alex ignored her. He slid his hands down her icy arms towards her hands, maintaining a firm grip. He suspected that the patient was telling the truth, but didn't want to spook the probable imposter while his back was turned. "I've got the situation in hand now," he told the nurse. "I have something else I need your help with. I need you to go get the head nurse."

His hands kept sliding down until he reached the patient's wrists. He cupped them and turned them over, feeling the soft underside with his fingers. He couldn't find a pulse. He shifted his grip and waited.

"There is no one else," the nurse said. It was as though her lungs were clogged with smoke. He was surprised she wasn't coughing.

Alex sighed in frustration. "I mean it. We have a situation that I need help with. Now, go get me someone senior on staff. I don't care who it is."

Alex dug his fingers deeper into the spot on the patient's wrist where the radial artery runs. He couldn't feel a thing. He looked at the patient closely for the first time, now noticing the extreme paleness of her face, the bluish tint to her lips, the fine network of purple veins that blemished her temples and spidered down her neck. He looked into her eyes. They were milky with cataracts.

"Please don't hurt me," she said. She didn't appear to be breathing. Her chest never rose. Alex let go of her wrists and began backing away.

The nurse followed him with her head. Her marble eyes searched the ceiling. "We need to find Eli," she whispered in her scorched voice. The skin at the corner of her mouth split slightly and clear fluid dribbled out.

The patient sat up in bed. "Eli's here?"

"What do you want with Dr. Alpert?"

The patient turned to the nurse, her opaque eyes opening wide, her blue lips expanding into a delighted smile. "Oh thank god. Eli. I get it now." She turned back towards Alex. "Can you take us to him?"

"I, uh…" Alex stammered, backstepping towards the door.

The lights dimmed, and a low hum began as if the electrical power was being drained. A tortured howling came from down the hallway – guttural and inhuman. It was nothing like the caterwauling so common among the patients. This was the sound of an animal – some beast – either angry or in pain.

"Please. You must help us," the nurse said, walking towards him. He couldn't tell whether or not she looked scared. Her face was incapable of expression. Shadows writhed across the indentations in her skin.

"I'll go check it out," he said, scrabbling backwards, feeling exposed as he turned to open the door.

Alex stumbled out into the hallway. The door shut behind him. He was breathing hard as he watched it, waiting for it to open, but it never did.

Yes, something was seriously wrong.

It's like a dream within a dream, he thought. He heard the guttural howl again, closer and coming his way. *But I think I prefer the other one. At least my brother was there.*

He saw a long shadow emerge at the far end of the hall, preceding whatever form it was cast from. It had long, ropy arms and a hunched back with a thin neck stretched forward. Its disfigured head grew up the wall, appearing to turn and look his way, as if of its own accord.

Alex turned and shuffled forward in a facsimile of a run. It was like his legs had been frostbitten. They were stiff and moved at odd angles. The walls reverberated with the guttural growl of the beast behind him.

The turn was over ten feet away. There was no way he would make it there in time. His shoes were slapping and squeaking against the floor, his legs pistoning as fast as he could pick them up and put them down, but his pace was painfully slow.

Then he heard its voice. But it wasn't at all what he'd expected to hear. It was a woman's voice, soft and somewhat scratchy. "Hey!" she cried. "Wait! Stop. Wait for me!"

He slowed and peered over his shoulder. A woman had emerged at the far end of the hallway, in the spot where the long shadow had appeared. The distance was too great for Alex to see her clearly. The lights were too dim, and growing dimmer still, so he could no longer see her shadow.

Her shadow? It couldn't have been hers.

But she appeared to be slender and young, somewhere in her mid-thirties. Despite not being able to clearly discern her features, he could somehow make out the color of her eyes – a pale and penetrating blue – the color of a frozen pool. Her eyes seemed to precede her face somehow, like cold candle flames held out to see through the fading light.

Alex turned, walking backwards. The woman was walking at a regular pace but appeared to be gaining ground at an impossible rate. It was like she was on a moving sidewalk, while he was standing still.

"Are you a doctor?" she yelled. "I need your help." The lights flickered and faltered. Her eyes flashed like sun on ice. She was halfway up the hallway now, moving much faster than her gait should allow.

He was not going to make it. She was going to be upon him in just a few more of her exponential steps. He saw her more clearly as she grew closer. She was ravishing, but also severe. Her face honed into sharp angles with a pinched, needy expression. It was like she was fighting to stay composed, resisting the urge to launch forward.

Alex spun around. He slipped and almost fell, saving himself by bracing his hand on the floor. There was a patient's door just up ahead on the right. *Safety,* his mind was screaming. *I need to get somewhere safe.*

The woman did not make a sound. He couldn't tell how fast she was approaching. He knew she had to be just a step or two behind him.

Alex lunged forward and grabbed the doorknob, swinging it open and spinning inside. He slammed it shut and leaned his weight against it, hoping to keep it closed.

A woman screamed. Then, still excited, said, "What's wrong?" The voice came from behind him, from within the room.

He didn't think his heart could take another shock. It was already past its maximum RPM. *Fine, kill me. I'll take a heart attack over this.*

He squeezed his eyes shut, hoping that whoever was in the room with him would simply go away.

Then, he heard a man's voice. This one easier to recognize. "What the hell's gotten into you, son?"

The woman with the icy-blue eyes had not attempted to open the door. He couldn't tell if she was on the other side of it or not. He turned his head, keeping his body pressed against the door, to look within the room.

It was impossible. He was back in the conference room. There's no way this door could have brought him here. Angela was next to Eli. It looked like she was trying to wake him. Bearman was pacing along the right side of the room by the wall. His shirt was so sweaty now it was see-through, revealing a matted pelt of curly, black hair. At least he now had his sleeves rolled up.

Alex staggered, his legs nearly giving out. "How did I get here?"

Angela and Bearman exchanged the same confused stare before directing it back his way.

"Come again?" Bearman said, looking annoyed.

Angela looked afraid. "Who's out there? What are you running from?" The others in the room all remained catatonic.

"Whatever's going on," Alex said, and swallowed, trying to catch his breath, "it's going on out there as well."

Alex pointed back towards the door. "Something's taken over Sugar Hill."

CHAPTER FIFTY-FOUR

This was not Eden. It had become hell.

Crosby had awoken between the cold and rigid corpses of the naked man and woman, whom he thought of as Adam and Eve. They were both perforated by swollen puncture wounds with ragged purple edges. It looked like the snake had bitten each of them at least a hundred times.

But, that wasn't the worst of it. They were sexless now. Their genitalia had been devoured by something other than a snake. The woman's chest featured two gaping wounds where her breasts should have been. The man's groin was a glistening pit.

The first man and woman would never give birth to humanity.

It was still dark outside. But there was no beauty to it now. No innocence. It was the darkness that conceals the demons who stalk the night. It was the dark that hides the shadows.

He no longer felt the omnipotent power that had filled him before. It was as if he had been drained, sucked dry by the snake of original sin. He had tried to manipulate this new reality, to bend it to his will, but had been unsuccessful. And so he was trapped in a world of his own creation, hunted by creatures that hungered for his soul.

The creatures emerged from the night. He saw them pass, lurching out of the garden and into the hospital realm. They wore human skin, but he saw them for what they really were. He had seen them in the hospital staffs' heads. But there was one whom he knew much more personally.

She hadn't come from the garden. At least, he hadn't seen her here yet. But she would walk to the border separating this world from the other one, and look inside as though searching for something. As though searching for him.

She had finally come back to find him. To erase her greatest mistake. Or, worse, to take him back home. He wouldn't let her, though. He couldn't. So he stayed hidden, deep within the darkness of the garden, under a dense thicket of bushes. Where he hoped he wouldn't be seen.

CHAPTER FIFTY-FIVE

"Well, did you think to call the cops?"

Shit! No, he hadn't. *I was too busy running from...from...*

From what, he didn't know.

Alex pulled out his cell phone. He stared at the blank screen. "Battery's dead."

Bearman and Angela both checked theirs.

"Well shit," Bearman said. "So go back out there and use the landline."

Alex still had his forearm barring the door. He expected the lady, the impossibly fast woman with the disfigured shadow, to test it at any moment. "There are people out there."

"Yeah, so? Let them know we need some help. What the hell is wrong with you?"

Alex didn't know how to explain what he'd just seen. It was all too surreal. Too insane. It felt like some elaborate fantasy concocted by a schizophrenic, not the sound observations of a rational mind.

"Wait, that's it," Alex said, an idea falling into place. He turned and pressed his back against the door, bracing with his legs. "What if we're all having some kind of psychotic episode?" He expected their eyes to light up once the revelation hit.

They simply stared back at him with the same blank expression.

Bearman shook his head, his bovine lips flapping as he exhaled in exasperation. "I ain't got time for this," he said, marching towards Alex and the door. "Move aside."

"Wait a minute," Alex said. He didn't want to open the door. He was afraid to let the lady in, although he wasn't sure why.

Bearman pressed forward, getting into Alex's face. He smelled like pickled lemons; his sweat betrayed his fear. But he hid it well. His eyes were narrow slits of anger, his mouth a scowl of disdain. "This has been a complete catastrophe," he said through clenched teeth. "And you're not doing a single thing to make it better. Get the fuck out of my way so that I can fix this. Be prepared to explain yourself when I get back."

Alex didn't move. His mind was trying to compute too much at once, paralyzing him in place.

Bearman placed a heavy hand on Alex's shoulder and pawed him aside. He pulled open the door.

Alex tucked his head like a turtle seeking protection within its shell. He waited for the woman to storm through. Then he heard the door slam shut. He turned.

Bearman was gone. He could hear his clomping tread storming down the hall, his booming voice calling, "Hello? Where the fuck is everyone?" His voice was fading.

Alex looked at Angela. She was sitting up straight in her chair, listening, her senses at full alert.

Then, faintly, he heard Bearman's voice change. "Hey! You! Hold up there a minute! Come here!" Seconds passed, then he heard his voice again, fainter still and unintelligible. A baritone murmur felt more than heard.

Alex strained his ears, pressing his head against the door. He held his breath in silence for a full minute, but didn't hear another sound.

From behind, Angela whispered, "Alex, what's going on?"

He turned. She was the only animated face in a row of mannequins. He wondered what was going on behind those placid masks.

"Shared psychosis," he said. "It's the only explanation that makes sense."

Angela frowned. "*Folie à deux*?" she said, reciting the technical term for the transfer of psychosis to people with otherwise healthy minds. "But how? It happened so suddenly. And it seems to be affecting all of us. That doesn't fit the profile."

Alex was hardly listening. He was distracted by the menacing silence emanating from out in the hall.

He's not coming back, Alex's mind said, and his first feeling was relief. His second was shame.

"What did you see out there?" Angela asked.

Alex tiptoed away from the door as though it were a ticking time bomb that could explode at any moment. He grabbed a chair and pulled it to the open spot across from Angela. When he sat down it felt like he'd unloaded two hundred extra pounds. *I'm not meant to be in charge*, he thought wearily. All he wanted to do was rest.

He told her about what he had seen, the abandoned nurses' station with the discarded cups and warm coffee. The two women in the patient's room. His descriptive abilities were incapable of relaying the severity of the nurse's burns, or her apparent ability to see despite her marble eyes. He told her about the third woman whom he had encountered. The one with the cold eyes that blazed in the darkness like blue flame. He struggled to explain why he had felt threatened by her.

"She started running towards me," he said, although that wasn't really true. She had calmly walked at a sprinter's speed. She had defied physics.

"Who were they?" Angela had begun glancing at the door and picking at the cuticle of her thumb. She pulled away a strip of skin without noticing, and it began to bleed.

"I think they were hallucinations."

"But, then, where is everyone else? Why isn't there anyone to help us?"

Alex turned to Eli. He would know how to help. He motioned towards him with his head. They both looked at his vacant face.

"Where did *you* go?" Alex said to Angela. "What did *you* see?"

The only sound in the room was Angela picking at her nails. Her eyes welled up, and she blinked back tears. "I can't explain it," she said. "I don't think I even want to talk about it. Not yet, anyway."

"I think we need to. It may help us figure this out. Offer some kind of clue."

Angela straightened in her chair. She raised her head a bit higher and stopped fingering her nails. "I was molested as a child," she said, looking frankly into Alex's face. "By my uncle who was a Catholic priest. It went on for several years, until we moved away.

"I thought I had left it behind when it ended. I tried to block it out. But I guess I carried it inside. Deep within my subconscious.

"That's where I went. I relived my molestation, but in a far more elaborate and nightmarish way."

Alex had often wondered what Angela harbored from her past or was like in her personal life. The piercings, the dyed hair and arm ink suggested an alternate persona, but she had always been a consummate professional at work. It made sense now.

"I didn't know," he said, fidgeting.

Her eyes left his. They seemed to gaze inside. Then she took a deep breath, her chest inflated, and she appeared confident and composed. "It was horrible. Like a dream, but real. A true living nightmare. But also cathartic. I feel better somehow. Like a thorn has been plucked from my psyche. I can't explain it. There's no possible way."

"You don't need to," he said. "I experienced the same thing." He attempted a smile, but it quivered and felt false, so he stopped. "Well, different, but the same in that it felt real."

She watched him, waiting for him to go on. After several false starts, he did. "I was in a prison somewhere. Bearman was there. He was the head guard locking me away. I was put in a cell with Devon. You know, the..."

Angela nodded. "The orderly who attacked Jerry."

"Right. But he didn't kill him. He couldn't have. I saw him here as I was rushing out to help Rachel, while Jerry was still alive. I was his alibi, but I didn't say anything. Let's just say that he wasn't very happy to see me. He nearly beat me to death."

Angela scooted forward in her seat. "Wait. Then that proves it."

Alex cocked his head. "What?"

"That it was a dream. You don't have any bruising. There's no sign that you were beaten."

He hadn't thought of that. He pressed his fingers against his face and felt no pain. "That shouldn't come as a surprise. Clearly, what we experienced was some sort of lucid dream or psychotic break."

"But I've never had a dream that felt so completely real. Not even close."

Alex closed his eyes, remembering. "Me either," he said.

He rubbed the bridge of his nose, relieved by the lack of pain, and continued. "My wife and father came to visit. They told me that I had been convicted of malpractice for testing my experimental medicine on unauthorized patients."

"But you had Bearman's permission. You had the support of the board."

"For Crosby, I did. Not for—" He cut off, realizing that he hadn't told anyone else about administering the medicine to Jerry.

Angela gave him time. Then gently... "Who?"

He tried to hold her eyes, but couldn't. He cowered into his hands. "Jerry." It was little more than a whisper, which quickly evaporated into the utter silence of the room. The air between them thrummed.

"I treated Jerry, and he got better. One hundred percent better. He was back to his old self. There were no negative side effects that I could detect. But he died before we could make any definitive conclusions."

A flush had crept up Alex's neck. It sat there and burned. "He was there too. In the cell with me, covered under a blanket like a corpse in a morgue. He was…in the dream, or whatever it was, he was dead. His throat cut." Alex dragged his thumb across this own throat as though slitting it.

Then he stopped speaking in the monotone voice of remembrance, focusing more intently on each word and its implications. "He told me that the medicine was responsible for his death. He accused me of 'conjuring his killer.' He said something about how the medicine opened up the mind. Something about how there was still time to create another world."

He rapped a knuckle atop the table and leaned back. "I don't know. It seemed to make more sense at the time. Sounds crazy now."

He looked up and winced when he saw the anger in Angela's eyes.

"On Jerry? You experimented on your own brother? Why?"

And then he felt angry himself, at Angela and her accusation. At himself. "Because there were no other options. He's been sick for half his life. He had just been dismissed from Sugar Hill for having another episode. And here I have a way to help him. What, am I supposed to hold out on my brother? Just because of some regulations made by organizations that care more about profits than patients? No, fuck that."

"Is that why? Or did you see an opportunity to fine-tune your formula without having to report the outcomes to a regulatory agency?"

Jerry's pale face flashed back from the prison cell. *"You…meant to…get rich…. You…meant to…get respect…. You didn't…think of…the consequences…. It was…at my…expense."*

The memory brought Alex a sensation of physical pain. Pain from fighting against the truth.

He shrank in his seat and slowly nodded his head. "Yes, that too. It was both. It was. I did it for personal reasons. For money. For prestige."

Angela leaned forward. She looked more excited now than angry. "So you were harboring guilt, if only subconsciously. Which is why in your dream sequence you were sent to prison. You were being punished for your crimes. And then you take a metaphorical beating for the wrong you committed against Devon, and are given a second chance by Jerry to make amends for experimenting on him."

Alex's chuckle contained as much humor as the rattling of chains. "I'd say that's a workable theory. Pretty fucking obvious when you lay it out like that. But," he said, scratching the back of his head, "that doesn't explain what caused it."

"But you already said that. *Folie à deux.*"

"Yeah, maybe," he said. "I suppose it could have been transferred by Crosby. But you're right. I don't see how it could have happened instantaneously and affected so many people at the exact same time."

Angela began picking her cuticle again. It sounded like a clock ticking.

They both glanced at the door, feeling a shared sense of dread. Bearman had been gone a long time.

"There is a connection, though," Alex said.

"Between?"

"Jerry and Crosby. They were both administered a refined version of the formula, and both have been subject to unexplainable experiences."

Angela nibbled her thumb, gazing inward. "Right," she said. "What was it that Jerry said in your dream? You conjured his killer?"

"And now...you've conjured...yours."

"Yes. And Rachel also experienced some kind of hallucinatory spell during the murder. She was convinced it was Devon who came and killed Jerry, which we know is impossible. She also claims to have—" He stopped.

"What?"

Alex sighed. "To have seen her dead dog. The one I ran over."

Angela groaned, but it was more from confusion than revulsion. "So what do we do now?"

What would Eli do? "I wish they would wake up."

"How would that help?"

"Strength in numbers."

Angela stood. She stretched her arms overhead, rising up onto her toes. She looked like a cat waking up from a nap. "We can't just stay in here. We've got to get help."

"That's what Bearman's doing."

"Well where did he go? He should be back by now. What if he's fallen back into that dream state?"

What if he's been killed, Alex thought. *By what? His imagination?*

Alex stood and stretched as well. Then stopped, wincing. He had almost pulled a muscle. "What if he ran into those women," he said, rubbing his lower back.

"So what if he did? They're just hallucinations, right?"

"You...conjured my...killer."

"Yes. They have to be."

Angela came around the table and stood next to him. They both stared at the door. "Then what do we have to be afraid of?" she said.

Alex didn't answer. He took a tentative step forward.

Angela followed.

Before he knew it, his hand was grasping the door handle. He pulled open the door on the empty hallway beyond.

CHAPTER FIFTY-SIX

Bearman had to bend over and rest his hands against his legs. He was panting, his heart performing a drum roll in his chest. He couldn't catch up to the lady. She kept darting around corners, always down at the far end of the hall. The strange thing about it was that it didn't look like she was running. She appeared to be taking a casual stroll.

That little twerp was going to pay for this. He would be the one to take the fall. He would reinstate Eli until he found a more appropriate replacement. Of all the fucked-up things he had seen while running the board of a loony bin, this one beat them all.

He looked up. There she was, waiting for him. Sweat dripped into his left eye and he blinked it away. "Wait," he wheezed, knowing she wouldn't listen.

I keep this up and I'll have a heart attack. His shirt was completely soaked through.

But there's no one else here, he thought, unbelievable as that was. And he was still shaken by the dream he had experienced while he was hypnotized. Or whatever the hell had happened to him. It was better to stay active, to keep his mind occupied, than to let it wander back to the hellish place it had been. Better to leave his first wife dead and buried where she belonged. He'd prefer a padded cell to facing her vengeful spirit again, and would probably need one if he did.

He pulled his right leg forward with his hands and lumbered on. As soon as he started moving the lady dashed around the corner. "Stupid bitch!" he yelled, and strode forward, bolstered by the resurgent strength of his voice.

A door opened halfway down the hall, and a doctor peeked out. He saw Bearman and his face turned stern. "What's the problem?" he said.

"The problem?" Bearman ran a hand through his sweaty hair, plastering it flat against his head. His laugh was like an engine revving, he was about to blow steam. "Where the fuck do you want me to start?"

The doctor straightened in surprise. He pushed his glasses higher on his nose and squinted, his upper lip rising like a rat's. "Excuse me?"

Bearman was several inches taller and was accustomed to using his height to his advantage. He looked down his nose at the doctor. "I've been all over this place looking for help for a good half hour now. Where is everyone?"

"I'm not sure what you mean. But you need to settle down. Come with me, please." The doctor turned to walk back through the door.

Bearman grabbed his arm. "Wait a fucking minute. I'm talking to you. Who are you?"

The doctor eyed Bearman's hand until he let go. He pinched a name tag on his white lapel and angled it up for Bearman to read.

"Dr. Francis?" Bearman said.

The doctor offered a terse nod. "Come with me. I can help you." He turned and walked back into the room before Bearman could grab him again.

Bearman balled his fists and followed.

It appeared to be an examination room. It was larger than he would have expected from the outside. A patient was lying in a contoured chair, restrained by rows of thick leather straps. A stool and instrument tray stood beside it. Low cabinets lined the walls, and two large orderlies loomed in the far corners.

"We're just finishing up here," the doctor said. He walked to the head of the patient and pulled the instrument tray towards him, retrieving a tool that looked like a staple gun. The patient began whimpering, pleading in gibberish. A white foam frothed from his mouth.

"Hush!" Dr. Francis said. He reached down and grabbed something hanging from the back of the headrest and pulled it upwards as though he were closing the lid on a mailbox.

Bearman shifted his position for a better view. He gasped. His stomach roiled in revulsion.

The doctor had just replaced the man's scalp, covering his gleaming, blood-smeared skull. He held it in place with one hand while he pressed the staple gun against the seam and began stapling the scalp in place. The man screamed every time a staple was fired.

"Christ, man! What are you doing?"

Dr. Francis never looked up. He fired the final staple and began unstrapping the restraints.

Once freed, the patient crossed his arms across his chest and curled into a fetal position. He was trembling, mewling.

Dr. Francis motioned to the orderlies, who moved forward, pulled the patient from the chair and dragged him out the door.

"Have a seat, please, and tell me what's the problem." Dr. Francis patted the chair. It left behind a red handprint strewn with a few strands of black hair.

Sweat trickled down the side of Bearman's face. He ran a hand through his damp hair and snuck a peek towards the door. Something was most certainly wrong here, but he wasn't sure what.

"What were you doing to that patient?"

Dr. Francis's face lacked expression. "Relieving him. Letting the demons out, you might say."

Bearman smirked. "I didn't think Dr. Alpert approved of such techniques."

"He may not. I'm not sure what that has to do with me." His head tilted slightly to the left. "Is that one of the problems you need help with?"

Bearman could hear his own labored breathing, a thin wheezing from deep within his lard-covered lungs. He felt lightheaded and his thoughts were muddled. He tried to cure all of this by clearing his throat. "Look, who's in charge here? We have a situation."

Dr. Francis furrowed his brow. He circled the bed and walked towards Bearman. "I thought you were in charge here."

Bearman wanted to back away from the man, but stood his ground. He puffed out his chest. "That's right. I am."

Dr. Francis put a bloodstained hand on Bearman's back and gently guided him towards the chair. "Here, rest for a minute. Let's get this all sorted out."

Bearman resisted, leaning back with all his weight, but still found himself taking steps forward, the chair getting closer. "Wait. Stop." He tried to turn. He tried to get away from the doctor's gentle guiding hand.

"Don't resist. Just have a seat."

Bearman's legs brushed against the chair. He grabbed an armrest and braced against it with both hands, pushing backwards. "I said let go of me!"

"A little help in here," Dr. Francis said calmly, quietly.

The door flew open and the two large orderlies rushed through. Dr. Francis backed away and they grabbed Bearman by his arms, wrenching his hands away from the armrest and cranking them behind his back. They wrestled him onto the chair, holding him in place as Dr. Francis began clasping the leather restraints, starting near Bearman's feet.

"This is for your protection as well as mine," he said. "I'll release them as soon as you've calmed down."

Bearman looked like a riding bull whose flank strap had just been pulled tight. He wasn't close to calming down. "What the fuck do you think you're doing? I'll have your fucking heads!"

Dr. Francis made a grunting sound as he pulled another strap taut and clamped it down, this one around Bearman's bulging belly. His wrists had been secured in padded cuffs. Only a few straps remained before he was fully restrained, but he was already immobilized.

The orderlies released him and returned to their stations in the corners. "There's no need to make such threats. I'm here to help you, remember. Please tell me what the problem is."

The door opened. A woman walked through. Bearman's neck strained as he looked around Dr. Francis to get a better view. She looked fierce. Her pale-blue eyes locked with his, and he shivered. It was like falling through ice into frigid water. While he hadn't gotten a good look at her earlier, this was the woman who had been running from him. He was sure of it.

"Ah, just in time," Dr. Francis said, cinching a strap against Bearman's chest.

It constricted his breathing. His arms were now pinned to his sides.

The woman smiled. It gleamed like the steel shaft of a knife. She was slight, but looked disproportionately strong. Her hands were like claws, with knotted knuckles and long, slender fingers tipped with sharp, talon-like nails.

"What's his condition?" She approached the chair and leaned over as though inspecting some strange and exotic bug.

Dr. Francis joined her, peering down, the impassive face of a professor beginning his lecture. "Well, he's sociopathic, for starters. He displays symptoms of grandeur and inflated self-importance. He places little to no value on others, seeing them merely as objects to manipulate or obstacles to overcome. He is the center of his own world, suffering from uncontrollable fits of anger, and is prone to extreme bouts of verbal and physical violence."

The woman placed a hand on Bearman's meaty thigh and squeezed. "He's one sick puppy."

Dr. Francis pushed his glasses up his nose and nodded.

She dragged her hand higher up his thigh, cupped his groin and squeezed. "Oh, and quite the man."

Bearman's eyes flashed wide. "The fuck!"

"Such a foul mouth," she said and tsk-tsked with her tongue. "No matter. He will do. He's the best we've found so far."

"I agree. Not much more needs to be done with this one," Dr. Francis said. "I'll prepare him, then."

She leaned over and looked into Bearman's bulging eyes. "Don't you worry about a thing. I'll take care of you, just as long as you help me get what I need."

Bearman's eyes narrowed. His face assumed the expression of hate that he had conditioned so exquisitely over time. "You have no idea how bad you have fucked up, you crazy cunt. I am the head of this hospital. If you don't unstrap me right this—"

She covered his mouth with one of her strong, bony hands. It was dry and cold. "My, my," she said, "I wish we could do something about the language. It's just awful."

"I could shut off his linguistic abilities."

The woman seemed to consider this. "No, so long as it's not directed towards me, I think I can manage. We'll want him to seem like himself."

"Right. Again, there's not much to change."

She looked up at the doctor, her hand still clamped over Bearman's mouth. "Let's begin."

Dr. Francis approached the instrument tray. He picked up an electric bone saw and turned it on. It whirred to life with a high-pitched whine, its serrated blades blurring.

Bearman tried to scream, but was stifled by the woman's hand.

Dr. Francis walked behind him. "Sorry, but we're all out of anesthetic," he said. He smiled and began to giggle as he reached down to the mask around his neck and pulled it up over his mouth. "There aren't any nerves in the brain, however. So this shouldn't hurt... much."

He lowered the saw to the top of Bearman's forehead. The blade sliced easily through his skin, ripping it wide.

The woman's blue eyes gleamed as blood and bone dust sprayed into the air. She removed her hand from his mouth and Bearman's voice commingled with the bone saw to create a single scream.

CHAPTER FIFTY-SEVEN

The lights flickered. Shadows danced in the hollows of Angela's cheeks and the sockets of her eyes. "This isn't Sugar Hill," she said.

Alex knew she was right, but wasn't ready to admit it.

The hallway shared the same general appearance as Sugar Hill, but there were vague differences, as those experienced in a dream. Only, now, they were obvious and felt more out of place. Most noticeable being the silence and absence of people.

Just wait until you see the ones who are *here,* Alex thought.

Then they heard the scream, faint and horrible. A howl, more animal than human.

Angela grabbed Alex by the arm so hard it hurt. "Okay, maybe we should go back."

"That's the same howl I heard last time I went out. Right before the woman started chasing me."

Angela began backpedaling towards the door, dragging Alex with her. When they reached it, she turned and pushed it open. It led into the cramped quarters of a patient's room. Her head was on a swivel. "Where's the conference room?" she said.

The howl came again, reverberating off the walls. They both spun back around.

"I don't know," Alex said. "It never should have been there in the first place. We're in a different part of the hospital."

"What do you mean?"

Alex shrugged. "Just what I said. I don't know how to explain it."

He pulled his arm free. His hand was tingling from lack of circulation. He shook it out as he started back down the hallway. "No sense in staying here. Besides…" he turned back and tried to smile – in the flickering light, it was a crypt keeper's grin, "…it's all just part of our imagination, right?"

"If this is what our patients go through, I regard them with a whole new level of respect. I'm not sure how much more of this I can take."

"I think we're just getting started," Alex said. He waited for her to join him, and then they shuffled down the hallway side by side.

Angela's legs were shaking. Her voice trembled. "Mind if I hold on to you?" She grabbed for his arm again.

"Just as long as you let some blood through."

She eased her grip and they shuffled along. Ahead was the nurses' station. They stopped to take a look.

Alex showed her the abandoned cups and the coffee that was still warm. He pointed towards the door halfway down the hallway. "That's where I saw the patient and the nurse. The one with the burns."

Angela's grip tightened again and Alex gasped. "Sorry," she said. She eased her grip, but remained frozen in place.

"Come on. Let's check it out." Alex pulled her forward. Reluctantly, she followed.

They came upon the door from the side. There was a window in its front that they couldn't yet look through. In order to peer in they would have to risk being seen. They crouched down and duck-walked underneath it, then pressed their ears to the door. They couldn't hear a thing.

"I'll check," Alex whispered. He took a few silent breaths and then started to rise.

Angela stopped him. *No,* she mouthed, shaking her head. She brought him back down to her level. "I need to break through this fear. Let me."

Alex held out his hand as if to say, *by all means.*

Angela let go of his arm. She balled her hands into fists, her face grew stern. She was nodding her head, psyching herself up. She began to rise, slowly, neck craned back in order to peek over the window's lower lip with the least amount of her head exposed.

She was just below the window when the booming voice echoed down from the far end of the hallway. "Hey! Where'd you guys go? I've been looking all over for you."

Angela lost her balance and landed on her butt.

Alex almost sprained his neck from turning his head so fast.

Bearman was at the other end of the hallway, half concealed in the shadow of the far dark corner. But his voice was unmistakable.

Angela sat up. "Thank god," she said.

Alex marched forward, staying hunched over until he was past the door, and then he began speed-walking away. The air felt cold behind him. He expected the door to swing open any second.

Bearman stayed put, waiting. "I found help," Bearman said. "They're this way." He pointed towards the turn.

"Thank god!" Angela said again. Alex heard her footsteps behind him as she started jogging to catch up. It looked like Bearman was holding something by his side. Something small, with a sharp, clawed end like a pickaxe.

Good, he has a weapon, Alex thought.

Bearman retreated as Alex drew closer, sinking deeper into shadow. He was but a black outline against the darker shade.

Alex slowed and stopped several steps away. "Who'd you find?" he said.

"Come here and I'll show you."

Angela's footsteps slapped against the linoleum floor as she arrived. "What's the plan? Did you call for help?"

"This way." Bearman pointed down the hallway leading off to his right, his other hand holding the object down by his side. "It's Crosby who's doing this," he said. "We have to find him. You need to help us."

Alex took a step closer. There was something wrong with Bearman's face. It looked wet, like he was bleeding. "Wait, help who? We need to get help back to Eli and the others."

"Stop with the fucking questions and get over here! I'll tell you what we need to do!"

Angela flinched from the outburst and took a step back. "We need to stay calm," she said.

"I'm telling you to get over here right fucking now," Bearman said. It sounded like a growl.

Alex took a reflexive step forward, and Bearman pounced. The dim yellow light illuminated his face. It was a mask of blood streaming down from a ragged wound running across the top of his head. It had been crudely stitched together with staples, the skin was rippled. Blood seeped through yawning gaps. Only one eye was open, gazing through the red sheen; his mouth was a crooked snarl.

Alex tried to scramble backwards, pinwheeling his arms. But

Bearman grabbed him. He spun Alex around, curling an arm around his neck, and brought the sharp end of the instrument to the front of his face. It scraped against his cheek, just under the eye, drawing blood.

"You too, darling," he said to Angela. "You're both coming with me."

Alex felt his stomach churn and his bladder loosen. More than fearing for his life, he prayed he wouldn't pee.

"Wait, wait. What are you doing?" Angela said, her hands held out in a defensive posture. She was backing up.

"There's evil here," Bearman said. "We need to get rid of it."

"Okay, look. We can help you. But this isn't the way."

"I'm not going to fucking tell you again!" He pushed Alex forward, still holding the instrument against his face. Both of their faces were now running with blood.

Alex tried to speak, but Bearman squeezed his neck harder so that all he could do was gurgle.

A door opened down the hallway. Angela turned.

Bearman hesitated.

The burned nurse walked out, the patient with the frizzy, blonde hair followed. "Get away from him," the blonde lady said.

"Don't listen to her," Bearman said. "Who knows where the fuck they came from."

★   ★   ★

Angela was caught in another nightmare.

On one side of the hallway was Bearman, who looked like he had just been lobotomized by some psychopath. On the other were too wraiths: a woman so severely burned she was hardly recognizable as human and another whose skin was the ghostly shade of blue seen only on the dead. But Bearman seemed like the more hostile of the two options.

He wiped blood from his open eye as he shuffled towards her. It was wide and deranged.

"What happened to you?" Angela said, still retreating. "What happened to your head?"

"I needed it. It helped me to understand."

"Hurry! Come with us!" the women called.

Bearman was closing the distance on Angela as she considered her options.

"We can't let him get too close!"

Bearman picked up his pace, pressing forward. Blood pattered from his face to the floor. The woman with the burns broke away from the other and rushed towards Angela. She was trapped, being descended upon by two monsters.

Angela froze, and then backed up against the wall. The burned nurse was closing the distance. Her unblinking eyes were staring up towards the ceiling.

Angela covered her face. She was too scared to scream.

Bearman was just steps away. Alex was backpedaling with his feet, trying to slow him down. But Bearman kept barreling forward. He removed the pickaxe-looking instrument from Alex's face. Grunting, he swung it towards Angela's head.

She was nearly yanked off her feet; her shoulder broke free from its socket. The pickaxe breezed through her hair and crashed into the wall where her head had just been. Chunks of stone went flying.

Now Angela screamed, but mostly from pain. Her shoulder socket was on fire.

The burned woman pulled her arm again to get her moving, then pushed her from behind. Together, they ran.

Bearman was screaming behind them. Angela looked to find him lurching forward, but fading into the distance.

They reached the blonde woman and Angela almost collapsed in fear. Her face was webbed with black veins, her skin blue, almost purple. Her eyes were covered in a milky film.

She looked more closely at the burned woman. Her eyes were blind too.

They're dead, she thought. *Both of them, dead.*

The blonde woman grabbed her by her good wrist. Angela's other arm dangled uselessly by her side. It sparked fire with every step. The three of them ran past the nurses' station. They turned the corner and sprinted to the end of the hallway.

They stopped and the two women stared at Angela with their unseeing eyes. "Open it," the burned woman rasped. It was like wind rustling through reeds.

"It's a dead end. A patient's room." Angela was fighting back hysteria, struggling against shock.

"Not anymore," the patient said.

"What?" Angela said. "No, wait. What about Dr. Drexler?"

Bearman's shout came from around the corner, as though in answer. "You go with them, you die!"

What do I do? What do I do? What do I do?

"Please open it. It has to be you." The woman's lipless mouth was charred black on the inside.

A shadow approached from the other end of the hallway. A writhing, shuffling mass – Alex in front, Bearman behind. Bearman's shadow looked misshapen. Long and hulking, with an oblong head and loping arms. He screamed again, but it sounded more like a howl.

"It's happening. Please, you must hurry."

Angela tried to raise her right arm, but it wouldn't budge. Pain streaked down her side. "I can't," she said, stifling a sob.

"Yes, you can. *We* can't." It was the blonde woman. She pressed her hands on her hips and shifted her weight as though mildly impatient. "But if you want to get turned into one of them, be my guest."

Bearman turned the corner. He still had Alex by the neck. Both of their faces were a bloody mess.

Seeing Angela trapped at the end of the hallway, Alex braced his feet against the floor and began pressing backwards, trying to block Bearman from advancing.

Bearman arched his back, lifting Alex's feet off the floor. Then he raised the pickaxe into the air and swung it into Alex's unprotected stomach. It sunk in up to its hilt, and Alex collapsed to the floor. Bearman leapt over him and began running their way, snarling, blood spraying from the ragged gash on his forehead.

The blonde lady began tapping her foot.

The burned one pleaded with a sigh, "Pleaaasse."

Angela grabbed the door handle with her left hand. She pushed it open and fell inside. The women squeezed in behind her.

The door slammed shut with a bang.

CHAPTER FIFTY-EIGHT

Angela could hear Bearman charging towards the door. He would burst inside any second now. She tried to push herself up off the ground but collapsed on her dislocated arm, crying out in pain. She flipped onto her back. "Bar the door!" she yelled.

The two women turned, but didn't move. All three of them watched the door as the foot stomps closed in. They heard the door open, and then silence descended. The door on their end remained shut.

The women turned back towards Angela, both looking nonchalant. Angela was hyperventilating. Her head fell back and hit the floor and she fought to catch her breath. Looking up at the ceiling, she realized where she was. Back in the conference room.

The two women leaned over, emerging into Angela's upside-down field of vision.

Those eyes. God, how do they see through those eyes?

"You're safe now," the patient said. When she spoke the black veins running up her neck pulsed darker. She held out a hand.

Angela took it. It was placid and cold.

Angela stood and turned. Sure enough, she was back in the conference room. Linda, Steve and Eli still sat with their catatonic stares. It was heart-wrenching to see Eli in this state. He looked old and senile and a little bit scared.

"What is going on?" Angela asked, mostly to herself.

"We're here for Eli," the two women said as one.

Angela shook her head. "None of this makes any sense." She looked at them. "Who are you? You're both…you're both dead."

The blonde patient chuckled. "There is no death, sweetheart. Just dying."

"But how are you real? This must be a hallucination."

The patient pointed at Angela's arm. "Does it feel like a hallucination?"

Angela grimaced. "What, then?"

"To be honest, we're not entirely sure. We're just as surprised to be here as you are to see us. It's true, we're both dead. At least, this version of us is. Eli brought us back."

Eli's face was blank. He blinked, and then it went slack again.

"How?"

"We don't know. We don't understand it all. It's still a mystery, even on the other side. But, somehow, reality is being manipulated on this level. In this dimension. We're all capable of manifesting our own reality; we just don't know how to control it. There must be a conduit, someone who has altered the frequency of this material plane. All we know is that Eli manifested us. And now we've found him."

The women walked towards him. They sat on either side and stared at him. There was a calmness that descended. A sense of peace. Perhaps even love. They shared the same look of happy adoration, evident despite their horrific appearance.

"My sweet Alpert-fish," said the burned nurse.

"My adoring doctor," whispered the one with blonde, frizzy hair.

They placed their hands on his arms, stroking him. They ran their fingers gently down his face. They spoke in low whispers that Angela couldn't hear, and didn't want to.

"It's okay," they said, alternately and together. "It wasn't your fault. There's nothing more you could have done. We forgive you. We love you still. We love you always. Come back to us. Come back, please."

They continued like this, caressing him, whispering their words of love while he maintained his vacant gaze.

And then the blonde one spoke alone. "You did it," she sighed. "Just like my letter said. You loved so hard it drove you insane."

Eli's chest began to hitch, his breath catching in his throat. His eyes glistened with tears. One fell and splashed against his cheek. He blinked. And then he came back.

Angela gasped, her good hand rising to her gaping mouth.

Eli blinked as though clearing debris from his eyes, looking around. He did not appear shocked or confused. His face lacked emotion. He was merely observing. He gazed at the woman with the blonde, frizzy hair. He turned to look at the mask of burned flesh. He revealed nothing, not even fear.

He peered up at Angela. "Extraordinary," he said.

She nodded. "Yeah, you could say that."

He turned back to the women. "I've let each of you die. So many times." His voice trailed off, turning into a contemplative whisper. His gaze went inward. "So many times. Why do you always return?"

"You're worth dying for," they said.

Tears returned to his eyes. "Why?"

"Because you have so much love to give," the nurse said.

"But you don't offer it to yourself," the patient continued.

"We'll keep coming back until you do."

Eli let that sink in. For a moment, he looked catatonic again. "But what good is love if it only leads to death?"

"It's all a part of learning. But, through it all, you always continue to love."

Eli remained stoic. Again he looked to Angela. "What have you learned?"

Angela mashed her knuckles against her mouth. Her face crumpled with emotion. "Much," she said. "A lifetime's worth."

Eli inhaled through his nose. He turned and looked at Linda and Steve. "What about them?"

Angela took her hand away from her mouth. A saliva bubble broke when she spoke. "Still learning?"

"And Dr. Drexler? The others?" Eli said.

Angela's eyes shot wide. "Alex!" she said.

She shuffled towards the door, then stopped and listened. "What if he's out there?"

"Who?" Eli asked.

"Bearman. He…he's changed. He came after us. He hurt Alex. Maybe killed him."

"Don't worry," the blonde woman said. "He can't come in here."

"How do you know?"

"Because he's not welcome," the nurse said.

Angela frowned. Her brows came together. Her lame arm hung limply. She reached out with the good one and grabbed the door handle. She braced herself as she eased open the door and looked out. She let out a relieved sigh. The hallway was empty.

But there was blood. A large pool of blood with a wide swath running away from it and bending around the corner.

"We've got to go help Dr. Drexler."

"Can we?" Eli asked.

"We can try," answered the nurse.

The two women stood. "You asked who we were," they said to Angela in unison.

Angela stared in stunned silence.

"I'm Miranda," said the patient, as she curtsied.

"I'm Lacy," said the nurse in her scorched voice. Her marble eyes smiled.

"But we're both really the same," they said.

"Okay," Angela said. "I'm just going to pretend like this will all make sense later. And concentrate on helping Alex for now."

Eli stood and stretched. "Sounds like the right attitude." He shook his head as though clearing it of cobwebs. Then his face went still, his eyes resolute. "Lead the way."

CHAPTER FIFTY-NINE

The trail of blood thinned as it progressed down the hallway, narrowing to two streaks where Alex's feet had dragged along the floor.

"It's not enough blood for him to have bled out," Eli said.

"Wow, quite the observation, Sherlock," Miranda said and snickered. "The more obvious clue may be the lack of a body."

Lacy elbowed her. "Stop it. Ghosts are supposed to be scary."

"Sorry, you're right. Whooooo—" Miranda held out her arms in a pantomime of Frankenstein's monster.

Angela figured it was supposed to be funny, but it was one of the most frightening things she'd ever seen.

The trail of blood disappeared altogether around the next turn, except for occasional drops and smears, which were hard to detect in the dim and flickering light. "Where would he have taken him?" Angela said.

"Anywhere he wants," the burned nurse said. "This place is malleable. This reality isn't fixed."

"Is that why the conference room changed places?"

Miranda skipped ahead, twirling as she went. "Convenient when you need a shortcut. Not so much when trying to track someone down."

Angela turned to Eli. He was focused on finding blood drops on the floor. She sidled up next to him. "How are you not freaking out right now? This is the most insane nightmare ever imagined and you act like it's completely normal."

He didn't answer for a while. Even after Angela prompted him again.

Lacy and Miranda were scouting ahead, giddy like two schoolgirls out on a class retreat.

Finally, he said, "I've had time to adapt to the insane. This *is* normal compared to where I've been, what I've been through."

Angela considered that for a moment. Yes, this was indeed saner than what she experienced during her fugue state. "You mean, in the dream, or whatever?"

"That was no dream. I've lived lifetimes between now and then."

"You could have ended it at any time," Miranda chirped in from ahead. "You were always in control."

"There was no way to control that place. I did the best I could."

Lacy turned her head. The twisted skin of her neck stretched like it was about to split. "For others, not for yourself."

Angela was dismayed. "So this makes sense to you?"

"Of course not. But I'm trying to make sense of it."

They were nearing Eli's office.

"Hey, stop here," he said.

The name tag to the right of the door lay in shards on the floor. There were divots in the stone wall where it had hung. Angela thought they could have come from Bearman's instrument.

★　★　★

Everyone quieted as they approached, Eli leading. He tried to peer through the pebbled glass but couldn't see within. Without further hesitation, he pulled open the door and walked through.

Everything was as he had left it. Or, it was how it had once been. In another lifetime that felt like millennia ago. Since then, it had taken on several forms. It had offered respites from grisly scenes of death and suffering. But, no matter what, it had always been a place of safety. A place to regain his sanity. He hoped it would be that once again.

The room was dark, quiet. But it warmed as they walked in – a subtle luminescence seemed to radiate from the walls. They shuffled around in a daze. Then Lacy broke the silence with a gasp. They all turned and watched her approach the wall ordained with Eli's pictures. The one with the two of them together.

Miranda came up behind her. "Ah, lucky," she said. "You got to have all the good times."

Angela came closer. "Is that you?" she said.

Lacy nodded. Her marble eyes were staring at a space above and to the left of the picture frame. "It was."

Eli was at his desk, gazing down into the intricate swirls of its wood, trying to comprehend the complexity of the current situation. "Tell me all you know," he said.

Angela waited to see if the two women would speak, but they remained fixated on the photos. She broke away from them and began filling him in on all that had happened since they had all fallen into their dream state. She told him about her dream, about how it had seemed to have been dredged up from her subconscious and pertained to a traumatic event from her past. She relayed Alex's dream, and its more significant points regarding his guilt surrounding his brother and the strange circumstances of his death. She told him about their speculations that Crosby was somehow involved with what was happening, and their encounter with the bloody and surgically scarred Bearman. She told him about the inhuman howls and the rumor of the strange woman roaming the halls.

Eli stood statuesque, listening, not once interrupting until Angela reached the end of her tale. And he stayed like that for minutes after, staring deep into the swirling pattern of the wood.

Finally, he raised his head. "There's another incident that's connected to this."

"What?"

"After Jerry had his last psychotic episode, Alex was in charge of his care. Then he made that miraculous recovery, like he was one hundred percent mentally sound. Now we know that was a result of whatever medicine Alex administered. His experimental compound."

Eli thumped his index finger against his lips – once, twice – then continued. "I met them for dinner. To see how Jerry was doing. I was amazed by his condition. That kind of recovery was completely unprecedented. I should have been more incredulous, but I was... preoccupied with other thoughts at the time.

"There was an incident at dinner. I noticed some anomalies with Jerry's eyes – extreme pupil dilation and contraction. And then, I don't know how best to explain this, but I experienced a hallucination. I thought that one of the servers resembled someone from my past. It was impossible, of course, but it was utterly convincing at the time. Had I not been having other stress-related issues, I would have given it more attention. Instead, I chose to suppress it. But now it makes a bit more sense. I don't think it was a case of mistaken identity or a stress-induced hallucination. I think it was the same thing that's happening here."

"Which is what, exactly?"

"I'm not sure yet. But I believe it is connected to Alex's formula. We know he administered it to both his brother and to Crosby, and that both patients have been subject to similar experiences. Jerry admitted as much to Alex in his dream. Or, that alternate dimension – I'm convinced it was no simple dream.

"Alex's wife identified Devon as the killer, and what was it that Jerry told him, 'You conjured my killer'? It seems as though he must have manifested it somehow."

Eli's words were picking up pace as he streamed his thoughts together, but he remained composed as he spoke. "Just like with Crosby. Alex told you that people with disfigured shadow selves are prowling the hallways. That fits Crosby's psychotic profile. The woman who chased after Alex could be Crosby's abusive mother." He stopped, seeming to run out of steam.

Angela had been nodding along, expecting Eli to follow the trail of crumbs all the way to its final conclusion. She held her breath as Eli paused, pleading for him to continue. She deflated when he didn't.

"But what about us? How does that account for our experiences? How does that account for them?" She pointed towards Lacy and Miranda, who were still marveling over the photos on the wall.

"You said Alex thought this may be shared psychosis? *Folie à deux*?"

Angela nodded.

"That's close. It's something like that. I'm just not convinced that this is all mere hallucination. It's too elaborate. It feels too real."

"Isn't that what our patients say?" Angela placed her good hand on her hip. It felt like the tables had been turned. The insane turned psychiatrist.

"But your dislocated arm isn't imaginary. Dr. Drexler's blood trail isn't a hallucination. The abandonment of the hospital isn't made up."

"We're all dead here. We're caught in the in-between."

Angela shrugged, and winced as pain shot down her injured arm. Eli arched a brow as though to say "see."

"Somehow reality is being manipulated. At least our perception of it. But hallucinations are rarely shared. The answer lies in Dr. Drexler's formula. We need to find him, or his formula, to learn more. And, unfortunately, we can't do that from here."

"Maybe we can," Angela said.

Eli furrowed his brow. The wrinkles on his forehead looked like dried riverbeds.

"It's like they said about this place being malleable. About our ability to manipulate our reality. We moved the location of the conference room to serve our purposes. Those women seem to have been manifested by you somehow. Maybe we can locate Dr. Drexler from here."

"Smart girl," Miranda said from afar. "You better not have designs on our man." Lacy laughed, and it sounded like the rustle of dry leaves.

"Interesting," Eli said. "But I'm not consciously controlling any of this. I couldn't bend the reality to my will in that fugue state. It may be possible. I just don't know how to do it." He paused, contemplating. "Do you?"

Angela shook her head. "No, I've never felt less in control in my life. I feel like I'm losing my mind."

Eli walked around the desk. He gripped her good arm. "You're not," he said. "I'm in this with you. You're doing remarkably well."

"Okay, lovebirds, that's enough pep talk. Let's shit or get off the pot." Miranda turned from the wall. Her face was starting to sag, decomposing further on the spot.

Angela stared up at Eli, her eyes wide and glistening wet. "I don't know how you do it," she said. "But I feel better having you here. No matter how crazy it is." She wiped tears from her eyes and sniffled, composing herself. "I just know I'm going to wake up in a straightjacket. And it's going to be the biggest relief of my life."

"I've thought that before," Eli said. "That insanity is the ultimate freedom. It's the people who adapt to this crazy world that we need to watch out for."

He released Angela and walked to the door, gripping the handle. "Should we split up?" he said.

"I'm going with you!" they all said at once.

He fought to keep the smile from his face. "All right then. Let's go."

CHAPTER SIXTY

The risk in playing dead is that you can lose the game without even knowing it.

Bear. *Bear man.* Bear. *Bear man.*

What do you do when attacked by a *Bearman? Play dead!*

This ridiculous jingle had been running through Alex's mind since he woke up while being dragged across the floor. Instinctively, he had remained motionless, letting his body be pulled along like a bag of sand. Like a corpse.

He could feel himself growing weaker. He wanted to examine himself, determine the extent of his injury, but was afraid to let Bearman know that he was alive.

He knows you're alive, idiot. Why would he bother to drag a dead body?

He couldn't get his mind to make sense. It felt like his brain's battery had been drained. But he decided that the safest thing to do at this point was stay compliant and let Bearman drag him as far as he'd like.

What do you do when attacked by a Bearman? *Play dead!*

If it weren't for that stupid saying, perhaps he could think.

Bearman was beginning to strain. He had already dragged him around several turns, covering the full length of each hallway without taking a break. And that was just as long as Alex had been conscious. He had no idea how long he'd been out. Bearman's movements were coming now in spurts; he was beginning to grunt with exertion. He was beginning to growl.

Alex could hear voices ahead. A man and a woman. They were drawing closer.

Bear. *Bear man.* Bear. *Bear man.* What do you do? *Play dead!*

They rounded another turn and Bearman dropped him with a final grunt. Alex's head bounced against the ground. Lights flashed behind his eyes, and a metallic tang filled his mouth. He had bitten his tongue.

"You're back," the woman said. "Where are the others?"

"They goddamn disappeared."

"Say again, Soldier!" a man said.

Alex kept his eyes closed. He kept his breathing as shallow as he could.

There was a pause.

"Who the fuck is this?" Bearman said.

"What did you say?" the man said. He sounded like a drill sergeant. "You better speak to me with respect!"

Alex could hear foot stomps and heavy shuffling, the sounds of two alpha dogs fighting for dominant position.

"You will stand down!"

"I don't take orders here!"

"Stop it. Both of you," the woman said.

The scuffling stopped.

"He's on our side," she continued, her voice flat and androgynous. More husky than feminine, like someone with emphysema. "He's going to help retrieve my son."

"I'm an expert in reconnaissance," the drill sergeant said. "I've smoked my share of gooks out of their gopher holes."

"Shut up," the woman said, and was greeted with silence. "What do you mean the others disappeared?"

"I chased them down. Had them cornered. They went back into a patient's room, but when I followed them in they were gone."

"Did you check for hiding places?" the sergeant said.

"There were three goddamn girls. I went in seconds after them. There was nowhere for them to go. I'm telling you, they just disappeared. I don't know what else to say."

"What happened to him?" the woman asked.

Alex could feel himself being looked at. He held his breath and remained still. After just a few seconds he felt like he was going to suffocate.

"He was slowing me down."

"And dragging him all across the hospital sped you up?"

"I mean earlier. When I was chasing the others." Alex heard pacing. "What are those other things, anyway? Those two women. They look dead."

"Have you looked at yourself lately?" the woman said, and the sergeant snickered. "Don't worry about it. They're not our friends."

Alex realized that if he continued to hold his breath much longer he was going to have to gasp for air. He slowly exhaled the carbon dioxide from his lungs and quietly sucked fresh air in. Blood was collecting in the back of his throat and he struggled not to gag.

"Is he dead?" asked the woman.

"What am I, a fucking doctor?"

Play dead, but don't lose the game.

Having had his eyes closed for so long, Alex's hearing had grown more acute. He could sense a resonant, echo-like quality in the sound of their voices, as though they were in a large space. That meant they were either in the dining hall or the rec room.

"Oh well. We don't need him. And we can deal with the others later. We know where he is."

"Yeah? Where?"

"In there."

Alex heard shuffling feet.

"In where?"

Silence, then, "Oh…" It had come out of Bearman's mouth in an awed and reverent tone.

"There're a bunch of spooks in there. I scouted it out already," the sergeant said.

"My poor son's scared." The woman moaned sensually, as though letting dark chocolate melt on her tongue. "And he should be."

Alex's body began to tingle. He was getting cold. But he was comfortable now. The voices were oddly melodic. He was content to lie here and listen. And he didn't notice as they began to fade. Or as the darkness grew deeper. Or as…

The risk in playing dead is that you can lose the game without even knowing it.

CHAPTER SIXTY-ONE

"Wait, stop." They had just left Eli's office. It felt like leaving the safety of a reinforced bunker to rescue a soldier from enemy fire. This, Eli would know. "Has anyone tried their phone?"

"Sorry, left mine back in the great beyond," Miranda said.

A pallid hue was blanching Angela's tan face. The sockets around her eyes looked bruised. "They don't work."

"What about the exits. Has anyone gone outside?"

They exchanged glances and then Angela shook her head.

"Let's start there," Eli said.

Eli took the lead, walking fast. There was an exit just beyond the nurses' station, which opened out onto the staff parking lot. Their footsteps echoed down the dimly lit hall.

The hospital felt empty, yet not, as though it were occupied by people just beyond their realm of observation. And there were just enough inconsistencies with the true architecture of Sugar Hill to suggest that they were somewhere else. It seemed incomplete, somehow. As though it had been recreated from memory with certain details left out.

The exit was just up ahead. Emergency floor lights offered a dull illumination of the door. It looked murky and smaller than it should.

He stopped in front of the door and the women crowded behind him, pressing forward, eager to get out. "Hold it," Eli said. He didn't bother trying to listen through the door. It was made with reinforced steel. But he wanted a moment to collect himself.

Sometimes it's better to just press on.

He opened the door.

It was like plunging underwater. The air was sucked from their lungs. Sound ceased. Eli's mouth moved, but nothing came out. He could feel pressure building between his ears.

Outside was erased. It was nothingness. An empty void, absent everything. No sight, no sound, no up, no down, nothing. It was reality in reverse. And, like a black hole, it seemed to have its own gravity. Eli felt like he was being pulled in.

Eli closed the door. It slammed against its frame as though caught in a backdraft. There was a moment of vertigo – *the building is floating through eternal dark* – and then Randall's words came back to him: *"We're all dead here. We're caught in the in-between."*

God help them if they are, Eli thought.

But Eli didn't think God was going to save them. It was up to him.

"Jesus!" Angela exclaimed as if sharing his thoughts on divine intervention. "What is this?"

"How long are you going to keep asking that?" Miranda said. She looked bored.

Lacy's scorched voice hissed like steam. "Out there hasn't been created yet."

"If you have all the answers, why don't you help us more?" Angela's voice was rising. She was fighting hysteria.

Lacy answered. "We're helping as much as we can. He brought us here. Only he knows why."

Miranda combed her fingers through her hair and a clump of it fell out. "Fiddly-fuck," she said.

Eli was thinking. "It hasn't been created yet?" He pondered. "Who's the creator, then? If you're here because of me, that suggests I am part creator."

"We all co-create our shared realities," Lacy said.

"Learning how to do it is the bitch," Miranda said.

The dim overhead lights flickered. The emergency lights near the floor flared and then went dead, casting them further into darkness. The silence of the hallway screamed.

"Fuck this," Eli heard Angela say. "I've overcome scarier shit than this before." She started out ahead, one arm swinging in a purposeful stride, the other swaying limply by her side. Eli and the others were forced to follow.

"Stay calm," Eli said. "We don't want to rush into anything."

"We're reacting too much," Angela said, speaking to the open hallway before her. The forceful march was pumping invigorating blood through her veins. "We need to be proactive. That's the only way to make anything happen. That's the only way to create something."

Eli trotted beside her. "Let's be balanced," he said. "Cautious."

"Being cautious has never gotten me anywhere good in my life." She clenched her fists and picked up the pace. Her dark eyes flashed under the flickering lights.

She passed Eli's office, the door blurring beside her. She reached the end of the hallway and turned. Her right foot almost slipped out from underneath her. She looked down. It was smeared in blood.

"He's down this way," she said, wiping her shoe clean before rushing on.

The blood trail was back. It looked like Bearman had slowed once they made it this far, allowing the blood to pool. It was even thicker up ahead, near the entrance to the rec room.

Angela was the first to reach the corner, which she rounded and stopped. Both hands went to her face.

Alex was on the floor. His eyes were closed, eyelids robin's egg blue. His face was pale and shiny with oily sweat. His bangs clung to his forehead in boyish curls.

Angela kneeled on one side, Eli the other. They lifted his shirt. Angela grimaced. The hole was triangular, just below the sternum. Blood oozed out in slow, pulsing waves.

"He's still bleeding. That means he's still alive," Eli said. He took off his white-cotton coat and crumpled it into a ball, laying it against the wound and applying pressure.

Alex stirred.

Angela brushed the hair from his brow. His forehead was so cool. She said his name, whispering it like a worried lover. Then louder, more urgent, like a nurse. "Alex. Wake up. Are you with us? Come on. Wake up!"

His eyes fluttered, then opened. His brow creased as he struggled to focus.

Eli adjusted his weight, pressing down harder against the wound.

Alex winced in pain. "Ow, shit." Alex shut his eyes and sucked air through his teeth.

Eli didn't let up. "Stay with us."

"I'm here, I'm here," Alex said, his head rising a few inches off the ground. "Holy shit. Where have you guys been?" He scanned their faces; then his eyes bulged wide.

"Hiya, handsome," Miranda said. Dark sludge had seeped into her irises, turning them black. "We're with Eli."

Lacy smiled, pulling her tortured skin tight against her skeletal face. Her nurse's cap had tilted back while running, revealing her ravaged head.

Angela guided Alex's attention back towards her. "Don't try. None of it makes sense. They're okay, though. They brought back Eli. They woke him up."

Eli leaned in. "I don't think you've lost too much blood. You're going to be okay. You need to stay strong, though. Focused."

Alex nodded. "It's…good to see you," he said.

Eli focused his attention on Alex's wound. He feared looking into his eyes. He wasn't sure what they would show. "You too," he said.

"Where did Bearman go?" Angela asked.

Eli began treating the wound, fixing a tourniquet as they talked.

Alex pointed towards the far wall. "In there."

They all looked. There was no exit that way. Only the wall covered by a large mural that a patient had once painted. Eli couldn't be sure in the dim light, but it looked like the mural had changed. *Hadn't there been a drawing of Adam and Eve before?* Now it was just a dark and ominous garden in the ghostly glow of twilight.

"Where?" Angela said.

Lacy and Miranda were both walking towards the mural to get a closer look.

"Oh wow," Miranda said as they approached.

"It's alive," Lacy said.

And even from here Eli and Angela could see. The limbs of the large apple tree were swaying, as if stirred by some impossible breeze. The tall grass fluttered; the full moon reflected a sepulchral light that seemed to radiate outward from the wall. Small creatures rustled quietly through the far shadows, and they could hear the faint chirrup of insects performing their nocturnal song.

"Why?" Eli said.

"They're going after Crosby," Alex said. His eyes rolled back in his head, then refocused.

Eli forced him to lie down on his back. Through shallow breaths Alex said, "His mom is here. She's the one who chased me. She's looking for her son."

"Crosby's mom? Impossible. She's dead," Angela said.

Lacy rejoined the group. "Not anymore," she said.

"Bearman's with her. But it's like he's been lobotomized. He's completely insane." Alex glanced down at his bloody stomach. "Obviously," he said. "And someone else. Some army asshole who looks like he's straight out of *Apocalypse Now*."

"Did you get a name?" Eli said.

Alex nodded. The stress of talking was weakening him. His forehead was dappled with sweat. "Wagner."

Eli's eyes swung back to the mural. He studied it for several seconds, listening to the night sounds emanating from the animated garden. "That's enough for now," Eli said. "You need medical treatment. Where are your supplies?"

"The nurses' storage room is fully stocked," Angela said.

"I know that," Eli said. "But they don't have everything I need."

He leaned down and whispered into Alex's ear.

Alex's eyes flickered from side to side, relaying his whirring thoughts. He shook his head, and Eli spoke again. Alex's lips paled as they pressed together, then he raised his head and spoke into Eli's ear.

Eli stood. There was a wheelchair stationed in a far corner. Walking towards it felt like navigating a balance beam. His equilibrium was off-center. The room kept trying to warp into a different shape.

He slowed. He turned his attention towards his breath and focused.

There has to be another way, his mind tried to convince him. *Take the time to think this through.*

But there is no time. I don't think time even exists here. Besides, no one else will die on my watch.

No one, that is, except me.

He grabbed the wheelchair and began rolling it back towards Alex and the others, his fingers digging into the foam handles. "Help me get him in," he said.

Gently, they lifted Alex into the wheelchair. His head was beginning to loll.

"You're doing great, Alex. Hang in there," Angela said. She grabbed the handlebars as Eli turned and strode away.

Eli led them back towards Alex's office.

"Why are we going this way?" Angela said. She had to trot to keep up. Her main focus was on Alex, but she was beginning to worry about Eli as well. He too looked pale, and was starting to wheeze. "Slow down," she said, as she herself sped up.

They arrived at Alex's office. Eli held the door open and ushered the two women through. He stopped Angela before she could enter. "I need you to go to the nurses' closet and get what we need to stabilize him."

Angela rolled her eyes. "That's what I was trying to tell you."

Eli disengaged her hands from the wheelchair handlebars. "Hurry. Bring them back here."

"I don't understand—"

"There's no time now. Hurry, please go." He wheeled Alex into the room, turning his back on her.

Angela stood in the hallway and watched the door close in her face.

She listened to the hum of the lights. Then, in the distance, she heard footsteps. A slow, steady tread coming closer. She looked both ways. The hallway was empty, but a shadow was emerging at the turn on her left-hand side.

She didn't wait to see what was coming. She turned the opposite way and sprinted towards the supply closet. It wasn't far, and she never knew she could run so fast. She flew on the legs of a little girl.

CHAPTER SIXTY-TWO

Crosby had been running for what seemed like hours, but he couldn't tell if he was covering any ground. The scenery never changed. It seemed like he kept passing the same group of bushes as he traversed the same uneven terrain. Overhead the pockmarked moon shone its sickly light down upon him as though tracking his location. And the beasts were forever nipping at his heels.

More and more of them had emerged from the depths of the garden as he had lain in hiding. Grisly, alien creatures bearing little resemblance to the real beasts of the natural world. Warthogs with horned tusks extending out from between crimson eyes. Tigers with long, distended necks and gaping jaws lined with disproportionately large fangs. Baboons swung between trees, throwing feces, shrieking from savage snouts with kaleidoscopic colors. They must have come from the wild imagination of the original artist. This world was no longer his own.

So he ran, never tiring, never traveling far, while the strange beasts followed. But he knew a place he could go to escape. He just didn't know how to get there. And he wasn't sure that it was safe.

He had seen her break through the threshold and enter into the garden, accompanied now by two men. It had been the final straw, causing him to flee deeper into this realm. He felt like his whole life had been spent running from monsters of his mother's making, and now was no different.

He knew, though, that he couldn't run forever. He had made a stand before. And he had conquered the evil forces in his life. Had conquered her. He could do it again.

He slowed. The snarling grew louder, closing in from behind. He stopped in an opening of a copse of trees and turned to face them.

They stalked forward, glossy fur shimmering in the moonlight, eyes glimmering green. Slowly, the exotic beasts circled, sniffing the air with chuffing snorts and tasting it with their dexterous tongues. They growled, and grumbled, and tittered. Their sharp teeth gleamed.

Behind them, the two men emerged. One was a strong and serious-looking man in army fatigues. The other was fat and splattered with blood. His forehead had been sliced open and stapled shut. Stark bone shone through the rippled skin. They both stopped, stood tall and smiled when they saw Crosby. Then they parted ways to create an opening for his mother to walk through.

"Told you I'd track the son of a bitch," the army man said.

"Indeed you did," Crosby's mother said. "Now keep your stupid mouth shut."

She looked radiant in the moonlit glow of the garden. Her blonde hair shone with a ghostly aura. Her face was sharp and severe, like he remembered. His eyes tracked down her long, wiry arms – which swung gracefully as she stalked forward – to what hung heavily below: her hands. Knotted and twisted with bulging veins, the gnarled fingers curled in like claws.

But it was *his* hands that had caused the most damage in the end. The last time he had seen his mother they had been wrapped around her slender neck, wrenching it as he pressed his weight against her, thumbs digging into the skin. Her icy-blue eyes had shown more hate than fear as they had gradually dimmed. Her final expression, as he stood trembling in shock over what he had done, had been a sneer of contempt. Or a look of baleful disgust.

You disappoint me to the very end.

"You don't look happy to see me," she said, still stalking forward, causing him to stumble back. He heard a warning snarl from behind and stopped. "But I'm so happy to see you." Her face suggested otherwise.

She pulled up a couple of feet before him, measuring him up and down with her frigid stare. She stood just beyond arm's reach.

Crosby thought about charging forward and grabbing her neck, choking her dead, as he'd done before. But he felt powerless and paralyzed in her presence. He knew that the beasts were on her side, just like they'd always been. And he knew that they wouldn't hesitate to hurt him, just as they always had.

"My little broken baby. All grown up." When she stopped speaking her mouth settled back into a scowl, its natural state. "Got himself put in a loony bin. No big surprise there. I always knew you were fucked in the head. What kind of sick kid has sex with his mother's boyfriends? Is that why you did what you did to me? So you could have them all to yourself?"

Crosby could feel himself shrinking in her presence, shriveling back into the body of the boy he'd once been. He looked at her hooked hands and shivered. He saw her shadow and began to cry. It was darkness deformed, a lopsided lunatic. It had come to seek her revenge.

"You made me do those things," Crosby said, his voice quivering as he cowered. "I only did what I did to make it stop."

Her laughter cackled, her shadow howled – the two sounds mingled together to create a psychotic wail. The beasts joined in, sending their discordant screams into the moonlit sky.

"They always place the blame on other people. The fault always lies with the parents, never themselves. Seen it all before." Bearman chuckled, enjoying the show.

"I know how to fix men who fall out of line, trust me on that," Sergeant Wagner said. "Just say the word."

"No. This is between me and my son," she said. She lifted her chin and Crosby could see the purple outline of his fingers imprinted on her neck and a splash of black where her trachea had burst. "It's my lesson to teach."

The shadow grew. It overwhelmed her, dwarfing her in size, casting her aside like molted skin, as it took on a third dimension. The beasts began baying into the night as it stretched taller and taller until it loomed overhead.

"Ho-lee-shit," Bearman said and began backing away.

Wagner followed, crouching down with his head angled up and his eyes opened wide.

"No," Crosby whimpered, watching it rise. "I killed you already. You're already dead."

The thing stopped growing and glowered down from on high – a dark stain that swallowed the light. *"I don't die."* He heard the words inside his head. They came as a ferocious whisper. *"But you do."* The last word stretched and then dissolved into the abrasive sound of static, expanding out from the center of his brain – a loud electronic hiss that was either a laugh or a scream, or something else entirely.

Crosby fell to his knees before it. Like he'd done with all the other beasts his mother had conjured and sent his way.

CHAPTER SIXTY-THREE

Eli held the vial in his hands, inspecting the clear liquid within. "Why didn't you tell me?"

Alex was chalky white. He held blood-crusted hands against the dark-red bandage. "I don't know, Eli. I didn't think you'd approve. And I didn't want to let you down."

"Why did you do it then?"

Alex blew out a long gust of air until his lungs emptied. He waited until it hurt before inhaling. "I wanted to do something important. I wanted to make a name for myself, something I could never do while working in your shadow." He paused, reflecting. "I wanted to make my parents proud." He smiled shamefully. "I wanted to get rich."

Eli turned the vial in his hands and held it up to the light. He popped the top and sniffed. "How does it work?"

Alex winced as he straightened in his chair. He rotated the right wheel to half turn towards Eli. "Its primary compound is a derivative of the neurotransmitter Dimethyltryptamine, which is a psychoactive chemical I studied in med school."

"I've heard of it," Eli said. "It's been coined the 'spirit molecule'."

Alex raised an eyebrow, impressed. "That's right. So, as you know, it's endogenous to our bodies. We create it in the pineal gland. It's renowned for its ability to produce extreme altered states of consciousness, perhaps even responsible for dreams during REM sleep and the visions that come during death."

Eli was nodding. He set the vial down and leaned back against the desk, facing Alex.

Alex continued, "My hypothesis was that people experiencing extreme hallucinations and distorted perceptions of reality were suffering from an unregulated release of neurochemicals, similar to, if not specifically, Dimethyltryptamine. My formula is designed to restore balance to the levels of these compounds released by the pineal gland, bringing them back to baseline, relieving the patient from what, in essence, can be described as an extraordinarily strong, self-induced hallucinogenic trip."

"Okay. I question the scientific accuracy of your hypothesis, but I'm following your point. How does that explain all of this?"

Alex shook his head. "I don't have a clue. I tested it extensively without anything remotely like this occurring. The only side effects that some test subjects experienced were intensified hallucinations."

"Then what was different about Jerry and Crosby?"

Alex spoke slowly, trying to work it out in his blood-deprived brain. "I modified the formula some. But not much. I administered the medicine under less-than-ideal conditions."

Then in his mind he saw the long seven-inch needle plunging into the vial, the syringe filling to the brim with liquid. "The dose," he said with a renewed sense of conviction, with the dawning of a revelation. "I increased the dose. By a lot."

"How much is a lot?"

"Double." Alex avoided Eli's stare. "Triple. The higher the dose, the better it seemed to work. At least, at first." He became silent, thinking. "But still. That wouldn't account for this." He waved an arm towards Lacy and Miranda.

"Hey!" Miranda said, feigning offense. "You'd be having your head examined by Dr. Lobotomy by now if it weren't for us."

Alex still couldn't look at them without showing disgust, so he averted his eyes.

Eli came off the desk and began to pace. "Or maybe it does," he said. "The pineal gland has held significance for certain societies stretching back to ancient times. Some have called it the seat of the soul, its resting place within the physical body while alive, and the channel through which it departs upon death.

"It has also been referred to as the third eye – the eye of true perception. In some reptiles, the pineal gland actually has a developed cornea, lens and retina, literally making it an eye inside the mind.

"If the pineal gland has anything to do with how our conscious minds interpret the world, then manipulating it could alter the way we perceive reality. Think of it like a radio antenna. Changing the channel allows you to pick up a different station. Or, in our case, a different wave of reality."

"But I don't think we're dealing with your standard hallucination here." Alex nodded towards the blood-soaked rag covering his stomach. "I'm not imagining this."

"No, you're not," Eli said. He looked towards the door, wondering what was taking Angela so long.

Lacy stepped forward. It sounded like a leaking tire when she spoke. "Reality is created by our consciousness. It exists in a state of perpetual potential until we dream it into being. It is eternal, it is multidimensional. If we co-create our physical reality through the power of our conscious minds, then by altering that perceptual filter, we alter the reality that we manifest."

"Look at you, smarty-pants," Miranda said, nudging her with her elbow. "Way to parrot a bunch of New Age mumbo jumbo."

"Not necessarily. There are people within the quantum physics community who propose the same thing," Eli said. "The world is a hologram that we call into existence through the power of observation. It's still a radical fringe theory. But this is a radical situation."

"There's a flaw in the logic, though," Alex said.

Miranda propped a hand on her hip and cocked out her elbow. "Oh yeah? What's that?"

"None of us have taken the medicine, yet we're experiencing the altered reality."

Their heads all turned as one when they heard the scream coming from down the hallway. It was Angela – an inarticulate wail of terror, coming closer, growing louder and more shrill. They could hear her feet pounding in a panicked run.

Then her shadow emerged on the other side of the pebbled-glass door. The knob began to rattle under her hand. It was locked. She began banging on the frame. "Open up! Hurry, open up!"

Eli rushed to the door and unlocked it. Angela almost knocked him over as she barged in. He could hear another set of footsteps bounding down the hallway.

"Oh god! Close it! Hurry!" Angela yelled.

Eli slammed the door shut and locked it.

A second later another shadow appeared on the other side, less than two feet from where Eli stood. It was a bulkier shape, the outline of a man.

"Who is it?" Eli said, more to Angela than the figure on the other side of the door.

But it was the man who answered. "Is that you, Eli? Chief Medical Director Dr. Alpert, I mean? My, haven't you come a long way."

Eli waited for Angela to answer. She was shaking. Her face was dripping sweat. "I don't know who it is. I've never seen him before. He looks like a doctor, but from a long time ago."

"Dr. Alpert. We have a situation out here that we could use your assistance with. You always were such a trusted hand. Loyal and obedient. One of our old patients is in there with you, I understand. We did such good work with her, together. Why don't you let me in? We're all on the same side here. There's nothing to fear."

"No, don't," Angela said.

Eli gripped the doorknob and tensed. He clenched his teeth so hard together his jawbone knotted and his molars squeaked.

"No, Eli, don't let him in." It was Miranda this time. She came up behind Eli and placed her hand over his. She turned her bloodless face towards him and batted her opaque eyes. "I always hoped I'd get a chance to see Dr. Francis again," she said with a hint of genteel charm. "I'll go out and greet him."

She bumped Eli aside with her hip and opened the door before he could stop her. She stepped out and slammed it shut. Dr. Francis issued a squeal of surprise as Miranda unleashed a scream of rage. They heard the sound of bodies colliding and then the hallway went silent. Their shadows disappeared.

Eli reopened the door. The hallway was empty.

He spun back around, surveying their faces, eyes wide with shock.

"Don't worry about her," Lacy said. "I can't say the same for him."

Angela dropped the medical bag and started jumping up and down, shaking her arms as if she had just walked through a spiderweb. "Ahhh!" she screamed. "I am so fucking over this! I don't know how much more I can take."

Lacy moved towards her with open arms, offering a hug.

Angela pushed her away. "No, please. I know you mean well. But...I just can't. Not right now."

"Well then. Where were we?" Alex said, his head bobbing slightly. He looked loopy and mildly amused.

Eli grabbed the medical kit and brought it over to Alex. He rifled through the bag to find cleaning supplies and gauze. He carefully removed the bandage and began dressing the wound.

"Hey, wait," Alex said, and Angela looked up. "What was your theory behind what all is happening?"

"That we've all lost our fucking minds?"

"Yeah, but...there's a name for it."

"Folie à deux," Eli said. Then he said it again with emphasis, "*Folie à deux*. That could actually explain how we're experiencing whatever this is without having taken the medicine. If we're somehow stuck in this alternate reality created by the rewiring of Crosby's brain, then perhaps we're capable of co-creating the experience on some smaller scale. Our conscious minds are adapting to the new environment and operating within the framework of a new set of rules."

"But it's still Crosby's world," Alex said, "which would explain why it's so damn..." he paused, searching for the proper word, "... insane," he finished, smiling like he'd nailed a punch line.

"Perhaps we can counteract that," Eli said, holding up the liquid vial, "with this."

Angela shuddered when she saw the vial. "I think that's the problem, not the solution."

"Besides," she said. "You already seem capable of manipulating this reality. All the people we've encountered so far are here because of you."

"But it's beyond my control."

"You think Crosby is controlling any of this? Do you think he conjured his mother back from the dead to hunt him down?"

Alex bolted upright in his chair, wincing in pain. "That's what Jerry said, 'You conjured my killer.'"

"Yes, but he also said something else. What was it?"

"'The medicine opens up the mind. You can create any world you choose.'"

"I will happily choose any world other than this," Angela said. She reached inside the medical bag and pulled out a bottle of pills. "Something for the pain?"

Eli reached out and grabbed them. "Not yet. We need him as clearheaded as possible."

"For what?"

Eli grabbed Alex's hand and placed the vial in his palm. "For this."

CHAPTER SIXTY-FOUR

Eli sat in a chair, slouched down with his neck bent against the headrest, face angled up towards the ceiling. Alex sat next to him holding the syringe. The chamber was completely full.

Angela held Eli's head steady in her hands. They'd had to wait for her to stop crying. The tears kept raining down on Eli's cheeks.

Angela sniffled. "How are you going to do it without the imaging equipment?"

"Very carefully," Alex said. The needle wavered slightly in his trembling hand. He waited for it to settle. "I've done this enough times to know where to angle it. The rest is up to fate."

"I thought you didn't believe in anything as metaphysical as fate," Eli said, showing a half smile.

Alex squirted a few drops from the syringe and leaned over Eli's head, bringing the needle towards the corner of his eye. "My beliefs are being redefined as we speak."

He placed the needle against Eli's tear duct. It made a tiny dimple. "Ready?" he said.

Eli closed his eyes in affirmation. He didn't risk nodding his head.

Fortune favors the bold, Alex thought automatically. It had become a rote saying for this stage of the procedure. Although it had never proven true.

He plunged the needle through the socket of Eli's eye.

Eli stiffened, but just slightly. Angela held his head steady in her hands, watching the steel shaft of the needle slide through.

"Almost there," Alex whispered, monitoring the length of the needle to gauge the distance to the pineal gland. He reached the point where the gland should be and closed his eyes. He felt the slightest resistance against the tip of the needle. He nudged it gently, sensing a microscopic pop, and depressed the plunger, emptying the syringe. He quickly pulled the needle out, and the operation was complete.

"Brace yourself," he said to Angela. "This part can get a little rough."

Eli's eyes rolled under his lids, like someone deep in REM sleep. His lips parted as if to whisper some dying secret. He looked peaceful, more youthful and serene than he had in many months, if not years.

Then his face contorted into a horrid mask of pain and he began to convulse violently in his seat, his feet kicking out and scrabbling against the ground, his back arching and bucking against the chair.

Angela wrapped an arm around his jaw, locking her hand into the elbow of her other arm, which she used to secure Eli's head. Alex grabbed his legs and held them down. Lacy pinned down his flailing arms.

Eli was grunting and making gurgling sounds, a white foam spilled from his lips.

"You gave him too much," Angela said, struggling to hold his head still.

"No. This is actually a good sign. It means I did it right."

Eli's eyes flew open as wide as the lids would allow. The pupils were fully dilated, just two black circles like gun-barrel holes. Alex watched the left one constrict down to a pinprick while he struggled to restrain Eli's bucking legs. Eli's lips contorted into a rictus, spraying white spittle, and he began making a choking sound interspersed with a prolonged groan.

"How is this a good sign?" Angela sounded panicked.

"It's—" Alex began.

Eli's face was turning a violent shade of red. His breathing was hitching in his throat, the groan weakening.

"Shit! Get him on the floor."

"He's dying," Lacy said as they shifted him from the chair to the floor.

"No he's not," Alex said, but he could tell Eli's systems were shutting down, the convulsions subsiding. His eyes, with their mismatched pupils, had become fixed in place.

Angela shifted from the top of Eli's head to his side. "He is, Alex. He's crashing."

Alex grabbed Eli's wrist. His pulse was weak, barely there. Alex dug his fingers into Eli's flesh, trying inanely to awaken Eli's pulse through pain. It beat softly. Once...twice...just the faintest flutter.

And then it stopped.

Alex held the lifeless wrist in his hand for a full minute, listening to the harsh breathing that he realized was his own. Angela watched him silently, her wide eyes glistening.

He let go of the wrist and it thunked to the floor. He looked down on Eli's body, which appeared even smaller and less substantial than before.

"We need to resuscitate him. Now. Start CPR!"

Angela reached out with trembling hands and placed them on Eli's chest. "Christ, Alex. What's happening?"

Lacy answered for him. "He's gone."

CHAPTER SIXTY-FIVE

All he sees is smoke. A grayish-white thread billowing up against the black. He can smell fumes from the ash, and it reeks of burnt cordite. It reeks of roasted flesh.

It's coming from his house. He doesn't know how he knows this. But he does.

The house comes into view as he steps towards it, its bland features emerging through a murky gloom. How is he walking? He has no legs, no feet. He is part of the darkness, insubstantial as a shadow.

The house sits all alone on a solitary plot of land, surrounded by haze. Or smoke. He can't tell. It's so hard to think right now.

Whose house? His house. Who is he?

He sees that the front door is ajar. The smell of smoke is stronger here.

This is wrong. He always keeps his house securely locked. Someone must have broken in. Someone is trying to burn it down.

He hesitates on the front landing – *Wait, there's something I'm supposed to be doing right now. I'm... I don't know. I don't remember* – and then he shakes his head. It would help if he could just see his own reflection. Then he could recall.

The door swings open on silent hinges, and he walks inside.

Walks?

He knows that this is his home, even though he has never been here before. He feels no connection to it.

Why, then, is he walking inside? Why is he here?

There is a reading room to his right. The walls are lined with bookshelves. A hazy light filters in through the tall windows, highlighting drifts of smoke coming from farther inside. He sees the side profile of a man in one of the high-backed chairs: a chest, one arm and a leg. The face is hidden.

"Hello?" The voice he hears is not his own, although he's not sure how he knows this. "Who's there?"

The man doesn't move. So he glides closer, orbiting the chair to reveal more of the man's body and face.

He circles around to the front. There is no face. It is covered in a thick sheet of dried blood that drained out of the man's nose and down from the open cavity at the top of his head. The pistol rests in the dead man's lap.

He has seen this pistol before. Has seen this man before. He used the pistol once to kill. And now the pistol has killed again.

The man's eyes peel open, staring at him accusingly. He feels as though he is being assessed. Black chunks coat the back of the chair, but the man's eyes retain some intelligence. *You couldn't kill me,* they say. *So I did it myself.*

He must close those eyes. Close them forever so that they may never seek out violence again. So that the man can finally rest in peace.

He reaches out without hands, or perhaps a shimmering outline of one, and the dead man reaches up and grabs hold of his nonexistent wrist.

"Don't you fucking touch me with your hypocritical hands."

The man pulls himself to his feet. He is tall. The face behind the blood is firm and handsome. He wears a military uniform with rows of shiny medals.

"You call me a killer? What about you? How did your hands get so clean?"

"I'm not clean!" he gasps. "I'm no cleaner than you!" He is looking at the bloody filth on the man's face.

"You're fucking-A right you're not. Because I'm in you. I am you."

The man is holding the gun in his other hand. He raises it and points it at the invisible face. The barrel hole looks like a dilated eye.

"You think you're some kind of saint or something?" the man says. "You're a killer worse than me. You did it despite your high-and-mighty morals."

"No." He hears the voice that's not his own, surprised by its defiance. "I am not that man. I am not that man anymore."

The hand holding the gun falters. The blood-smeared eyes squint.

"Yes you are," he says, but he doesn't sound sure. "I know what you did."

"No, that man died when he shot that young boy and gave birth to someone new." There is an accent in the voice he hears. One he cannot place. "You died too," he continues, "and have lived in hell ever since."

"Ha!" the man's laugh is full of mirth. "You're talking fairy tales." The man's lips quiver in an attempt to smile, but they do not know how. A face has never shown such pain.

It hurts his heart. *Whose heart?*

He looks again at the gun and realizes it isn't real. It can kill him, but not hurt him. He reaches out with his free hand, which he can hardly see, and pulls it easily from the man's faltering grasp.

"Give that back," the man says, but his voice is weak, a whimper. They stand there, connected hand to wrist. "You can't take that from me. It's mine."

"You look tired," the accented voice says. He pulls the man towards him, and the man stumbles forward on the sleepy feet of a little boy. "Come, rest." They embrace.

Darkness falls as he closes his eyes. There is a pain somewhere that feels like his center, and then it slowly melts away.

A loud, booming voice causes his eyes to spring open. "The fuck are you doing?" it says.

A large, overweight man in a dark suit is standing in the corridor. "Your fucking house is burning down, you dipshit! What the hell are you standing around like an idiot for?"

The military man is gone. The chair where he sat is now clean. He blinks his eyes that aren't there and focuses on the angry, overweight man now yelling at him.

"My house?" he says.

The large man shakes his head in disgust, points a fat finger. "Your house. It's burning right to the fucking ground."

The acrid smell of smoke is stronger now. The air is growing hot. A pulsating glow is coming from the far end of the hallway, and he can hear a crackling sound.

"Are you just going to stand there while your whole fucking house burns down around you?"

Am I? I...? I am. I am Eli. I AM ELI!

And just like that he remembers who he is. Or was. Or both.

He is Eli, and this is his house.

He starts walking towards the hallway.

The large man steps in his way. "Oh, now you're going to do something about it? No, too late. Your house is going to burn."

The man is twice Eli's size, his hulking frame fills the hallway from wall to wall. But Eli can see the glow from the fire coming through the large man's body. "You're not really here," Eli says.

The man puts his hand on Eli's chest and shoves, sending Eli stumbling back. "Don't talk crazy, old man. I'm here, all right. I've always been here, waiting for this whole thing to come crumbling down."

Eli's right hand feels heavy. He raises it and realizes he's still holding the gun. The grip feels rough against his skin. He points it at the big man, walking forward.

The man does not budge. If anything, he leans forward. "You put that down, you hear me? You put that away, right fucking now!"

Eli presses the barrel against the man's heart. He doesn't want to kill. Not again.

"You're not in charge," he says. *Why does his voice still sound so strange?* "You're not in charge of anything."

The large man smiles. His parting lips are but folds within folds. "I own you," he says. "And I—"

Eli squeezes the trigger.

The large man falls to the ground, grunting as he lands, and the smell of burnt cordite fills the air.

"You own nothing," Eli says, looking down on him. "Nobody does."

He can hear the fire as he moves farther down the hallway. Smoke is seeping through the doorframe that leads to his meditation room. The walls are shimmering with flickering light.

He sees his shadow for a second – the narrow frame, the long, bushy face, the cone rising up from his head – and is stunned. It looks nothing like him.

He scalds his hand as he grabs the doorknob and turns it, coughing against the smoke.

There is a man inside, feverishly working to smother the fire. "Help me!" he cries in an all too familiar voice. "Please! Help me!"

It's him. It's Eli.

Then who am I?

The floor is on fire. Orange flames are climbing up the walls. Eli is frantic in his attempts to stomp it out, to suppress the ascending flames.

He throws a thick blanket on the fire that seems to work for a moment and then it begins to burn. "Help!" he screams.

And then the fire is right before him, singeing his skin. "Help!" he hears himself yell, the voice now his own. "Help!" He turns around to plead with the man who has just entered the room, but no one is there. He is all alone.

I'm going crazy, he thinks. *Seeing things. Seeing things that aren't really there. I've got to stop the fire. I've got to put it out.*

The heat from the fire is not as painful as he first feared. In fact, it's almost pleasant. A comforting warmth. He looks down and sees that the flames have subsided a bit. The fire is more manageable now.

Okay. Okay. This isn't so bad. I can keep this under control.

He has time to breathe, to think. *I've got to get back. I have patients who rely on me. They need me. What am I doing here?*

Smoke from the smoldering fire blinds his eyes.

Or do they? Do they really? Maybe they need someone else. Someone younger. Someone who doesn't have so many issues of his own. Do I even really make a difference? Or do I only pretend to make people sane?

He can no longer even feel the heat. He has forgotten about the fire altogether. He's got to figure this out. Get to the bottom of it. No time for fires now.

Must get back. Back to work. Back to where I belong. I've got to make it all right. My legacy. I've got to secure my legacy.

His body radiates with warmth. It is neither pleasant or painful. It is just there, where it's always been.

Wait. What's so bad about a little fire? Didn't she...? Didn't she burn?

The warmth inside flares, singeing with a painful heat.

No, no. Fire hurts. Tamp it down. Stomp it out.

But he doesn't. He opens to it, just a little. Giving it room to breathe. He hears it hiss as it tastes air. It sounds a little like a woman he once knew saying, *"Yessssss."*

And then the pain returns, igniting his whole body. Yes, his body. He can feel it now. God, it hurts.

Come on, Eli! Come on! The voice. He knows that voice. *Don't give up! Come on, don't let go!*

The fire is back, roaring loudly in his ears. The voice inside his head is trying to tell him something, and he has to strain to hear it. Something legacy. Something responsibility. Something about his sanity.

He's never felt anything like this fire. He doesn't know if he can continue to hold it back. It's burning his whole body. His whole body hurts.

End it now, he thinks. *Just let...*

And for once he stops fighting and gives in to the flames.

CHAPTER SIXTY-SIX

"Come on, Eli!" Angela said between breaths, pumping Eli's chest. "Don't give up on us!"

"Wait, stop," Alex said, resisting the urge to push Angela aside. "I think—"

Eli's chest rose as he took a shallow breath. His head rolled to one side, his eyes fluttering. He issued a reedy exhale and then took another breath.

"Move back," Alex said, giving Eli room.

Eli's head rolled back to the other side. Then he blinked and tried to sit up.

Alex grabbed his arms. "No, no. Take it easy."

Eli looked straight through him, his eyes unfocused. He tried to sit up again, but Alex held him down.

"Let him go," Angela said. She reached down and pulled Alex away. "Just give him a minute to come back."

Eli scanned the room in a daze, his eyes roaming past Alex and Angela without the slightest pause. He attempted to sit up, but failed. Then tried again and made it.

"Eli," Alex said, but Eli didn't respond. He was staring at something past him.

Then Eli's eyes narrowed, the crevices beside his mouth deepened, his wrinkled skin appeared to sag. He stood up.

"Easy," Alex said, offering his arm for support. But Eli ignored him and started walking towards the...

CHAPTER SIXTY-SEVEN

...fire bathes the night in its amber glow, its roiling flames reaching towards the glimmering sky. Towards the blazing stars which died eons ago.

He can hear chanting. It is sanctimonious in its sincerity. Muted and indecipherable, yet as timeless and essential as blood.

A family approaches the fire and offers a body to its flames, sending sparks tumbling into the night.

"*Many lifetimes,*" he hears the accented voice of the man beside him. "*Many lifetimes.*"

And then he sees the people emerging from the flames, walking towards him. Shadowed outlines flickering against the blistering haze of the funeral pyre.

He goes to greet them, compelled by something beyond rational thought.

"*Many lifetimes,*" the voice maintains.

CHAPTER SIXTY-EIGHT

The night sky is bright against the shadow's blackness. It sends the moonlight scurrying.

Crosby bends his head. He is resigned against this evil thing. The static noise inside his mind is driving him insane. That's what it is supposed to do.

But then he hears another sound. A beautiful sound, distant yet approaching. The sound of people joined in song. The sound of people rejoicing. Someone playing guitar with such harmonic wonder as to validate the perfection of its design.

The music is overwhelming the insane static, shoving it aside. And he senses a change in the force before him. Not fear, exactly, but something like contempt.

Crosby raises his head. From the edge of the trees shadowed shapes are approaching, outlined against a ruddy glow. But these shadows show no sign of the demonic possession he's so accustomed to seeing. They exude peaceful kindness, a promise of pleasant companionship.

Contrasted against the encroaching light, the large shadow beast begins to fade, showing itself as nothing more than a figment of his imagination. A subtle trick of the eye.

His mother stands before him, gazing upon some distant point, listening. Her perpetual scowl nearly transforming into a smile.

The static hiss within his head is fading, fading, fading, until it is just the sound of crickets in the distance. An external thing, calming and serene.

His mother senses the shift at the same time as he, and shudders with relief. It is like being brought in out of the cold.

And in the continuing shift her face softens. Her eyes glow warm in the ruddy light accompanying the emerging shadows. Her hands dangle down from her delicate arms. But they are just hands now, knuckled and gnarled and twisted with veins, but incapable of delivering harm of their own accord. They are the same hands that held him once, and guided his mouth to her breast, and combed the curly hair that he once had.

They were a little girl's hands at one point in time, tiny and unblemished. And a baby's before that.

But then they were forced to be used as a method of defense. To ward off the blows cast down from an abusive father, drunk because he doesn't know how else to quiet the voices in his head. They scream at him all day long to do horrible things, and he doesn't. He fights against them as long as he can until he can't take it any longer and then he drinks until the world goes dark and he loses time. But he never meant to hurt his little girl.

Just like she never meant to hurt her little boy.

The voices are in her head too. She never learned to quiet them either. And he was always there, her little baby burden. And the voices would get too loud until she couldn't take it anymore.

And once you do it once, you do it again and again. It becomes a punishment against oneself. *What's the worst thing I can do? How can I hate myself more? I'll destroy the thing I brought into the world. The last piece of my innocence.*

But it didn't start out that way. And it wasn't the way she wanted it. And she'd take it all back if she could.

And the happiest moment of her life, since before she could remember, is when you killed her. It is what she wanted. It is what she deserved. She was so proud of you. And so, so sorry for what she made you do.

But you don't have to carry it with you. You can let it go. Even something as horrible as that, you can let it go, like it never even happened. Because the only way to make it worse is to keep it inside and let the cycle continue.

We're sick. We're all sick. But we can be cured. And we can be kind. And we don't have to let our lives be ruled by the shadows of the past. Not if we act through love.

The light is growing brighter. So bright it burns. He must close his eyes against it.

His mother is becoming consumed with white heat. And the

singing is rising. And the guitarist strums the perfect tune.

And the white light grows ever brighter, and in it his mother burns.

CHAPTER SIXTY-NINE

The sounds began to return in small increments, like the volume on a stereo slowly being raised. At the same time, phantom outlines of people bustling by began to emerge, as though seen through a thin sheet of falling water. The faces were familiar, the scene immediately recognizable – this was an ordinary day inside the halls of Sugar Hill.

But they were outside of it somehow, a few frequencies farther down the dial. It was clear, as they followed Eli down the hallway, that they were not visible to any of the phantom people walking past, some passing straight through.

"It's working," Angela said, smiling as she recognized a nurse. "It's all coming back."

"Don't get your hopes up just yet," Alex said. "I've been disappointed before." But now he at least felt the contrition to cringe. *Disappointed* by his medicine was too mild a word.

Eli ambled on in his fugue state, occasionally mumbling to himself. Occasionally smiling with psychotic glee. His mind appeared to have been fried by the medicine, but something had to be working. People were returning to this plane of reality. Or, perhaps, it was they who were returning to the real Sugar Hill.

Eli clasped his hands together in a gesture of blessing as tears spilled from his manic eyes.

Angela sensed that someone was missing. She looked to find that Lacy was gone. She hadn't seen her disappear. She hoped they hadn't left her behind, somehow. Back in that barren and hopeless place.

The volume around them continued to increase. The phantom images grew more concrete. Eli continued on, blessing each one in turn.

They came to the entrance of the recreation room, and Eli looked in, his wide eyes roaming with delirium.

Alex and Angela came up behind him.

Amidst a room full of spectral bodies, Crosby stood. He was as solid and real as they were. His arms were raised in some sort of triumphant pose. He was crying freely. There appeared to be a white aura engulfing him, radiating out across the sea of bodies surrounding him and rebounding back.

These were patients, Alex realized. He recognized their faces.

And then he heard their singing. And the sound of a guitar.

He could see Randall strumming the one Eli had given him. Several of the spectral patients looked their way and smiled and waved. They could see Eli, Alex and Angela through whatever veil currently separated them. It was as though their special minds were open to an expanded field of reality.

And through this thin film of separation, Alex saw them in a different light. They no longer looked deranged or dangerous or mentally unhinged.

They looked like regular people, happy and hopeful and full of purpose and great potential. Mothers and sons, and sisters and brothers. Saints and sinners, and shamans. Strong and weak and imperfect, but real and worthy of kindness and compassionate attention.

These weren't accidents or defective creations. Rather, these were respectable people battling hardships like anyone else, fighting to overcome their illnesses, working to get well. And they deserved the best care that he could give. Just as Jerry had.

Crosby turned and looked their way. Behind the tears his eyes were coherent. He opened his mouth and strings of saliva stretched between his lips. "No more fear," Alex heard him say, his voice distant, as though traveling across a great divide. "Only love." He began to cry heavily, painfully, his whole body convulsing against its intensity, but it was the antithesis of sadness. A white aura surrounded him, burning the darkness away.

Eli began chanting, low and indecipherable, seemingly in some foreign tongue that sounded like Hindi. He started to shuffle his feet and gyrate his arms in a kind of ritualistic dance. He waltzed away from the recreation room, bounding towards the doors that exited onto the gardens out back.

The sunlight was blinding, Alex blinked against it and held up a hand to shade his eyes. A few phantom shapes mulled across the lawn, growing in solidity.

Eli twirled, his face a garish mask of lunacy, and clapped his hands.

Tap. Tap.

He was walking towards the fountain, where the maiden was pouring her bottomless bucket into the pool that was forever full. Eli stopped by the bench before it. He swayed on unsteady feet, then lost his balance and fell onto the bench seat.

Slowly, his eyes raised and he stared at the face of the fountain maiden. His was the expression of a devout saint reveling in the true presence of divinity.

Alex grabbed Eli gently by the arm. "Hey, are you there? Can you hear me?"

Eli offered no reaction. His lips gleamed wet with drool.

Alex felt his own arm grabbed gently from behind.

"Hey, look," Angela said. Her finger was pointing towards the face on the fountain statue.

It was shimmering with the faintest double image, and both of the faces were beautiful. Miranda no longer wore her death mask. Lacy was no longer disfigured by her burns. While they watched, the two solidified into one.

"Was that them?" Alex asked.

"Her," Angela said, softly. "I think there was only ever one."

And as the face on the statue solidified, Eli's did too. It became fixed in place as though paralyzed. As though set in stone. Yet, still the lunatic smile remained on his face, and his chest continued to rise and fall with each rhythmic breath.

The yell startled both of them. It came from the entrance back into Sugar Hill. "Dr. Drexler! Lord, there you are. We need you!"

Alex's head spun around. Angela's nails nearly punctured his skin.

A nurse was leaning outside the doorway, waving to get their attention. She appeared as clear and solid as she had ever been. And she could obviously see them. "Hurry! Come quick!"

Alex and Angela exchanged a glance. He grabbed her by the same arm that was holding his, wanting to pull her into a hug, but resisting. "Stay here," he said, guiding her towards Eli, "with him."

A dull pain burned just below his lungs when he pulled Angela's arm. He looked down. The blood was gone. He felt underneath his sternum where Bearman had stabbed him. The dressing was gone too.

As was the wound. He could feel a raised knot of scar tissue, though, that hadn't been there before. And he could feel a slight ache.

He raced up to where the nurse was waiting, feeling weightless on his feet. But then he saw the urgency in her face and he knew that something was wrong. They weren't out of the woods yet.

"What is it?" he said, bracing himself for her response.

"Come with me. We have a problem." She turned and began speed-walking away.

Alex caught up to her. "What is it?" he asked again.

"It's Mr. Bearman. They're having a board meeting, but something's wrong. I thought you all were in there with him?"

They hurried past the recreation room. Alex glanced in as they rushed by. A group of orderlies was attempting to separate the patients and calm them down. They were all huddled around Crosby in some sort of celebratory scrum. They were laughing hysterically and beaming with smiles.

Just another outburst from the crazies here at Sugar Hill, Alex thought, and almost started laughing himself.

"We…" Alex's mind was whirring; he could hardly think, "…we were. But we had to leave," he said. "What's the matter?"

"I don't know. I'll let you see for yourself."

They turned a corner, then another. Alex was marveling at each room he passed that contained a familiar patient. He almost cheered as they scurried by the nurses' station and saw their bored expressions.

Finally, they reached the conference room. "You should go in first," she said. From outside the door Alex could hear Bearman's booming voice shouting. He opened the door and entered.

Bearman had his shirt off, exposing his rotund belly and hairy chest. He looked just like a—

What do you do when attacked by a Bearman? Play dead!

Again, Alex had to suppress a series of giggles coming from his overexcited mind.

Bearman was slick with sweat and yelling at the top of his lungs, pointing at Linda and Steve who were both crying in hysterics. "And it's in you! And it's in you! And it's in all of our black and sooty sinners' souls! We can't escape it! It's inside us! It's inside all of us!"

From across the room, Alex could make out a faint purple line that traversed the top of Bearman's large, gleaming forehead.

He turned and saw Alex standing in the doorway. His eyes opened in shock and recognition. "You!" he shouted. "You're the one who did all this! You let the demon out!" Bearman's face contorted in rage and he charged towards Alex.

Alex pushed the nurse back through the door. He closed it and held the handle tight. He could feel a dull throbbing under his chest from the exertion.

"Help!" they both called out together. "Code red!"

And to Alex's delight, he could hear the sound of footsteps running his way. Within seconds they were joined by a group of large orderlies.

Where's Devon? Alex thought. *Shit, I'll have to clear his name.*

The orderlies replaced his position at the door, looking to him for instructions.

"Mr. Bearman is having what appears to be a psychotic episode, perhaps brought on by extreme stress. He'll need to be subdued and detained. Sedate him, if needed."

"You got it," the lead orderly said. "Back on up, we'll handle this."

They opened the door and barged in, wrestling Bearman to the ground. Alex could hear his ranting, his psychotic claims.

He suppressed his smile as he turned back towards the nurse, who was trying not to ogle at the sight of Bearman being restrained. "Never a dull moment," Alex said.

"Not here, there sure isn't," she said, and shook her head.

Alex was anxious to get back to Eli. "I can't stay. Can you handle this from here?"

"I suppose. I'll come find you when the poor man's settled down."

"Thanks." He half turned then stopped. "The other two may need help too."

"I imagine so, the way he was berating them."

There's a bit more to it than that, Alex thought, but kept it to himself. He made his way back towards the exit where Angela was sitting with Eli by the fountain.

★   ★   ★

Angela was pretending to talk to Eli, shielding him from any onlookers. Alex walked up. "Any change?"

Angela moved her head, revealing Eli's face. It was still stuck in that vacant grin.

"What should we do?" she said.

"Other than wait, I don't know," Alex said. "He's obviously conscious on some level. I don't know how he did it, but he brought us back here. Maybe he's stuck wherever he is."

"I don't think so," Angela said. She wiped away a string of drool that was running down Eli's chin. "He's smiling."

"Sure, but we have no way of knowing whether that's voluntary or not. I don't think he's consciously aware of the way he looks right now."

"And she disappeared too," Angela said.

"The nurse with the burns?"

Angela nodded. "I think that was Eli's wife."

"How do you know that?"

"The pictures in Eli's office. I recognized her."

Alex looked around. "Well, we need to try and revive him. We can't hide him out here much longer."

"What if he doesn't want to come back?" Angela was gazing at the fountain. "It's like Jerry said about the medicine, 'You can create any world you choose.' Maybe he chose another one."

Alex squinted against the sun. It felt sublime on his face. "Or maybe the medicine pushed him over the edge. Maybe he snapped."

"You mean, like he's gone insane?" Angela studied Alex through one squinty eye.

Alex shrugged.

"Well, what would be so wrong with that?" she said, and a smile spread across her face. "Because I'm a fucking lunatic. And you're so batshit crazy it's downright scary."

Alex sounded like he was just now learning to laugh; it was a choked, gargling noise that lasted for a long time.

"Can't argue that," he said, once he was able to compose himself. "I have no idea how to assimilate what we've been through. What we're still going through."

"I don't think we can," Angela said. She leaned her head back and let her face bask in the sun. "God, that feels good."

"Holy shit," he said. "There's a lot of work to be done. I don't even know where to start."

But that wasn't true. He realized that he knew exactly where to start. It spoke to him from a place in the same proximity as his heart.

My most important work is waiting for me at home.

And as he let the warm sun shine against his face, he thought about his father and the people in his life who mattered to him most. He now knew what needed to be healed.

FINAL CHAPTER

He can hear them talking. It is distracting and he wants it to go away. He focuses on his breathing – *in and out, in and out* – and that helps a little.

They are worried about him, but they don't need to be. Part of him wants to tell them that, but it would mean he would have to return. And he doesn't want to. The fire here is too beautiful. The singing too important. Here, death and rebirth are happening all at once.

"It is not so serious," the man beside him says. He is smiling, as always. "Go. Stay. It's all the same."

Eli does not contemplate how the man can read his mind, or his enigmatic words. He just nods his head.

The parade of spirits emerging from the fire has stopped. They have all moved on.

But, then, he sees another walking his way. Tall and slender, with a graceful gait. The figure is backlit by the amber fire, so he cannot see its face.

Rajamadja titters as the figure draws closer.

"Look-ee, look-ee," he says like a child.

Heat waves are undulating up from its shadowed form. It walks straight, with undeterred purpose. It takes another step forward and starlight illuminates its features.

And it's her. His beloved wife, Lacy. The way she was before she got sick. Before she put on the veil.

She stops and they consider each other without words. She reaches out her hand, and he takes it. Their hands clasp together in an embrace that feels like a hug. She tugs gently, but she doesn't need to. He wants to go, and doesn't hesitate.

He can still hear the voices. Will they ever stop? If not, that's okay. He's lived with them for this long. He can make do as long as he must.

The heat from the blazing funeral pyre feels good. A comforting warmth, a bit like a womb. His skin begins to tighten as he walks towards it, but that doesn't stop him. He squeezes Lacy's hand and she squeezes back.

They are close now. The singing is much louder. Everyone here is so happy.

There's no turning back. He wouldn't, even if he could. And so they keep walking, hand in hand. The fire before them looms large. Together, they walk into the flames.

And the sound of voices goes silent.

FLAME TREE PRESS
FICTION WITHOUT FRONTIERS
Award-Winning Authors & Original Voices

Flame Tree Press is the trade fiction imprint of Flame Tree Publishing, focusing on excellent writing in horror and the supernatural, crime and mystery, science fiction and fantasy. Our aim is to explore beyond the boundaries of the everyday, with tales from both award-winning authors and original voices.

•

Other titles by Brian Kirk:
Will Haunt You

Other horror titles available include:
Snowball by Gregory Bastianelli
Thirteen Days by Sunset Beach by Ramsey Campbell
Think Yourself Lucky by Ramsey Campbell
The Hungry Moon by Ramsey Campbell
The Influence by Ramsey Campbell
The Haunting of Henderson Close by Catherine Cavendish
The House by the Cemetery by John Everson
The Devil's Equinox by John Everson
Hellrider by JG Faherty
The Toy Thief by D.W. Gillespie
One By One by D.W. Gillespie
Black Wings by Megan Hart
Hearthstone Cottage by Frazer Lee
Those Who Came Before by J.H. Moncrieff
Stoker's Wilde by Steven Hopstaken & Melissa Prusi
The Playing Card Killer by Russell James
The Siren and the Specter by Jonathan Janz
The Sorrows by Jonathan Janz
Castle of Sorrows by Jonathan Janz
The Dark Game by Jonathan Janz
House of Skin by Jonathan Janz
Dust Devils by Jonathan Janz
The Darkest Lullaby by Jonathan Janz
Creature by Hunter Shea
Ghost Mine by Hunter Shea
Slash by Hunter Shea
The Mouth of the Dark by Tim Waggoner
They Kill by Tim Waggoner

•

Join our mailing list for free short stories, new release details, news about our authors and special promotions:

flametreepress.com